A Long Way from Home
– with '776 LAC Andy Marshall

A Long Way from Home
– with '776 LAC Andy Marshall

Nigel Springthorpe

Matador
9 Priory Business Park, Wistow Road
Kibworth Beauchamp
Leicester LE8 0RX, UK
Tel: (+44) 116 279 2299
Fax: (+44) 116 279 2277
Email: books@troubador.co.uk
Web: www.troubador.co.uk/matador

ISBN 978 1780881 003

British Library Cataloguing in Publication Data.
A catalogue record for this book is available from the British Library.

Typeset by Troubador Publishing Ltd, Leicester, UK
Printed and bound in Great Britain by TJ International Ltd., Padstow, Cornwall.

Matador is an imprint of Troubador Publishing Ltd

For Norman, J. J, Doug, Keith, Tony, Alan, Eddie, George and the many other equally unforgettable characters with whom I served and to Jeanne, without whose encouragement this story would never have reached the printed page.

1

An Island in the South China Sea, 1955
With just a bump or two, a twin-engine aircraft of Royal Air Force, Far East Transport Wing, touches down on a crushed coral airstrip after a four hour flight from Singapore. Then, at a more leisurely speed, it takes a turn to port, exiting the runway before working its way along to the dispersal area. With a proud sweep of its tail, the Vickers Valetta showers the solitary, corrugated-iron servicing shed with a huge cloud of dust before coming to a halt. Inside the shed, with the temperature gauge nudging 95 degrees Fahrenheit, a servicing crew of four wait for the dust to clear. Shortly, they will emerge to carry out the re-fuelling before the 'plane continues its onward flight to Clark Field Air Base in the Philippines. But for one of the passengers on board, 2752776 Leading Aircraftman (LAC) Andy Marshall, this is as far as he goes. The slim, dark-haired, eighteen year old National Serviceman leans forward anxiously in his improvised seat unit to catch a first glimpse of the Island that will be both his workplace and tropical home for the next nine months.

The propellers spin to a halt. Almost immediately, beneath the fuselage, chocks are being slammed against the wheels. "This is it, young man," shouts the Signaller from the front of the 'plane. "Out you get!"

Andy exits into blinding sunshine, kitbag slung uncomfortably over his shoulder, and is directed across a patch of arid, stony ground, towards a waiting jeep. The driver, stripped to the waist, is staring straight ahead, engine running, fingers tapping impatiently on the steering wheel. There is no welcoming eye contact as he speaks.

"Are you Finnegan's replacement?"

"What?"

"Are you – or are you not – the fireman taking over from Finnegan?" comes the sharp reply.

"Not likely, I'm replacing the admin bod!" smiles Andy.

"Great! That's ten dollars I've won from the Irishman."

1

"Sorry, I don't follow."

The driver grins. "Forget it, just get in."

"Christ, it's hot," Andy mutters with a grimace, as he climbs into the passenger seat.

"You'll get used to it," comes the abrupt response. With the help of a clumsy gear change, the jeep lurches forward and is soon bouncing along the perimeter of the airstrip.

Andy struggles to take in the surroundings. In front of him, the only building is a modestly built white, wooden control tower. But for a pair of sparkling, silver aerials sprouting from its roof, the construction could so easily be mistaken for one of the many village green cricket pavilions to be found back home in England, now some seven thousand miles away.

Above, hangs a cloudless, powder blue sky. The area cleared for the airfield is bordered completely by clusters of palm trees and bush which, in the absence of any wind, stand motionless. The only movement is from the heat waves, shimmering at the far end of a runway, now lying silent between two lines of white-washed stones trailing into the distance.

"Is it true some of the chaps here are rejects from other camps in the Far East?" enquires Andy, as his driver struggles to negotiate the rutted track. "You know, the oddballs who…"

"What d'ya mean?" interrupts the driver, adjusting his sunglasses and tilting his head towards his passenger to catch the conversation above the engine noise.

"So, what's it like here then?" asks Andy, anxious to change the subject while rising in his seat in an unsuccessful attempt to ride yet another hump.

"What you make of it. Some don't get on, don't get accepted. Others love it, sign on for another tour, can't get enough of the place. Don't forget only some thirty of us here, so everyone knows everyone. Some say it's the remotest outpost in the Far East."

"And you've been here for…?"

"Coming up for two years," comes the casual reply.

"Should've known that from your tan."

Andy lurches forward in his seat as the driver fails to negotiate the vehicle around a series of potholes on the dusty track.

"Hope you don't suffer from the heat. We had a ginger-haired wireless operator flown out last week, horizontal on a stretcher – just three days after he arrived! Saw him being lifted into the plane, the colour of a flaming lobster."

"That's horrible," says Andy.

"Silly sod brought it on himself. Second day here he went sunbathing."

En route, Andy casts an anxious eye at the modest collection of single-storey stone buildings and wooden huts, reminding him of the prefabricated bungalow-style dwellings that had sprouted at home immediately after the War.

The jeep comes to an almost emergency-style stop outside a wooden billet, which is long overdue for a couple more coats of green paint. A desperately thin, grey coloured dog, with a leg cocked up against a fire extinguisher at the side of the hut, throws a furtive look at the couple before scurrying out of sight.

"This is it, lad, your new home. Well, yours and the others you'll be sharing with. Don't forget your gear in the back. Jock, the storeman, is in there and he'll fix you up with bedding and a 'mossie' net. Make sure you get a good one, we're very close to the swamp. Get some nasty bites in this place. Oh yeh! don't forget to see the medic first thing in the morning to get your paludrine tablets. Those are for your malaria."

"But I don't have malaria! Might have picked up something in Singapore but it ain't malaria," Andy grins.

"Tell that to the Doc," chuckles the driver, working noisily through the gears before completing a laboured u-turn.

"Thanks for the lift..." Andy's words of appreciation are lost in an engine roar and a cloud of exhaust fumes.

Stepping over a couple of planks that straddle an empty monsoon ditch, the new arrival enters his new home, casting an anxious look around him.

Despite the laboured efforts of the creaking overhead fans, and the open wooden shutters, doubling up as ventilation, there is a musty, stale smell about the place. A few prostrate bodies, one totally naked, lie motionless on their beds. The walls are decorated with pictures of glamorous, scantily-clothed female film stars, a few instantly-recognisable professional footballers and a host of calendars carrying clearly-ringed dates. Positioned on the stone floor at the foot of most of the beds is a black-painted, wooden deep sea box, carrying the stencilled rank, name and service number of the owner. Boxes destined to be shipped back to the UK at the end of each Airman's tour of duty.

Raffles, this is not, thinks Andy, throwing his bag down onto a vacant bed.

He wonders why, in mid-afternoon, the prostrate Airmen are not working.

"You'll never get off the island!" comes a sudden cry from immediately behind them.

Andy spins around to catch sight of an overweight figure, stripped to the waist, breaking into a bout of uncontrolled laughter. A well-soiled apron hangs over a baggy pair of white trousers. His footwear consists of a pair of flip-flops, non-Service issue. Sweat has matted what remains of his thinning hair and he sports a complexion which suggests he is in permanent hiding from the sun.

"Christ, you made me jump!" recoils Andy, slapping a sticky right hand across his chest.

"You the new boy? 'Cos I'm one of the camp cooks. The name's Ken. Always ready to do something for a birthday special, anniversaries and all that. Not the usual stuff I serve up in the Mess, though. Couple of dollars on the side will do it. Don't forget now. But I'll need a day's notice."

"What's that about never getting off the island?"enquires Andy, ignoring the sales pitch.

"Only joking," comes the laughing reply. "Oh yes, grub at six in the Mess – and that's for free, every day, just like breakfast. Don't listen to what the others say about my grub. Innocent till proved guilty is my motto. Forget anything else you might hear."

"What you got lined up for us tonight, then? I'm hungry already," says Andy.

"If I can borrow a boat, it'll be fish and chips," comes a straight-faced reply, followed by a weakly suppressed grin.

"Usually count on me to come up with a surprise or two!"

Andy watches in silence as the cook turns and waddles out of the billet and into the blistering sun.

Late afternoon sees the return to the billet of other Airmen at the end of their working day, flopping out onto their beds to a musical accompaniment of singing and whistling from the outside shower. Strolling past, a few throw a nod in the direction of the new arrival, as if in token acknowledgement of Andy's presence.

One breaks from a group and ambles back. "Are you my relief, fireman Henry Forbes-whatsit?"

"No," answers Andy.

"Are you sure?"

"Quite sure."

"Bastards! They promised my replacement would be coming up today. Bastards!"

"Sorry."

"No, not your fault, it's down to that lying little bastard who worked for the C.O."

"Actually, I'm his replacement," Andy responds tentatively.

"Thanks for the gen, but I'm still gonna get that bastard. I'll hunt him down wherever he's hiding. And he's lost me money."

"You mean he's already gone, he's not here? But I'm supposed to have a handover period, what's gone wrong?" enquires Andy anxiously.

"I'm sure he made that name up just to keep me quiet," continues the disappointed fireman, side-stepping the questions. "Ever heard of a fireman being called Henry-Forbes? Nah! 'course you haven't, didn't sound right to me either. The bastard made it up. Should have known. Anyway, I'm Corporal Finnegan, Fergus Finnegan that is. The boys sometimes call me Fergie but 'Finnegan' will do. I'm in charge of the fire crew."

Andy can't fail to notice the thick silver chain draped around the Corporal's neck. Standing over six feet tall, feet well apart, his threatening stance could be mistaken as one of a boxer in the ring being introduced to his opponent. High on one arm, he carries a large heart-shaped tattoo, complete with a couple of fading arrows and blurred initials.

"Nice, isn't it? Worth a bit I can tell you," boasts Finnegan, proudly running his fingers over the links of the chain.

"Come to think of it, Finnegan, can't recall seeing any of your crew up at the airstrip when we landed," says Andy.

"Put it this way, my friend, we always *try* to get up there before the kite lands – and we usually do – but not always."

Andy takes a deep gulp in disbelief as the Corporal strolls away into the darkening bowels of the billet. Not much discipline here then, so very different to the organisation at RAF Changi, Singapore, the parent Station he has just left.

Early evening passes quietly as Andy stretches out on his lumpy mattress, trying to adjust to his new surroundings. His first day in Borneo and one he is unlikely to forget. He decides to give dinner a miss, choosing to reflect on the characters he has met in the short time since his plane touched down. Somehow they seem a different breed: a bit detached – except for the jocular cook, Ken. Suddenly, he views the prospect of a nine month detachment at this remote station with some apprehension. His thoughts return to that fateful day at the square-bashing camp in Shropshire, when he was suddenly ordered to report to SHQ (Station Headquarters) to discover that, instead of being sent on a six-week radar course to Yatesbury in Wiltshire, he was being posted to the Far East. The explanation given was of an urgent need to fill a number of administrative posts out there, and his experience in the Civil Service made him eminently and immediately suitable. How different it all could have been. A home posting within striking distance of where he lived, close to his girl, weekend passes... And now this.

"Here's your net!"

Andy is shaken from his reflective mood. He looks up to find someone stretching over him, struggling to attach a mosquito net to a hook above and behind his bed.

"You must be Jock?"

"Aye, that's me."

The Scotsman's tubby body is sweating profusely. Finally the net unfurls.

"Hey! there's a couple of big holes up there," cries Andy, pointing upwards to a couple of tears in the black netting.

"They've all got a few wee holes in them, this is one of the better ones though, trust me," answers Jock in a deep, baritone, Glaswegian accent.

Andy slumps back on the bed. But his attention is almost immediately distracted by the sobbing of someone in the bed directly across the gangway.

"Jock, Jock – just before you go," whispers Andy. "Not ill, is he?" fixing his eyes on the naked body in distress.

"Naw, his wee girlee dumped 'im. You'll find his 'Dear John' letter on the notice board at the end of the billet. We've told 'im he's betta off without her. Nasty bitch canna even spell and her writing's a joke. But I tell you, Billy took it bad so he's sleeping it off and drying out at the same time. Had a wee drink to blot it out, ye know. Betta off without the girlee, though."

Their conversation is broken by what sounds like a grumbling engine, revving up immediately behind the billet.

6

"Christ, what's that?" exclaims Andy, in the midst of flattening out the bumps in his mattress.

"Ah, that's the camp generator," Jock explains. "Got some local civilians in there now, trying to sort it out. Problem is they dinna ken what they're doing. We dinna pay them enough so they'll be clocking up overtime to give themselves a wee bit extra. Can't blame 'em, can ye? Crazy, isn't it? You'll get used to the noise. At times, it's a wee bit like living in the ticket office of a railway station!"

Andy drops his head back, slow motion style, in astonishment, thumping the pillow. "Thanks for that! All this way, miles from anywhere, and I'm sleeping next to a bloody railway line."

His thoughts turn to the job he has been sent to do: working as the Admin man for the Commanding Officer, Flight Lieutenant Charles Munro. He is anxious to learn more of the C.O, about whom he has heard some disturbing rumours prior to leaving Singapore.

He walks further down the billet, hoping to elicit some information from Jock.

The Scotsman now lies on his stomach, engrossed in a well-thumbed paperback, the reddened skin on his back in an advanced stage of peeling.

"'Scuse me, Jock, a word about the C.O, if I may."

"Can we leave it till the mornin?"

"Prefer not to. Haven't even met him yet but I've heard the rumours, you know."

"Which ones?" laughs Jock.

"What? Whether he's AC / DC?" smiles fireman Finnegan, moving from an adjacent bed space to join the conversation. "Forget that one, boys. I've heard on the grapevine the Old Man's bride-to-be is coming out from the UK and he's planning the wedding in Singapore. Rumour is he was on flying duties a couple of years back and something went wrong, badly wrong. Not exactly a court martial but something like that – and he got posted out here as a sort of punishment. The man is bitter. Definitely an odd bugger. Goes rambling on about the War, which bores the ass off anyone in range. Our Section here is not far away from his office, so I see quite a bit of him. Calls me 'Paddy' – 'cause I'm Irish – all friendly like when we're alone but when anyone else is around he changes tack, all nasty like, calling me 'You!' or 'Corporal!' And then I'm back to being an 'Erk'."

"Thanks for the warning," says Andy.

"And him being queer? I tell you, one of the washerwomen who comes in from the village, sometimes stays overnight at his place – and we know she's not doing any washing! Mind you, I've heard he's also taken a shine to the Doc," adds Jock.

"OK lads, thanks for that. I get the picture," replies Andy making his way thoughtfully back to his bed space.

He flops onto his mattress, looking upwards through the mosquito net at the whirring fan. He notices that every now and then one of the blades appears to dip.

"Should mention that to someone in the morning," he mutters to himself. Apart from an occasional snore or cough, the only sound is the purring of the now repaired, but still close-at-hand, generator.

Andy's thoughts turn to his family and home, and to the stone built cottage on the edge of Dartmoor in Devon, which now feel a million miles away. Taking account of the time difference, he knows that back in England it is mid-morning. In his mind's eye, his mother is returning with their two labradors from a stroll over the neighbouring fields. It is raining and the two dogs have just come into the porch and are trying to shake themselves dry, while she is attempting to settle them down.

Andy's pensive mood is rudely shattered by a sudden blast from a gramophone further up the billet.

"Turn that damn racket off, will you!" "For Christ's sake!" "Not again!" The chorus of cries immediately silences the music.

"O.K fellows, I accept your total non-appreciation of all levels of civilised music. Accordingly, I will desist from sharing my discerning musical choice with you. Your loss, gentlemen, not mine."

There follows a ripple of cynical applause.

Andy rises from his bed in an attempt to discover the speaker with the educated voice, which strikes him as somewhat out of place. His curiosity is aroused.

He wanders down the billet, in search of a gramophone and its owner. En route passing what appears to be the closing stages of a serious card game, the outcome of which is clearly attracting the interest of a growing group of non-participants, clustering around one of the beds. Andy finally stops alongside an Airman, on his knees in front of his bedside locker, carefully re-arranging a box of vinyl records.

With his back to Andy, the man of music speaks:

"If you're here to complain about the music, please move on."

"No, I was just interested in what you were playing – and what else you've got. I collect records at home and my dad has an enormous haul, mostly classical though."

The Airman stands up, turning to face Andy.

His appearance seems strangely out of place at this remote detachment. He is wearing a maroon, silk dressing gown and a pair of tennis shoes. He sports a central parting for his well-greased black hair, similar in style to the departing generation of male ballroom dancers. On his bedside locker stands a wood-framed photo of an elderly couple and an egg timer. He emanates an overpowering smell of after-shave.

"Tell me more, tell me more. I'm Martin, known affectionately to all and sundry as the 'Music Man.' And you're…hold on, don't tell me!…Andrew Marshall? The C.O's new side-kick?"

"Dead right."

"No offence intended, but I can pick 'em a mile off. Grab a seat, fancy a warm Carlsberg?" adds Martin with a welcoming pat on his mattress.

"Thanks, what do you do here?"

"I'm one of the wireless ops, morse code and all that, receiving and sending out signals."

"Sounds interesting."

"What? Doing a shift alone in a wooden hut, sweating like a pig. Dot, dot, dash, dash, dot. Interesting? No, 'interesting' is not the word I would have chosen. Anyway, what's your taste in music? Who knows, I might just be able to oblige."

"Got any Guy Mitchell – or Jo Stafford?" asks Andy tentatively.

"Not in my collection at the moment, shall we say," smiles Martin. "Basically, my collection is classical and modern jazz. Did you know that most of the leading jazz pianists have studied classical music? Didn't you ever give your dad's music a chance? Did you ever really *listen* to it? Well, now's your opportunity to give it all a try. You'll find you have the time. Be my guest – but not when these Philistines are around!"

Andy detects a trace of a West Country accent within the Music Man's voice.

"Where d'you come from?"

"Near Bristol, don't tell me you're from that part of the world."

"Yes, Plymouth. Not that far away really."

"Listen, Andy, my shifts mean I'm sometimes off duty during the day. That's when I listen to my music, without anyone here to moan. If you manage to get away from your office, come back here and join me."

"Thanks, I'll remember that."

Before returning to his bed space, Andy's bladder reminds him of the need to visit the latrine. Not surprisingly, being the latest newcomer to the camp, his bed is the one positioned closest to the outside toilet and adjoining shower. He leaves the billet and returns almost immediately, his fingers acting as a peg on his nose.

"Sorry, about that mate. My gut's been playing up something awful."

The words come from the adjacent bed, where the pale-faced occupant is grimacing in discomfort.

"It's Cookie, you know. That fish he served up tonight was as tough as leather and just as difficult to digest," continues the stricken Airman.

"Anything I can get you?" offers Andy.

"No, just leave me alone to get some kip. Sorry."

A series of cries and yelps from the other end of the billet suggests that the card game is finally over.

Andy tidies up his bedside locker.

He gives a fond squeeze to his Service issue 'Housewife,' the small bag of needles and thread issued to him at his square-bashing camp in Shropshire. On the lower shelf, lies a pair of well-polished, black Service issue shoes and socks and, tied neatly in a red ribbon, the entire, treasured collection of the read – and much re-read – letters he has received so far from the UK.

It has been an eventful day. He wonders how he will cope over the next nine months. Hopefully, the time won't drag. And how is Sandra, his fiancée, adjusting to life at home without him? She seemed genuinely upset at his leaving for Singapore but that was almost three months ago. And her letters are somehow becoming less emotive and more factual. Would another year apart prove too great a strain on their relationship? After all, she was a good-looking girl who couldn't be blamed for taking up with someone else. And didn't people say something about 'out of sight…?' Could he end up getting a 'Dear John', just like the naked and now disorientated body on the other side of the billet? He turns to look at the circular, silver-framed photograph on his bedside locker, and blows a gentle, silent kiss to his beautiful, ever-smiling Sandra. Simultaneously, the ailing occupant from the adjacent bed lets rip with an explosive fart.

Andy toys with the idea of sleeping without his lightweight pyjamas, something he has never done before; but the twin threat of the mosquitoes and bed bugs force him to change his mind.

What did I do to deserve ending up here? he asks himself, drawing a deep sigh and pushing a now clammy leg out from under the bed sheet. But before he has had a chance to answer his own question, his tired body is already beginning to switch off. Soon Andy is fast asleep.

2

"Welcome, Airman. They took their time coming up with you, so I hope it's been worth the wait," snaps Flight Lieutenant Charles Munro, leaning back from his desk to ease his small frame into his rattan chair. His cap rests uneasily close to his ears, suggesting a smaller size would have sufficed. Immediately above his upper lip, there appear signs of 'work in progress' on a ginger moustache. Directly behind him, hanging slightly askew, is a black and white picture of the Queen against an otherwise bare wall. Above them, a squeaking fan is sending out a SOS call for a touch of oil.

It's Andy's first day of duty and he pauses, standing almost to attention in front of his new Commanding Officer, hoping the right words will somehow arrive. Momentarily, it feels no different from being summoned to the headmaster, except now he is having to explain himself to a dapper, bespectacled, impatient-looking individual in military dress, sporting a pair of oversized, khaki drill shorts below which protrude his spindly, white legs.

"I don't know what you've been told about this detachment but I'll spell it out. Our complement numbers just over thirty, which includes a handful of Sergeants. Our job here on this island is to provide an efficient staging post at which aircraft can be re-fuelled before proceeding to their final destinations. Except for emergencies, we don't get any landings after dark."

"Sir, I caught sight of a couple of chaps from the Australian Air Force on my way from the Mess this morning and I wondered…"

"Don't wonder, Airman. They're here on special duties, nothing to do with you, it's all very hush-hush."

Andy feels rebuffed but his curiosity is immediately aroused.

The C.O rises to his feet, then circles the latest addition to his staff, continuing to debrief.

"We do have a few civilian flights coming through and, occasionally, an American Air Force kite from Clark Air Base will drop in after air sea rescue operations. The monsoons can prove a bit tricky when 'planes get grounded but that's not really your concern. You'll find the quarters for the men are first class – in fact I can't recall hearing a single complaint from anyone since I arrived. Security-wise, this is an open camp, so there is no guard or fire picket duty. I take it you've settled into your billet?"

"Yes, Sir," answers Andy without hesitation.

"And your tour of duty here is the standard nine months which, as it happens, will almost coincide with my return to Changi."

The C.O returns to his chair, before taking a deep breath. Andy senses he has something important to say.

"Unfortunately, we have a mixed bag of personnel: the servicing crew are certainly up to standard but the fire crew need shaking up. And the rest of them need watching. We have no Police presence, so you will be my extra pair of 'eyes and ears' – but I'll come back to that. Now, let's hear what you've got to say. Well …? Speak up, young man, I won't bite you. Not yet, anyway."

"Sir, I'm a National Serviceman – in for two years…"

"Good God, I know all that – already got your Service Record here. What did you do before you were conscripted?"

"Civil Service, Sir," replies Andy in an apologetic tone.

"Poor chap," smirks the C.O. "I've seen some of your sort at the Air Ministry back in London. A motley, miserable pin-striped crew. Are you actually planning to continue with that for the rest of your life? If not, think seriously about signing on. Damn sight better life than being a civil servant. Who knows – you might even get a commission!"

"Yes, Sir," says Andy, simultaneously casting a quick look around the sparsely furnished office. Fixed to one wall is a small safe, on which hangs a multi-coloured umbrella; on another hangs a faded, black and white aerial photo of the camp. The top of the C.O's desk is flanked by a couple of empty, wooden filing trays. In the centre stands an almost empty jug of iced water with a sad-looking, sunken slice of lemon.

"Impressive picture, isn't it?" says the C.O, noticing that Andy's attention has wandered to the aerial picture. "Not sure whether it was already here when the Australian Ninth Division re-took this island from the Japs in '45. Probably not, given the notoriously short-sighted Nips were incapable of taking a decent snap. More to the point, what do the Japs know about photography?"

The dialogue is interrupted by the noise of one of the gardeners

13

pecking at the rock-hard ground immediately outside the hut, causing the C.O to raise his voice.

"Just remembered, Airman. Tomorrow's Pay Day for the locally-engaged staff here. The gardeners and …"

"And the washer women?" adds Andy mischievously, recalling his chat with the fireman.

"So that's your first job, young man: Pay Parade for the civvies. I'll be in the background – just this once – to see it's done properly, then you'll be on your own next time. Try not to cock it up. Your predecessor never really mastered it."

"Your coffee, Sir."

Andy swivels around to see the formidable figure of Ken, the cook, stripped to the waist, standing in the doorway, holding up a large brown mug.

"Put it down there, man. And cover yourself up, that's an order! You look more like a sumo wrestler than a cook on active Service. And leave the door open," bawls the C.O.

"Yes, Sir, of course Sir," comes the swift reply.

The cook exits, closing the door behind him.

"Have to watch him, and as I said, that will be one of your tasks here, Airman. You will be my third eye. Not just the cooks – because they have the capacity to immobilise the whole camp with one dodgy meal – but the others. I don't trust them. As I've said, this is one of the very few RAF Stations in the Far East without a Police presence, so it's our job to take their place. I've still got a few tricks up my sleeve, I can assure you."

The C.O's pale face is beginning to redden.

"But Sir, I'm just an LAC, surely the Sergeants should fill those duties. That's going to make life difficult for me, I can't pull rank."

"Listen, I live 'off camp' so I can't be aware of everything that goes on here. So that's where you come in. Follow me?"

"Yes, Sir, you mean a bit like an informer?"

"That's perhaps a bit strong but something on those lines," replies the C.O with a wry but barely concealed smile.

"Understood, Sir," replies Andy with a confirmatory nod. He had not expected this and is becoming increasingly concerned about the role he is expected to play.

"And don't forget young man, there could be a promotion or two if you perform to standard. I have my connections with Personnel back in

Singapore. Oh yes, almost forgot! When we had a spot of bother a month or two back, I told the chap before you to dust off the Charge Sheets, Form 252, if I recall. Silly blighter couldn't find them, then told me he'd ordered some more from Changi. Didn't believe him. You should check to see if they ever arrived."

"Yes, of course, Sir," answers Andy.

"What you must understand, Airman, is that we have a vital strategic presence here. We're not just a staging post, a refuelling point between here Singapore and the Philippines. We're a vital piece in a crucially important military jigsaw. This is not Butlins!"

"I don't quite follow, Sir,"

"No, I don't suppose you do. Listen, this is the Far Eastern theatre of War, and our new enemy is Communism, with a capital C. Just because that shindig has ended in Korea, don't think it's all over. Oh no, not by a long chalk! Don't you know about all the trouble they've been causing in Malaya?"

"Who's 'they' exactly, Sir?"

"The damn Commies, of course," barks the C.O.

"First we see off those dreadful Nips, then up pop these awful Commies!"

"But aren't we a bit too far away from anywhere to be involved, Sir?" questions Andy.

"That's exactly what the shallow-minded think. But don't forget we're just off the coast of North Borneo and you know how important Borneo was to the Japs, don't you?"

"Not exactly, Sir."

"Well, in the last war, forty per cent of the Japanese oil supplies came from Borneo. Bet you didn't know that either," replies the C.O, sporting a smug and knowledgeable expression.

"No, Sir, I didn't."

"And goodness knows what's brewing over in China. Don't think for a moment we can trust that lot. Wouldn't be surprised if they're already trying to infiltrate our camp," continues the C.O.

"What, at this moment, Sir?"

"Wouldn't put it past them, cunning load of monkeys," replies the C.O.

Andy switches his weight from one foot to the other. He is beginning to tire of both the military and political lesson. But the C.O is in full flow as he returns to his chair.

"I was at the fall of Singapore in '42. Know what I'm talking about. Oh yes, lucky to get out of there alive."

"Did you actually see the Japs close up, Sir?"

"Err….mm… not exactly, but I was there in the thick of it when the place was being bombed just before they invaded the island…"

"Bit like my Gran, Sir! She was in Plymouth, in the city, when the Germans bombed it," interrupts Andy, seizing on the sudden opportunity to make a contribution to the almost one-sided conversation.

"No, Airman, certainly *not at all* like your grandmother!" bellows the C.O, realising that the conversation has run its course. "She was a mere civilian, for goodness sake. I was on active Service and right in the damn thick of it!"

The Flight Lieutenant rises angrily from his chair, pushes his chest out and stands erect to his full five and a half feet. "Now off you go to your office next door and clean it up. It's a damn disgrace."

Andy steps through an arched gap in the wall, dragging a beaded curtain to one side, and enters his working area. His predecessor had made a token attempt at tidying up.

A trestle table, with clean, newly-laid brown wrapping paper tacked with a collection of mostly blunt drawing pins, serves as a desk. On it sits a typewriter, with the faded letters on the keyboard betraying its age. A fold-up chair lies on the floor behind the desk, resting on an untidy pile of crumpled newspapers. A couple of ants are engaged in what seems a detailed inspection of the interior of a cracked and discarded cup. A badly scarred, metal filing cabinet is positioned in a corner of the room, with a couple of broken drawers gaping open.

"What's your typing like, how many words to the minute?" barks the C.O, poking his head through the beaded curtain.

"Not too good, Sir, but I'm sure I'll quicken up with practice."

"You'll damn well have to! I've got this urgent letter for you to type – right this minute. There's a kite due out for Singapore in about twenty minutes and my letter has got to be on it."

The C.O thrusts his hastily written manuscript into Andy's hand.

"Don't bother to read it, Airman – you haven't got time. Just type it!"

Andy, a two-finger man at best, struggles with the temperamental machine before handing the typed page to the C.O.

"I suppose it'll have to do," groans the Flight Lieutenant, as he takes his pen to scratch a few manuscript corrections. "Now put it in this mail bag, seal it with this wax – here's the matches – and get your backside up to the strip, double quick. If necessary, get a lift on the fire tender."

Nervously, Andy applies the red wax, almost burning his fingers in the process, then scampers out of the office. The C.O stands in the doorway, hands on hips, watching as the National Serviceman breaks into a trot.

"Run, man, run," screams the Flight Lieutenant, dabbing the perspiration on his forehead with first his forearm and then a badly soiled handkerchief.

Andy stops to draw breath. He can hear the roar of an aircraft in the distance, hoping it's not the one destined to carry the urgent document. As he rounds the Mess, he catches sight of the fire crew boarding the already moving tender. A couple of the men are hurriedly donning their green jackets as they clamber into the vehicle. Finnegan stands at the rear of the vehicle screaming at his colleagues to hurry up.

"Wait! Hold on!" comes Andy's plea but his waving arm to the departing vehicle goes unnoticed. "Shit! what have I done to deserve this lot?" he mutters to himself, before breaking into a run. But within less than another hundred yards his legs begin to buckle. Ahead of him on the stony track he suddenly notices the fire tender has come to an abrupt stop.

Finnegan's head emerges from the driver's window, simultaneously dropping a beckoning hand. "Hurry up, if you want a lift," he shouts back to the breathless clerk. Within minutes the fire tender arrives at the airstrip.

The propellers of the Singapore-bound aircraft are already in motion and the steps are being rolled back. Andy rushes forward to throw the mail bag towards the plane's open door. The Valetta's silver fuselage glints in the fierce sunlight, forcing him first to squint and then shield his eyes. One of the aircrew appears from within and stands in the still open doorway.

"Let's have it! Throw the bloody thing, man!"

Andy draws his right arm back, then forward, releasing the small bag. The letter is finally on its way, sailing through the air and coming to rest in a safe pair of hands.

"Now, stand well back!" comes the cry, the door closes and the engines burst into a full-blooded roar. The camp's latest arrival follows the path of the aircraft as it taxies out to the runway, making a laboured ascent before climbing slowly into the open sky.

In four hours it will be landing in Singapore. "Four hours closer to home," mutters Andy, feeling a lump coming to his throat.

He turns away, mission accomplished, a sweat-sodden jacket clinging to his chest.

"Your first bit of excitement then," smiles Finnegan, draping a consoling arm across the damp shoulders of the newly arrived National Serviceman. "Can't give you a lift back 'cause now we're waiting for a flight in from Clark Field," adds the Irishman. "Due within the next half hour – and Andy, my friend, do everything to get my bloody replacement up here quick. I'll make it worth your while."

"That's O.K, I'll take a stroll back," replies Andy.

As he walks past the servicing shed, an ambulance draws alongside.

"Think you're bloody well immune to malaria, do you?" shouts the driver.

Andy spins around. "Sorry, you talking to me?"

"Too bloody right I am. Everyone here – and that includes you – needs medication. You should have reported to me as soon as you arrived. Just wait until the next kite arrives and I'll take you back to the Medical Centre."

The short ride back to the camp is an eventful one with Andy wincing as his driver also manages, unerringly, to visit almost every pothole on the rocky, unmade road.

"Can you drive? If not, you can learn here. I give cheap lessons in this ambulance, just a few dollars. Cost you a fortune back home."

"No, I don't drive," replies Andy quietly.

"Well, that's fixed. I'll fit you in. Lessons are at dusk up on the strip, after all flights have finished. Plenty of room up there and nothing to hit!"

The journey ends outside the Medical Centre, a wooden hut, less than fifty yards from Andy's billet.

"Oh, by the way, I'm Doc Todd, 'Sweeney' to the lads."

The Doc is sporting a black, bushy moustache. His tanned body and muscular physique suggests he is setting a healthy example to the rest of the camp.

Inside the hut, the dilapidated remains of a long, brown leather settee with some of its interior padding on view serves as the main item of furniture. Dusty wooden shelves carry a few broken cardboard boxes but also endless rows of what appear to be coloured sea shells. Life-size anatomical charts almost cover one of the walls. A pair of weight scales lie on top of the patient's table.

"Here's your paludrine tablets. One a day, in the morning – and don't forget to take them. If you go down with malaria you'll be flown back to Singapore. Can't deal with it here. O.K?"

Andy slips the strip of pills into the back pocket of his shorts, and makes for the door.

"Is that it, then?" he asks.

"Not quite. Have you seen the VD film?"

"Oh yes, during square-bashing."

"No, since you've been out here?" asks the Doc.

"No."

"Not pretty but it serves a purpose. O.K, you can get a viewing with the other new arrivals. This film's a bit different, so be prepared 'cause it's gruesome."

"Thanks," replies Andy. "Can I go now, the C.O will be waiting for me?"

"Fuck the C.O!" comes the explosive reply. "Listen, mate – and listen hard, particularly if you're a beach boy. I take it you like a swim?"

"Sure, they talked at Changi about how good these beaches were."

"Yes, the beaches are good, the shells down there are spectacular but the sea snakes are lethal."

"Sea snakes? No one said anything about them."

"Take my word for it, if you get bitten it's curtains."

The Doc hands Andy a coloured drawing of the sea snake.

"You see this little striped, greyish blue fellow. He can deliver ten to fifteen mgees of venom. Given one and a half mgees is enough to be fatal, you could have a problem."

"Does it have a name?"

"Well, not one it answers to! Sorry, only joking. Yep, it's a krait."

"I won't forget that in a hurry. Thanks for the gen."

The Doc walks Andy to the door, giving him a firm pat on the buttocks before he steps outside. "And don't worry about the tea tasting funny, lad. Cookie's been ordered to put a touch of bromide in it, just to stop us all getting too frisky. Yeh, and I'll be in touch soon about the driving lessons."

"Thanks Doc," answers Andy without turning around, hoping the medic's farewell hand on the backside was nothing more than a friendly, innocent gesture.

He hurries back towards his office, anticipating the C.O will be anxious to know the fate of his urgent letter to Singapore. His pace quickens as he nears the Mess. Overhead, the RAF flag hangs limply against a whitewashed, wooden pole standing in a rectangular plot bordered by stones. Ken, the cook, stands with his formidable frame almost blocking the Mess doorway.

"Come in and join the boys, we're having a cuppa."

"Sorry, can't, got to get back to the C.O," replies Andy.

"Don't worry, pal, the Old Man has just gone off camp."

As he approaches the entrance to the Mess, Andy's attention is drawn to what appears to be the skeletal figure of a mongrel, laying prostrate in the monsoon drain just a few feet away.

"Is she... ?"

"You mean a gonner?" suggests Ken.

"Well, yes, poor gal. Must be the heat."

The cook breaks into a bout of laughter, the trembling flab on his chest suggesting he should be wearing a bra.

"It's a bitch. Pissed, that's all. We call her Carlsberg 'cause that's her favourite drink."

"Is that what's in her bowl?" asks Andy. "But that's cruel. She could become an alcoholic."

"She already is. Like that when I came here over a year ago, so don't worry about it."

3

As an experienced Serviceman, Flight Lieutenant Munro is expected to know all about fighting his corner but on this early morning he is engaged in a totally different type of struggle: to recover the space lost in his own bed. Alongside him, face down, lies the naked, ample frame of Fatimah, one of the three washerwomen from the camp.

Her clothes lie, neatly-folded, upon an adjacent bamboo chair.

"Don't push me like that, Coomandah! Uddavise, you get no more jig-jig."

As usual, Fatimah is directing operations.

"My sweet, there's something I must tell you…" begins the C.O.

"Come here, you naughty man," she orders, rolling over onto her back with her hands coming together behind her neck.

The Commander pauses before gazing down at her voluminous brown breasts.

"My God, you really have got the finest pair of tits I've ever seen."

"Is it that what you must tell me?"

"No, no, it's something different, very different…"

"Then come close, Coomandah, get between my legs and show you vant me,"smiles Fatimah, flashing her sparkling white teeth as a bonus.

With a helping hand from his partner, the C.O clambers aboard, pumping his pink, frail body furiously into her flesh, his open-mouthed head flopping over her left shoulder.

"Why you no look at me, Coomandah, when we jig-jig?"

Momentarily, the C.O loses his position, then pushes a hand downward into the pillow in a clumsy attempt to lever himself up.

"What's that, my sweet?" he asks breathlessly.

"Why you no look?" she repeats.

"You know I don't talk or look when we're doing it, my sweet. Never have."

The C.O finds himself forced to drop a couple of gears, as he struggles to regain some composure.

Effortlessly, Fatimah slides her partner's frail, panting body back onto the sheets.

"Now, velly special treat for Coomandah."

The C.O groans in expectation and, with an outstretched arm, reaches for his spectacles on the bedside table.

Fatimah is now astride him, her tongue snaking a line of saliva down his perspiring chest, heading due south.

"My God, woman, you're positively evil!"

"But you like treat, Coomandah, I can tell."

"That is a 'Roger'!" giggles the C.O.

"Our little friend Roger soon become big Roger. Yes? Fatimah give more kisses. Yes?"

"Most definitely," comes the swift and obedient reply.

Minutes later, the couple lie a foot apart, on their backs, looking up and smiling together at a couple of pink lizards darting backwards and forwards across the ceiling.

"Never quite worked out how the little devils manage that, scampering around upside down. Defies the basic laws of gravity, you know," comments the C.O.

"You say funny things, Coomandah. I no understand."

"Seriously, my sweet, one would expect one of the blighters up there to fall down on us."

Fatimah slips out of the bed and stands with her back to him, still naked, gazing out from the window of the bungalow onto the manicured lawn. He watches closely as she pushes up her raven coloured hair from the back of her neck before stretching her arms out horizontally. Aware she is being observed, Fatimah treats her partner to a naughty wiggle of her buttocks. Despite bearing four children, her waist is still remarkably trim and enticing. No doubt about it, thinks Charles Munro, a formidable and exciting woman. Not much idea with the camp's washing but, at moments such as this, her occupational shortcomings can be overlooked.

"Your money is on the table, my sweet, with a bit extra this time for the kids."

"You like them, you vant to see them, I arrange?"

It is a question to which Fatimah already knows the answer.

The C.O clears his throat before replying.

"Not for the moment, my sweet. Something to look forward to."

"You vant me go now – no shower?" asks Fatimah.

"Yes, it's running late and I'm due at the camp for the locally-engaged Pay Parade."

"So you have more to give Fatimah today?" she giggles mischievously.

"No, I've got a young chap in from Changi and want to see how he copes – just once."

"I see you there, Coomandah, might give you naughty vink," teases Fatimah.

"Certainly not, woman, our liaison must remain a top priority secret. Understand?"

She dresses without speaking further, realising she is in danger of upsetting her lover.

With a backward wave, the Indian washerwoman leaves the room before slipping out through the bushes at the rear of the C.O's bungalow towards the swampy ground, her short cut route to the camp.

It has just turned ten in the morning as Andy waits in his office for the C.O to arrive.

He takes yet another look at his wrist watch before once more counting the overlapping, brown envelopes laid out on his desk. Outside, in the scorching heat, the locally-engaged staff await their weekly payment.

The two Chinese washerwomen are deep in conversation, waiting for their Indian colleague to appear. Standing apart, the team of male grass cutters are grouped together, excitedly comparing their respective pickings of discarded cigarette butts collected from around the camp. From the look on their faces, it appears to have been a lucrative haul. Suddenly, the breathless Fatimah rushes across the square to join them.

Meanwhile, a short distance behind, and from a quite different direction, Flight Lieutenant Munro is pedalling hard as he approaches the entrance to the camp.

"Good morning, Sir," calls out one of his men, accompanied by a mocking, American-style military salute.

The C.O ignores the greeting as he rounds the Mess building, coming into view of the local workers outside his office.

"At last he's here," mutters Andy to himself.

Using one foot to brake, the C.O dismounts, throwing his bike against the side of the hut and steps inside.

"Another damn slow puncture, Airman. Get it fixed!"

"They're all here, Sir."

"So, what the hell you waiting for, Airman? It's your job, not mine. Call them in. Get on with it!"

Andy moves to the doorway, pausing while he contemplates how best to address the local workforce. Finally, he calls out: "This way please, ladies and gentlemen, for the weekly Pay Parade."

The workers stand flat-footed for a few moments, not understanding or expecting the invitation. They look quizzically at the young Airman and then each other.

Fatimah comes to the rescue, in a language completely alien to Andy, before ushering the flock forward into the office.

The three washerwomen are first in line. In turn, each one approaches the trestle table, takes a respectful bow and, without lifting her head, holds out a hand to receive the brown envelope. This is followed by another equally deep bow as they leave the office. The same procedure is repeated by each of the trio of male grass cutters.

Andy turns to the C.O with a look of incredulity after the last of the workers has left.

"Sir, does that happen every time? I mean the bowing. I felt like laughing!"

"You have to remember, Airman, their last employer here was the Imperial Japanese Army. The Nips treated the people here in a brutal manner and, in a way, they've still not taken to us, despite the fact we were their saviours and are now their protectors. Leave them to respect us in their own way. They'll come to their senses. So, no laughing! Got it, Airman?" explains the C.O.

"Yes Sir. By the way, can I ask how exactly my predecessor managed to cock up a Pay Parade?"

"Sometimes one of the girls got a bit more than the others, which usually led to a bit of an undignified scuffle. I'll leave you to work that one out. And tell the cook, I'm still waiting for my coffee. But first, before you go…"

From the serious look on his face, Andy senses the C.O has some highly important information to impart.

"Sir?"

"Come through to my office, Airman."

Andy follows, pencil and note pad in hand, dipping his head through the beaded curtain.

"No need to write anything down, what I have to tell you is in the strictest confidence. Understand?"

"Of course, Sir."

"I shall be flying to Singapore tomorrow to rendezvous with my bride-to-be, who will be arriving from the UK. The wedding will be at St. Andrews, of course, then we'll take a short break up country in Malaya. In all, I will be away for some ten days. We'll both return here. I'll leave you a note of the dates. Got that?"

"Both of you, Sir?"

"Yes, we will be living at my bungalow. And one of your immediate tasks, while I'm away, is to get the place cleaned up and sparkling. The cooks can help by sorting out the kitchen and I won't complain if they surprise us by leaving a few goodies. I'll give it a thorough inspection on my return. Not a word to them, of course, about my plans. All this is top secret: the first the men will know of all this is *after* we've arrived back. Got it?"

"Understood, Sir," replies Andy.

"Right, I'm off to the strip. But, first, where's that signal about the complaint from the Squadron Leader of that Bristol Freighter that came through last month?"

"Haven't seen it, Sir," replies Andy.

"Course you haven't because it arrived before you came here. But you should find it filed away in that cabinet over there. Your predecessor employed what he considered to be a very sophisticated filing system: all the typed letters in one folder, manuscript ones in another and signals somewhere else. Didn't seem right to me but it sometimes worked."

"I prefer to file by subject matter, Sir."

"As long as you can find it – it was a complaint – do what you damn well like in future."

"What was the complaint about, Sir?"

"Well, it appears that the Bristol Freighter had already touched down when the pilot caught sight of our fire crew and ambulance tearing along the perimeter track on its way up to the strip. Damned incompetence."

"And what if the aircraft had crashed and there had been no one there... ?"

"Exactly, young man. Now, not a word to anyone, but I'll be up there most of today, incognito, dressed as a local, complete with my ultra high definition binoculars to do some random checks on Finnegan and his gang. Did a bit of amateur dramatics at university, so I know all about disguise. Someone said at the time I was a natural."

"Of course, Sir, not a word to anyone."

Andy, now alone, quietly works out the remainder of the day, his only visitors being Martin, with a handful of signals requiring the C.O's attention, and Ken with a mug of scalding hot coffee.

The fading light reminds him that it's time to return to the billet. Peering out through a wooden shutter, the sky is presenting a glorious, closing chapter to the day. With a sudden sweep of his arms, the shutters are thrown fully open. The colours lie softly and delightfully in tiers. A subtle orange tinge hangs over the outbuildings of the camp and, above them, a purple haze is slowly giving way to a deepening blue. He watches, almost spellbound, until the silent hand of darkness drops the curtain on the show. As a boy, living close to Dartmoor, he had often walked with his parents as they attempted to introduce him to the world of the beautiful and ever-changing patterns the sky can bring to delight the eye. 'Therapeutic' was the word his father had used repeatedly to describe his own feelings of dramatic sunsets. But Andy knows this is different, much different and on a grander scale. The slowly-changing colours leave him breathless. It is the first time he has fully appreciated a sunset and it registers as a moving, almost spiritual, experience. *Must get a camera,* he reminds himself.

He returns to the billet to find the atmosphere subdued. A group has gathered around the bed of Billy, the recent recipient of the latest 'Dear John' letter, and everyone is in serious discussion with the unhappy lad. Andy is inquisitive and moves closer to the action. Advice for the unfortunate young man is coming thick and fast.

"Let's face it, Billy, I've seen your picture of her – she's no oil painting."

"Plenty more fish in the sea. Any girl who waits for you to come out here before dumping you…"

"Billy, just look at her writing and spelling – it's real bad. Don't want to get stuck for the rest of your life with someone who ain't been to school."

"And everyone knows that tiny, joined-up writing means the person is, well, 'mean'."

"That's enough, fellas, just leave me alone. I need some kip," pleads Billy.

The group disbands, except for fireman Finnegan and Andy.

"Billy, my friend, I know you must feel hurt," begins the Irishman. "So…you have to get back at the bitch."

"How the hell do I do that, being thousands of miles away? Come on, Finnegan, tell me!" asks Billy in desperation.

"Simple."

"Oh, yeah?"

"First, we go round the billets collecting up all the spare photos of anyone's mum or, even better, granny. Second, you write the bitch a nice letter, enclosing the photos, ending up by saying you can't quite remember what she looks like. Then – and here's the punch line – you tell her to pick out her own photo from amongst the pictures of the old biddies – and ask her to send the others back!"

"Finnegan, you're a bloody genius!" beams Billy, looking better by the second.

"Anytime, my friend. Now get off your arse and start collecting those photos."

"You bet," Billy replies, casting off the bed sheet and slipping his feet into flip-flops.

The Irishman catches Andy turning away.

"Hope you heard that, too. Good advice if you ever get the same treatment."

"Whose fiendish idea was that, Finnegan?" asks Andy.

"Something I learnt while I was at Changi. And it worked a treat, I tell you. Mind you, the bloke who told me was worse off than Billy."

"How come? How could it possibly be worse?"

"Well, he was married to the woman who dumped 'im – and there were kids."

Andy winces as the explanation sinks home and returns to his bed space.

His thoughts are now of Sandra.

She would never send him a 'Dear John' – or would she? She wasn't that sort of girl, or was she?

But no doubt Billy had thought just the same, until the postal bombshell arrived.

And just how long had it been since the last letter from Sandra?

Her father had never really taken to him and perhaps now would be the right time for his daughter to offload her suitor. Literally on the other side of the world, he was already well out of sight. How soon before he also became 'out of mind'? Andy senses the odds are being stacked against him.

He comforts himself with the thought that Sandra has assured him she would be waiting for him on his return; but that still left another twenty months of waiting.

He would not have changed, of course. But would she?

In the background, he can hear Billy excitedly bartering a bottle of beer for a photograph of someone's ailing grandmother, shuffling along with the aid of a stick. Clearly his mood is now in the ascendancy.

Tonight, the billet lies strangely silent. The Music Man is fast asleep, snoring, along with most of the others. The temperature has soared during the day and Andy wonders just how long it will take him to adjust.

A few large, moth-like creatures are busy overhead, circling the light like excited kids at a fairground enjoying a never-ending, free ride on the merry-go-round. From outside, comes the chorus of crickets happily chirping the night away

4

"She's here! They're about to land!" shouts Martin from the doorway, before disappearing.

Andy drops his hands to either side of the typewriter and looks up in disbelief.

"No, can't be, not until tomorrow. Hold on."

His words are in vain. The messenger is now hot-footing it up to the airstrip to join a reception group of Airmen awaiting a late afternoon flight from Hong Kong.

Andy grabs his beret and prepares to join the party.

Ken appears holding a mug of coffee he has brought from the cookhouse.

"S'pose you won't be needing this now."

"No, just leave it there, Ken, I'll have it when I come back."

"What's the bleeding panic? All the lads rushing up to meet this 'plane. Anyone would think it's the flaming Queen."

"Well, perhaps not quite Her Majesty but pretty damn close. If it's who I think it is…"

"So who is it, Andy?"

"Not sure. Could just be the C.O with his new wife."

"Straight up? Right, I'm coming with you."

"But they must have changed their flight, Ken. Actually they're due up from Changi tomorrow on the early morning flight. Come on, let's see if we can grab a lift in the ambulance."

Both the ambulance and fire crew have already left, so the duo are forced to leg it.

They pause en route to take a break, hands on hips, taking deep breaths.

"If you want to go on ahead, I'll understand," suggests Ken. "This heat buggers me, I wasn't built for running. Eating and drinking perhaps, not running."

A couple of the more athletic lads from the Signals Section, anxious not to be late for the arrival, race past on foot.

"This could turn out to be a false alarm," warns Andy.

"Perhaps, but my money's on the Music Man, he's pretty sharp," suggests Ken.

"His finger is usually on the pulse. He told me the storeman spent last weekend cleaning up the C.O's bungalow; and the grass cutters have been tarting up the lawn and all the plants – and that was spot on. He reckoned it all pointed to the Old Man bringing a bird back with him."

"Yes, I was aware of that," replies Andy smugly, not wishing to appear uninformed.

"And he said the washerwomen were also there, putting in some hours," continues Ken.

"Really?"

"I reckon the Old Man is going over the top for this woman. He must be keen to impress her."

"Perhaps he's going to offer her a commission," suggests Andy, in an attempt to lighten the discussion.

"I'd be surprised if he's got anything else to offer her. Can't think what any woman would see in him."

As they approach the airstrip, they catch sight of a Valetta at the far end of the airfield coming in above the palm trees, quickly losing height as it prepares to land.

"I still reckon they won't be on this flight."

"Well, you should know," says Ken.

The landing is a smooth one and the aircraft taxies in.

The breathless pair reach the servicing shed, joining a group of some twenty Airmen, most of whom are stripped to the waist, waiting anxiously for the passengers to disembark. Virtually all activity on the camp is now on hold. The mood of anticipation heightens as the steps are being moved into position alongside the aircraft door.

A few move forward to be closer to the action.

"Oh! the suspense," remarks the Doc cynically, as there is a delay in positioning the steps.

Finnegan gives Andy a nudge with his shoulder, before whispering in his ear, "Can't wait to see what the Old Man's bit of stuff looks like."

"I think it's quite sad, people coming up here just to ogle at her," adds the Music Man, while pushing himself forward in front of the pair of them to reach pole position.

The door finally opens and a slender, reddish-haired female, in a knee-length, lemon dress appears.

"Not bad, not bad at all," comes a softly spoken compliment from the rear.

As if anticipating the reception party, the object of everyone's attention smiles demurely at the men and slowly descends the steps. A number of men edge forward to the foot of the steps.

"Well, she ain't Diana Dors, is she?" mutters Finnegan.

"Nice legs though," suggests Billy.

"She certainly likes an audience, I'll say that for her," adds the Music Man.

"And I wouldn't climb over her to get to you, that's for sure," adds Ken.

Behind her, follows her recently acquired husband, Flight Lieutenant Munro, smartly dressed in his KD and shorts and carrying a brown leather suitcase. He pauses on the steps to throw a disapproving glare at the unwelcome and unexpected reception party.

"What the hell are you lot doing here? Get back to work immediately – and that's an order!"

The lady of the moment continues to hold a friendly smile, as if dissociating herself from her husband's hostile outburst.

The welcoming party begin to disperse.

The C.O points an accusing finger directly at Andy.

"And you, Airman. I'll see you in my office in exactly one hour."

"Yes, Sir."

Andy watches as the C.O and his wife are driven away by jeep.

"What's all that about, Andy?" asks Finnegan.

"No idea but the Old Man isn't happy. Don't think he expected to see us all up here."

"Bugger him, quite natural for us to want to see his new bit of stuff. What's her first name, Andy, you must know?"

"Haven't a clue – but I'll soon find out."

Sergeant Curtis, in charge of the Signals Section, leans across to whisper in Andy's ear.

"Her name? It's bloody obvious, isn't it?"

"How d'you work that one out?" asks Finnegan.

"Simple. Think first of her new surname – come on! come on… ! Munro, Munro," adds the impatient Curtis.

There is a pause.

"Sorry still don't get it," concedes the fireman.

"Munro, Munro…so it's got to be *Marilyn* hasn't it, you daft sods!"

Andy groans and prepares to make his way to the office to face his Commanding Officer. As he turns, he catches the familiar face of Fatimah, the washerwoman, standing alone, partially hidden behind a parked petrol bowser. He pauses before offering a half-hearted wave of acknowledgement. But she wheels away immediately, as if not wishing to be seen and disappears quickly from view. He wonders what she is thinking. Will she be able to accept that circumstances have changed, given the arrival of the C.O's wife? If not, could he find himself caught up in the emotional cross fire? Or possibly cast in the role of spectator to a real life eternal triangle?

Back in the office, a single sip from the mug of coffee tells Andy the milk has curdled. All the paperwork is up to date so he relaxes, thumbing through a collection of back copies of the *Straits Times* that have been flown up from Singapore. The rush to the airstrip in the uncomfortable heat has taken its toll and he is feeling exhausted.

Any thoughts of taking a quick nap are broken by the sound of a bicycle banging against the wooden frame of the office. The C.O has arrived earlier than expected.

"In here, Airman!" comes the shout.

Andy follows, pencil and pad in hand.

"Tell me," the C.O continues, "who revealed the information about my flight arrival?"

"I don't know, Sir. I honestly thought you would be flying in tomorrow from Changi, not this afternoon, from the opposite direction, from Hong Kong."

"Exactly, as per the note I left you; and that was what I anticipated you leaking to all and sundry. You damn well let me down, Airman. I worked on the assumption that my ETA (estimated time of arrival) here tomorrow would soon become common knowledge, so I decided upon a classic outflanking manoeuvre by arriving here a day earlier, from Hong Kong – not Singapore. Yet somehow, someone found out about my change of plan."

"Yes Sir," replies Andy apologetically.

"Can you imagine how embarrassing it was for Dorothy – my wife, I should say – to be gawped at by a bunch of leering men?"

"No, Sir."

"Well I certainly can, it must have been dreadful. I'll get to the bottom of this, Airman, mark my words. I have my suspicions. Off you go – and in preparation you can start by dusting off the Charge Sheets – Form 252, if I recall correctly."

Talk of the C.O's wife dominates a lively conversation during dinner in the Mess.

"Suppose we won't be seeing much of them for the next few weeks," comments Jock.

"Don't bank on it, they've already had their honeymoon up country in Malaya," counters Andy.

"Listen, the longer he's off camp the better," adds Finnegan, devouring one of Ken's fancy cakes in a single mouthful.

"Who knows, he might end up needing some medical treatment," laughs the Doc.

"From exhaustion, you mean," suggests the Music Man.

Mindful of his allegiance to the C.O, Andy decides to avoid being drawn further into the discussion. He picks up his irons and makes for the door.

"Hey! Andy, give us a bit of gen before you go," Billy asks.

"You're his right hand man – so what's happening? Is his wife actually planning to stay on here?"

Billy persists, following Andy outside.

"She's staying for a while. I'm saying nothing more."

"O.K, mate, it's just that the lads are a bit curious. Personally, I couldn't give a bugger."

Andy decides, conveniently, to change the subject.

"Oh, Billy, have you managed to collect any decent photos to send back to your ex?"

"Indecent, you mean. Yeah, I've got a few corkers. Cost me a few dollars, mind you! One is of a Gran, complete with stick, and another of an old dear who could double as Quasimodo's sister. Finnegan reckons they're spot on."

Billy's mood is now firmly in the ascendancy. His 'Dear John' will remain on the notice board, long enough to be suitably and comprehensively annotated by the other men.

Andy catches sight of the C.O cycling away, homeward bound to his wife. He decides to take the opportunity to return to the billet. The post has arrived. He immediately spots a letter resting on his bed. At last, the first word from Sandra since his arrival on the camp. He grabs the letter. But the manuscript written address on the envelope is in the hand of his mother, not Sandra. Andy slips the letter inside his locker.

Meanwhile, a couple of miles away, Dorothy Munro is taking a first look around her new home. An only child, with parents equipped with the financial means to pander to her every need or whim, she had met with few of life's disappointments. Standing now in a cramped, improvised Asian kitchen, devoid of the latest Western gadgetry, her body language suggests she is facing one of those rare moments. Her mind flashes back to her first meeting with the dashing flier at a Christmas Charity Ball. Hard on the heels of an earlier painful, broken romance, Charles had more than filled a void in her life. She had been showered with his caring love notes and impressed by his attentiveness.

Perhaps the deciding factor in accepting his proposal of marriage had been the extent to which her parents had taken to the Flight Lieutenant. They had welcomed him as if he had single-handedly won the Battle of Britain; and his reluctance to engage in any discussion or recall of past military exploits had been accepted as an admirable example of genuine modesty. Any doubts about the disparity in their ages had been ignored. At the same time, closing in on her thirtieth birthday, Dorothy was becoming aware that an increasing number from her circle of friends had either married or become engaged. Matrimonial opportunities were likely only to lessen. Events had somehow conspired to develop their own head of steam, and she had felt powerless to control the direction they had taken her: into the welcoming arms of Flight Lieutenant Charles Howard Munro.

More worryingly, the honeymoon in Malaya had in many aspects been a bitter disappointment. His outbursts of impatience with the hotel staff had revealed a previously unseen side to his character; and his sexual behaviour had shown a disregard for her feelings. Was this, perhaps, a foretaste of marriage? And to compound her feelings of unease she was, much to her surprise, already missing her ever-attentive and doting mum and dad.

"You all right darling, you've gone rather quiet."

"It's clean, I'll grant you," comes Dorothy's qualified approval.

"Yes, darling, it's been thoroughly fumigated and, as soon as the smell had gone, the chaps from the camp were straight in giving the whole place another good lick of paint."

"And that's the problem, Charles. It still reeks from the first coat of paint."

"Don't worry, darling, we can leave the shutters open."

"Not at night we can't! We'll both be bitten to death by those awful insects," replies Dorothy as she makes her way into the garden.

Charles follows a few steps behind.

"Well stocked with plants, isn't it?"

"I suppose the men from the camp were brought in to do this as well?"

"Uh, yes. Enjoyed it immensely I'm told. Labour of love, so to speak. And it hasn't cost us a penny – or should I say a dollar?"

"Charles, I must say you were rather beastly towards them when we arrived."

"Not at all, darling, there are times when they have to be put in their place – and that was one of them. That's how an Officer earns respect from his subordinates."

Charles slaps his knee in an unsuccessful attempt to destroy a persistent mosquito.

"Was it really surprising that they were inquisitive? They weren't rude or offensive, I smiled at them and they smiled back. Quite flattering in a way. No one booed! Perhaps, in a sub-conscious way, I was seen as a link with home."

"Sorry, but I have no wish to discuss the subject further. Consider it closed."

"But apart from the washerwomen, how long is it since they last saw a white woman? Don't forget they are full-blooded men with natural instincts."

Charles clears his throat with a manufactured cough and turns away.

"It's just the eight months you've got left to do up here, isn't it Charles?"

"Yes, darling, eight months and four days to be precise."

"Well, can I suggest we make the very best of it. Try not to be so grumpy with the men. After all, I'm sure they're all probably counting the days till their return."

Charles offers no comment.

Together, they walk slowly around the garden without exchanging a word.

Dorothy pauses to admire a splash of white gardenia.

Overhead, the laboured drone of a departing Hastings breaks the silence.

"Let's go inside, shall we? I'll prepare a couple of my very special iced lemon teas," suggests Charles.

"And I'll just pop into the bedroom, dear."

Charles rummages through a plate of Ken's fancy cakes, awaiting his wife's return.

"Everything to your liking in there, darling?"

"I'm not really sure," comes the reply delivered slowly in a monotone.

Dorothy is now standing in the doorway and appears to be holding something behind her back.

She breaks into a wicked smile, before thrusting her hands in the air.

"Charles Munro, you are a surprise package! Where on earth did you get these? I found them in one of the drawers."

Dorothy is dangling a pair of black stockings and matching suspenders above her head.

"Um… Ah…got them in… Hong Kong yesterday Ah… while you were having your hair done," stutters Charles.

"Well, I must say, full marks for trying; but like most men you haven't a clue about women's sizes. These would fit a much, much larger women than me. But you are a sweetie for making the effort. And! If it's not too hot this evening…"

Dorothy leans forward and delivers a robust kiss on her husband's reddening face.

Charles makes an immediate mental note to double-check the entire bungalow to ensure no further items belonging to Fatimah are discovered by his wife.

"I take it we're not going out for dinner this evening," teases Dorothy.

"Nowhere to go actually, apart from the D.O's spread."

"D.O?"

"Yes, darling, that's the District Officer. One of us, English speaking. His post is a sort of legacy from our colonial days."

"And what exactly does he do?"

"Not quite sure, very much doubt if anyone else does. Probably doesn't even know himself! But he throws a first class party and plays a mean hand at Bridge."

"Is he married?"

"I should say. She's a good looker but with a suspicion of Indian blood somewhere down the line. No kids, that's probably deliberate though. Amelia is her name, probably a false one. I'll fix something up once we get settled here."

"So what's for dinner tonight?"

"Thought we'd keep it simple: spam fritters, followed by a few slices of pomelo – that's a sort of fruity, green grapefruit. Washed down by one of those expensive bottles of that red wine I picked up in Hong Kong."

"I can hardly wait," replies Dorothy with more than a hint of sarcasm.

"Excellent, my darling, I'll get cracking straight away."

"Charles, before you go, what about that huge packet of candles in the kitchen? Do we really need so many?"

"Strictly an emergency back-up to the rather temperamental lighting we have here. Anyway, don't you think they lend a rather romantic touch to dinner?"

Without offering a comment, Dorothy turns and heads for the bathroom.

5

Mother Nature has dipped into her palette to stunning effect. As the men gather in the square, the day is closing with a colourful marriage of orange and gold in the sky above.

Another Borneo sunset to behold. But its beauty is lost on the diminutive figure of Flight Lieutenant Munro as he steps authoritatively onto the top of a wooden crate to address the gathering. He clears his throat before speaking:

"Men, tomorrow is an important, very important, day in the year. It is an opportunity to pay our heart-felt respect and thanks to those of our fellow countrymen, and many others, who gave their lives so that we – and those who follow us – would remain free to enjoy ours. We owe them a debt we can never repay. Tomorrow is Remembrance Day.

For those who don't already know, a few miles from here is a Memorial Park where some three thousand of the fallen are at rest. Some of them, like you, were young men. They left their wives, mothers and loved ones behind, never to return. We're the fortunate ones: we will be returning to our families.

Tomorrow, we will be at the park to pay our respects. I want you all to remember my words as you stand proud and tall in your ceremonial dress. This is *not* another square-bashing parade where a Drill Instructor is trying to catch you out with an unpolished buckle or dirty toecaps.

All newcomers, pay attention. I give you advance warning, you will be standing for over an hour directly exposed to the sun. If, at any stage, you feel dizzy or affected by the heat, remember to throw your rifle to one side before you go down. This is particularly important if, at that point, you happen to have your bayonet fixed. We don't want a repetition of last year when one Airman stabbed himself in the thigh and another sliced his upper arm. We will be there to represent the Royal Air Force, not to spill unnecessary blood. Our forefathers spilt enough for us all.

So, I'll see you all here, for inspection, at zero eight hundred hours. Oh! and one point I almost forgot: I understand that, for the first time since the War, a party of Aussies have made the long trip from their homeland. No doubt some may actually be survivors, POWs, hoping to pay their respects to their fallen comrades. Let's put on a damn good show. Any questions? Fully understood?"

A mumbling chorus of "Yes Sir," follows the C.O's solemn words. The gathering breaks up. There is little talk among the parade party.

Andy and Finnegan look pensively at each other, before strolling back to the billet.

"First time, I've ever heard the Old Man speak like that, sounded almost human," says the fireman.

"Yeah, struck me that way, too," replies Andy.

"Did you know this place saw a bit of action in World War Two?" adds Finnegan.

"Yes, the C.O mentioned it – at some length – when I first got here."

"Well, this airstrip was built by the Japs in '42 and, if you look closely in the undergrowth at the far end of the runway, you'll find the skeletons of a couple of their Mitsubishi Zero fighter aircraft," continues Finnegan.

"Right, I'll make sure I get up there and take a peep. Must get a camera first, though."

"What's more, at the end of the War, this was the exact spot where some Japanese prisoners were flown in from the mainland, before they were shipped out. And a lot of Australian POW traffic came through here as well. One 'plane might land with a few Nips, the next with our blokes, straight from the prison camps."

"Bit like a transit station, you mean?"

"Not really, 'cause *not all* the Japs who flew in, flew out."

"How come?"

"Some evenings, there was a 'turkey shoot'. After our people had endured the distressing sight of the skeleton bodies of the Aussies and our blokes who had been liberated from the POW camps, the next 'plane would arrive with captured Nips. So, with emotions running high, sometimes the Japs were taken straight up to the far end of the airfield at dusk and simply blown away. Can't really blame 'em, can you?"

"What about the Geneva Convention?" asks Andy.

"What's that got to do with it? Bastards got what they deserved!" snaps Finnegan.

"Any more for tonight's card school?" shouts Billy, attempting to bring the conversation back to the present.

In the billet, most of the men are preparing themselves for the morning, either polishing up their shoes or cleaning their belts. The mood is subdued. Now and then, a cockroach scuttles across the stone floor, seeking safety under a bed.

Andy stretches out on his mattress and wonders what was really happening on this camp – perhaps in this very billet – ten years ago. And how true was it, as Finnegan claimed, that the Japanese POWs had been executed here without trial? Despite the brutality they had inflicted on our Forces and the locals, was that defensible? An eye for an eye? Compared with what had gone before, the inconvenience of his leaving home and doing National Service on a now peaceful tropical island no longer seems a hardship.

Morning arrives. A Bedford truck pulls up outside the billet, the rear flap drops, and the twenty members of the camp's ceremonial guard clamber aboard. The driver slowly moves them another fifty yards to park outside the storeroom. The men pile out to collect their Enfield 303 rifles from Jock, the storeman. "Don't look so bloody serious, fellas, yees lot are going to a pussy-footing parade, not a bleeding War," mocks the Scotsman.

"Just as well," answers Billy, "we've got no ammunition!"

"Over here, men!" barks the C.O, jumping out of his Land Rover. The squad react slowly to the order, fearing another speech is about to be delivered.

"Stop Press, so to speak. Three of the Australian Air Force personnel, who are here on special duties with us, will now be taking their place in our parade this morning. Another reason for you all to turn in a first class show: don't want a bunch of colonials descended from convicts to show us up, do we? Eh? I'll spare you the embarrassment of a final inspection. Now get back in the truck. And don't forget what I told you all yesterday."

"Should be able to manage that, after all it is Remembrance Day," whispers Martin, in an attempt to lighten the mood.

The vehicle winds its way for a couple of miles along a narrow cart track, with the overhanging branches occasionally brushing the canvas roof and sides of the vehicle.

"Do you think the driver's lost?" asks Andy, struggling to maintain his balance.

"He found it last year!" laughs Finnegan.

The truck comes into a clearing and to a halt at the gates to the park, where a group of priests from the local area, some in white gowns, are deep in conversation. The men spill out and are led by the C.O into the welcome shade of a colonnade, the walls of which record the countless columns of names. After a few minutes, Flight Lieutenant Munro beckons the men to follow him out onto the central lawn. The men form up in three lines in front of a towering white memorial in the form of a cross, glittering like a diamond in the morning sun. Standing erect, their KD trousers smartly pressed and belt buckles shining, the ceremonial guard are at once the focal point of attention for the gathering onlookers.

Already damp patches of perspiration are appearing on the jackets. Turning his head from side to side, Andy is shocked by the sight of the endless lines of small, square white stones, each covered by a brown, metal name plaque. Before the parade is brought to attention, he glances to admire the riot of colour from the assortment of plants and the trees that border the park. The whole area is beautifully landscaped; and there is an undeniable air of tranquillity. In his short life he had struggled to envisage a picture of heaven; but now he somehow feels better prepared for the task.

The Service, with each priest delivering a reading, is punctuated by the men carrying out their necessary ceremonial drill to the cries of: "Order Arms!" "Present Arms!" and "Fix Bayonets!" The heat becomes intense as Andy finds sweat pouring from his body.

His arms begin to ache and the rifle almost slips from his grasp. His jacket is now stuck to his chest, like a piece of used blotting paper, and his KD trousers are keeping his legs uncomfortably hot. The peak of his UK issue cap is managing to minimise the glare from above but his hair is now wringing wet. Out of the corner of his eye, he can see the sizeable Australian contingent, in civilian clothes, some holding aloft an umbrella to shield themselves from the unrelenting sun. A couple of the older looking men in their party are displaying medals pinned to their jackets. Suddenly, a voice from behind Andy whispers, "How much longer? Shit! I think I'm going down."

"Start counting then, start counting," comes the immediate and anonymous advice.

Mercifully, the C.O gives the final "At Ease" call, followed by the welcome order "Dismiss." Amongst the men, there is a an unspoken sense of both relief and pride they have all remained standing.

The tired group file away, quickly making for the shade. A ripple of applause comes from the visiting Australians who have clearly been moved by the occasion. They appear to be a mix of middle-aged and elderly people, but no children.

The C.O has disappeared, which allows Andy and the others to move to the shade and willingly accept an apparently endless supply of chilled beer which the Aussies have brought with them. To their complete surprise, most of the men are being congratulated by the male visitors with a hearty handshake or a slap on their sweat-sodden backs, while the luckier ones are treated to an unsolicited onslaught of unrestrained female hugs and kisses. The decibels rise and soon laughter begins to lighten the mood. Andy slips away, deciding to look more closely at the individual gravestones.

Slowly, he makes his way between the lines, pausing to read the names. He is moved to discover the number of teenagers who are at rest. But he is finally brought to tears when he comes across the first bronze plaque bearing the words: 'Known unto God.' As he continues, he finds that the unidentified appear to account for at least half of the total buried.

During this walk, Andy is aware of a woman following some distance behind him.

In an attempt to conceal his emotions, he takes a sharp turn towards a sheltered area beneath a clutch of palm trees. His back is turned to his pursuer.

But the lady is not to be shaken off and remains striding directly towards him.

"Excuse me," come her softly-spoken words.

Andy stops, wiping a hand across his eyes, before looking around to face the woman.

"Excuse me, but I wanted to thank you."

There is no mistaking her Australian accent.

"I was watching you during the Service," she continues.

"Well, I apologise but never been much good at rifle drill. Genuinely sorry about that. Secretly, I was hoping no one was watching me – but I got the front row."

"No apologies needed. You boys were marvellous. There was a reason why I noticed you."

"Really?" says a surprised Andy.

"Yes, in a way you look very much like my son. Not quite as muscular but the same age, height, dark hair and young face."

The remark leaves him struggling to respond. Slowly, they walk together in silence for a few yards.

"Is your son here today?" asks Andy casting a glance at the group of visiting Aussies.

"Yes, he's here. I'll take you to him."

The woman leads the way across the immaculately cut lawns.

Suddenly she stops in front of a grave, upon which lays a circular, floral wreath arranged in Australia's national colours of green and yellow.

"Here he is. My son, my only child." Her head drops.

Andy searches desperately but unsuccessfully for words to express his sadness.

His immediate instinct is to console the woman but she is a total stranger.

"I'm sorry, so sorry," says Andy, lowering his head in a gesture of respect.

The woman remains surprisingly composed, without any outward sign of distress.

Suddenly, she takes a deep breath, raising a hand to her freckled forehead. Her small frame is modestly dressed, without much apparent thought for the unrelenting heat. A slightly crumpled white bowling hat lies perched on a thatch of greying hair. Her faded, floral dress reaches down almost to her ankles. She struggles to offer a smile, as if to prove that her emotions are under control.

"My friends think I've taken it all remarkably well. Others just say I'm a hard bitch. His father has never been the same since we got the telegram. I cried myself out many years ago. Now I just hurt inside."

Although desperate to offer some comfort, Andy remains lost for the right words.

"I only found out a couple of years ago that our boy is here, and it's taken me that time to put the money together to make the trip. But I'm so glad I came. It's such a beautiful place, don't you think? Oh, the flowering trees and shrubs – such colours! – and the way its all been looked after. The gardeners have done a wonderful job. I didn't know what to expect. I'm so glad I came."

She shakes her head, as if trying to quell her emotions. They stand together silently for a minute or two.

"What's your name?"

"Andy...Andy Marshall."

"Can you do me a favour, young Andy?"

"Of course, if I possibly can."

"Well, if you ever come to Oz, make sure you visit me in Melbourne. Now I'll give you my name and address. I don't have a telephone."

The woman's fingers scratch feverishly through her handbag before producing a crumpled piece of headed note paper, bearing the name of a hotel in Jesselton on the mainland.

Her tongue slides slowly back and forth across her lips as she puts pencil to paper. The writing is child-like.

"Sure you can you read it? I'm not the best writer."

"Yes, that's fine."

"Now is that a promise, young Andy?"

"It's a promise."

"Good – and don't lose that piece of paper!"

For a fleeting moment, the lady's tone of voice reminds him of his mother telling him to wash behind both ears.

The pair stroll back to join the rest of the party.

Billy strides out towards them, holding out a brown bottle of beer, frothing at the neck. Andy stops to accept it, while the woman breaks away to re-join her party.

"Bit old for you isn't she, Andy?"

"Shut up, Billy," comes the sharp response

The park staff have left and Finnegan can be heard breaking into a tuneless song.

"What the hell have you been up to? You've been missing all the free beer. Those Aussies are really pushing the boat out and – guess what?"

"Go on, Billy, tell me."

"They've invited all the lads to one of their 'Barbees' They've brought a load of huge steaks in cooler boxes and they're going to set it up close to the park."

"Impossible to feed us all, surely," replies Andy.

"They don't seem to think so. If you ask me, I reckon they planned it in advance," smiles Billy, followed by an enthusiastic dig in the ribs. "What with a free piss-up, it's turning into a day to enjoy, don't you think?"

Andy looks away, shocked at the flippancy of his colleague's remark.

Young lives cut short, their bodies at rest in a foreign land thousands of miles from home. Their families left to grieve. No, this is not a day to enjoy but a day to remember.

"You're a worrier, Andy, taking it all too serious. Don't look so miserable. Relax, take each day as it comes. Hold on now, didn't lose anyone in your family in the War, did you?"

The question is met with a stony glare.

"Christ, haven't put my bloody foot in it, have I?"

Andy counters with a question of his own.

"By the way, where did the C.O disappear to?"

"We reckon his wife was expecting him home for Sunday lunch, so forget about him for the rest of the day."

Andy relaxes and makes for the barbecue. One of the Aussie men, boasting a bush hat, approaches him, "Fancy a cool un, young man? And take that flaming jacket off for starters, you won't upset any of our women – might even excite them. Some of them need cheering up."

Andy's right hand almost disappears under the involuntary bone-crunching handshake from the lanky visitor with a weather-beaten face and bushy eyebrows.

"The name's Jake. Not my real one, mind you, but a nickname I'm stuck with."

"Pleased to meet you, Jake. How did you manage to get here?" enquires Andy.

"Long story. Do you really want to hear it? Well, we first flew to Singapore, then caught another 'plane to Jesselton. Then the fun began. We had to find a way over to this island. We wanted to stay over here, stay the night, have a look around. So…we ended up hiring a motor launch! After all, there's some twenty of us. But I tell you this, Sport, we'll be back in bigger numbers next year, once the word gets around. You can count on it."

Andy throws his head back to take a swig of beer.

"Plenty more where that one came from," comes Jake's immediate response.

Martin and Finnegan, bottle in hand, join Andy and the Aussie.

Jake steps forward and gives each of them a welcoming, fatherly hug.

"You boys did us proud, couldn't have done any more today."

"I think we possibly could," suggests Martin.

"How come?" asks Billy.

"We could have had some music. Perhaps…"

"Give it a rest, Martin, we hear enough of your music in the billet," interrupts Finnegan, "Can you imagine a whole band standing out here in this heat, with some poor bugger banging a bloody great drum strapped to his belly? We'd end up digging another grave before the day was out!"

"Come on now, boys, over here and enjoy a *real* steak," says Jake, sensing an argument might develop.

Not surprisingly, the Aussies circulate first amongst their fellow countryman who serve on the camp, then gradually break away to other parts of the park to pay their respects. But as the afternoon passes they return and their attention turns again to the men from the UK. Andy watches and listens. Those who have recently emigrated seem eager to find someone associated with a particular city or county they or their parents have left behind and enquire about recent developments there. Addresses are being exchanged and generous invitations to Australia flow freely. To the young National Serviceman, it seems fitting that this remote yet idyllic resting ground for the dead could now become the birthplace for future friendships.

The lads finally say their 'goodbyes' before boarding the truck. Andy catches sight of the woman with whom he had spoken. During the afternoon she had sat alone, and seemed content to do so. He wonders whether he should have made the effort to speak further with her, to console her. Now he feels he should say something but words are hard to find. She gives him a tender smile as he drives away, followed by a hesitant wave.

In the fading light, the rest of the Aussie party are now breaking into full song but pause to give the departing parade three hearty cheers.

Back in the billet, Andy tries to sleep, but the words 'My son, my only child' continue to echo in his ears. And with it, his first thoughts on the justification for the 1945 'turkey shoot' of captured Japanese Forces are being viewed in a different light.

6

A blanket of silence covers the billet. Not even the Music Man dares to offer a sound. The post has arrived.

Andy lies horizontal on his bed, eyes eagerly racing through sentence after sentence of Sandra's latest typed letter, a letter destined to be read and re-read a dozen times more before the day closes.

Around him, his colleagues are similarly engrossed, their thoughts no doubt thousands of miles away. A time for both reflection and for thoughts of the future.

"So what are you planning to do for Christmas, Andy?"

Finnegan stands, beer bottle in hand, looking down at the young Airman.

"Later, not now," pleads Andy, without turning his head.

"Sorry mate, didn't mean to interrupt. You're a lucky bastard with the post. I'll come back later."

"Hold on, Finnegan. Christmas? Haven't even thought about it yet. Now then let's think. First, I'll see what Santa has put in my stocking, collect my presents from around the tree, then pop outside and build myself a couple of snowmen, then…"

"All right, all right, don't be daft. Just been talking to the Music Man who's come up with a gem of an idea."

"Which is?".

"We take off, leave the island," says Finnegan with a wild flourish of his arms.

"Who's 'we'? And where are *we* taking off to?"

"We is: yours truly, the Music Man, yourself – perhaps Billy. Our secret destination will be one of the neighbouring islands. And, just in case you're wondering how we're going to get there, that's all in hand."

"Sounds great, but we'll need a boat, Finnegan."

"Exactly, and that's already fixed."

"Count me in!" comes the enthusiastic response.

Andy returns to Sandra's letter, deciding to go back to the

beginning. It reads:

Dear Andrew,

Received your letter this morning. Posted 'Airmail' but it's taken an eternity to reach me. Your local Post Office needs a real talking to.

Loved the photos you sent. Next time, scribble the names of the men on the back. Then I'll be able to put names to faces. Don't forget now, will you?

Must say, I do envy you the sunshine and warmth. Find it hard to believe that you miss our frosts and Spring showers. The weather here's been ghastly. We've just had our first fall of snow and it's played total havoc with my getting to and from work. Daddy got blocked in on our driveway and couldn't get out for a couple of days, it was so icy and slippery. In desperation, he drove out sideways over one of Mum's flower beds. She's hardly spoken to him since. Daddy's back in the spare bedroom again. Nothing's changed!

Anyway, enough of our problems. How are you? I bet you've got a really impressive tan by now. The girls in the Office think it's so exciting I have a boyfriend in Borneo, land of the head hunters, they keep reminding me. Have you seen any yet?

Daddy is very excited about the opening of his third Branch. Hopes to have it up and running before Christmas. Are you still planning on going back into the Civil Service? Daddy says that when you come back and get demobbed, he might offer you a proper job, running one of his Branches. That would be more exciting, wouldn't it?

I know you had doubts about him but he's not a bad old sort really. Once you are prepared to make allowances and get to know him, I'm sure we'll all get along just fine. Bark worse than bite, you might say.

Everyone seems to be getting so excited about Christmas. I've been invited to so many parties it's difficult to know which ones to accept. What are you doing for Christmas, my dear Andrew? Not much snow around out there with you, I bet!

I've sent you a card, plus a special present. Hope you like them both, and hope even more they reach you before the twenty fifth!

Finally, I have an apology to make. Brace yourself, Andrew, because it's something I'm so ashamed about. I've lost my engagement ring. It was our Office Party and I'm sure someone must have put something very naughty in my glass. I became rather silly and, so I'm told, made a bit of a spectacle of myself. Ended up with a dreadful hangover.

Can't even remember going home. I've hunted high and low for the ring, but without success. Can you ever forgive me? I know it cost you such a lot of money and now it means you'll have to buy me another one. I feel so awful about it. I overheard one unkind soul at work suggesting it meant our engagement was now, technically speaking, off. What a cheek! The sooner I have a replacement, the better. Hope you'll forgive me.

Must dash, Daddy's waiting for me in the car outside. We're going down to the stables.

Love as always, Sandra

Andy carefully folds the letter back into the envelope, before placing it inside his bedside locker. Its content fills him with dismay. Did he really need to know that Sandra was making a spectacle of herself; and was it necessary, at this point in time, to mention the lost engagement ring? Cast away on the other side of the world, what the hell could he possibly do about it? That news could have waited. And the mention of him being the boyfriend! Had she forgotten to remind her pals they were engaged to be married?

And, for the first time, there was no mention of the wedding and its guest list – nor *the dress*. Perhaps more worrying is the fact that the letter runs only to three pages, the shortest to date. He walks down the billet and stands in the doorway, looking out at a couple of lads knocking a football back and forth on a dusty patch of ground.

Andy is deep in thought: for the first time he harbours doubts about his future with Sandra.

He gazes upwards at the clear blue sky, failing to realise that a ball has come to rest at his feet.

"Come on Andy, kick it over here!" comes the cry.

"Wake up!" comes another shout.

With a clumsy shuffle of his legs, Andy prods the ball away in the direction of the players. He turns quickly, almost bumping into Finnegan.

"Bad news from home?" asks the fireman.

"No, not really."

"Sure about that? My friend, I'm a good listener. If you want a second opinion…"

Andy decides to change the topic of conversation.

"About the island holiday, Finnegan, put me down as a definite."

"Good man!"

"So what's on the island?"

"I'm told a few natives live there. And I mean a few."

"And food?"

"We'll take our own. I reckon I can do a deal with Cookie."

"Why not take him with us?" asks Andy.

"He's not good company after a few drinks, and we'll be taking a few bottles with us."

"And the sleeping arrangements?"

"We'll take a cut down parachute. Tried it before – and it works."

"Is Billy coming?"

"We can count him out. The Music Man spoke to him yesterday and reckons he's had a relapse after his 'Dear John.' He was chuffed to death sending back that put-down letter and those hideous photos to his ex-girl friend. But now he's got second thoughts about having hurt the cow. Gone quiet, hardly talks to anyone and goes out alone for late night walks."

"So that's just the three of us, right?"

"Correct."

"A suggestion, Finnegan: why wait for Christmas? Why not take off this weekend?"

"You mean a trial run?"

"Yeh."

"Why not indeed! I'll square it with the Music Man."

"Is Martin planning to take his gramophone?" jokes Andy.

"Not a snowball's chance in hell! His gramophone's never been a problem: it's that bloody mournful sound that keeps coming out of it. Come to think of it, we could take it with us – then sling it overboard."

"Now that would be cruel."

"I know, but a bloody relief to the rest of us in the billet, 'specially when we're trying to get some kip. Hey! the lads would pay us just to drop it into the South China Sea."

There is an unusual spring in Finnegan's step as he makes towards the prostrate body of Ken.

Andy's eyes follow the Irishman as he makes for the cook's bed space. He catches just the opening words of their conversation: "Cookie, got a deal you might be interested in..." before the strains of the Music Man's latest attempt to convert a captive audience to one of his favourite classical records envelops the billet.

"Turn that bloody racket off!" "Not again!" "I'm trying to read!" comes the almost immediate chorus of complaints. Martin bows to the hostile response, then walks the length of the billet to join Andy.

"Philistines, the lot of them," comes his dismissive comment as they meet.

"Martin, have you been to this island?"

"No, but I caught an overhead view of most of the islands on a landing approach. And I spotted one no more than a few miles from here, directly across from our local beach.

From the air it looked uninhabited but positively beautiful. I thought it might be fun to pop over. What worries me is whether we can get a reliable boat. I've seen the death traps the local fishermen use!"

"I can swim, a little," replies Andy.

"That might just come in handy," smiles Martin.

"Shades of 'Robinson Crusoe', don't you think?"

"As long as one of us doesn't end up like 'Man Friday!'"

Meanwhile, Dorothy Munro is waiting, in her new home, for the right moment to sound out her husband on an idea which she anticipates will tax her powers of persuasion.

She circles the Commanding Officer, seated in an well-worn leather armchair recently gifted to him by the District Officer. Off-duty, he sports a pair of cream slacks and a pillar box red silk shirt, topped off with a scarlet neckerchief.

"I think your glass needs topping up, dear."

"You're spoiling me, darling, but please don't stop. And not so much tonic this time."

"I've got an idea, Charles," says Dorothy tentatively.

"What now?"

"Well, you did mention there might be a problem with morale on the camp."

"I wouldn't call it a problem. More a negative attitude by the men. So what's the idea?"

"A party, or a get-together – here. You, me…and the men."

"Never get them all in here!"

"No, no, but a few at a time might work. Sergeants one night, Corporals another, and then perhaps a selection from the rest. Off duty, casual gear. Could work wonders."

"Umm, let me think about it."

"Can we think about it now?" insists Dorothy.

"Not a good idea, darling."

"Because?"

The C.O rises, pushing his footstool away with a angry stab of his foot.

"Because… we don't have to pander to them. In the UK, Officers don't entertain or fraternise in their homes with Other Ranks. That is a well established military principle. And what applies in the UK applies equally here."

"But that's the whole point, my dear, we're not in the UK. They don't go home at weekends. They must miss seeing their families, particularly the married men."

"You've missed the point entirely. They are all Servicemen, serving Queen and Country. Didn't have men flying backwards and forwards from here in the last War because they were homesick, did we? Just imagine, the Fall of Singapore in '42: the Japs at the ready on the other side of the causeway, poised to strike across the water, and all action is put on hold while we sift through applications from men wanting to go home to see their families! Totally bizarre! They had a job to do then and they have one to do now, and that includes those disruptive National Servicemen. Compared to what I went through, this is Butlins! I'm sorry, but I don't think a social gathering would make any sense."

"Sorry, Charles, but I still think it *does* makes sense."

"As I've already said, I'll think about it, darling."

The C.O turns his back on his wife and walks towards one of the shuttered windows.

"Which means we forget the idea, does it?" snaps Dorothy.

"No but…"

"My dear, I'll do all the preparation and I'll enlist the help of that young man of yours, Andrew, is that his name? There'll be nothing for you to do at all, apart from holding court which is, of course, your forte."

"Come to think of it, darling, that is the sort of role which comes naturally to me. You may have a good point there. But as I said, leave it with me."

Dorothy is quick to pounce on a possible weakening of her husband's position.

"Precisely. You could entertain them with your exciting recollections of your time at the fall of Singapore and your early flying days in the Air Force. I'm sure they would find it every bit as interesting as I did. I very much doubt if any of them have – or ever will - experience such incredible times."

"Yes darling, there is some merit in what you say. But I'd prefer to let the matter rest for the moment, if you don't mind."

"Just one extra thought if I may, my dear," adds Dorothy. "I've noticed those rather sad looking locally-engaged staff who work on the camp. They strike me as rather emaciated, particularly the grass cutters. Also those poor washerwomen…"

"Good God, you're not suggesting we invite them along as well, are you?"

"No, but someone should be thinking of their welfare and perhaps making them feel more appreciated."

"They get jolly well paid. What's more we lost thousands of men liberating them from the Japs. In my book that's payment enough," counters the C.O.

"At some convenient time, perhaps you could introduce them to me. I've noticed in particular the Indian washerwoman who never fails to stop and greet me with a big, toothy smile. Never speaks, just smiles. I take it they all come from the village."

"Wouldn't have a clue," replies the C.O, realising that a swift change of topic is called for.

"To be brutally honest, Charles, I'm getting a bit bored here. The amah and the houseboy are very good, so there's little left for me to do. I read a bit, potter about in the garden, take a short nap in the afternoon but it's not really enough. I think these get-togethers with the men would be a jolly good idea for all concerned. What do you say?"

"I say it's time for bed, darling," comes the roguish reply.

7

It is shortly after dawn and the sun is waiting patiently to break through.

Andy, Finnegan and the Music Man stand together alone on the beach, looking out over the open sea. Around their bare feet lay clutches of seaweed and pieces of broken driftwood. There is hardly a ripple on the water but there is an undeniable note of apprehension in their voices.

"How far d'you think it is over to the island?" asks Andy, pointing an outstretched arm toward the horizon.

"A damn sight nearer if we'd managed to get hold of a boat with an outboard motor!" replies Martin.

"Listen, we've a boat, two oars and three men – so let's get on with it," shouts Finnegan.

The Irishman seizes the initiative by moving to the front of the stationary rowing boat, attempting to drag it along by its chunky rope. The weight soon forces him into a drunken-like stagger before stumbling then falling onto the wet sand. The trio break into laughter.

"Careful, you silly sod," shouts Martin. "You'll rip the bottom out on the coral, so let's all carry it out into the water. Got it?"

Andy suggests a final check on their supplies. "Got my list here."

"*You* would have!" laughs Finnegan.

"Right, food: bananas, pineapple, pomelo, tinned spam and corned beef, flakes, biscuits, bananas, tea, powdered milk, fags, water and…beer!"

Martin is peeling away the tarpaulin at the back of the boat, barking a mocking military call as each item is identified.

"Also one makeshift parachute tent, together with mugs and irons," he adds.

"Great, let's go!"

With a man on each side, and one at the front, the boat is hoisted into the air and carried to the water's edge.

"Come on, a bit further," pleads Finnegan as their ankles catch up with the receding tide.

The boat rocks violently from side to side as the crew finally clamber aboard.

Finnegan takes immediate charge: "Take an oar each, I'll be cox. The object of the exercise is to use it to sweep the water, not remove it. Row together. We don't want to end up going round in bloody circles! Got it?"

After a few tentative strokes, the boat slowly begins to edge forward into deeper water.

"Hope you two can swim?" smiles the Irishman.

There is no response, the only sound being the oars scraping as they swivel in the rowlocks.

"I'll take that as a negative then."

Soon, the inexperienced rowers begin to lose their rhythm and their oars begin to drag and chop the water. The cox suggests they take a break.

Andy and Martin try to relax by opening their shoulders. They throw their heads back, take deep breaths and let their hands trail in the water.

The sun is breaking through and the crew take the opportunity to discard their shirts.

"Further than I thought," admits Finnegan raising himself from a crouched position at the back of the boat, to train the C.O's borrowed binoculars in the direction of their destination.

"Right men," Finnegan intones, "put your backs and shoulders into it. It's not that far really."

"Cheeky, lazy Oirish bastard," groans Martin. "I'll be cox on the return journey!"

"Time for a song, I think," the Irishman grins, in an attempt to lift the spirits of his crew.

"How about the Eton Boating song?" gasps Martin.

"You'll be singing on your own, 'cause I don't know the words,"

"I do!" shouts Andy.

"Ah, but not be the words I'll be singing," laughs Martin.

"Come on then Music Man, give us a solo – if we don't like it we'll throw you overboard!"

Martin clears his throat, takes a deep breath and lets rip:

When Judith goes out to make water

She passes a powerful stream
She pees for an hour and a quarter
You can't see poor Judith for steam
Now the sexual life of a camel
Is stranger than anyone thinks
In the height of the mating season
It tried to bugger the sphinx
But the sphinx's posterior orifice
Is blocked by the sands of the Nile
Which accounts for the hump on the camel
And the sphinx's inscrutable smile

The song is delivered in a rich tenor voice, a voice previously unheard by his fellow men. There is a brief moment of silence before Finnegan and Andy burst into laughter.

"Never thought we'd hear that sort of stuff from you of all people, Music Man. All that classical and jazz stuff back in the billet – and now this!"

Andy reflects on their bizarre situation. Sailing off to an unknown island, singing dirty songs without a soul within earshot to offend. No compass and not a life jacket between them. Quite a tale to tell when he gets home and, as an added bonus, he's almost forgotten Sandra's latest letter.

The boat is now on its intended path with the shoreline of the island coming into clearer focus. Suddenly the men are hit with a strong cross current. Finnegan rises to his feet, shouting a number of contradictory orders which serve only to confuse the flustered rowers.

"You're drifting again, men, straighten up!" "Stop rowing, Martin." "Just you now, Andy, bring it round." "Good man, that's better." "Martin start rowing again."

The stream of instructions are brought to an abrupt close when the Irishman's feet slip on the greasy floor of the boat. He tumbles backwards, hitting his head on the wooden box of provisions but swiftly regains his balance to resume an upright stance.

Together, Martin and Andy manage to retrieve the situation. Some water has entered the boat but insufficient to present any danger to its passengers.

"Well done, shipmates," shouts Finnegan.

"No thanks to you," snaps Martin. "You should have seen whatever that was coming."

The Irishman ignores the rebuke.

"This will have taken us just under the hour. We'll have to try and beat that time coming back," says Finnegan, still rubbing the back of his head from the blow sustained in his fall.

"Thought we were coming to relax and get away from it all, not trying to break rowing records," replies Martin.

"Something to aim at, so why not?" counters Finnegan.

"Watch out for the rocks on our right," shouts Andy.

"You mean starboard, don't you?"

"I mean over there, whatever you call it," groans Andy, slackening his grip on his oar and simultaneously nodding his head in the direction of a row of boulders guarding one of the approaches to the beach.

The sun is now bearing down on the boat and its crew.

"Right men, use your oars to keep us off the rocks. We'll need this damn piece of wood to get us back," shouts Finnegan.

The oarsmen respond as they slip through a narrow neck of jagged rock and close in on a deserted beach.

As the boat reaches shallow water, Finnegan jumps overboard, showering his two crew mates in the process. He strides on ahead, splashing his legs in the water while pulling hard on the rope tied to the front of the boat. Andy and Martin slide their oars back under the seat, enjoying the luxury of an effortless ride.

"Faster! Faster!" they shout at the Irishman.

"Cheeky bastards," comes his reply. "Remember I navigated you here."

"And we just did the rowing, did we?"

The oarsmen disembark onto the deserted beach and look for a spot to secure the boat.

The trio find themselves pushing their feet through the powdery white sand to the back of the beach. They stop in the welcome shade of the undergrowth.

"So what do you think of 'Treasure Island' men?" asks Finnegan.

"I'll let you know tomorrow, after we've met 'Man Friday'!" replies Martin with a deadpan response.

"Well," adds Andy, "let's have a look around first."

"You pair of miserable sods! I reckon it's bloody marvellous, beautiful unspoilt beach, not a deck chair – or C.O – in sight. What more could you ask for? All we're missing are women," says Finnegan with a toothy grin.

"We'll bring the boat up here, it's far enough away not to be dragged out in the tide," advises Martin.

"Good thinking," says Andy. "Now who's for a beer?"

Immediately, the Irishman walks away in the direction of the boat, then sprints back holding three brown bottles.

"Let's drink a toast to the Royal Air Force," suggests Martin.

"What the hell for?" asks Finnegan.

"Because without them we wouldn't be here today on 'Treasure Island', that's why."

"Can't argue with that," laughs Andy.

The trio lay on their backs, beers in hand, enjoying the moment.

Though their journey has not required sophisticated skills of seamanship, it could so easily have gone horribly wrong and ended in disaster, despite the waters being reasonably calm and unthreatening. But there is an unspoken belief, amongst all three, that an hour's rowing in the South China Sea, successfully reaching an unknown island, has shown a degree of trust in each other and certainly represents a major navigational achievement.

Their improvised tent, consisting of parachute material and six wooden poles, is pitched and the men move inside for a well-earned nap. Space is at a premium as the trio prepare for their first evening away from the comparative comfort of the camp. Reprises of the uncensored version of the Eton Boating song, coupled with the occasional bout of unrestrained laughter, fill the air. Soon, the area immediately outside the tent is being littered with empty, brown beer bottles.

Behaving more like schoolboys on a weekend scout camp than men on active Service, they see the day out to the background music of waves softly lapping on the otherwise deserted shoreline.

The following morning, Martin awakes to find himself alone. Opening the tent flap, he looks out in both directions along the beach. Some distance away, Andy and Finnegan appear to be deep in conversation, sitting facing each other astride a fallen tree trunk.

"Why d'you choose to be a fireman? You don't seem to enjoy it," says Andy.

"Me da', he's responsible."

"How come?"

"He used to be one, always talking about it as a cushy number. Either sleeping or playing cards in the fire station – and getting paid for it!"

"He must have had some scary moments."

"If he did, he never talked about 'em. So, when I joined up for National Service I went for fireman. No vacancies at the time but signing on for the extra years did the trick."

"D'you enjoy it?"

"It's a job."

"Will you be signing on for more?"

"Who knows."

"Can I ask a personal question?" asks Andy.

"Why stop now?"

"It's something you said back on the camp about me being lucky with the post. Couldn't work that one out. How can anyone be lucky with post?"

"You bloody well are!" laughs the Irishman.

"Come to think of it, Finnegan, can't ever recall you receiving a letter. Oh dear, sorry, forget I said that."

"Don't start feeling sorry for me, my friend, I don't need anyone's pity," replies Finnegan sharply.

Andy hesitates, then asks: "Got any brothers and sisters?"

"Nope."

"Mum and dad…?"

"Just mum, dad left us a long time ago. What's with all the questions then?"

"Just curious," replies Andy, deciding not to enquire about the initials on the Irishman's tattooed arm.

Finnegan rises to his feet and looks towards the advancing Martin, adding in a whisper:

"Now this bloke coming up here is worth questioning. It must be an odd bastard who can wear a woman's dressing gown with plimsolls, plays posh music, sings rude songs and then feels able to look down on the rest of us. Don't look the part today though, does he? Underpants and sandals, I ask you!"

"Sorry, mate, didn't mean to upset you," apologises Andy, sensing that his questions had been unwelcome.

"Don't worry, my friend, you didn't get anywhere near."

It is the first time Andy is aware of a more sensitive, vulnerable side to the fireman.

The men stand together for a few minutes, gazing out across the sea back towards the island they have left. Finnegan takes the initiative as the Music Man joins them.

"Right, lads, we're wasting valuable time – let's take a look around. Pith helmets at the ready!"

They first head for the shade of the undergrowth, looking for a break in the trees which hopefully might provide a footpath inland.

"Christ it's hot, I'm wringing wet!" sighs Andy.

"Keep up, you softies," comes the demand from Finnegan, striding on ahead through a break in the waist-high ferns. He stops to let the two stragglers catch up.

"Where exactly are we going?" enquires Andy.

"No idea – today we're explorers and we might even strike gold."

"Let's slow down," suggests Martin. "There's no point in going on aimlessly in this heat."

"Aren't you curious about what's here?" counters the Irishman.

"Not really, if we just keep to the shoreline we'd probably see just as much and, what's more important, we won't get lost," suggests Martin with a hint of rebellion in his voice.

"Give it another ten minutes and if we've seen nothing different by then, we'll go back. How about that?" says the ever diplomatic Andy. Martin groans.

The party's progress becomes increasingly difficult as they find themselves having to pick their way through a host of fallen trees either covered in moss or wrapped in creepers. Fortunately, most of the higher-hanging branches above are inter-twined, offering welcome protection from the sun. Finnegan remains in the lead as they approach a clearing. He stops suddenly, spinning around to face the others. "Shut up and listen."

"What's the problem?" whispers Andy.

"Keep quiet and listen, I think I can hear someone singing."

"Trying to sing, you mean. That voice is badly out of tune, trust me," adds Martin.

"You two stay here, I'll go on ahead and have a peep."

The Irishman ducks his head and weaves through the undergrowth before disappearing out of sight.

"Knew this was a mistake. Told you we should have kept to the shoreline," says Martin.

Andy takes a swig of water from his flask. He finds it difficult to understand why, within such a short period of time, the Music Man is showing so much concern. So different from the suave, self-assured character who graces the billet. After all, it was his idea to make the trip.

The pair decide to rest their weary limbs on a log, awaiting the return of Finnegan.

"Who d'you reckon that was singing?"

Martin responds with a casual shrug of the shoulders.

"Andy, as long as it wasn't a hungry head-hunter, I couldn't care less. Quite frankly, I don't feel comfortable here. Off the beaten track. Sure to be crawling with snakes, insects and God knows what. Much safer being back near the beach."

Ahead of them, there is rustling in the bushes. To their relief, it is the figure of Finnegan that emerges, sporting an ear-to-ear grin. His unprotected forearms and legs reveal numerous scratches inflicted by his foray into the unfriendly undergrowth.

"Follow me, Men, told you it was 'Treasure Island', didn't I?" laughs the Irishman, spinning around to face the direction from which he had just come.

"D'you find 'Man Friday' then?" enquires Andy enthusiastically.

"Did you see the singer?" asks Martin.

Finnegan ignores the questions and quickly opens a gap between himself and the other two, whose expressions suggest an increasing lack of enthusiasm in the expedition.

The Irishman slows then stops before turning around to shout: "No lagging, keep up, almost there!"

The trio finally come together.

"Now take a look at this!" says Finnegan proudly.

The men have reached a clearing and are looking up at a bamboo house resting on a dozen or so wooden stilts, with a shingle covered roof. It is surrounded by towering palm trees. There are no windows, only blinds of matting hanging at full stretch to foil the penetrating heat. Bamboo steps lead up from ground level through to the verandah floor. In the shaded area underneath the house, partially covered by a canvas cover, sits what appears to be the remains of a car. In the background, two young native girls on their knees, tending the surrounding plants, rise gracefully to greet their surprise visitors with a welcoming smile.

One of the blinds is hastily reeled up.

"Good afternoon, gentlemen!" comes a booming call from the verandah above.

Looking down on them is a deeply tanned, Santa Claus-style bearded face holding a beaming smile. His trailing locks, bleached by the sun, lay over his shoulders.

"Welcome, gentlemen, I'll be straight down."

The trio look at each other in surprise.

"What the hell is this bloke doing here?" asks Andy.

"It could be his home, he probably lives here," suggests Martin.

"Why don't we just ask him when he comes down?" adds Finnegan.

The host descends the steps before greeting each of the visitors with a vigorous handshake.

"Pleased to meet you, gentlemen. I take it you're from the RAF camp across the water."

"Yes, we rowed over actually," says Martin with a hint of pride in his voice. "We're taking a pre-Christmas break."

"I know. My house boy spotted you coming over. He doesn't miss much with our military binoculars."

It is the first time that the Irishman has faced a man wearing a sarong, and he is finding it difficult to take in. Meanwhile, Andy and Martin's attention is being distracted by the antics of a couple of hens engaged in what seems a bad-tempered dispute. Angrily, they circle each other clucking noisily within their wired-off pen. For a few moments conversation is on hold as all eyes focus on the two combatants.

"Would you care for a drink?" asks the host. "I must say you all look pretty whacked."

Together they climb the steps. Andy catches sight of a line of coconut shells acting as hanging baskets for a colourful display of butterfly orchids.

"Now sit yourselves down and tell me what you each do across the water. But first a drink."

Aware of the need not to disclose military information to a stranger, Martin ignores the question and decides to take the initiative by asking a question of his own.

"So how long have you been living here?"

"Longer than I care to remember," comes the evasive response. There is an awkward silence before the host rises and moves to a drinks cabinet in the corner of the room.

"Now then, gentlemen, I can offer you a rather special brandy – or anything else you might fancy in the form of spirits. Apologies, but I don't carry beer."

Martin and Finnegan settle for a large brandy. Leaning back, they are grateful for the cool air coming from a whirring fan directly overhead.

Andy, a teenager and, by comparison still teetotal, is more interested in the vast collection of books which fill shelves on all sides of the room. He steals away to have a closer look.

Reaching up, his finger runs along a dust-ridden ledge before coming to rest at 'Great Expectations.'

Suddenly he is aware of the man of the house standing close behind him.

"You like Dickens then?"

"Set book at school, actually."

"Well now, that's something you'll never forget, trust me."

Andy looks across at his two mates slumped in a pair of rattan chairs; one now asleep and the other clearly headed in that direction. The walk from the beach and an unexpected but generous intake of brandy has left its mark.

"Andrew, are you and the boys going back tonight?" enquires Santa Claus.

"Well, the plan was to spend the weekend here."

"What? On the beach!"

"We've got a damn good tent,"

"Pity I haven't the room to put you all up. Could perhaps manage one."

The suggestion is whispered in Andy's ear, who senses a change of subject is called for.

"Noticed the car below. Looks like a goner to me."

"On the contrary," replies the host, moving ever closer.

"Surely there are no roads here to drive it on," adds Andy.

"It's a rather special old Ford which, over the years, has fallen into disrepair. My ambition is just to hear the engine roar again. It's been silent for too long."

"Are you a car mechanic, then? If not, I'm sure we have some lads back on camp that would come over to help, providing you made it worth their while."

"Thanks for the offer, but I regard it as a personal challenge. On each of my monthly trips to the mainland, I manage to pick up a spare part or two. I'm slowly, very slowly, getting there. Creeping up on it, you might say. And I do have a copy of the original handbook and manual for the car which, believe it or not, was left in the glove compartment."

Andy catches sight of an antique-looking record player. "Good heavens, that looks like a golden oldie, a collector's item if you don't mind me saying."

"Not at all young man. 'Fraid it doesn't work, now it's more a piece of furniture. I have a collection of records but the only music you'll hear in this house is me singing."

Behind them comes the explosive sound of breaking glass. An outstretched leg from the careless Irishman has toppled the decanter from one of the small bamboo tables.

"Clumsy bastard, Finnegan!" shouts Martin.

"Time to go, my friends," declares the Irishman, jumping to his feet.

"Must you, gentlemen? I've still got so many questions to ask you."

Meanwhile, one of the girls, now dressed in a cherry red, wide-sleeved robe fastened with a black sash, comes from an adjoining room to remove the broken glass and clean the floor. With just a few elegant hand movements, all traces of the accident disappear.

The eyes of all three Airmen are trained on her slender, inviting body. She smiles at each of them, in turn, bows and exits. Martin and Finnegan exchange a knowing glance.

Their bearded host turns to Andy.

"My boy, before you go, a question or two. Have you ever been to Cambridge?"

"No, not yet."

"You see, that's where I come from and I often wonder whether it's changed much. Look, you haven't even seen around the house, why the rush to go? Have I offended you?"

Martin and the Irishman move to the top of the steps. Andy is aware they are waiting for him to leave with them. Their host continues to hold Andy in conversation.

"Are you sure about Cambridge?"

"Quite sure, I'm from near Plymouth, other side of the country."

"Let the others go, join them later. You can stay here overnight," comes the surprise invitation, accompanied by a warm smile.

"Andy! Time to head back for the beach," comes the call from the Irishman.

"Nice to have met you, Mr... uh," stutters Andy almost apologetically.

"And you too young man," comes the host's reply. "If you change your mind..."

"Sorry, must go."

The master of the house, with two girls at his side, watches from above as the trio descend the rickety steps, cross the compound and make for the undergrowth.

The houseboy, binoculars strung around his neck, follows them for the first part of their return to the beach, before slipping out of sight.

Back on the beach, bottle in hand, the men sit by their tent.

"Well, what the hell did you make of all that?" asks Finnegan.

"You mean the bloke in the bungalow?" replies Martin.

"Who else? I was more interested in the ceremonial Japanese sword that was hanging in his kitchen," adds the Irishman. "I was going to ask him to get it down so we could have a closer look."

"Didn't notice it. How the hell did Santa got hold of one of those?" muses Andy.

Martin rises to his feet to deliver his thoughts.

"Let's think about this rationally. He's in his fifties or sixties, which means that ten to fifteen years ago he could have been in the Forces. Let's face it, he could have been a deserter – or even a collaborator – which would account for the Japanese sword. And did you notice the way that girl was dressed? She was wearing a damn kimono?"

"Unless he was working in this part of the world as a civilian when the War started," suggests Andy.

"Yeh but, if he was, why is Santa roughing it here now instead of living in style with the other ex-pats on the mainland. And did you notice that huge radio he threw a cloth over soon after we went into the room? Long range job that one, could probably tune into Radio Tokyo! My money's on him ducking out, which is why he's stuck here and unable to go home," insists Martin.

"I wouldn't call it 'roughing it' with those two girls," laughs Finnegan.

"And where do those girls spend the night?" smiles Martin.

"He was a friendly sort of bloke," adds Andy.

"We could see he took a shine to you. Did I hear him asking you stay the night?" enquires the Irishman.

Andy chooses to ignore the embarrassing question before walking away from the other two.

Finnegan lets him walk a few yards ahead along the beach before joining him.

"Sorry, my friend, didn't mean to upset you?"

"Don't worry. You didn't get anywhere near," replies Andy, returning the words he had received from the Irishman earlier in the day.

The pair exchange smiles and return to their beachside tent. The visit to 'Treasure Island' has not been a disappointment.

8

"Airman! Airman!" Andy remains seated at his desk, pencil lodged over his ear. The tone of his Commanding Officer's voice suggests that it is a matter of some importance.

"In here – and quick!" comes the order.

Andy takes a deep breath, rises to his feet and instinctively reaches for his notepad.

"Sir?"

"I've decided to hold a social evening for the men."

"In the Mess, Sir?"

"No. At my home. We'll kick off with the Sergeants for the first evening, then the Corporals and finally, possibly, a few of what's left."

"How soon, Sir?"

"This weekend, Airman, and you'll be needed."

"Me, Sir?"

"Yes, *you* Sir."

"We'll need someone to pour the drinks and change the records. By the way, do you know if any of the men have any gramophone records?"

"I'll have a word with the Music Man, Sir."

"Well, you tell your Music Man chappy that we'll need some Bing Crosby and Victor Sylvester."

"I'll see what I can arrange, Sir."

"Knock out an invitation on your typewriter and I'll OK it before you send it out."

"Will there be food?"

"No need, the men will have eaten earlier in the day. My wife will have a couple of plates of bit and pieces, but nothing substantial."

"Will it be casual dress, Sir?"

"Certainly, except for you and me. That'll remind them they're on active Service, not on holiday at Butlins. Don't want them thinking above their station, do we?"

"No Sir."

"Now off you go and get moving on that invitation."

Andy returns to his office to contemplate the occasion. He wonders how the C.O will cope with an invitation declined? His abrasive attitude towards the men will surely undermine any attempt at a relaxed get-together. Broadside in particular will need watching – and Curtis – and Ashton, in fact all three!

Time perhaps to search again for those elusive 'Charge Sheets' – just in case. But first, a word with the Sergeants!

It's just after midday as Andy returns to the billet to find the Music Man lying on his bed; eyes closed Martin is not alone: he is sharing the moment with Tchaikovsky.

"Excuse me, Martin?"

There is no response. Andy moves closer to the prostrate body and leans down to adjust the volume control on the bedside gramophone.

The prostrate body opens one eye.

"No need for that, young man. If you were at a concert, would you leave the audience, walk up to the conductor, tap him on the shoulder and tell him to turn it down, would you?"

"No, I wouldn't."

"So, it's either 'on' or 'off', one or the other, there's no in-between," replies Martin, rising from his mattress.

"Hope you're going to be able to help me with some records," Andy says tentatively.

"I'm impressed, you're finally beginning to appreciate my collection. Now then, what would you like to hear?"

"Martin, I need to borrow some records for the C.O's social evening."

"What social evening?"

"The C.O is planning to start with our three Sergeants, then the Corporals and so on."

"You mean a musical evening, 'cause that's what my records are suitable for."

"Actually, Martin, he's after Crosby and Victor Sylvester records. Got anything on those lines?"

"Not at the moment. But I think I know where I can get hold of some seventy-eights of Victor Sylvester – might even muster a few Gracie Fields favourites. I have my contacts."

"Great! How soon?"

"A day or two, leave it with me."

"Thanks, Martin, that's great news," says Andy with a relaxed sigh. "Whose idea is the social evening?"

"The C.O's, of course," replies Andy.

"Don't you believe it. It's his missus, Marilyn. Tell you now, it's a disaster waiting to happen."

"Why?"

"'Course it'll be, just take my word for it. Anyway, I'll have the Sylvester music by the morning; Crosby might take a bit longer."

As Andy leaves the billet, he catches a rare glimpse of Sergeant Broadside, staggering back to his workplace in the Mess, managing somehow to defy the laws of gravity and narrowly avoiding the indignity of dropping into one of the monsoon drains. A number of camp personnel have already testified to his epic drinking sessions both here and in Singapore. Andy has already noted his Service Record which reads more like a crime sheet, with additional pages documenting being found by the RAF Police in numerous houses of ill repute elsewhere in the Far East. Together with his punished liver, Broadside, a native of Glasgow, is now coming to the end of his Service career.

His blotchy face bears the scars of many years of over-indulgence, with wandering eyes always appearing to be in search of some elusive and seemingly non-existent object. Meanwhile, Ken, his deputy in the cookhouse, being very much left on his own, performs minor culinary miracles each day while at the same time protecting his Sergeant from the unwelcome attention of the C.O.

"Sarge!" shouts Andy. "A quick word, please."

Broadside stops, sways to one side and then back again, before turning around.

"Whaa 'ya want?" he slurs.

"Just to warn you, the C.O's having a social evening at his place on Saturday evening."

"'Ope he has a nice time," comes the reply, accompanied by a hiccup.

"Sarge, you'll be getting an invitation, it's a 'Do' just for Sergeants," shouts Andy, aware that his words are being ignored.

He watches as the Sergeant's legs become entangled before crashing through the doorway of the Mess. Andy rushes to his rescue, propping his sagging body up against a couple of wooden benches which have been stacked against the wall.

"Thaas champion, pal, juss leave me here. I'll be right," sighs Broadside, eyes closing as he speaks.

Andy decides to make for the second of the camp's three billets, hoping to warn the Signals Sergeant of the special evening.

Sergeant Curtis, a tall, humorous character, always wearing a welcoming smile, is deep in concentration as Andy enters the billet. A popular figure on the camp, he is in charge of the Signals Sections but rarely seen during the working day. Now, about to unleash his all important third and final dart, he is clearly not a man to be interrupted. Seconds later, the missile hangs limply from a strip of wood a foot above the board.

"Just a matter of inches away from glory, eighteen inches to be exact," he laughs.

"Here's the C.O's man, lads, watch your pockets!" jokes one of the players.

"Got a moment, Sarge, in private?"

"Excuse me, gentlemen."

Andy takes Curtis to the doorway.

"Just to warn you, Sarge, that you'll be getting an invite to the C.O's social evening on Saturday."

"About bloody time that miserable bastard mixed with the men. Great! I'll be there."

"But, Sarge, Saturday evening is just for the Sergeants, there'll be a separate get together for the Corporals and then…"

"Oh! so he's not mixing with *all* the men then? What time do we have to be in the Mess?"

"No, not here – it's at his place. His wife will be there and the District Officer might come along."

"Thanks for that, Andy. My diary's probably clear, count me in."

Andy's thoughts now turn to the third invitee, Harry Ashton, in charge of motor transport, and holding the precarious, temporary rank of acting Sergeant. Harry is a shy, bald-headed Brummie whose passion is collecting butterflies and moths, with little time for the mainstream interests of his colleagues. A permanent squint in his left eye seems to question whether he should have been given a driving licence.

"Harry!" shouts Andy as the acting Sergeant from the Midlands, wearing only a towel around his waist, bounds, kangaroo style in the direction of the showers.

"Sorry, can't stop," comes the reply.

Andy stands outside the shower and shouts his message against a background of running water.

"Saturday night, Harry, you're invited to an elite gathering at the C.O's place."

"Invited to what?"

"A social evening with the C.O and his wife."

"Bugger off! I'd rather spend an evening in the dentist's chair."

"I'll show you the invitation later, it's pukka gen."

Andy feels he is wasting his time and returns to the office. There is no doubt that the C.O is unpopular with the men and little enthusiasm exists for the opportunity to spend an evening with him; and it is difficult to imagine that a single social event would change their opinion of him. The Flight Lieutenant and his men have so little in common. In Andy's mind, the greatest threat to the success of the evening is the possibility of a hostile reaction from a captive audience subjected to yet another monologue from their C.O about his exaggerated exploits during the Second World War.

Dorothy Munro has spent most of the day preparing for her social debut in the role of the Commanding Officer's wife. Experienced in hosting dinners, such an event should hold no fears; but somehow she feels uneasy. The men are not the type with whom she has previously had much contact and it will be essential to avoid talking down to them. She has decided that her appearance and dress will be of paramount importance. Her nails have demanded most attention but now it is time to remove the rollers from her flame-coloured hair, which has drawn many a compliment since she was a young girl. She steps back from the mirror to take a full-length look at herself. It is decision time for Dorothy. What to wear? Something 'nice' but not too 'dressy'? After much deliberation, she opts for one of her as yet unworn 'honeymoon' outfits. It is a cool, silk, patterned dress she bought in Singapore, immediately prior to her wedding. It has a neat 'boat' neck, cap sleeves and the full circle skirt is great fun, and shows off her neat waistline. With the hour of judgement drawing near, she stands in front of her husband.

"How do I look, dear? Will I do?" asks Dorothy.

"Exquisite, as usual, darling."

"Charles! How can you see me hidden behind that damn *Straits Times*?"

She moves even closer to her husband, hands on hips.

"Charles!" she repeats in a raised voice.

"Sorry, darling, jolly interesting piece here about a Jap soldier who's just come out of the jungle, totally unaware the War ended ten years ago! Could be the last one for us to pop in the net. Not very bright, was he? Quite comical really."

"Actually, I find that rather sad. So…will I do?"

"Positively stunning, belle of the ball."

"Except this is a social evening, not a ball. And I'll be the only belle on show."

"Of course, darling."

"Charles, the men were due at eight and it's just gone ten past. Are you sure they know the way here? And it might be a good idea if you make that drink your last one."

"Our young man in the office is rounding them up and they'll be arriving in the Land Rover. Don't worry, darling, anyone who fails to appear will be on a Charge."

From the driveway outside, can be heard the back-firing of a vehicle.

"That's no Land Rover!" cries the C.O, rising from his chair.

"It could be the District Officer, dear, my surprise guest," explains Dorothy tentatively. "Thought he'd stop you and the other men from talking shop all night."

Dorothy opens the door to greet the imposing frame of Malcolm Prenderghast, sporting a badly creased, lightweight fawn blazer, panama hat and a polka-dotted bow tie peeping out from below a double chin.

"Good evening, absolutely delighted and privileged to be invited. 'Fraid to report my good lady is still laid low by a dreadful insect bite. Absolutely mortified she can't be here. She was so looking forward to meeting you."

In a more intimate tone, the D.O adds: "… and may I just say how positively delightful you look this evening, Dorothy. Charles is indeed a fortunate man."

The C.O closes in to offer an immediate welcoming drink.

"Malcolm, just as you like it, with more G than T. The men will be along shortly."

"Yes, Charles, I passed them on the way in. Looked like a tyre change to me."

Before they have a chance to sit down, there is a resounding knock at the door.

"I'll take this one, darling," says the C.O firmly. He decides to have a private word at the door with his men before letting them in. "Poor show, men. Eighteen minutes late – and only one tie between the three of you. And a word of warning: behave yourselves."

The C.O glares at Andy who stands at the rear of the guests.

"Don't just stand there, Airman. You're on duty and supposed to be organising the drinks and the music, get moving!"

Once inside, the Sergeants stand grouped together. Across the room, the District Officer and Dorothy are locked in a whispered conversation. After sinking a few generously-sized mouthfuls from his glass, the seated Flight Lieutenant Munro calls for music.

"Managed to find some Victor Sylvester, Sir, but failed with Bing Crosby," explains Andy.

"Good man!" shouts the C.O. "So let's hear it! My wife will show you to the gramophone, and how to handle the replacement stylus needles we bought in Singapore. Dorothy! the Airman is in need of technical assistance," comes a further demand.

She breaks away from the D.O, moving quickly to her husband's side. "Darling, time to make the men welcome, they're being left out."

"The D.O will be happy to talk to himself, he usually does," sniggers the C.O.

Meanwhile, the youthful looking Sergeant Curtis, displaying his finely greased head of black hair and renowned for his joke-telling and impersonations, already has his fellow Sergeants hanging expectantly on yet another punch line. It duly arrives and a burst of explosive laughter fills the room.

Dorothy throws a glance at her husband who is now scowling at the men; but his glazed eyes and almost empty glass suggest he will soon be losing touch with the proceedings.

Suddenly the unmistakeable sound of Victor Sylvester's Orchestra joins the party.

Dorothy moves quickly towards the Sergeants, tapping her feet to the beat.

"Any of you gentleman care to 'cut a rug'?"

Harry Ashton immediately distances himself from the invitation.

"Sorry, Mrs M, don't know much about carpets. I'm just a motor transport. man."

"But you also have a sense of humour, don't you?"

Harry looks nonplussed at her response, while Sergeant Curtis intervenes to take control.

"May *I* have the privilege, Mrs Munro?"

"Smooth bastard, that one," mutters Ashton, looking enviously as the invitation is accepted with a gracious smile. He moves towards Andy for a re-fill of wine.

Meanwhile, the dancing duo close together as one, moving elegantly across the floor, neatly side-stepping a fallen chair. "That Curtis is a creeping sod," mutters Sergeant Broadside as he makes yet another sortie towards Andy, holding forth an empty glass.

Glass in hand, Ashton decides to make conversation with his C.O, whose head is rolling from side to side in a laboured attempt to keep in tune with the music.

"Sir, nice place you have here," leaning down to catch the ear of his Commanding Officer.

"'Course it's nice. As befits an Officer of the Crown."

"Yes, Sir," comes the obedient response.

"Sergeant, did you hear about that dumb Jap soldier who's just come out of the jungle? Silly blighter didn't know the War was over. No hope for that race, no hope at all."

"Will he get paid for the last ten years, Sir?"

"Only God knows. Correction: make that only the Devil knows."

"Very funny, Sir. I like that, Sir."

"Tell you what," slurs the C.O, "we should have gone for the hat trick with the Atomic Bomb."

"Don't quite follow, Sir."

"Should have dropped a third one for good measure. Hiroshima, Nagasaki, then bingo! The final one slap on top of the Emperor's Palace. And while you're on your feet, Sergeant, get me another drink."

"Yes, Sir."

Ashton returns with a large gin, only to find the C.O is now asleep, slumped in his chair.

He turns to Andy. "I think the Old Man is sinking."

"I'm more worried about Curtis, take a look at him and Marilyn," suggests Andy.

"The C.O asked me to put on some smoochy music. Now look at the pair of them."

Sergeant Ashton and Andy watch, open-mouthed as the dancing couple are slowly becoming locked in an embrace, with Curtis's hand drifting inexorably towards his partner's buttocks. Ignoring the tempo of the accompanying music, the pair have reduced their dance to a laboured shuffle.

"Where's Broadside?" gasps Andy. "Think he's out the back – being sick."

"Oh, no! go out and help him – quick."

"How dare you!" comes a high-pitched cry, followed immediately by the sound of a resounding slap.

Dorothy is now distancing herself from her short-term dancing partner, before fixing Curtis with a threatening stare. The Sergeant looks downward, rubbing the side of his face.

"Sorry, Marilyn – sorry, er….erm… I mean Mrs Munro – but my hand must have slipped."

Somehow, the sudden silence seems to have woken her husband.

"Who stopped the music? Put it back on, that's an order!" shouts the C.O, unaware of what has happened and making an unsuccessful attempt to rise from his chair, before sliding backwards.

"I think it's time for everyone to go home," declares Dorothy in a firm tone.

The three Sergeants make for the door without offering any comment.

Andy breaks the uneasy silence by offering to tidy up.

"It's really no trouble, Mrs Munro."

"No, thank you. Anyway, you must be the only one sober enough to take the Land Rover back to camp. Off you go now."

"Except I can't drive, Mrs Munro."

The C.O's wife ignores the comment and heads for the kitchen.

Andy takes a last look around the room. In the background, he can hear his transport is already on its way back to the camp. The C.O is now snoring loudly. Victor Sylvester's Orchestra has been demoted to a whisper and the amah has appeared with a tray to remove the spread of largely uneaten food from the trestle table. As he makes his way, on foot, back to the camp, Andy views the prospect of any further social evenings as dead in the water.

9

Early evening: the light is fading but the humidity persists. The only sound is the constant humming of the overhead fans. Most of the lads lie stretched out on their beds, waiting for the temperature to drop before taking a shower, except for one sad soul standing by his locker, energetically scratching off another day of his life from a self-made demob chart. Suddenly, the tranquillity is shattered by shrieks of female laughter, coming from the neighbouring block.

Andy levers himself up by the elbows from his sweat-sodden pillow and looks out through the open doorway. "What the hell was that?" he shouts.

"It's those Chinese washerwomen," comes an anonymous voice from further down the billet.

"They should have gone home hours ago."

"They did. But they're back for the show," comes a louder voice.

"What show?"

"Cookie, our Ken. They're waiting to see him go out to the shower."

"I don't understand," says a puzzled Andy.

Finnegan is now standing at the foot of his bed, wearing a roguish smile and a time-expired, almost 'see-through' pair of underpants, ready to explain.

"Come on, Andy, don't be stupid. The women are waiting to watch him do the ten yard sprint out to the shower hut."

"But we all wrap a towel around us when we go out there, so what's the attraction?"

"His tits!"

"His what?" laughs Andy.

"Andy, you don't get it, do you? Listen. Compared with our birds back home, Chinese women are flat-chested. So when the biggest pair of knockers they'll ever see are on a bloke, they just fall about."

Meanwhile, Ken, cast in the reluctant role of top billing and tipping the scales at over fourteen stone, waits impatiently in the aisle of the billet, silently cursing all things Chinese.

"Go on, Cookie! Flash your boobs! Give 'em a treat!" come the cries of his mates as, in turn, they rise from their beds to gather around him.

"If these bloody women keep this up, I'll give 'em a real surprise, trust me. Fucking Chinese!" threatens Ken in his broad Yorkshire accent.

It's now almost ten minutes since he left his bed space, and his mood is darkening.

He waddles out to the doorway, soap in hand, pausing to shake a defiant fist at the three waiting women, before breaking into a laboured dash to the shower hut, exposing his wobbling and voluminous breasts as his flat feet slap over the concrete slabs.

The short journey is completed in a matter of seconds but is accompanied by even louder screams of laughter and hand clapping from the uninvited spectators.

Andy moves to the doorway and realises that the women will not be moving until Ken embarks on his return leg. It's a tricky situation and one in which he'd prefer to have no involvement.

The situation is crying out to be defused. He decides to walk across to speak to them, in the process deliberately obscuring their view of the hut – and the unfortunate Cookie. The star attraction has disappeared from view but the women are clearly still desperate for an encore.

"Ladies, you shouldn't be here now, please go home," pleads Andy.

"Fat man look like lady," comes the initial response through the gold teeth of one of the pencil-slim washerwomen.

Her colleague attempts to hide her giggling by first ducking her head and then putting both hands across her face. Her amusement quickly gives way to a serious-sounding question.

Her composure restored, she asks: "Is fat man – lady?"

While Andy ponders his response, Ken, sensing that Andy has momentarily distracted the spectators, seizes his moment of opportunity. He scampers from the shower hut and back to the safe haven of the billet.

Andy quickly follows him in.

"Thanks, mate," gasps Ken. "But guess what? I've left me soap out there."

"Don't worry, I'll get it for you."

"Sod that, I'll get my own soap. I'll give those Chinese whores something to look at."

Ken spins round in the doorway to face the washer women. Centre stage, arms aloft, he proceeds to vigorously shake his wobbling chest. Their laughter erupts again, followed by an enthusiastic stamping of feet. "That's it! You've asked for it," he shouts loudly.

Standing proud, thrusting his legs apart, Ken allows his towel to drop to the ground.

To his surprise, the women take a step forward and stare in silence. Slowly, their shocked expressions turn from gasps of amazement into wide grins, then into another bout of uncontrolled shrieking.

Finnegan decides to intervene, pulling the now naked cook away from the doorway.

Ken, with a new-found spring in his step, returns confidently to the billet, only to be met by a barrage of mixed comment from his colleagues.

"What the hell did you do that for?" "Those bloody women will be back for sure - every flaming night!"

"I don't shower every night," comes his immediate response.

"And they'll be bringing up their mates from the village," adds Billy.

"Don't you realise Ken, that's indecent exposure – even in this part of the world?"

"Just wait until the C.O hears about it!"

"Good man, Cookie, you certainly showed 'em what's what!"

"Should have hung your towel on it!"

The cook dismisses the remarks with a reverse-handed Churchillian gesture, then strides away, triumphantly, down the billet before slumping onto his bed.

Outside, the washerwomen seat themselves on the ground, still giggling, somehow hoping the show has not closed. Andy moves outside and towards them. With a dismissive wave of the hand, he encourages them to leave. One of the ladies rises to her bare feet to shout: "Fat man no lady! Fat man no lady!" Then covers her mouth quickly before bursting into a muffled bout of laughter.

Inside the billet, the Music Man attempts to soothe the discordant atmosphere with an interjection of one of Mahler's lesser known works. His ploy is met with spontaneous shouts of disapproval. With a philosophical shrug of the shoulders, he carefully removes the record from the turntable, slips it into its brown paper sleeve and consigns it to his bedside locker.

Finnegan and Martin stroll down the billet to stop at the foot of Andy's bed.

"I think it's time our Cookie moved on. Why don't you mention it to the Old Man?" suggests the Irishman.

"What makes you say that?" questions Andy.

"He's been here too long. The food he serves up is rubbish, not always properly cooked. I've also heard he makes a bit on the side, using our emergency rations, for birthdays and special occasions. And now tonight he's flashing at those washer women," adds Finnegan.

"Exactly," says Martin.

"Have a word in the C.O's ear in the morning, Andy. Get him out tomorrow on the next flight."

"Well if he was, you could be his escort on the same kite, Finnegan?" suggests Andy.

The Irishman takes a step back, open-mouthed, as a wide grin breaks across his face.

"Are you saying?…Oh no! … You don't mean my replacement is actually coming?"

"Yep! Not sure when, but they're under strength back at Changi and you're needed there ASAP. You'll probably be off before your replacement arrives."

Finnegan punches the air in delight at the news.

"Signal came in this morning. You've finally got your wish!"

"Thanks, thanks, Andy. Let's get the beers in! Tuborg for me."

The trio hotfoot it to the Mess for a celebratory beer.

"You're a lucky bastard, Finnegan, but I suppose that's 'cos you're Irish," laughs Martin.

"Well, Music Man, you know the best thing about leaving this place?"

"No idea, tell me."

"Not being brainwashed by that awful music of yours."

"And the worst thing?" asks Andy.

"Not now being able to make a return boat visit to our island. Secretly, I was hoping to take a closer look at those two girls that Santa had running around for him. With those birds tucking him in, it must feel like Christmas every night."

"But couldn't work him out. Didn't talk about the War but then there was that Japanese ceremonial sword hanging up," adds Martin.

"If he was proud to give it pride of place, why not mention it? He kept on about his collection of books, too, but never mentioned his radio," questions Andy.

"Perhaps he was in with the Japs, like a collaborator," suggests Finnegan.

"Or a deserter who opted out for the duration of the hostilities," says Martin.

"I felt a bit sad for him," interrupts Andy. "Kept wanting to know how things were back in Cambridge. I reckon he's homesick."

"Yeh, and I reckon he took a right shine to you, too!"

Empty bottles of beer soon litter the Mess table; cigarette smoke fills the air.

Andy is the first to wilt under the twin onslaught of alcohol and fumes.

"I'm feeling a bit queasy, lads. Mind if I slope off?"

"Shall we let him go, Finnegan?" asks Martin.

"It's my farewell do, I'm calling the shots, so I'm afraid you'll have to stay."

"Really?" gasps Andy.

Finnegan slowly breaks into a teasing grin.

"Go on, bugger off then. And when I wake up in the morning, don't tell me this posting back to Singapore is all a joke. 'Cos I'll rip your bleedin' head off!"

Andy totters off into the darkness and back towards the billet, leaving the duo to get down to some serious drinking.

Behind him, the discordant strains of the now familiar song of 'Judith' carry through the still night air.

Meanwhile, Martin and the Irishman are surveying the limited stock of drink at their disposal. Only a few bottles of Tuborg remain. The ammunition is running dry.

"Look here, Music Man, I reckon it's time to crack open one of those bottles,"suggests Finnegan, pointing up to a collection of green bottles on a dusty shelf."

"I'm not pouring that rocket fuel down my throat! The labels are unreadable so you don't even know what the hell you're having. Could even have been left behind by the Japs. Could be booby-trapped. Don't you know that even the locals don't touch it?"

"Perhaps they're just not up to it. You know, they can't take a drink."

"Listen, those bottles are probably only for display, not for drinking."

"Chicken! Chicken!" teases the Irishman, accompanied by a flapping of arms.

"Finnegan, I'm pretty open-minded about drinking but I draw the line at that stuff."

"Well my friend, bugger you, I'm going to have a sip. Tomorrow, I'm on the first stage of going home. Just another three months to do in Singapore then – home. Yippie! Things are looking good at last."

The Irishman reaches up, almost losing his balance in the process, and grabs one of the bottles.

"Here goes!" comes the shout as he uses his teeth to remove the cork. After circling the bottle beneath his nostrils, Finnegan throws his head back to take a vigorous swig.

His drinking companion shakes his head in disbelief as the Irishman's eyes close and his complexion momentarily loses its usually florid appearance. Finnegan drops his head before coming up for air.

"Not bad, not bad at all. Go on, try it."

"Don't be daft," replies Martin.

"The trouble with you, Music Man is that you don't ever let yourself go. All that funeral music you keep playing has turned you into a right miserable bastard."

The Irishman awakes late the following morning. Immediately, a voice within tells him to stay put. He is sweating heavily as a result of the previous evening, with a persistent throbbing in his head. Levering himself up from the mattress, he looks slowly from side to side to discover the billet is empty. He takes a deep breath, before resuming his sleep mode. But his solitude is broken by the sudden arrival of Andy at the foot of his bed.

"Got you on the flight due in from Clark Field at fourteen hundred. How's that for service?"

Keeping one eye shut, Finnegan slowly gets to his feet.. "Today?" he croaks.

"Yep! Today. You'll be back in Singapore before dark. Imagine that."

"I'd rather spend today in bed – here," replies the Irishman.

"You don't look too good, shall I get the Doc?"

"Not bloody likely! That clown with the wandering hands, not flaming likely. I'll be fine shortly, don't worry."

"Call in at the office before you go up to the strip, I've got some papers for you to take. Don't forget." Andy leaves, smiling to himself with the knowledge of the further surprise he has in store for his departing friend.

The news that the Irishman is leaving has spread like wildfire through the camp.

The thought of anyone taking a step closer to home strikes a chord with all of the men; and Finnegan has never failed to make known his wish to return to the UK. The Irishman is a character and will be missed. No doubt about it, there'll be a few up at the strip to see him off.

The Valetta from the Philippines, en route to Changi, touches down a few minutes after two o'clock. Apart from the ever-present servicing crew, Finnegan's fire crew have turned up, uncharacteristically early, to bid farewell to their leader. With his deep sea box already safely on board, the Irishman prepares to board the aircraft. There is a hint of emotion in his voice as he pauses to turn to address the group.

"Well, I suppose that's it. You lot have got my address back home. If you're anywhere near, you're all welcome to look in – and just remember this: *you'll never get off the island."*

A chorus of boos and cheers, in equal measure, reach Finnegan's ears as he is about to enter the aircraft.

"Leaving your kit bag behind are you?" shouts Andy from the foot of the steps.

The Irishman spins around in the doorway.

"Don't be an idiot, give it here quick – they're almost ready to go."

"Hold on then, I'll bring it up," adds Andy.

"They don't want you on board."

"They do, 'cause I'm also on this flight. I'm taking the weekend as leave in Singapore. I'll be staying in the Transit Block on Changi."

"You artful, cheeky sod," laughs Finnegan as the engines roar into life.

"Somebody had to make sure you got off the island!" smiles Andy.

Minutes later, the Irishman leans across to the window and is looking down on the island as the aircraft begins its climb, heading out in a south-westerly direction over the South China Sea towards Singapore.

"Suppose it wasn't all bad," he reflects.

"Come off it, Finnegan, you've left some friends behind."

"Let's say, I haven't left too many enemies. Don't get all soft about it. Anyway, you're the one I'm sorry for – you've got to go back!"

Despite the bravado, Andy senses a touch of sadness in the Irishman's voice.

As the aircraft continues its ascent, the pair remain silent. They are the only passengers, seated amidst an assortment of boxed freight and metal cylinders. The temperature has dropped considerably since take-off, and there is now an uncomfortable chill around them.

"Quite a view from up here, isn't it?" says Andy.

"I'd settle for a couple of 'Wafs' (WRAF) up here as stewardesses!" laughs the Irishman.

"See that boat down there, Finnegan, could be innocent fishermen but they could just as easily be pirates, I've been told they do operate in these waters. Look, they're waving up to us ..." Andy's words fall on deaf ears: his travelling companion is already asleep, mouth open, breathing heavily. Last night's farewell drink has finally taken its toll.

Meanwhile, back in Borneo, the camp is under siege from a prolonged downpour.

The normally barren areas between and surrounding the billets are flooded, and brown pools of muddy water are flowing over some of the paths. Up on the airstrip, a Valetta stands alone, being buffeted by an unforgiving wind. There will be no more flight departures today. The weather, however, is of little interest to the three Sergeants who stand to attention, facing Flight Lieutenant Munro in his office. The temperamental, overhead fan is once again out of action and the men are beginning to sweat profusely.

"I consider the events at my house on Saturday evening a pretty poor show," comes the C.O's opening comment. "I'm given to understand that one of you – and I intend to discover who it actually was – left a dreadful mess in my bathroom. Furthermore, there was little food eaten. A damn waste, when one thinks of all those starving children in Africa. More importantly, there was no genuine attempt by any of you to join in the spirit of the evening, apart from Curtis. Have you anything to say?"

Curtis clears his throat, preparing to offer a grovelling apology, but

Broadside from the cookhouse is the first to speak. "It was me, Sir."

"It was you? – you who what? Explain yourself, man," demands the C.O.

"It was me, me in the bathroom, Sir, the mess and all that."

Flight Lieutenant Munro registers his disgust with a prolonged head-to-toe stare at the offender.

"And what have you to say for yourself, Ashton?"

The Sergeant's only response is to look down at his feet.

"Nothing! – it seems," snaps the C.O.

"And you, Curtis? Well... don't dither, man. Spit it out!"

"Sir, I am deeply sorry..."

The C.O rises from his chair before the Sergeant can offer an explanation, slamming a glass paperweight hard against the top of his desk. "Well, you shabby lot haven't got much to say for yourselves, have you?"

There is an embarrassing silence.

"My wife is upset by your conduct. In fact she can't even bring herself to discuss the matter with me, so I'll just have to hope that the passage of time will serve to loosen her tongue. Unfortunately, I must have dozed off when it all happened. In the meantime the jury is out, so to speak. You haven't heard the last of this, oh no, not by a long chalk. Back to work, you apologies for members of the Royal Air Force. This isn't Butlins! Go on, out of my sight. Dismiss!"

Once outside, the Sergeants agree immediately to meet in the Mess to discuss a strategy, in the event of the facts becoming known to the C.O. A worried looking Curtis is the first to arrive, followed closely by Broadside. They make for a table away from the others.

"What are the chances of the Old Man finding out what actually happened?" whispers Curtis.

"Pretty high, I think," comes Broadside's sombre reply. "What I do know, Curtis, is that you're bloody lucky to get away with it – so far. It all depends on his missus. If Marilyn spills the beans, you're done for."

"Do you think I should have a quiet, apologetic word with her?" asks Curtis.

"Don't be bloody daft! She never comes here, so it would mean you having to go to the bungalow. And, if you did, and the C.O found out, you'd end up in chains," warns Broadside.

Ashton, arriving late, joins the discussion.

"Curtis, you must be the jammiest sod alive," says the acting Sergeant.

"If the C.O hadn't been sloshed at the time and knew what was going on, you'd be on an almighty charge."

"And on the next flight out to Singapore," adds Broadside.

"Groping the C.O's wife! What do you get for that?" roars Ashton.

"Hey! keep your voice down," pleads Curtis, placing a finger to his lips.

"Dead lucky the D.O had left and the C.O was smashed. It's just the three of us – and Andy – who were party to the incident."

"So what now?" asks Broadside.

"Right, lads, so we agree a common line. If the Old Man starts ferreting around to find out what happened, we all have the same story. Right?" suggests Curtis.

"Which is?" asks Ashton.

"Nothing happened, simple as that," replies Curtis. "Her word against ours."

"And the slapped face?"

"Didn't hear or see a thing," adds Broadside.

"That goes for me, too," says Ashton.

"Thanks, lads, appreciate your support. Meeting over, gentlemen," declares Curtis, rising up from the bench. "I'll have a word with Andy soon as he gets back, we need him on board. By the way, what is that cheeky young sod doing nipping off to Singapore with Finnegan?"

"Don't worry, the Irishman will teach him a thing or two. He'll end up in some sort of a scrape. Anyone care to take a bet on it?" invites Ashton.

"Come on, I'm hungry," says Broadside.

The trio make for the counter. Awaiting them are spam fritters, mashed potatoes with a generous helping of tinned tomatoes. Sliced pomelo fruit to follow. The sad face of a low-profile Ken is there to greet them, a plate in each hand.

"Been thinking about your shower problem, Cookie," says Ashton in a loud voice, while banging his irons on the top of the counter.

"You should have a word with the C.O.'s wife. Ask her to lend you one of her bras!"

"But make sure it's big enough," adds Curtis.

The other diners join in the laughter as Ken retreats into the kitchen. Broadside appears to bring the raucous noise to an abrupt halt, turning sharply to face the diners.

"That's not funny. The young man dinna deserve it. Leave him alone 'cause he's ma 'wee' deputy – taught him all I know – and he's also my friend. Got it?"

10

A cool beer in hand, Andy sits patiently in a wicker chair, close to the door of the Malcolm Club at RAF Changi. He is waiting for Finnegan to return from Block 140, where he has been visiting one of his fire crew chums with whom he served in the UK.

Alone, Andy reflects on his five months on detachment in Borneo. His time there is passing more quickly than anticipated. The C.O, although at first appearing a threatening figure, has turned out to be relatively harmless, although more than a touch eccentric and with a hugely inflated ego. His first impressions of what seemed a lonely, unfriendly outpost staffed in part by misfits now seem misplaced. Furthermore, he has struck up good relationships with the other lads on the camp. Finnegan and the Music Man in particular have proved to be his closest friends. Despite both of them being older and from different backgrounds, they have somehow gravitated towards each other. Their boat trip to the neighbouring island is an adventure which Andy feels will live long in his memory. There will be no need to talk it up. Since their return, he has heard talk on the camp of an eccentric expat character called *'Educated Edwards,'* a professor who, after the War, had sought a life of seclusion on a nearby island. Could this just be the bearded Santa that they had inadvertently visited?

Subconsciously, he is aware of a growing fund of Asian experiences that he will be telling and re-telling throughout his later life. And perhaps his dad did have a point when, just before his departure for the Far East, he reminded Andy that 'seeing the world in the Services, at the country's expense,' represents a real bargain.

Characteristically, the Irishman is late. Finnegan finally bounces in, a familiar look of mock apology on his face. "Sorry, my friend, got caught up with some of my old pals. Haven't even had time for a shower!" His sweat-soaked bush jacket clings tightly to his chest.

"I'd never have known," replies Andy with a touch of sarcasm.

The Irishman drops his large hands on the circular table, taking deep breaths after his short sprint. "Now then, my friend, what you drinking?" he gasps.

Andy ignores the apology and the offer of a beer. He is more concerned with the speed with which the place is filling up. "Bloody 'ell, look, they're still flooding in."

The shouting from an adjacent table forces him to raise his voice an octave as he asks, "What the hell's going on?"

"Boat party – in fact two parties tonight. The lads in 140 mentioned a couple of lucky lads are going home," explains Finnegan. "And – wait for it! – a number of 'Wafs' might be coming in later. Could just be worth hanging around."

"Too noisy for me, don't fancy just sitting here all evening getting shot away," says Andy.

"Never been much of a drinker have you, lad? Don't worry though, still time for you."

"Fact is, Finnegan, I just don't really like the taste of the stuff."

"You'll grow to love it. Granted some of it can taste a bit off, 'specially if it's flat, but in my book you always feel better after you've sunk a few. For me, can't beat it, particularly with the thought of some crumpet dropping in later. We might just get lucky, Andy boy. Drink up!"

In front of them, one of the crew of the boat party is now standing precariously on a table littered with glasses and empty bottles, struggling to shed his trousers. His colleagues are whistling and chanting his name. Behind the bar, a petite young Chinese girl, her jet black hair tied neatly in a bun, looks on impassively.

"Why don't we go into Singapore?" asks Andy.

"'Cause we'll waste valuable drinking time getting there – and what's more it's cheaper here," counters the Irishman.

"I've got a few dollars saved up."

"O.K, you've convinced me Andy, so where do we go?"

"First, the village?"

"That'll do for starters. Let's go! Then Bedok Corner? From there, we can go on into Singapore."

Andy is seeking to impress Finnegan with his knowledge of the area, despite having spent only a couple of months on Changi before being detached to Borneo.

"One place at a time, young man, if you've got the dough, we'll get a cab from the village," smiles Finnegan. The duo make their way out of the now over-crowded club. Andy takes one final look behind him. A member of the boat party crew, clearly the central character in the event, and thus the major recipient of a seemingly endless flow of free beers, has slumped to the floor, hitting his head in the process, and is about to be carried outside.

The Chinese girl behind the bar continues to observe the antics with the indifferent expression of someone who has witnessed the scene countless times before.

There is a welcome breeze as they walk down into the village, with its bars and restaurants facing each other in two rows of wooden, zinc-roofed shops and houses. Resting in the middle of the road, in a cordoned off area serving as a bus terminal, are two single-decker, red and white painted coaches from the fleet that run between Changi Village and Singapore City. The white knuckle ride that the coaches provide has, justifiably, earned them the nickname of the 'Changi Flyer.' A number of those from the camp who have sampled the nerve-racking experience of being taken around the twisting, hairpin route into Singapore City are in little doubt they have been driven by born-again Japanese kamikaze pilots from World War Two.

The aromas of Chinese and Indian cuisine hang heavily in the air. A group of local children are chasing each other around a huge tree, engaged in a boisterous and highly vocal version of tag. Village trade is heavily reliant on Service personnel and their families, and the traders have developed a sophisticated and cunning sales approach. Andy catches sight of one of the shopkeepers reaching for a complimentary drink to delay the departure of an impatient father clearly anxious to move on, while his wife and children continue to browse. Behind the counter, the shopkeeper's own children stand ready to be brought into the action to amuse and play with the visiting kids should they become bored and threaten to leave. With her husband and children occupied, the wife can relax and the prospect of another sale is kept alive. A bulky, turbaned Indian shopkeeper, his shy young daughter clinging tenaciously to his trouser leg, is quick to engage Finnegan in conversation, as the Irishman pauses outside his shop to look at the colourful display of silks, shirts and slacks on offer.

"Special price for you today, Sir."

"No thanks, just looking."

"Come inside, Sir, and look around. We make suit for you –velly quick, velly cheap. Twenty four hour – all made. Lovely cloth. You tell me vitch material you like? Come inside."

Finnegan declines the offer and turns to see Andy has moved on ahead and is now crossing the dusty, unmade road. The Irishman rushes to join him.

"So where's it going to be then?" he shouts. "Let's try Tong Sing's, doesn't look like too many in there, should get decent service," replies Andy.

"Don't you worry about that, my friend, these blokes know how to look after us. I've been here before."

They make for a table in a corner of the restaurant, well away from the throbbing jukebox. The only other customers are a couple of fellow Servicemen, sitting close to the machine, their feet tapping in tune with Elvis Presley and their hands armed with a ready supply of coins.

"Christ, that'd be just the ideal birthday present for the Music Man: a bloody juke box!" laughs Finnegan.

"Shall we move on?" asks Andy.

"Don't see why, thought we were going to loosen up here with a few beers."

The Irishman suddenly thrusts his arm up in the air. "Waiter! John! two big Tuborgs over here – and quick!" To ensure the order for the larger bottles has been understood, Finnegan positions one hand directly above the other, a foot apart.

The pair feeding the jukebox react with a rather shocked response to the Irishman's shouted order by immediately asking for their bill. The stooped figure of an elderly Chinese man soon appears with a tray carrying a couple of chilled bottles and tall glasses.

"Thank you, John," says Finnegan. "Now you can get us the menu."

"That's taken care of Elvis, then," suggests Andy, as he watches the only two other people head for the door. He is already harbouring doubts about the wisdom of his decision to spend a weekend in Singapore with this Irishman, a character known to enjoy a drink more than most. Tonight could be one of the defining evenings of his Service life.

Another waiter who was standing in the doorway, touting for passing trade, comes back into the restaurant to resuscitate the silent jukebox and a high-pitched female voice bursts into song. Andy and Finnegan examine the menu in some detail, with the waiter hovering close at hand. "Another two beers, John, while we decide."

"Bloody hell, she's got a pair of lungs on her!" says the Irishman.

"Who? Where?" asks Andy, spinning around in an a hundred and eighty degree turn to catch a glimpse.

"It's the music I'm talking about, you daft sod, nothing to see," laughs Finnegan. The waiter returns with the drinks.

"Who's that singing, John? Don't recognise the voice?" enquires Andy.

The Chinese man nods obligingly.

"I find out," he replies obediently, before scampering across to the jukebox.

He returns almost breathless.

"Lady in box Caterina Valente, song 'Breeze and I '," comes the answer.

"John here knows everything, don't you, John?" says the seated Irishman, wrapping a friendly arm around the waiter's waist. The waiter appears uncomfortable with the unsolicited gesture and steps to one side. Andy and Finnegan settle for steak and chips at one dollar fifty. The preparation of their order sparks a sudden frenzy of shouting from the kitchen.

"Not bad this Tuborg," comments Andy, wiping the froth from above his upper lip.

The Irishman smiles knowingly. The meal is soon despatched and the pair pay up, leaving a generous fifty cent tip.

"Right, my friend, Bedok Corner it is." The pair step out into a village now sporting all the lights of evening. Andy spots 'George's Photographic' shop sign further along the road.

"Must get a decent camera before I go back."

"Not now, my friend," replies Finnegan, steering his companion in the direction of the taxi rank.

An Indian driver greets them with a generous smile. After taking their seats in the back of his car, and before the engine is turned on, there follows the usual prolonged negotiation of agreeing the fare. The driver's pleas of poverty, followed by his dubious estimates of the cost of feeding his children are ignored. The presence of a growing number of fellow drivers standing idly by their motors serve only to weaken his bargaining position. The fare is agreed and the pair relax as the vehicle heads away from the village. In the Irishman's opinion, tonight is to be enjoyed, to be savoured.

Very soon, in the gathering darkness and a few miles away from the camp, Finnegan thrusts an arm across Andy's chest pointing to the outline of an infamous building where thousands of Allied servicemen were incarcerated during the Second World War.

"Look, out to our left, that's Changi Prison. And those fields over there are where the prisoners were allowed out to the allotments, where they could grow their own food," explains the Irishman.

"Would have thought such a horrible place would have been reduced to rubble as soon as we got our poor sods out. Wonder why they haven't...?"

"Because they need it for a civilian prison," continues Finnegan. "Apparently they have so many robbers, like taxi drivers don't they, John?" adds the Irishman, raising his voice, simultaneously leaning forward to deliver the comment close to the ear of the driver immediately in front of him.

The man at the wheel pretends to ignore the remark by breaking into a soft, tuneless whistle.

Tonight, Bedok Corner is lit up as if it were Christmas. Lining one side of the road, facing the sea, are open air food stalls, tucked closely together. The busier and more popular ones boast lamps hanging from their overhead tin canopies. Customers jostle to view what's on offer. It's a popular spot with Servicemen. Perhaps not a place for the gourmet, with the local cuisine being taken straight from steaming buckets and wrapped in newspaper, but tasty Chinese grub at bargain prices. Across the road lies the beach and from it drifts the soothing sound of waves lapping onto the sand, before coming to rest amongst the sleeping fishing boats. Most of the local shopkeepers have closed for the day and their frontage has long since been boarded up, leaving the food stalls to cash in. The duo, who have already eaten, are able to pass along without being tempted by the culinary delights on display. They cross the road.

"Had enough to eat in the village, don't you think?" suggests Finnegan, "time for a drink, time to relax."

"Hold on!" Andy stops suddenly to thrust a hand into his trouser pocket, then stares open-mouthed at the Irishman.

"I've lost my money!"

"Where? Calm down, don't panic. Now where did you lose it?"

"Either back in the village – or here when I took the notes out in the taxi to pay the driver."

"Sorry, mate, but you can kiss that goodbye," replies Finnegan, "but don't worry – I know a place where we can get a free beer or two. Follow me!"

"Finnegan, stop!" shouts Andy, a smile slowly filling his face.

The Irishman spins around.

"Guess what? The dosh was in my back pocket all the time, can you believe it? Panic over."

"This way, you daft sod."

With Finnegan leading, the pair make towards a gap between an unlit cluster of huts. The Irishman hesitates, seemingly uncertain of the direction, before moving off again through the semi-darkness.

"And down here – yes, that's it," he adds, as if slowly retrieving the route from memory.

Andy recalls the advice all Service personnel have received about keeping out of the bad and potentially dangerous districts of Singapore. Could this just be one of them, a visit to regret into an 'Out of Bounds' area?

"Where the hell we going, Finnegan?" he asks anxiously.

"Patience, my friend."

Suddenly, they are aware of footsteps behind them.

"Quick! – in here and don't breathe a fucking word," comes the warning as Andy feels the Irishman grabbing his arm, then his stomach being pressed back against a wooden doorway.

The sound of pounding footsteps draw ever closer then, just as quickly, pass by.

"A couple of bleeding 'Pongos'," whispers Finnegan as the strangers disappear from sight and sound further down the path.

"How d'you know?"

"Smell 'em a mile off," laughs Finnegan. "And I bet I know where they're going. Off we go now."

Andy finds himself being led deeper into the gloom, now out of earshot of the diners at Bedok Corner. The pair pick their way along a path littered with rubbish and holding the strong smell of fish.

"Almost there," sighs the Irishman.

In front of them, a wooden door is being slowly dragged open, scraping noisily on the gravel but throwing a welcome shaft of light onto their path.

"Good evening, gentlemen, come inside and sit down."

Holding one side of the door is a portly Chinese man, sporting a

Hawaiian–style shirt and a billowing pair of white slacks.

They enter a shed which, from the scattered oil deposits on the ground, suggests it can only be a garage. The smell of petrol hangs heavily in the air. In one corner, already seated on a row of collapsible canvas chairs, are a couple looking every inch like fellow Servicemen. One has his clean shaven head slumped between his shoulders; the other clearly suffering from an excess of alcohol and struggling to remain seated. The bald one spins around, glaring at Andy.

"You blokes geeze us the slip. We were following you. What's your game?"

The accent and the threatening tone suggests that the speaker and his pal are members of the Army's King's Own Scottish Borderers, stationed close to RAF Changi.

"You all friends together then?" intervenes the Chinese host with an innocent look, clearly aiming to defuse a potentially difficult situation.

"Yep, course we are," replies Finnegan immediately, in a friendly tone designed to smooth things over.

"You boys no fight tonight over my ladies, OK? They give plenty action for all boys."

The two representatives from the Army hesitate before offering a confirmatory nod.

The host returns quickly, hastily pouring out the beers with a shaking hand, causing the froth to overflow each glass.

"First, drink for gentlemen, then I bring you lovely ladies. Good time tonight for everyone. Now, I get beautiful ladies for you."

Andy prods the Irishman in the ribs before whispering: "Are we in a brothel?"

"Course not, it's a bloody garage. The brothel's upstairs!"

"That's it, I'm off," replies Andy.

But Finnegan grabs the back of his shirt before he can raise himself from his seat.

"Hold on, this is the place where we get free drinks."

The host reappears. A line of women trail obediently behind him.

They stand uncomfortably, a few feet apart, with the look of condemned prisoners.

Unlike prisoners, however, there is no uniform.

Leading the line is a smartly dressed Chinese woman in a body-hugging cheongsam, allowing a glimpse of her leg up to the thigh. Following her is a short, plump lady with a loose-fitting blouse and skirt which suggests she could be in the early stages of pregnancy. Tip-toeing behind them is an innocent looking Indian girl, probably in her early teens, looking down solemnly at her bare feet. Two much older looking women, bringing up the rear, complete what is on offer for an amorous evening.

"Lovely ladies for you. I introduce them all," announces the host.

Their names, including an animated description of their individual speciality, are announced.

The fourth in line smells strongly of perfume and, with more than a generous application of make up, takes up her position immediately in front of Andy.

He is aware of her proximity but is determined to avoid any eye contact.

She thrusts out a stockinged leg, tapping the foot of his chair. She giggles.

"I think she likes you," teases Finnegan.

Andy gulps in embarrassment, continuing to keep his head down.

Meanwhile, the two other customers are quickly on their feet, in heated negotiation about a price for the cheongsam woman. Agreement is reached and together all three disappear together into the upstairs darkness.

Finnegan points to the heavily perfumed woman. "And this one?"

"Fifteen dollar for short time," insists the owner. "She know plenty tricks, and lotta saucy new ones, too."

"What about this podgy bird?" enquires the Irishman.

"I see you good judge of lovely lady, Sir," purrs the owner.

"Don't bullshit me. How much?"

The woman in question tilts her head to one side, offering a complimentary 'come hither' smile. Her tight, scarlet silk dress and pouting lips leave little to the imagination.

"Very pretty lady, you could be lucky, lucky tonight."

"For Christ's sake, man, how much?" repeats Finnegan.

"Ten dollar short time – and she show you hospital card to prove she clean. O.K? You like?"

The Irishman winces and runs his eye back along the line.

"And this one?" Finnegan points to the young Indian girl.

"Oh! this one – she special. No short time for this special lady. Thirty dollar."

"Make it twenty five and you've a deal."

The Chinese man feigns a pained expression before replying.

"I have business to run, but tonight you lucky, lucky man."

Finnegan rises, wrapping an arm around the pencil-slim waist of his chosen one before throwing a wide grin at Andy.

"Won't be too long, and don't forget – free drinks for you while I'm upstairs."

The three remaining unwanted women shuffle out through the rear of the shed, leaving Andy alone with the owner.

"You no like my ladies?"

"Oh yes! – but I have a skin complaint that's contagious, you know catching."

"You kind man. Not wish to spoil my lovely ladies, yes?"

"That's right," replies Andy.

"So now I give you special 'on house' drink. No charge."

Andy quickly despatches another complimentary glass of warm beer but his thoughts are of the fate of his Irish companion. He glances around the shed while the owner once again fills his glass. A few empty bottles lie beneath the chairs, together with discarded and torn copies of the *Straits Times* and *Free Press*.

The erratic movement of a solitary light bulb, hanging from the ceiling, suggests business is well under way upstairs.

With a couple of badly worn tyres fixed to each wall, Andy wonders whether the owner runs a garage repair service during the day and supplements his income with his ladies of the night. Or is he just an evening operator, with no motoring interests? He decides it is a question better not broached, particularly as his head is beginning to spin.

"Your friend be back shortly, don't worry. Next time lovely lady for you, too, at special price."

Andy nods in thanks, inwardly praying there will be no return for him. For a moment, he thinks of his parents and how they would react if they ever became aware of his visit to a place such as this. And what on earth would Sandra think? No doubt about it: this must remain a secret to take to the grave.

The host continues to talk, stopping only to show pictures of his family.

One snap looks suspiciously like one of the women who had been paraded in front of him. Andy decides against asking the obvious question. Finnegan appears, tucking his shirt into his trousers and tightening his belt.

"That was a waste of fucking time," comes his verdict.

"Come on, let's go," presses Andy.

The pair leave, threading their way through a cluster of huts towards the main road.

"You didn't enjoy that, then?" enquires Andy.

There is no reply from the Irishman.

"You had the best looker there," persists Andy.

"Don't want to talk about it, all right?"

"Sorry, just wondered what went wrong."

"Look, the deal in those places is that it's free drinks all round, providing a number of the lads are going to take a woman. Understand? You got a few beers for nothing and so did I, let's leave it at that."

"Didn't see those two 'Pongos' come down, did you?"

"Nope, they always make sure they get their money's worth. Mind you, I heard someone up there being sick. Could have been the woman. Who knows, who cares?"

A few minutes later they reach the beach and decide to rest on the side of a broken fishing boat. Across the road, the stallholders are closing up and only a few people remain.

"Thought I might try and 'phone Sandra tomorrow – from here," suggests Andy.

"What the hell for?"

"Well, can't do it from the island."

"Cost you a fortune from here as well! Why not send her another letter but this time post it from here."

"Be a real surprise to actually speak to her from here, wouldn't it?" insists Andy.

"Forget it, save your money. No woman's worth that."

"But you don't know her like I do, Finnegan."

"I don't have to, my friend. Keep 'em guessing, and with a Singapore and not a Borneo stamp on the envelope that'll probably keep her thinking till you go home!"

Their conversation is interrupted by the sudden arrival of a jeep with a couple of Army Police on board. The vehicle screeches to a halt in front of the stalls. The driver and his partner jump out and race along the road before disappearing through the same gap taken earlier by Andy and Finnegan.

"You don't suppose…" begins Andy.

"Yep, I bet our two *friends* have caused some bother back there in the shed. I noticed the Chinese bloke had a 'phone under the staircase."

"Lucky we got out in time," says a relieved Andy.

The Irishman chuckles to himself, as they leave the beach and look to get a cab back to camp.

"What's funny about that?"

"Andy, smart people make their own luck. Remember that."

"Tell you what, Finnegan, did you see that woman with all that make-up. Looked more like a Geisha girl, don't you think?"

"Don't feel sorry for her: probably makes her money up during the day as a plasterer!"

"So what went wrong with your woman back there? Go on, tell me," presses Andy.

"If you must know, we were really getting it together, getting my money's worth then, all of a sudden, I hear this rustling of paper alongside the bed."

"And?"

"Thought it must be a cat or mouse under the bed. Then I lean over the girl and see what's happening…"

"And …?"

"Her arm's hanging down and she's dipping into a crisp packet, while we've been at it!"

"But didn't you hear her munching away?"

"No, she was doing a lot of groaning at the time – all part of the service, I suppose."

"Another thing, Finnegan, that Chinese bloke wasn't doing the best for himself. I mean, a tatty old garage with a single light, hardly the best way to show off his women, is it?"

"He's no mug. That garage will cost him next to nothing, and if the place was properly lit and you saw 'em close up you'd run a bloody mile. And if you saw any of 'em in the daylight – you'd never stop running."

11

Saturday morning. Andy awakes to a fierce argument raging in a nearby bed space. It takes just a moment or two for him to realise that he is no longer on detachment at a remote island in the South China Sea, but on the largest and most populated Air Force Station in the Far East. This is his weekend home in the Transit Block at RAF Station, Changi. Accommodation destined to hold a mismatch of occupants.

It is the temporary resting place for those having just arrived from the UK and who wait, often apprehensively, to be moved on to their permanent station elsewhere in the Far East; and simultaneously the final stepping stone for those tour or time-expired men waiting to be sent home, either by troopship or 'plane. People moving in opposite directions, with different moods, hopes and expectations.

Andy returns from the shower to discover his slacks and shirt have picked up some dirt and oil stains from the previous evening, and his casual shoes are full of sand. Today, he has no alternative but to wear his uniform.

"Own up, you bastard!" comes the cry.

"Don't talk rubbish, who in their right mind would want to steal a pink shirt and tie?"

"You stole it, I want it back," replies an impressively tanned figure.

The pair are now locked in an angry dialogue and their voices are rising. The accused, with an equally brown torso, decides to turn and walk away.

"What's all that about?" asks Andy to the occupant of the next bed.

"Those two? They've been at each others' throats for the past two weeks. They're both waiting for a flight home, both long-term Regulars with no priority for a seat, both spending all their time and money in the village looking at new gear for going home. Nothing else to do."

"How sad," mutters Andy.

The dispute suddenly re-ignites. The feuding pair are again face to face, with the accuser prodding the other in his chest with a finger.

"Come on, where is it?" he shouts, "Tell me now!"

"Bugger off," is the immediate and equally loud response.

A couple of onlookers jump in between them.

"Any more trouble or noise from the pair of you, and I'll get the 'Snowdrops' – that means the Police in case you didn't know – down here, got it?" comes the warning. The stance and authority of the voice suggests the speaker, dressed only in a shirt, could himself be a Policeman. The warring couple return to their respective beds.

"Problem is the bloody National Servicemen: they get priority when it comes to going home," comes another voice.

As someone who has been conscripted, Andy moves discreetly outside onto the balcony of the second floor.

He joins a group who are looking out towards the main road.

"What's going on down there?" he asks.

"The troopship 'Devonshire' docked this morning and we're waiting for the arrival of the Moon Men," comes the reply.

"Moon Men?"

"Yeh, you'll soon see what I'm talking about. Look, that's the welcome party forming up below."

Andy glances down at the small crowd that is congregating, clearly not all from the Transit Block. Some are holding sticks and dustbin lids, others don party hats and are blowing whistles. There is a carnival atmosphere in the air.

A pale blue Bedford coach lumbers into sight, pumping out exhaust fumes, passing the Mess where a few of the catering staff have emerged to acknowledge the newcomers with their own shower of derisive comments.

As the vehicle comes to a halt, the party revellers move into action. Bedlam ensues.

Sticks hammer against dustbin lids as the chants continue to grow. Men gather around the coach for a closer look at the new arrivals from the UK, now looking out uneasily from within and bemused at what they have done to deserve such a reception.

"Here come the Moon Men!" comes the cry as the passengers disembark. After over a month on a troopship, they are looking far from their best. Their ill-fitting and creased KD issue does them no favours; but the most noticeable features of their appearance are the lily white knees and arms and the almost ghostly looking pink faces.

The newly-arrived are slowly being surrounded as they file out of the vehicle against a background of derisive shouts: "What's it like on the Moon?" "Getcha knees brown." "Get some in!" "I think that one's dead!" "Don't go near 'em, lads!" "Could catch something."

The Sergeant who has collected them from the Docks calls for silence as his flock are shepherded into the Transit Block, looking every inch like strangers from another planet. Andy is grateful that he was spared this initiation. Only his arrival in Singapore by 'plane, rather than boat, had denied him experiencing this unique welcome. "Poor bastards," he mutters quietly to himself.

"Today, my friend, will be a quiet day," says Finnegan, rising from the adjoining bed.

The pair decide to make for the nearby Mess. They amble slowly as the Irishman is still suffering the effects of the previous evening. Although the camp rests in cloud cover, he is wearing sunglasses.

"How about a quiet trip into Singapore?" asks Finnegan, taking a gulp of iced water.

"Suits me fine," replies Andy. "Didn't make it there yesterday, so why not today."

"Excellent, we'll take the bus in, have a stroll down Orchard Road, perhaps take in a film then head back."

"And we'll give the booze a miss, O.K?" cautions Andy.

"Yep, I'll drink to that," laughs Finnegan.

Apart from the occasional emergency stop, the journey to Singapore aboard the 'Changi Flyer' is relatively uneventful. They reach the Geylang Terminus. The passengers become impatient after the driver and then conductor disappear from the coach. The minutes pass and there is no sign of their return. In their absence, the bus continues to fill. All the seats are soon taken, followed by a bad-tempered jostling in the doorway from those attempting to come on board and win a standing place.

The Irishman attempts to discover the reason for the delay. He stands up from his seat and, for a few moments, surveys the mayhem before elbowing his way out to the front of the bus through the line of crowded passengers now blocking the aisle. Finnegan's empty seat is quickly taken by a Chinese man, holding a large, square wooden box. He offers a weak smile as Andy reels back in his seat in response to its unpleasant, farmyard smell.

The holder of the box raps his knuckle hard on the wood, before gently opening the top by a few inches. Andy recoils as the head of a chicken suddenly appears, accompanied by two high-pitched squawks. The owner immediately snap shuts the lid to the sound of muffled cries of protest from the imprisoned bird. The Irishman returns and there follows an exchange of animated sign language with the Chinese man, resulting in Finnegan regaining his seat. In the course of this heated exchange, the box hits the floor, causing its owner to drop to his knees and engage in a whispered and seemingly sympathetic dialogue with its occupant.

"Cows are kings in India; chickens in Singapore," observes Andy dryly.

The driver and conductor finally return and the coach resumes its single-handed battle with the other vehicles on the road, now muscling its way through heavier traffic and showing scant regard for either pedestrian or cyclist. Not a yard, not an inch, is surrendered by the man at the wheel. The horn is in constant use, as trishaw men scamper for the safety of the nearby pavement. Without realising it, the driver is ensuring that the dubious reputation of the 'Changi Flyer' remains intact.

Andy gazes out through the window, smiling to himself as he reflects on this trip and the years of his comparatively uneventful rides on the school bus in Plymouth.

The pair finally reach Singapore and make their way on foot to Orchard Road, passing the towering Cathay building. They stop to admire its impressive architecture, which houses shops, restaurants, a cinema and topped by an open-air sun terrace.

Anxious to avoid a repetition of the previous evening, Andy suggests taking in a film.

"Good idea, my friend, but later," comes the response.

It is now early afternoon and the temperature and humidity are rocketing. They pause in front of a car showroom displaying the revolutionary new 'Bubble Car', with a door opening both outwards and upwards.

"Christ, in this climate you'd probably be fried alive in that tiny thing – and you'd need both hands to work the door!" laughs the Irishman.

"Easy to handle on the road, though," adds Andy.

"Let's face it, if you were inside that and clashed with the 'Changi Flyer' you'd be reduced to a flattened sardine tin. By the way, what made you wear your uniform today. It's our day off. Hold on a minute, you're not enjoying your National Service that much, are you?"

"No, I'm damn well not."

"You are, my friend, and something tells me you're going to sign on as a Regular."

"Don't be daft, I've got a pensionable job to go back to, and a lovely girl. Look, I've got her photo here."

"Don't bother, I've seen it on your locker," comes the dismissive response.

The heat is beginning to bite and Finnegan suggests seeking refuge in the shade of a bar.

"Didn't think we were drinking today," says Andy.

"We're not – just thinking it might be worth putting some liquid back into our parched bodies."

"How long have you signed on for?" enquires Andy tentatively, aiming to change the subject.

"Too long, but what's the alternative?"

"Being a fireman in civvy- life, back home?"

"Still be in uniform and the only travel would be local. Be too late to get to overseas fires, wouldn't it?" laughs the Irishman.

Andy attempts another approach in trying to break through the Irishman's tough exterior.

"Just think, only a couple more months before you fly home. Bet your folks are looking forward to seeing you again." Finnegan fails to take the bait.

The pair continue their stroll along Orchard Road.

Andy spots a camera shop on the other side of the road.

"Sorry, my friend, I need to rest my legs. Off you go. I'll be waiting for you down there," explains Finnegan pointing through a narrow gap between the shops to a back street restaurant. "And don't forget to bargain with the bastards!" adds the Irishman as Andy crosses over, skipping daringly between a couple of motor cyclists.

Some twenty minutes elapse before the duo are back together, sipping a couple of beers.

The restaurant is in semi-darkness, without any other customers, lit only by the few working bulbs that have survived within a galaxy of

Chinese lanterns. The wallpaper, a mix of ruby red and burnt orange, does little to relieve the gloom.

"Another Tuborg?" enquires Andy, nodding at his partner's glass.

"What else? Get your camera?"

"Too expensive."

"Didn't you try to knock 'em down?"

"No, they kept saying 'special price.'"

"'Course they bloody well did, man. Tell you what, try the lost property back at Changi. Any gear not collected after three months, is sold off cheap. Might just have some cameras there," suggests Finnegan.

"How d'you know about this place?" asks Andy casting an eye around the empty chairs.

"I didn't, but once you get off the main roads in Singapore, the prices always get cheaper."

They are joined by a Chinese man, almost certainly the manager, dressed immaculately in a lightweight, charcoal grey suit.

"Just in time, my friend," says the Irishman. "A couple more – and one for yourself."

"Suggest this drink last one," comes a warning in a firm tone.

"Don't you want our business then?" replies Finnegan.

"No, not at all. For your own good. Very soon, Army boys from Nee Soon come in for Saturday night drink."

"So?"

"You no problem, Sir, but your friend in uniform – but not Army one. Understand?"

"I think he's got a point," interjects Andy, rising quickly to his feet.

"Don't worry, we'll go as soon as I've finished this drink – not before."

Their conversation is broken by the sudden and noisy arrival of a group of young men.

They stand together menacingly in the doorway.

"Hello, what have we here?" shouts one, pointing in an aggressive manner.

"It's a real Brylcreem Boy," sniggers another.

"You two can buy us all a drink before we throw you out," comes the command from their six foot plus leader.

"Let's not waste time, throw 'em out – now," suggests his pal.

The Army advance threateningly towards the seated pair.

"You two realise where you are?" comes a whisper in Andy's ear. He spins round to confront an aggressive looking face.

Andy decides to offer no comment, feeling instinctively that whatever he utters will be taken as provocative. Finnegan moves off quickly in the direction of the toilet as the unwelcome arrivals begin to form a circle of chairs around the now trapped Airmen.

"Back in a moment, lads. Don't go away now," comes his flippant remark.

Although no doubt taken aback by the audacity of the Irishman's remark, the Army boys detail one of their men to follow their prey. A tactical withdrawal by the Royal Air Force is clearly off the menu in this restaurant.

Alone, Andy is aware of chairs being moved ever closer towards him, scratching and scoring the restaurant's wooden floor.

"Don't have much to say, do you, Brylcreem Boy?" comes the unwelcome question in his ear.

Andy ignores the remark, simultaneously wondering why he ever agreed to follow his pal into this restaurant. Surely buying an expensive camera – and taking his time in doing so – would have avoided this impending disaster. Bugger the cost. A damn sight cheaper than getting a hiding from the 'Pongos'. Too late now!

Finnegan returns to find the table he left is now completely encircled by seated bodies sporting hostile faces. Strategically, the Army are in a commanding position. Andy cuts a vulnerable figure, sitting still and not daring to look up, his fingers running nervously around the rim of his empty glass. The Irishman throws up both arms in a gesture of submission. "No sweat, boys. We're going now so…"

But his words are brought to a premature and sudden close.

Andy looks up in horror as a chair comes crashing down on the back of Finnegan's head, causing him to crumple in a heap beside the table. The soldiers swarm in for the kill, grabbing hold of their victim's defenceless arms and legs. Simultaneously, Andy is hit. His body slithers down effortlessly between chair and table before hitting the floor.

The waiters, usually content to assume the role of spectator in such circumstances, decide to move into action. While the Irishman is the immediate and sole object of the soldiers attention, Andy's body is being pulled from beneath the table and swiftly dragged across the floor and into the safety of the kitchen. Meanwhile, Finnegan struggles helplessly to fend off the blows. There is a momentary pause in the action. One of the pacifist waiters, armed with a broom, chooses the break in the proceedings to tidy up; another staff member, seemingly oblivious to the mayhem is attending to the empty tables, totally engrossed in the laboured ritual of carefully laying the cutlery and napkins for the evening customers.

"Where's the other bastard gone?" comes the cry from one of the soldiers, rubbing a sore knuckle. The hunt is now on for Andy, with the boys from Nee Soon anxious to score another hit. They storm into the kitchen, leaving behind a trail of broken restaurant furniture. Then pause for a quick look around before disappearing out of sight into a courtyard filled with empty boxes and finally clambering over a wall at the rear of the building.

Finnegan lies beside the table groaning, an arm still protecting his ribs. Slowly he levers himself up with the aid of a broken chair leg. He runs a hand across his already swollen face. One eye is closing fast and his beaten rib cage is making breathing difficult. His tongue makes a quick dental inventory. "Andy? Andy! Where the hell are you?" he croaks.

A couple of white-jacketed waiters stand over him.

"Where's my mate, you silly bastards?"

"Your friend O.K, he outside in kitchen."

Shoulders hunched and with a grimace born of pain, Finnegan stumbles towards the kitchen, followed closely by the staff. His shirt is torn and blood stained. One of his trampled shoes remains under the table. "Where is he then?"

"He sleep now behind big freezer."

"I can't see him. Where?"

"Look down there, see leg under boxes?"

"Give us a hand, lads. Get him on his feet and we'll take a look at him."

Slowly the waiters lift a shaking Andy to his feet.

"You poor bastard. Get a grip! The Pongos have gone and won't be coming back," come the Irishman's reassuring words.

Still shaking from head to toe, Andy breaks into a fragile smile while rubbing the back of his neck. "Finnegan, I'm not shaking with fright – I'm shaking because I'm fucking frozen."

The manager intervenes to explain to the Irishman. "Army boys would have given your friend big kicking. When fight start, we take your friend to kitchen. After finish with you, Army boys come look for him and then run through kitchen into courtyard which lead to street at back. They think he run away but all time he in here."

"Behind the freezer, you mean?"

"Oh no! your friend *inside* freezer. Safe place."

"So didn't they come back?"

"No, no, Army boys always know: when big trouble, we ring Police."

"Did they whack you on the neck, Andy?"

"Someone did."

The manager steps forward to explain.

"Very sorry. When trouble start, I do quick karate chop on boy's neck, he make no noise and we put him in kitchen freezer. He lucky boy: we had short time as Army men always take big man first."

"Oh! thanks for that. Always glad to be your decoy, Andy," grins the Irishman.

"How long was I in that thing?" gasps Andy, pointing to the huge, cream coloured freezer, boasting a chipped chrome handle.

The manager's response is an inscrutable smile.

"Christ, what if you had forgotten me! I'd have been frozen to death."

"No, not possible. Every night, before go home, we check meat OK."

"See, Andy, you were never in danger with these smart fellas," laughs Finnegan.

"Once again, it's all part of the service in Singapore!"

"Part of the service, my arse," replies Andy.

"Your *frozen* arse, my friend, get it right," smiles the Irishman.

12

Andy is asleep for most of the Sunday flight back to Borneo. It had been an eventful weekend with Finnegan and now, as the only passenger, he can relax with the luxury of both legs draped across two improvised seat units. Unlike his maiden flight from Singapore over the South China Sea, there is no feeling of apprehension as to what the destination holds in store. Soon he will be re-joining the lads, his friends. No surprises this time, although there remains a nagging doubt about possible developments following the fateful evening when the C.O invited the Sergeants to his home. Has the C.O's wife spilt the beans over what actually happened? If so, it'll mean another abortive search for those elusive Charge Sheets.

These thoughts run through his mind as the Valetta ceases its drone and begins to lose altitude in preparation for landing. It's not like the feeling of returning home but, for a teenage National Serviceman who finds himself posted to the Far East, it's the next best thing. As he disembarks, the servicing crew stand waiting to fire the predictable broadside of questions.

"Finnegan show you the sights then, Andy?" "Catch anything, young man?" "What d'you think of Lavender Street, eh?" "D'you get down to Bugis Street?"

To his surprise, Andy finds himself holding a convincing, nonchalant 'man of the world' facial expression which somehow brings the comments to a halt. He strolls back to the billet, acknowledging a few nods and waves en route. The Music Man is waiting in the doorway, arms folded, sporting a welcoming smile.

"Enjoy yourself, then?"

"Oh, yeh. Got into a couple of scrapes…"

"What the hell did you expect, you daft sod? The Oirishman's middle name is 'Trouble'."

"Anything happen here?" asks Andy.

"Everyone wants to know what really happened at the C.O's party for the Sergeants, but they're saying nothing. Plenty of rumours flying around but I thought I'd hear it straight from the horse's mouth. You were there, weren't you?"

"Leave it, for the moment? Need to get my head down for an hour or two."

"Sure, and you'll find a couple of letters on the top of your locker."

"They can wait, too," says Andy, as he makes for his bed. He releases his sweaty grip on the handles of his holdall, letting it fall with a thud on the floor. Stretching out on the mattress, he cups his hands behind his head. Within minutes he is snoring.

Martin returns to his bed space, opens his locker and dips into his collection of music.

He is looking, mischievously, for a sound that is guaranteed to raise the returning sleeper from his slumber. Minutes later, the cannon fire from Tchaikovsky's 1812 overture fills the air.

"That's bloody unnecessary," Andy screams, rolling off his mattress and jumping to his feet.

"Well, give me the gen about the Sergeants Party and you won't hear another note."

"Martin, give it a rest, please, I'll be in trouble if I say anything. Whole idea was daft from the start."

The familiar handwriting on the envelopes tells Andy immediately that one of the letters is from his mother, the other from Sandra. As usual, he is about to look first at the one from his fiancée; but something tells him to first read the news from his parents.

As usual, his mother's words are full of predictable and totally unnecessary advice, little different from the words he was receiving as a ten year old. There is news of the dogs with some slightly out of focus black and white snaps of them playing together on the moors. His father has a touch of 'flu. But what registers is the brief mention of Sandra: "….She hasn't been in touch with us lately. Both your dad and I have rung her at home but there's been no reply. We know her family sometimes take off for a short skiing holiday abroad when the bad weather sets in, so that's probably the explanation. As long as she keeps in touch with you, dear, that's all that really matters."

Andy hopes that Sandra's letter will carry the explanation. She certainly hadn't mentioned that a skiing holiday was in prospect. Had she perhaps fallen out with his parents? It had happened before. He decides to leave the billet to read her letter in private.

Tchaikovsky's overture has ended with an abrupt and unscheduled ceasefire. Martin attempts to follow Andy outside to apologise but, after just a few steps, decides otherwise.

Andy makes for the camp cinema, located in the heart of the camp. A modest wood construction, open to the elements on two sides and boasting a corrugated iron roof.

Today, it is both silent and empty. Andy takes his place at the back, immediately in front of the projectionist's position. With no one else in sight, slowly and deliberately, he opens the envelope. It reads:

Dear Andrew,

We've had some heavy falls of snow this month, followed by some awful rain and now the roads are slushy. Dread taking the car out in these wicked conditions and the battery will probably be flat next time out! Just my luck.

As you know, this is the quiet season for estate agents so I'm taking some leave putting my feet up and tidying my room. I was even tempted to change the wallpaper and treat the woodwork to a lick of paint but Daddy tells me he'll get someone in to do it properly. With the luxury of extra time on my hands I've been thinking about our future. What really got me thinking was my lost engagement ring. Still hasn't turned up. I was heartbroken when it went missing and dreaded telling you about it. You were so understanding and somehow that made me feel even worse, but I did just wonder whether fate was sending a message to us both that we should not rush into things and perhaps our engagement was a touch too hasty. Perhaps losing the ring was an omen. Everything happened in such a rush before you left. It seemed so exciting and romantic at the time. Don't get me wrong, I'll never forget it – and the pictures of that day are among my favourites. I spoke to Daddy about us and he agreed that our enforced separation might well be for the good, something of a breathing space for us both. He thought it would prove a jolly good test, like a trial period. Eighteen months is a long time apart and, who knows, we might both have changed so much by the time we meet up again. Of course I still want you to write to me and tell me all your news and I'll do the same. This has been such a difficult letter to write and I hope you'll understand why I had to send it. Whatever happens, you'll always be a dear, dear friend. Love, Sandra

Andy slumps forward, almost losing his balance on the wooden bench. Stunned, he takes a deep breath before slowly folding the typed, one and a half page letter, and slipping it back inside the envelope. Almost immediately, he decides to give it a second reading. This is the shortest letter he has received from his fiancée since he left home. It is not just its brevity that shocks the young man, but the fact that such an important decision about their future together has been settled in consultation with his potential father-in-law.

"Sod the lost engagement ring," mutters Andy to himself. Jewellery can be replaced, not the love of his life. A torrent of thoughts flood his now confused mind. Has she met someone else? How the hell can they continue being 'friends' after implying that their engagement was a mistake? Should he ignore the letter and wait for Sandra to come to her senses? "Damn it," he curses. This would never have happened if he had been given a sensible posting in the UK, not thrown seven thousand miles from home, helpless to take any effective action. He sits quietly for a while and then ambles back to the billet.

Martin is waiting outside. "Sorry about the music."

"Forget it."

"Bad news from home?" enquires the Music Man in a tentative tone.

"Not sure," answers Andy.

"Well, you walked out of here half an hour ago with that letter in your hand and you're still carrying it. If you want to talk, that's fine. Only trying to help."

There is an uncomfortable pause as the men look at each other. Andy breaks the silence.

"Think I've got a 'Dear John'."

Martin raises his eyebrows. "*Think?* Good heavens, man. *Think!* Either it is or it isn't. Want a second opinion?"

"No thanks, and the letter is definitely not for the notice board," comes Andy's firm reply.

"Does she mention the bit about wanting to remain 'friends'?"

"Yes, she does actually. Why?"

"From the ones I've read, that's usually a dead giveaway. Pity Finnegan isn't here. Just the man for moments like these."

"Thanks, but can we leave it for the moment."

"Just a word of advice, Andy."

"Which is?"

"First, change the picture in that silver frame straight away. Let's see your mum and dad's face for a change. Second, let's take a stroll up to the runway and join the lads for a kick-about. Take your mind off it."

Andy hesitates.

"Come on, pal, take it out on the bloody football," insists Martin.

The pair make for the edge of the airstrip, which boasts a welcome spread of green weed upon which some of the lads are engaged in a competitive five-a-side game of soccer. The heat dictates that the playing gear is down to swimming trunks and plimsolls. Discarded, punctured, black oil drums serve as goalposts. Each goal scored is followed by both unrestrained celebration and simultaneous recrimination.

"Hey, Andy! We need a goalie. Get your jacket off and help us." The cry of desperation comes from an exhausted player who has just returned from a demanding walk to retrieve the ball from behind the servicing shed.

Reluctantly, Andy decides to join in, dropping his jacket on top of a foul-smelling and badly dented oil drum. The tempo of the game soon falls and Andy is tempted to dribble the ball up field towards the opposition. Soon he adapts to the surface and finds himself at ease, evading clumsy tackles and remaining upright. It's the first time he has kicked a ball since leaving the UK – and he is enjoying it. Unlike Sandra, his touch has not deserted him. The match comes to an end and a couple of the players compliment him on his impromptu performance. Martin emerges from the shade of the servicing shed. He walks towards Andy, nodding his head in appreciation.

"You've played a bit before, haven't you?"

"Yeh, played regularly back home, for my school and with Plymouth Schoolboys, loved running out on Argyle's pitch," replies Andy.

Ken, the cook, comes racing towards them.

"Listen," he begins, before dropping his head in a laboured attempt to recover his breathing. "Listen, we could certainly use you for our camp team. There's a local league. Only four or five sides but it is a league – and we start next week," explains Ken enthusiastically.

"You in the team, Ken?"

"Yeh, I'm the keeper. They reckon I'm worth my place because I'm big enough to block out most of the goal."

"I can understand that," smiles Martin.

"Some of those locals are pretty quick but they can't take a tackle, not even a fair one."

"I reckon you should lose a bit of that flab, Cookie," suggests Martin.

"Thanks, as long as I can get some off the top half, I'll be happy."

Andy and the Music Man stroll back to the billet.

"Did you a bit of good belting that ball around, don't you think?"

There is no reply. Thoughts of Sandra are re-surfacing.

Andy spends the rest of the day avoiding the other men in the billet. At first, he tries to lose himself in a thriller but somehow he lacks the conviction to follow the story. His mind is elsewhere, a world away. Only a couple of days ago it was the excitement of Singapore. Today, he is left alone to try and understand – or just guess – why his relationship with Sandra has hit the rocks. His thoughts slip back to his first day on the camp when he caught the sight of Billy sobbing his heart out having received a 'Dear John'. At the time, Andy couldn't help thinking it was all rather bizarre, almost comical. Today, he has a better understanding.

13

"Airman! Airman!" comes the piercing cry from the adjoining room. Andy grabs his notepad, opens the beaded curtain with a now well practised sweep of his hand, and stands to attention in front of his C.O.

"No need to write this down: this is strictly confidential and for your ears only."

"Of course, Sir."

"While you were on your jolly in Singapore, my wife received some distressing family news from home."

"Sorry to hear that, Sir…"

"Don't interrupt! The upshot of it all is that she will be returning to the UK immediately and I doubt if she will be coming back."

"Sorry to hear that, Sir."

"No, you clearly don't understand what I'm saying. Your sympathy is not required. What I've told you is the official line, and that is exactly what you will feed to the others. The truth of the matter is that she has found it difficult to settle here. Hasn't come to terms with the climate and has a problem sleeping, even with the fan on all night. Finally, she moved into the spare room."

"Oh dear, Sir."

"Yes, oh dear it certainly is. I'm telling you this now because I don't want anyone on the camp thinking she wasn't able to adapt or couldn't cope. If something on those lines got out it would bring into question my judgement in deciding to bring her out here."

"When will she be going, Sir?"

"Tomorrow, on the first flight out to Singapore. I'll drive her up to the strip to see her off. There'll be no repeat of that circus that greeted us here after our marriage. Understand? If there is, I'll know who to blame, won't I?"

"Of course, Sir."

"So, in a few days time, start dropping the word that it's been some sort of sudden family bereavement – but you haven't dared to enquire.

That should give them the message that it's hush-hush. And not a word at all about the timing of her departure. Got it?"

"Exactly, Sir."

"Good. Now find out what that over-sized cook has done with my coffee. Last time I saw him, he looked as if he had just consumed all our emergency rations. Which reminds me, when is the next inventory check of the emergency grub?"

"I'll check that, Sir," replies Andy cautiously, fully aware of the continuing and unauthorised cookhouse practice to dip into the food store reserves for special occasions.

Andy returns to his desk and contemplates the repercussions of the departure of the C.O's wife. Could it mean that no further action will be taken following the events of that disastrous party given for the Sergeants? Will Fatimah be restored to favour? Will the C.O now be spending more time on the camp and less at home? And could that mean the C.O would become even more difficult to work with during the remaining months of his tour?

While these questions occupy his thoughts, Ken appears in the doorway, holding the C.O's cup of coffee.

"Shall I take it straight through?" he asks.

"No, just leave it there, on top of the post bag. The C.O's had some bad news from home, best not to disturb him."

Ken leans forward to whisper in Andy's ear: "Old Man's not leaving us, is he?"

"No, not yet."

"By the way, Andy, you're in the team for tomorrow night. Down in the village, match against the Indian Brotherhood. Five o'clock kick off, truck leaves half past four. We've got a team shirt, shorts and socks for you, just bring your boots."

"Thanks, Ken, I'll be ready."

The cook leaves, breaking into his customary tuneless whistle.

Momentarily, Andy's thoughts of Sandra have been put to one side; but now he wonders whether he should send a reply. By leaving her letter unanswered it might appear that he accepted what she had said. On the other hand, any response would require careful preparation and drafting. "If only I could speak to her," he mutters to himself.

Any ideas on a future course of action are immediately disturbed by the unexpected arrival of the Music Man, waving a piece of paper above his ear.

"Leaving your post, tut-tut. So to what do we owe this rare visit?" smiles Andy, rising from his chair.

"Only when there's hot news," smiles Martin.

"What is it?"

"Priority signal for the C.O straight off the press – and the Old Man won't like it!"

"Come on, let's have a look before I take it in," pleads Andy.

But Flight Lieutenant Munro has already picked up the ripples of the conversation and now stands peering through the beaded curtain at the two men.

"What won't I like, Airman? Give it to me!"

The content of the signal from RAF Changi is scanned in seconds.

"Back to your post immediately," barks the C.O pointing a finger at the Music Man before turning to face Andy.

"And you, Airman, get the Sergeants down here straight away – whatever they're doing."

"Yes, Sir," responds Andy, still unaware what has triggered the sudden flurry of activity.

A mere ten minutes later, the Sergeants have been rounded up and stand together facing their Commanding Officer.

"Right then, men, relax and brace yourself for some important news."

"It's got to be World War Three," comes a whispered aside from Sergeant Curtis.

Flight Lieutenant Munro leaps to his feet, staring directly at the Sergeant.

"What did you say, Curtis?" he demands.

"About the heat, Sir. I said 'got to be ninety three'."

"Be that as it may," continues the C.O, "the news is that on Wednesday – a mere forty eight hours from now – Wing Commander Harding from Changi will be landing here, en route for Hong Kong. The purpose of his visit will be to carry out a brief inspection of this detachment. He will be leaving on a later flight that same day, giving him about three hours here. It is imperative the Wing Commander leaves this place in the knowledge that we are an effective, fighting force standing ready to meet any emergency or unexpected hostility, not merely a staging post. A chance for us all to shine, to impress our distinguished visitor. It will be on your heads if he leaves with any doubts about our capability. To borrow a nautical term, everything here must be shipshape. Butlins this is not! Do I make myself absolutely clear?"

"Anything in particular, Sir?" asks Curtis tentatively.

"Everything in particular, man! The MT and Fire Sections will have their vehicles spotless, sparkling in the sun. The billets will be a model of cleanliness and order. The cooks will get their act together in the kitchen. Each man will carry a look of dedication and professionalism. Yes, Curtis, there is a lot of work for you three to organise and do, both today and tomorrow, I shall carry out a final pre-inspection at eighteen hundred hours on Tuesday. Off you go – get cracking!"

Andy watches as the Sergeants slowly file out of the office. Their body language suggests a distinct lack of enthusiasm for the Wing Commander's forthcoming visit.

"And now your urgent tasks, Airman."

The C.O is standing directly behind Andy, reading from a manuscript.

"Sir?"

"The scrub and grass need attention, so get the locals in to tidy it up."

"We'll have to pay them extra, won't we, Sir."

"Good grief, man, certainly not. We rescued them from the hands of the Japs, set them free. They owe us everything: we owe them nothing."

Andy struggles to stifle a smile. "Right, Sir."

"And the paths around the camp need cleaning up. All paths leading to the billets will be lined with sizeable stones which are to be whitewashed. That will be your second task. Understand?"

The C.O slips quietly back to his desk.

"Something I wanted to show you," says Martin, having waited alone outside to eavesdrop. He pulls up one side of his shorts to reveal a nasty looking rash on the inside of his thigh.

"Good heavens, that looks bad."

"It feels bad, too," says Martin. "What do you think it is? Thought you might know."

"Well, I remember seeing something like that years ago…"

"And?"

"I think it was ringworm. You'd better see the Doc – and quick."

"Not bloody likely!"

"He'll certainly have something for it," insists Andy.

117

"You bet. Like a wandering hand up inside my shorts, followed by a phoney apology. No thank you." Without a further word, the Music Man shuffles off to his hut.

Andy finds it difficult to focus on his work: his mind unable to shake off thoughts of the distant Sandra. What would she be doing at this very moment, early morning at home?

Waking to another fall of snow, relieved in the knowledge that she had finally summoned up the courage to dump her unwanted fiancé? Her dad would be pleased to hear that. Sandra had often intimated that, on his return from National Service, a special place would be found for him in her father's estate agency business; but perhaps significantly there had been no further mention of a job after their hastily arranged, last minute engagement. Anyway, why worry? Whatever happened, there would be a job in the Civil Service to go back to. Nothing too exciting but, as his parents had never stopped reminding him, it was both safe and pensionable. Andy suddenly realises he is suffering a similar fate to that of the C.O: both dropped by their loved ones. He breaks into a smile at the thought of their shared experience. How unlikely they would ever have anything in common!

Meanwhile there is an eerie silence from the C.O's office. Andy hesitates to disturb his boss, knowing his tendency to over-react whenever interrupted. Instead he moves to the doorway to admire the graceful and seemingly effortless manner with which one of the local gardeners is using his curved hand-held blade to cut into the scrub. The gardener smiles back as if in acknowledgement. Ten years ago, this man was probably performing the same job here, almost certainly unpaid, for the Imperial Japanese Army. Andy wonders what memories he and his family hold of that period and whether they resent the continued occupation of their island by a foreign power. What did he make of the occasional drunken behaviour of the lads on the camp? And what of Flight Lieutenant Charles Munro, who treats the locals with scant respect?

A quick glance to the side of the hut offers the explanation for the C.O's silence: his bicycle has disappeared and, more to the point, the owner with it.

That's it for the day, decides Andy.

On his way back to the billet, he suddenly becomes aware of a stinging sensation on the inside of his left leg. He stops to take a closer look, pulling up his shorts.

"Bloody hell, it's ringworm!"

118

14

Andy stands beside his Commanding Officer, watching closely as the passengers exit from the Hastings aircraft. They each raise a hand to shield their eyes as a strong wind blows clouds of dust towards them. With mounting tension, they await a first sighting of their visiting V.I.P: Wing Commander Harding, DFC and Bar.

"He'll be last out, you can damn well bet on it," whispers the C.O, "we'll probably have to wait while he thanks each of the aircrew for a decent flight up here."

Almost immediately, a tall, well built figure appears at the door. As if to ignore the welcoming party of two, the Wing Commander slowly descends the aircraft steps, pausing to look over their heads at the area surrounding the airfield. As befits a seasoned and decorated flyer, there is a determined look about him: shoulders thrown well back and a square jaw jutting forward. It is not difficult to imagine him at the height of the Battle of Britain, seated at the controls of a Spitfire, against a background of a sky criss-crossed with vapour trails, calmly giving orders to the rest of his squadron as they prepare to swoop upon an unsuspecting and doomed pack of German bombers.

The C.O is clearly nervous. He steps forward, then quickly back, unsure at what moment to salute.

"At ease, Flight Lieutenant," comes the command, as the C.O's right hand is caught in mid-salute.

"Good flight, Sir?"

The Wing Commander ignores the question, and instead points to the Land Rover.

"This yours, Munro?"

The C.O nods repeatedly before opening the passenger door for his unwelcome visitor.

"Right, let's get moving, time is at a premium. Where do we start?"

"Thought we might first pop into my office for tea and biscuits – or something a touch stronger – while I show you the programme I've drawn up for your visit..."

"My mission here, Flight Lieutenant, is to assess strengths and weaknesses, it's not a social outing. It is to conduct an inspection."

"Of course, Sir."

Within minutes they arrive at SHQ. Andy is left to return to the camp on foot.

"That was your clerk standing with you at the airstrip?" enquires the Wing Commander.

"Yes, Sir. National Serviceman – but seems to cope."

"Looks awfully young to me. Might just have a word with him, see what he thinks of the place."

"Oh, he's very happy here. Good soccer player by all accounts, comes from somewhere near er..."

"I'd still like to speak to him," insists the Wing Commander.

"Sure I can't interest you in a coffee – or perhaps something stronger – before you start, Sir? Thought it might be useful, while you're here, for you to meet the District Officer. Really interesting fellow, plays a mean hand of Bridge."

The C.O has spent a sleepless night worrying about the inspection and is planning, wherever possible, to distract the Wing Commander from the purpose of his visit. The invitation is rebuffed.

"No, I'll get moving straight away. Just give me a map of the layout of the camp, the programme you've prepared and I'll take it from there."

"I thought it might just help, Sir, if I came along to add a little background, introduce the personnel, so to speak," adds the C.O somewhat tentatively.

"Not necessary. I prefer to speak directly to the men. My experience has been that the presence of a Commanding Officer during inspections can inhibit a frank and honest response."

"Of course, Sir."

The Wing Commander runs a swift eye over the plan of the camp, turns and strides authoritatively towards the Fire Section.

Inside the shed, the men are giving a last-minute polish to the fire tender.

The Wing Commander pauses outside to look up at the holes in the corrugated iron roof.

Finnegan's replacement, a burly, blond haired corporal from Grimsby, is the first to notice the arrival of their distinguished visitor.

"Aaaa...tenshun!" he screams as the crew scramble into an untidy line.

The reactive "At ease men," is delivered in a friendly tone, together with a hint of a smile.

"What's the grub like here?" asks the Wing Commander.

There is an award silence, as the men are caught off guard by the totally unexpected question, unrelated to their official duties.

"Well, do I have to repeat myself – or are your ears full of sand? You, Corporal, can you speak up for your men?"

"Oh, the food, Sir? Excellent, very good..."

"And what do you think, young man?" enquires the Wing Commander, pointing to the youngest member of the crew, a ginger-haired lad from Brighton whose bare, reddened shoulders suggest he is fighting a losing battle with the sun.

"Is there enough of it, young man? Speak up!"

"Oh, yes, Sir."

The Wing Commander takes a step back, thrusting his hands down hard onto his hips.

"Listen, men, I want your honest opinion. Not what you *think* I should hear."

"Now, once more, the food. I'll make it simple. Give me your marks out of ten. From the left!"

"Six," "Eight," "Five," come the figures.

"And you, Corporal?"

"Five, Sir."

"That's better," replies the Wing Commander. "So we've now established the food comes up with a sixty per cent rating. I note the polished vehicles. Just remember that an unpolished vehicle, in position *at the airstrip* waiting for the aircraft to land, is better than a polished tender still sitting *here* while the aircraft is in the act of landing."

The Corporal winces, fully aware that the recent complaints from visiting aircrews of the camp's firemen not being on standby, have now well and truly been registered in Singapore.

Meanwhile, the Wing Commander's movements around the camp are being closely observed by the C.O from SHQ. He is trying hard to remind himself that, this time tomorrow, the inspection will be history. Andy joins his boss as they look out across the compound towards the cookhouse. A further ten minutes elapse before the fire crew are stood down.

"This could be the defining moment of the visit, the blighter is going into the kitchen," groans the C.O, reaching anxiously for his binoculars.

"You did tell the cook to cover his body up, didn't you, Airman?"

"Yes indeed, Sir. Mind you it does get hot in there."

"No excuses, man. For inspections, he wears what he's told to wear. If I tell him to wear a fur coat in the cookhouse, he'll wear a fur coat in the cookhouse."

Meanwhile, the Wing Commander is attempting to engage Broadside in a meaningful discussion about calories and the availability of vegetables on the island but meets with little response. He decides to change tack.

"And now, Sergeant, your proposed menus for, say, the next three days?"

"Three days, Sir? Don't really look that far ahead."

"But you will do in future, understand?"

"Yes, Sir."

"Oh, and congratulations on cleaning up the kitchen. You and your chaps must have put in a lot of hours. Finally, I won't embarrass you both by asking to see your stock of reserve rations. Just remember that when the monsoon season hits here, and supplies can't get through, you'll be the only people starving."

"How long has he been in there, Airman?" asks the C.O with a nervous tremble in his voice, his eyes still focused on the cookhouse.

"At least quarter of an hour, Sir," replies Andy.

"Good God, you don't think they're going to feed him, do you? If they do, we're done for. Get over there straight away, man, and tell him I need to speak to him – urgently. Tell him anything but get him out of that place before he starts eating anything!"

The remark serves only to reinforce Andy's opinion that the C.O has scant regard for the welfare of his men.

"Quickly, off you go! Wait! Hold on, stay where you are – he's coming out!"

"Where's he off to now, Sir?" asks Andy.

"In the direction of your billet it seems. Yes… yes, that's where he's heading."

"No problems there, Sir, the men did a thorough clean up job last night."

"I hope they took down any pictures of lewd women," replies the C.O anxiously.

"Most of them, Sir."

The C.O offers a soft grunt.

"And were all the stones whitewashed on those new paths, as ordered?"

"Yes, Sir, we almost finished it last night. Got up 'specially early this morning to finish it off but, unfortunately, we ran out of whitewash."

The C.O sighs, holds his head in his hands and moves through the beaded curtain to the solitude of his office.

Wing Commander Harding stands in the doorway of Andy's billet. Overhead, a hand-painted sign tells him he has arrived at 'Everest.' He enters, glancing to his left and right to observe the rows of unoccupied but neatly-made beds, the pillows having been squared off in readiness for inspection. The rolled up mosquito nets quiver against the wall as a welcome breeze blows through the billet.

A faint sound, similar to that of a snore, is coming from the far end of the billet.

The Wing Commander decides to investigate. He reaches the last bed to discover a badly-swollen, pink ankle protruding from beneath the sheet. A swift rap on the leg, brings the occupant into full view.

Junior Technician Tony Blake, a slender fresh-faced lad from Whitstable in Kent, leaps out of bed and stands smartly to attention.

The naked Airman is not only lost for clothes but for words.

"Not a pretty sight, not a pretty sight at all," barks the Wing Commander. "My only advice to you is to get the M.O to take a look at your ankle."

"Certainly, Sir."

"And where precisely is your Medical Officer? I note his hut is locked."

"Ah, at this time of day, he might be down at the beach, Sir," replies Tony.

"And the reason for that is…?"

"He collects shells, Sir. Got a simply wonderful collection."

"What is your trade, Airman, and why are you not on duty?"

"RTDF Operator, Sir. On shifts. We've got our place at the far end of the runway."

"And to whom were you giving a fix last night?"

"Sunderlands, Sir, out on pirate patrol."

"Interesting, wonder if they spotted any in the dark. Now get dressed while I take a look around. I'll be back in a few minutes."

The Wing Commander slips out of the billet and towards the shower hut, the very stage for Ken's involuntary performances for the washerwomen.

He returns to further question Tony, who is now standing upright and fully clothed, alongside his bed.

"So how do you normally spend your off duty, non-sleeping time?"

"Read quite a bit, Sir. And I've made friends with some people from the local church."

"Really?"

"Yes, Sir, I make full use of my bicycle. Not just to go to work at the end of the runway but to get round the island."

"And that's Service issue being used for recreational purposes, is it?" replies the Wing Commander, thrusting his chin forward..

"Yes, Sir," replies Blake, suddenly aware of his faux pas.

"How do you manage the reading after dark, with only these central lights operating."

"We manage, Sir. Not ideal but we manage."

"And the beach? Is that where most men go?"

"Bit too much coral down there for me, Sir. Got some nasty cuts on my feet. But, yes, it is popular with the lads."

"How long have you been here on detachment?"

"Just over a year, Sir."

"Enjoying it?"

"I've got used to it, Sir, couldn't say I've *always* enjoyed it."

"Are you married?"

"No, Sir," comes the emphatic reply, accompanied by an embarrassed smile.

"Thank you, Airman, for being open with your comments. Feel free to resume horizontal mode. Oh, and I've already forgotten anything you said about the off-duty use of your Service pushbike."

"Thank you, Sir," replies Blake gratefully.

The Wing Commander has left a favourable impression on Tony. Nice chap, he thinks as he watches the Officer stride out of the billet.

Waiting outside Everest stands the C.O, with the now distinct feeling of having been cast in the role of the unwanted host.

"Everything going O.K, Sir? Wondered if you'd like to take a break. Something to drink, perhaps?"

The Wing Commander brushes past the C.O in a dismissive

fashion. "All in good time, all in good time. Is this the way to the MT Section?"

"Yes, Sir, straight through there," points the C.O with a fully extended arm.

Meanwhile, in anticipation of the Wing Commander's return to SHQ, Andy is replacing the coffee-stained paper covering on his trestle table style desk with a fresh strip of brown wrapping paper. The application of a handful of mostly bent drawing pins, completes the transformation.

Ken, the cook, appears in the doorway, wearing a jacket and holding the C.O's regular morning coffee.

"How did it go in the cookhouse? The Wing Commander was in with you for a long time," says Andy.

"He seemed a really nice bloke, no side. Said we had done a good clean up job for the inspection. That was good to hear. Broadside seemed pleased enough and offered him toast and a cuppa."

"Did he actually eat anything? The C.O will need to know," enquires Andy anxiously.

"Nah, said he had to move on. Tell you what, learnt a lot from him about calories. Knows his stuff about grub, I'll tell you."

Increasingly determined to monitor every movement of his distinguished visitor, the C.O is waiting for the Wing Commander as he finally emerges from his visit to the MT Section.

"Everything in order I trust, Sir?"

The question is met with, first, a long pause and then a meaningful stare.

"My report will be despatched to you in due course. Today is not the time to discuss its likely content."

"Just wondered, Sir, whether there were any points we should address with immediate effect?"

"All in good time, Munro, all in good time. Now might be the time to take a look at your accommodation."

"Yes, Sir, just right. Only a few minutes away in the Land Rover."

The two officers take the bumpy two mile ride to the C.O's bungalow, picking their way along the narrow track.

"Heard your wife had to make a sudden return to the U.K. Apparently shortly after she had arrived here. How are things working out? Will she be back soon?"

"Could be a little while, Sir. Pity, because she so enjoyed it here."

"No problem with the climate then?"

"Not at all, Sir, she can't wait to come back."

"And she's quite happy living in this somewhat remote spot?"

"Certainly, Sir, perfectly happy."

The C.O is feeling increasingly uncomfortable as he allows lie after lie to fall from his lips.

"Pleased to hear that. Would be pretty lonely for a chap like you if she failed to return."

"No problem there, Sir. I'm a pretty resourceful and adaptable when the occasion demands."

They arrive at the bungalow. The C.O leads his distinguished guest through the main room and out onto the patio, where they seat themselves in the shade of a badly faded sunblind, one discarded by a previous District Officer and gratefully accepted by the RAF.

The Indian servant appears with a tumbler of iced water, lime and two large glasses.

The C.O reacts immediately, jumping to his feet. "Good heavens, Boy. Not water for the Wing Commander!"

In one neat movement the servant both apologises and bows before shuffling away.

"Off you go, Boy, and bring me my usual. Chop, chop!"

The servant returns in a few moments with a beaming smile and a bottle from the C.O's stock of gin, suitably reinforced following his visit to Singapore and Hong Kong.

"This one you must sample, Sir," suggests Flight Lieutenant Munro.

"Thank you…. oh! steady on, old man," comes the cry as the C.O attempts to pour an over-generous measure. "Still work to do before I go."

"Really?" comes the C.O's response.

"Yes, I must pay a visit to the Signals people."

The Wing Commander watches closely as the C.O sinks his drink and almost immediately reaches for the bottle.

"Helps you unwind, does it?"

"Yes, Sir, just now and then – of course."

"Anything you want to ask me, Flight Lieutenant?"

"Just one thing, Sir."

"Fire away!"

"About my promotion. I suspect nothing will happen till I get back

126

home but I wondered how I stood. Anything on the proverbial grapevine, so to speak? Or anything you could suggest, Sir?"

The Wing Commander leans back in his chair to furrow his brow.

"Well, bit tricky at the moment, Munro. The Royal Air Force is looking more to the future these days and that means the younger officers have the edge. I know you have the experience but that doesn't necessarily mean…"

"I'd be willing to fill most slots, Sir. My strength has always tended to be on the personnel side but I'd be happy to have a crack at *any* administrative post. Any chance of feeding that into the system, Sir?"

"I won't forget what you've said."

"Thank you, Sir. Sure you won't have a refill? I'm having another."

"No, but don't let me stop you," replies the Wing Commander.

15

Sunday morning. A couple of Airmen are leaving the camp by bicycle to visit the local Christian church, a number are using their day off to remain in bed but the majority wait impatiently to learn the weekend soccer scores from home. Since local time is eight hours ahead of UK time, it means that the outcome of games played at home on a Saturday does not get through until the following morning. Martin, the morse code wireless operator, is busily picking up the results through his link with Singapore. For operational reasons, Airmen are refused entry to his wooden hut, so the arrangement is that Martin leaves his desk to post the results on the notice board in the Mess.

Andy, a devoted follower of his local team, Plymouth Argyle, waits nervously with a group of supporters of the more fashionable and successful clubs to learn his side's fate.

"Here he comes!" is the cry from an Arsenal fan as Martin is spotted strolling across the stretch of open land between his hut and the Mess.

"Don't hurry yourself, will ya," comes the impatient call from a Manchester United devotee.

With a theatrical flourish, Martin enters the Mess and makes his way to the notice board. "Stand back, lads, for Christ's sake! Give me some room."

The men cluster around him as the results are pinned up, then immediately scanned. A mixed chorus of cheers and groans fills the air.

"Hey you, Music Man, you've no got the Scottish results agin!" comes a cry of disappointment from Jock, previously a regular spectator at games north of the border.

Andy is reluctant to come forward, almost sensing yet another disappointing score line for his hometown club. For the past two seasons, Argyle have been floundering in the bowels of the Second Division, narrowly escaping relegation. This season is proving no different.

Martin comes over to console his friend, who sits alone.

"Don't bother to look, Andy," he says softly. "Your lot lost again, rather heavily. Sorry to be the bearer of bad tidings."

Andy breaks away to take a look for himself. A quick glance at the posted sheet brings a grimace. For this exiled teenage National Serviceman, yet another Sunday is getting off to a miserable start. All the anticipation of a winning result dashed in a few seconds.

"Cheer up, mate. You look as if someone has died."

The words come from Martin.

"Feels just like it," he replies softly.

"If we go down, we'll never get back. I dread going home and watching my team hacking around in the bottom Division."

"Look, I'm not a soccer fan – never will be – but you've got to keep it all in perspective. Would you rather have your girlfriend back or your team not get relegated?"

"That's a difficult one, I'll have to think about it," replies Andy, struggling to suppress a smile.

The mention of Sandra reminds him that there has been no letter from her since the 'Dear John' arrived.

"You never talk of girls, Martin. Don't you care for them?"

"Not part of my life, as it happens."

"No girlfriend to go back to then?"

"Nope."

"Mind you, Finnegan seemed to have 'em taped. He gave me some useful tips."

"Good for him," says Martin curtly.

Meanwhile, Andy overhears a few lads talking of a possible visit to the local beach as he trudges back to the billet. The UK soccer scores are being analysed, together with the likely scorers and possible League positions.

"All right if I join you?" asks Andy.

"Down boy! We're not going out until it cools down. Don't worry, we'll let you know."

An hour later, a dozen Airmen find themselves engaged in a heated contest on the beach.

The battle is for possession of a tattered, leather football soaked by its occasional, involuntary foray into the South China Sea. Andy's rediscovered touch with the round ball serves him well. For the moment, the disappointment of the Plymouth Argyle result lies dormant, pushed to the back of his mind. The game is gradually reduced to 'three-a-side' as, one by one, the players drop onto the sand to take a breather. A welcome breeze comes to their aid.

On either side of the men, a deserted stretch of sand tails off into the distance. Behind them, shuffling around in the undergrowth, 'Sweeney' Todd, the camp's demon doctor, is busy examining the shells he collected earlier in the day. The 'Doc', a non-swimmer and the longest serving man on the camp, has in recent months gradually become a withdrawn figure. He now prefers to sleep in his dilapidated sick bay rather than in one of the billets. He has also developed a worrying tendency to talk to himself and concern is being expressed among the men about his health.

As the sole medic on the camp, the problem is: who is capable of taking a serious look at him? Andy decides to take a stroll along the beach. The tide is coming in slowly as he moves to the water's edge to allow nature to wash the sand from his feet. He has already learnt that it was along this coastal strip in 1945 that the Ninth Division of the Australian Army made their landings to liberate the islanders from the Japanese. He pauses to look out over the sea towards the horizon, then turns to admire the line of waving palms that every now and then seem to lean out from the back of the beach.

Some ten years ago this was the scene of gunfire and death, of the final moments of the lives of men whose misfortune was to be in the wrong place at the wrong time. Today all is well. The only aggressive sounds are sudden outbreaks of laughter from his fellow Airmen relaxing on the sand, after hearing the punch lines from a rapid-fire onslaught of jokes.

The only conflict on view is a struggle between a couple of stray dogs on the wet sand, contesting ownership of a dead fish. Andy's thoughts are triggered back to Remembrance Day on the island and his poignant memory of an Australian mother gazing down upon her son's grave. The men make their way slowly from the beach, leaving the 'Doc' shuffling along in the deeper sand searching for yet another special shell to add to his collection.

Back in the billet, preparing for a shower, Andy once more catches sight of the rash on his inside leg.

"Hey, Martin!" he shouts to the Music Man, who is being roundly rebuked for attempting to convert his captive audience with a record containing an intricate piece of jazz improvisation.

"Never knows when to give up, does he?" comes an unsolicited comment from across the aisle.

As the noise from the banter subsides, Martin arrives to look at Andy's problem leg.

"Mine's just as bad. Right, that's it. We'll go straight round to the Doc."

"Not sure whether he's back from the beach. We left him down there in the trees, muttering to himself," says Andy.

"Doesn't matter. We'll sit outside his hut till the bugger turns up."

The pair don't have long to wait.

The Doc arrives holding what sounds like a bag full of shells rattling together.

"What you two 'Erberts' want?" he scowls.

"It's our legs. Could be ringworm, Doc."

"It's Sunday. Remember? You know damn well that I only see people on my day off when it's urgent. That rash can wait till the morning – and the same goes for both of you! Anyway, I examine patients individually, not in pairs."

"That because of patient confidentiality, is it?" suggests Martin.

"Yeh, bit of that as well."

The Doc turns his back on the pair, slips the padlock on his door and is about to enter the hut.

"Let's have a look at your shells then?" asks Martin.

"Not taking the mick? You'd really like to see them?"

"Me too, used to collect them when I was a kid," adds Andy.

"Fine, come inside," comes the Doc's invitation, inspired by a possible interest in his latest acquisitions.

The Doc's mood is changing by the second as he dips his hand in the bag.

"Tell you what, I'll line 'em all up on the table and you point out your favourites."

The duo of would-be patients look at each other in disbelief at their medic's seemingly unbridled enthusiasm for his collection of pickings from the beach. They notice that most of the overhead shelves now boast an endless row of shells.

The Doc reaches up to grasp a large, brown and white speckled shell. Proudly, he passes it down to Martin.

"Real beauty, isn't it? Now then, as a reputed lover of music, hold it to your ear and tell me exactly what you hear."

Hands clasped tightly together, the Doc waits for the verdict.

"Not a lot," is the Music Man's reply, as he switches the shell from ear to ear.

The Doc snatches the shell from Martin's hand and passes it to Andy.

"You listen!"

"Yes, just a faint noise."

"Ah! now *your* ear is properly tuned," explains the Doc.

Martin raises his eyebrows and makes for the door, stung by the inference that his ear is not 'tuned' and with it his reputation as a connoisseur of music has been so rudely brought into question.

"Come on, Andy, let's leave the doctor to his shells. See you in the morning, Doc."

The patients of tomorrow stand in the doorway, taking a final look at the haul of shells collected from the local beach.

"Goin' on at this rate, you'll soon have more shells than pills in here!" mocks Martin.

"And how about this little beauty?" beams the Doc, ignoring the comment. "You don't have to go, lads," comes his despairing call. "Hold on, what about your legs? I can take a look now, chaps. By the way, did you know that over the centuries shells have been used as currency, for medicine and…"

The door slams shut. The Doc is left alone in mid-sentence.

16

Andy is a worried soul this morning as he sits at his desk. For the third day in succession, the C.O's dapper Indian servant has jogged in from his master's bungalow with the breathless message that Flight Lieutenant Munro will not be on duty at the camp: "Masta no well... but Masta say no docta needed."

The lamented departure of his wife, coupled with the stress of the recent Wing Commander's inspection, has had an unsettling effect upon the C.O. Also the discovery of an almost empty bottle of gin in the office safe has done little to ease Andy's concern about the condition of his boss.

A few minutes later, Ken appears in the doorway, holding the C.O's morning coffee.

"Sorry, Cookie, should have told you. The Old Man won't be in today."

"What again! Put him on a Charge, the lazy bastard!"

"No, I think he's genuinely a bit down," replies Andy.

"Aah. I feel really upset," comes the unsympathetic response.

"No need to be like that. He's really not well."

"Could have told you that ages ago."

"Anyway, must get on with my work, see you later. Oh, and you can leave the coffee for me, thanks."

"You know what the lads are saying, don't you?" says Ken solemnly. "They reckon the Old Man's been on the jungle juice since Marilyn left."

"Well, thanks for that bit of gen, Ken. Must get on."

Andy spends the rest of the morning dealing with the paperwork and preparing for the weekly Pay Parade for locally-engaged staff, but all the time his mind is occupied with thoughts of his boss. Does he need medical attention? If he's really back on the bottle, then it's best to know. He wonders whether he should pay him a visit. Should he take the Doc, perhaps, to give a second opinion? No need stay too long.

Perhaps take along a few signals, not requiring action, to keep the C.O in the picture and to ease him back slowly. And, he must include the formal invitation just received from the District Officer, inviting the C.O to a cocktail party? That could prove the perfect opportunity to get him back into the social swim. Andy also thinks he should have a word with one of the Sergeants – or indeed all three? For operational reasons, they should know if he is likely to remain incapacitated. Who would take over then? As he struggles to find answers to these questions, the 'phone rings.

"Charles? That you, Charles?"

The polished, middle class accent is immediately identifiable: it's the voice of the District Officer, Malcom Prenderghast. Andy has never been sure whether or not to address the D.O as 'Sir', in fact he has never been able to discover what the man actually does. But on this occasion he decides to play safe.

"No, Sir, you're speaking to Leading Aircraftman Marshall."

"Yes, we met briefly at that party Charles and Dorothy threw for some of his men. You were the chap pouring drinks. Correct?"

"Spot on Sir, that was me."

"By the way, just between you and me, when is she coming back? On second thoughts, don't answer that!"

"Are you ringing about the invite to your cocktail party, Sir?" enquires Andy attempting to move the conversation to less sensitive ground.

"Not at all. Tricky problem brewing up for tomorrow and I wanted some help from your gang. But first I need to speak to Charles." An uncomfortable silence follows. "Take it he's not there then?" continues the D.O. "Ask him to give me a ring ASAP, there's a good fellow."

Some ten minutes later, Andy is taking a welcome swig from a bottle of water as the 'phone rings again. He anticipates it's the District Officer.

"Malcolm Prenderghast, here again. I need to speak with your Commanding Officer immediately. Can you put him on?" The normally measured tone of his voice has become more assertive, more urgent.

"'Fraid he's still not here, Sir. Still out on camp somewhere. Hoping to see him shortly. Can I give him a message?"

"Don't bother, it's now rather urgent. I'll come up to the camp straight away." The D.O hangs up without a further word.

Andy wonders whether the C.O should be disturbed. But accepts in the event of an emergency there would be little choice but to pay him a visit.

The District Officer duly arrives outside SHQ, driven by the Police Inspector in an aged but gleaming, royal blue open-top car.

As both men alight, Andy stands ready to meet them.

"Where's the Station Commander? Is he back? We've got to see him now," snaps the D.O.

Andy is immediately impressed with the appearance of the slim, Indian policeman. From his neatly angled black beret, sporting a well polished silver badge, down to his highly polished pair of tan shoes, he would pass muster for any Service parade.

"Yes, a rather dicey problem involving the Japanese," explains the D.O.

"Oh, so extremely dicey," adds the Inspector.

"What sort of problem, if I may ask?" enquires Andy. "Can't recollect ever hearing of or seeing any Japanese on the island."

"Well, there were quite a few right here during the War, young man, take my word for it," replies the Inspector with more than a hint of sarcasm.

"But that's not the immediate problem in hand," adds the D.O, stepping forward.

"We've had a radio message through from a cruise ship, one that's dropped anchor a couple of miles out from here. On board are a party of Japanese civilians who wish to visit the Memorial Park to pay their respects to their countrymen – tomorrow!"

Andy's body stiffens at the thought of the C.O's likely reaction to any group of Japanese, albeit civilians, setting foot on the island.

"Japanese dead – buried here?" questions Andy.

"That's the first problem, young man, they're *not* buried here, none of them. My predecessor told me they were put in the ground where they lay, without any of the formalities. Certainly not alongside our chaps," replies the D.O.

The Police Inspector intervenes.

"Immigration were prepared to let them through for a brief escorted visit, but unfortunately news of all this has somehow leaked out."

"And that's the second problem," adds the D.O. "I've just left the village and the locals are in uproar. Lot of anger brewing down there.

Placards are being painted with anti-Japanese slogans. The memories of what happened during the Occupation – only ten years ago, mark you – will live on for a long, long time to come. My assessment of the position is that any Japanese – even civilians – who try to land are in danger of being lynched. And with tomorrow being a public holiday, the locals have time on their hands. Could turn into a veritable bloodbath."

"So we need to see your Flight Lieutenant straight away," insists the Inspector.

"Yes, of course. He's a touch off colour at the moment, so we'll have to go to the bungalow where he's resting."

Andy is forced to accept his C.O must be informed of a situation that could develop into a major diplomatic incident.

The trio are soon driving towards the C.O's bungalow.

"How many Police can you raise?" the Inspector is asked by the D.O as the car bounces along the rutted track.

"Not counting me, just my clerk. Possibly another two raw trainees, both women, not yet in uniform," comes the reply.

"So that will mean a sizeable turn out for your Air Force chaps, I'm afraid," adds the D.O, turning to face Andy in the back seat.

They arrive to find the bungalow door open. They walk through into the lounge area. Lying full length, face down on the settee, is the snoring body of Flight Lieutenant Munro. On a nearby coffee table stands a half empty gin bottle and a single broken glass.

The D.O looks to Andy. "You'd better wake him up, young man."

Andy drops to his knees.

"Sir, you've got visitors." The words are delivered softly in the C.O's left ear, then repeated. There is a pause before the message hits home. Slowly, the partially dressed body begins to turn, revealing a reddened face but then, in the same movement, reverts to slumber mode.

The D.O steps forward. "Charles, it's me, Malcolm, the District Officer!" comes the booming voice.

The body stirs.

The D.O bends down on one knee to continue the one-sided conversation.

"Need your help, old chap. What you Service chaps call a real flap. But you'll need to sit up and listen."

With the assistance of the Inspector, the C.O is lifted into a slouched position, hands hanging limply by his side. His eyes are slowly opening and then almost immediately closing.

The D.O persists. "Charles – wake up! wake up! – we have a big, big problem, can you understand what I am saying?"

The C.O retracts his outstretched legs, lifts his head and looks directly at the D.O.

He purses his lips before uttering: "Dorothy's left me, you know. Couldn't damn well put up with me. Separate beds and all that."

The D.O grimaces before giving a nod to Andy. Together they retreat to the doorway, leaving the Inspector looking down at the C.O whose speech is now reduced to an incoherent mumble.

"Damn chap's pretty drunk. Think we'll have to decide on a course of action without him. Better get your medic to have an early look at him," suggests the D.O.

"So, how can our men help?" asks Andy.

"Quite simple. If the Japs have the temerity to land, we'll need the Royal Air Force to be on the jetty in a threatening pose, bayonets fixed and loaded guns at the ready to pitch them straight back into the sea. At the same time, any such action must be taken in a tactful and restrained manner."

Andy is taken aback at the aggressive attitude towards a group of possibly harmless, elderly civilians wishing to pay their final respects.

"The Inspector and I will be up at the camp first thing in the morning," says the D.O.

"Given the state of your C.O – who will be in no condition to lead your men – I respectfully suggest you give immediate thought as to who will be in charge. I'll need to have his name. London will expect a comprehensive report on all this, it's too big a matter to await my monthly report."

On his return to the camp, Andy immediately contacts the three Sergeants, informing them of the position and the urgent need to discuss a strategy for the following day.

It is early evening before the three wise men finally gather around Andy in his office. After a frantic search, Jock, the storeman, who has the added responsibility of being the custodian of the armoury, has been located close to the nearby swamp, his regular spot for collecting butterflies.

"Hope this won't take too long 'cause we've got a card school starting soon," comes the opening remark from Sergeant Curtis.

Andy explains, at length, the threat posed and the request for an Air Force presence at the jetty, adding rather nonchalantly, "unfortunately, the C.O is confined to bed with a stomach upset so he won't be involved."

"Christ! He must be in a bad way," shouts Curtis. "Silly old sod is always banging on about how, single-handed, he held back the Japanese in Singapore. My money's on him making a rapid recovery as soon as he hears about this. Just you watch him. He'll explode!"

Broadside nudges Curtis on the arm. "Actually, in his absence, as the senior N.C.O *you'll* be in charge."

"That's no problem for me," replies Curtis in a confident tone.

"Could be fun!" laughs Harry Ashton. "My old man was in Burma during the War but saw no action. He'll be chuffed to bits to hear I've knocked out a few Nips to make up for it."

"Really? Your dad in Burma?" says Andy.

"Yeh, and he told me all about the morale-boosting, duff gen our men were given by the Army about the Japs. You know, their slit eyes meant defective eyesight so they couldn't shoot straight and they had no sense of balance because all babies in Japan are carried on their mother's back..."

"Very interesting, I'm sure, but what's the timing on all this?" interrupts the uncharacteristically sober Broadside.

"The ship radioed the Police that it would be mid-morning, before breakfast ends – but they'd inform us when the party were being transferred onto the motor launch," explains Andy.

"Why don't the three of us go out to the ship first thing, rifles at the ready, get a free slap-up breakfast on board then say their trip's been cancelled?" suggests Curtis before slowly breaking into laughter.

"Can I say something?" says Jock.

"Tell you what, Andy, will we get a campaign medal for this?" questions Ashton.

"Mention in Despatches, at the very minimum," adds Curtis.

"Hold on, can I say something?" insists Jock, attempting again to break into the conversation.

"How many Japs planning to land?" enquires Curtis.

"For Christ sakes, listen to me!" comes the anguished plea from the storeman.

"Spit it out then, Jock."

"It's the ammunition for our 303s."

"What about the ammo?"

"There is none," explains the Scotsman, lowering his head in shame.

The group are reduced to silence.

"But only last month you told the C.O, in front of me, that…," says Andy, rising to his feet.

"Well, we haven't any ammo, I'm telling you," admits Jock.

The three Sergeants, stunned by the news, fire off a volley of questions at the Scotsman.

"Where the hell has it gone, man?" "Haven't heard any gunfire lately?" "You know it's a court martial offence if it's gone missing."

"Honest to God, fellas, most of it had already gone when I came here," explains Jock. "The bloke before me said he had sold off a couple of dud rifles to one of the farmers. Surely canna be no harm with that – if they're nae good," argues Jock manfully.

"And he sold off some ammo with it, did he?" suggests Curtis.

"But makes sense, doesn't it? A rifle's nae good without bullets."

"What the hell do farmers need with rifles?" asks Ashton.

"Perhaps they're planning to run us off the island – or they think the War is still going on," sniggers Curtis.

"So what use are a couple of dud rifles to them unless they repaired them?"

"The bloke before me said it was for shooting animals, scaring away birds," explains Jock.

"That sounds more like it," says Curtis.

"The D.O wants as many of us as possible down there. Leaving aside essential staff needed here, we could manage twenty," advises Andy.

"All depends on how many Japs turn up. Let's wait until they radio through the number getting into the boat. If there's only two or three of them, we'll look a bit stupid."

"Be too late then. Never know, the crafty buggers might at this very moment be talking other passengers into joining them. We all know how many Aussies came over for Remembrance Day," warns Curtis.

"I agree," says Ashton. "Let's leave it at twenty of us being down there."

"Hey! just thought of it: anyone speak Japanese?" asks Broadside.

"And what happens if they don't speak English?" poses Curtis.

"That's a good point. We're all going to look a bit daft just pointing empty rifles at them.

Hey, what if we knock up a banner like they use for riots, that would help with the language problem," suggests Broadside.

"What bloody use would it be if the Japanese can actually read the wording: 'Disperse or we fire!' Just imagine, they decide not to disperse but we can't fire because we've got no ammo!" laughs Curtis. "It's getting crazier by the minute. That's it, no banner!"

"I've an idea, the D.O has a Japanese servant who might be useful," suggests Andy.

"As the acting leader of our welcoming party, I hereby instruct you, LAC Marshall, to pursue that with the D.O. In fact, I might just have a word with that colonial misfit myself," chuckles Curtis. "What's his name, again? Poltergeist?"

"Prenderghast," replies Andy with a grin.

"Now, let's knock up a list of those who'll be needed tomorrow and tell them straight away so they can get their ceremonial gear out for the morning," orders Curtis, clearly warming to his new-found role as acting officer in charge. He stands, walks slowly to the doorway then spins around in an almost theatrical flourish to further establish his authority.

"Right, Jock, you'll spend the rest of the day bulling up those twenty rifles and helmets so we'll be ready to leave for the village and jetty at a moment's notice in the morning."

"And, Broadside, get Cookie to have breakfast finished by 0830."

"And the Doc?" interrupts Andy.

"Yeh, almost forgot. The sight of the ambulance being parked up on the jetty, close to the water's edge, might just give the Japs something to think about. Good thinking, you speak to him tonight."

"O.K, Sarge – or should that be 'Sir'?"

"Watch it, Marshall, you cheeky bugger. And one last thing, do what's necessary to keep the Old Man in his bungalow tomorrow. If he gets involved, it'll be a massacre. Now that's it, meeting closed."

Andy is left to reflect on the events of the day. To his surprise he has drawn some personal satisfaction from his active role in the planning and preparation for this unusual chain of events. Tomorrow could prove even more dramatic. Is he perhaps experiencing similar eve-of-battle emotions to those who master-minded the 'D Day' invasion? So, so different from his daily routine in the Civil Service. For just a moment or two, his thoughts are of his colleagues in the office back home. Given the time difference, they would now probably be breaking for lunch. The more adventurous making their way to the local pub, the more sober-minded and frugal to the nearby park to nibble away at sandwiches brought from home. But in total contrast here, tomorrow, he could get his first taste of unarmed conflict!

Suddenly, remembering his undertaking to speak with the Doc, Andy quickens his pace and is soon striding out towards Sick Quarters. A solitary, dim light remains on, suggesting the Doc might already be in bed.

A couple of tentative knocks on the wooden door fail to bring a reaction.

Andy slips around to the back of the hut and peers through the rear window. A number of boxes impede a clear sight of action within.

The Doc appears to be sitting on his bed, with a colourful selection of shells spread over the bed sheet. Andy returns to the front door and applies a more vigorous rap.

"Unless it's an emergency, bugger off," comes an angry voice.

"It certainly is, so please open up," replies Andy sharply.

"Oh, it's you!" says the Doc. "Not bloody sunburn or ringworm again, is it?"

"No, it's about tomorrow. There might be some trouble with the Japs – and the message is that you and the ambulance will be needed down at the jetty."

"Listen, mate, the Japs left here some ten years ago. Somebody's pulling the wool over your eyes. Go back to the billet and get your head down – unless you want to see the latest shells I picked up on the beach. And some of them are really good, I can tell you."

"I'm dead serious, Doc," insists Andy.

"Yeh, yeh, I'm sure you are. Just accept they've taken the mick out of you. Come inside, I'll make you a coffee. The real stuff."

Andy hesitates but realises the Doc must be made to take his warning seriously.

The Doc turns and makes for his bed, pointing towards a couple of purple speckled shells.

"Do you know, the Wing Commander on his visit here considered those two as the most attractive he'd ever seen?"

"Doc, what I said *is* serious. Please listen, all pukka gen. It's not the Japanese Army, Air Force or Navy. It's some of their civilians planning to go to the Memorial Park. We're going to try and stop them landing and turn them back 'cause the locals are angry and might decide to attack them."

"Sure the Japs won't be armed?" smiles the Doc.

"Pretty sure. They're on a cruise ship at the moment but will be transferred into a small boat which is expected to come in at the jetty."

"How many? And what time?"

"The ship is planning to radio through to the Police Station when the Japs leave the cruise boat. Can you be down for an early breakfast, Doc? We'll be leaving soon after."

"O.K, I'll be there, don't you worry."

"Thanks, Doc," sighs a relieved Andy

"Now, one last question before I make the coffee. What do you think of this beauty I picked up yesterday?"

17

There is a heightened air of expectancy in the Mess as the lads gather for breakfast, transcending the anticipation reserved for a day when the camp's soccer team clashes with one of the local village sides. This morning all talk is of the impending visit of the civilian Japanese, hoping to pay their respects to their fallen men from World War Two.

"Got an idea, Andy," says Martin, pushing his half-eaten bowl of soggy corn flakes and diluted powdered milk to one side. "If it's true we got no ammo, why can't we simulate the noise? You know, like we did when we were kids back home, playing soldiers."

"Don't be daft," replies Andy.

"I mean we could have an audition before we went down, those making the most realistic sound of gunfire could be in the front row…"

"Stop that. It's not funny," says Andy.

"Or perhaps I could take my record player down and put on the 1812 Overture. The gunfire alone would send the Japs packing."

"Give it a rest, Martin, the Doc has just come in. If he finds out we've got no ammo, the man might refuse to come down with us."

Their conversation is cut short by the sudden appearance of Sergeant Curtis, who is clearly relishing his temporary role in charge.

"Right, those men detailed for duty at the jetty: outside, in threes. Move!" comes the order.

The men, unaccustomed to obeying the camp's number one comedian, joke teller and mimic of their Commanding Officer, pause for a moment before responding.

The barked order of "Come on lads, Chop, chop!" succeeds in clearing the remaining benches.

Sergeant Curtis leads his party outside into the square, then stands precariously on the box normally used by the diminutive Flight Lieutenant Munro when addressing the men.

The detail are in a relaxed manner looking up at their 'stand in' leader, unsure of what is coming next.

"Go on, Sarge, give us an impersonation of the Old Man," comes a request from the front row, followed by a ripple of laughter.

"Not today lads. Today's serious business. We could be threatened by the Japanese and our job is twofold: to make their visit as short as possible and thus prevent a possible outbreak of civil violence."

"How many of them planning to land, Sarge?"

"No idea but there'll be twenty of us and we'll have our rifles."

"Is it true we've got no ammo?" comes the inevitable question.

"We're sorting that one out. Now pick up your rifles from Jock and get into the truck. We'll be leaving in the next ten minutes."

Meanwhile alongside the jetty, the villagers are growing in number by the minute. The mood is becoming increasingly hostile. A party of predominantly middle-aged Chinese are at the forefront, pushing hard against a rope wrapped around a line of rusted iron stakes, positioned strategically by the Police to prevent any locals getting too close to the action. All other eyes are cast anxiously towards the open sea. Despite the early morning haze, the cruise ship is clearly visible. A little further back from the action, a group of students have found a spot to put the finishing grammatical touches to a banner prepared overnight. They are surrounded by a gaggle of local children, caught up in the excitement but unaware of what is really going on. A Union Jack is draped across one of the barriers at the top of the concrete steps leading down to the water's edge. The Police Inspector paces nervously back and forth in front of the roped-off area, every now and then using his baton to prod back the more enthusiastic spectators. A couple of young boys attempt to duck underneath the rope, but a withering glance from the uniformed Inspector sends them scurrying back. The gathering is soon joined by a couple of local traders on foot, pushing bicycles laden with food and fruit. A golden opportunity to make money is clearly not going to be missed.

The arrival of the Bedford truck, carrying the RAF personnel, brings a hearty cheer from the District Officer's party, who have taken a privileged viewing position at the front of the crowd. It triggers a burst of applause from the rest. As the Airmen drop from the truck, the moment is proving too emotional for Mrs Amelia Prenderghast, the D.O's wife, wearing a sleeveless, floral dress boasting a riot of red roses. Her hair is swept up beneath a wide-brimmed black straw hat. Stepping forward to greet Sergeant Curtis, with an almost regal flourish, she breaks into song: "God Save our Gracious Queen". As she struggles to hit the higher notes, tears begin to fill her eyes. The national anthem is immediately picked up by the Police Inspector's Malayan wife and a couple of British expats. The locals look on in surprise before breaking into an aggressive chant in their own language.

Taking up their position on the jetty, Martin tugs Andy by the arm. "This is turning into a bloody carnival!"

"More like a pantomime!" comes the reply. "And we've already got the 'Ugly Sister.'"

The D.O reaches for his binoculars. "No sign of any boat coming in. I wonder what's going on?" he mutters to himself.

The Police Inspector is soon at his side, pointing seaward. "Can you see anything happening out there?"

"More worried about what's happening here! The locals are in a nasty mood. I think that's another anti-Japanese chant they're making," says the D.O.

"Can't blame them, given what happened here in the War."

Despite the absence of any sighting of a launch, Sergeant Curtis's twenty strong squad form a single line close to the water's edge.

"Pay attention, men," he shouts, raising his voice to be heard against the rising background noise from the crowd. "When the Japs land, you'll be called to attention."

"Don't forget they might be armed, Sarge," interrupts the Music Man with more than a touch of sarcasm.

"Yeh, and the last time they landed here they had ammo!" laughs Ken.

"Shut up, you jokers," shouts Curtis, stamping an angry foot on the ground. "As I was saying, you'll be called to attention, then you'll be ordered to fix bayonets and take two steps forward. That should be enough to frighten 'em off, we won't need bullets."

The D.O and Police Inspector distance themselves from the instructions for action and are soon locked together in animated conversation. The Inspector breaks away, hurrying off in the direction of his nearby Station.

Their discussion has not been lost on Curtis who moves quickly towards the D.O to discover what is happening. "What's going on? Where's he going?" he enquires anxiously.

"The Inspector is now checking with his Station whether there has been a message from the ship. Something's not right. The Nips – sorry, the Japanese – should be on their way by now."

"Wonder if the bastards have sunk?" suggests Broadside with a broad grin.

"Could be coming in by submarine, couldn't trust 'em ten years ago, why trust 'em now?" comments the Doc to one of the local traders.

Another twenty uneventful minutes pass. Some of the crowd are beginning to leave.

The intermittent chanting is tailing off, and even the line of Airmen has broken up with the unexpected lull in action. Some of the metal stakes now lie flat on the ground. Andy and Martin are in dispute as to whether the banners are written in Chinese or Japanese. Ken and Broadside have strayed away and appear to be interested in the contents of one of the local trader's buckets. A couple of Airmen are engaged in a seemingly flirtatious chat with two young local girls.

The Doc joins Andy and Martin.

"I'll give this another ten minutes, then I'm off back to the camp!" comes his sharp comment.

"Hold on," replies Andy. "At least wait until the Inspector has heard from the ship."

The Doc throws a dismissive look at the C.O's right-hand man.

"Got up really early this morning, got all the bandages sorted out – even found the morphine – and now it looks like it's all off. In a funny sort of way, I was looking forward to today. Even put a new film in the camera. Now it's all gone flat."

The Inspector is spotted sprinting back, a beaming smile covering his face.

The D.O and Sergeant Curtis are soon at his side, waiting expectantly as he struggles to recover his breath.

"What's happened?"

"Great news. It's all off. The Royal Air Force can be stood down."

"How? Why?" presses the D.O.

"The message from the ship's Captain was that there were only eight Japanese, consisting of two married couples, three grandparents and a teenage girl. Apparently the Captain was worried about the risk of an unnecessary delay in his ship sailing, and he talked the party out of making the trip."

"Excellent," smiles the D.O.

"A triumph for diplomacy, darling. I'm so proud of you," smiles Amelia stepping forward to plant a vigorous kiss on her husband's cheek.

"And London will have to be informed immediately, of course" counters the D.O as he leads his family in triumph towards his parked Ford Consul.

"Darling, let's have a party tonight at our place to celebrate! We can invite the Bannisters and …"

Meanwhile, some five miles away, totally unaware of the drama that has unfolded, Flight Lieutenant Munro lies motionless on his bed, a damp flannel draped across his brow. Overhead a whirring fan offers added relief to a body still hung over from a heavy intake of gin.

"Boy!" comes the sudden cry.

His servant, ten years his senior, answers the call without a moment's hesitation.

"Yes Masta?"

"Get my clothes together PDQ, I'm going into camp."

"But I told office you still have fevah – and Masta no work today."

"And I've still got that damn fever but I'm going in to check on them. When the cat's away, and all that."

"Not understand, Masta – no cats in bungalow today. I put poison in bowl, like you say."

"Course you don't understand, you bloody idiot! That's why you're nothing more than a servant," chuckles the C.O to himself.

The Flight Lieutenant rises and struggles into his KD, simultaneously unzipping a banana before walking out to his Land Rover.

His blotchy face begins to burn as he drives directly into the sun. En route he ponders which part of the camp he should approach first.

"No, play it straight, first stop the office," he mutters to himself.

The Land Rover screeches to a halt outside SHQ.

"Airman!" he screams at the closed door.

No response. He moves to one side and peers through a crack in the shuttered window.

"You in there, Marshall?"

One of the grass cutters appears from behind the hut.

"So what's going on, man?" demands the C.O.

Not conversant with the English language, the local employee can offer only a shake of the head and a courteous smile.

"Fat lot of good you are, too," snaps the C.O, throwing up his hands in despair.

He takes a quick glance at his watch. It's fast approaching midday.

The sudden sound of a engine roar from a nearby petrol bowser causes him to head for the Fire Section. Sweat is pouring freely from his brow and he is beginning to question the wisdom of his impromptu visit.

The bowser lumbers out from beneath the shade of its matted canopy. The driver appears to be the only person on duty.

The C.O steps out smartly in front of the vehicle.

"Out you get, Airman!" comes the command.

The driver pauses before clambering down from behind the wheel.

"Sir?"

"Where are the rest of the men?"

"Down in the village, Sir, down at the jetty?"

"What the hell for?"

"The Japs, Sir."

"Good God, man, what are you babbling on about? Where's young Marshall?"

"I'm sure he's gone down with the others, Sir."

Flight Lieutenant Munro stands, hands on hip, struggling to understand what is going on.

The camp is strangely quiet. The only sounds are of a clattering of pots and pans, coming from the nearby cookhouse.

The C.O decides to return to SHQ, hoping a stiff drink will allow him to assimilate the position more clearly. The locked door offers little resistance to a few hefty kicks from his right foot. Inside his office, his sweaty hands fumble to open the safe. He tries again, and again, without success. The temperamental overhead fan is once more out of action as he begins to curse the manufacturers of the safe. To his relief, the safe door finally flies open, only to reveal that his reserve bottle of gin is almost empty.

"Damn!" he shouts angrily, slamming the door shut.

In despair, he strides out from the office to survey his almost deserted camp. Even the normally active cookhouse area now lies silent.

A sudden realisation that there is always a wireless operator on duty, sends the C.O scurrying in the direction of the Signals hut.

He bursts into semi-darkness to confront the operator who is in the process of receiving a signal.

"What the hell is going on, Corporal? You must know. Speak up!"

With his back to Flight Lieutenant Munro, the operator, with ear phones clamped to his head, continues to receive a signal. The C.O's question is, unwittingly, being ignored.

"Damn you, too," he rants, slamming the door and stepping out into the glaring sunlight.

The sounds of distant male voices in song are beginning to fill the air.

The C.O is instinctively drawn towards the noise, coming from the entrance to the camp.

He watches open-mouthed and partially hidden in the shade of the Mess, as the Bedford truck comes to a halt outside the Bedding Store.

The squad disembark, unaware of the C.O lurking nearby. Sergeant Curtis brings the motley squad to order.

"Well done, men. Couldn't have asked for more. I shall be recommending a number of you for the prestigious and much-coveted VD and scar. Now dismiss, bugger off and resume your normal duties."

"Well done, Sarge!" comes the immediate response from one of the Airmen, followed by a chorus from others of "Why was he born so beautiful, why was he..."

Flight Lieutenant Munro remains out of view, tight-lipped and angry, before quietly slipping back to his office. The men return to their billets. Andy takes a quick shower, changes and slowly makes his way to the SHQ. As he approaches, he notices the bottom of the door has been kicked in.

"Oh no, not a bloody break in!"

He hesitates, wondering whether to alert someone and enlist support from the nearby cookhouse. Tentatively, Andy steps inside, aware that someone might still be in the C.O's room. Momentarily, he regrets having just handed in his rifle and bayonet.

Standing to one side of the beaded curtain separating the two rooms, he shouts, "Advance and be recognised! Whoever you are, come out!"

There follows an uncomfortable silence.

"Don't be such an arse, Marshall. It's me in here, your Commanding Officer," comes the sharp reply.

Andy gulps with shock, before stepping into the C.O's room.

Flight Lieutenant Munro is swaying in his chair, struggling to keep his eyes open.

He rises to his feet, then walks unsteadily around his desk to a point where the pair are standing no more than two feet apart.

"Sorry, Sir, I thought…" begins Andy.

"Yes, I know exactly what you thought. What I want to know is what the hell has been going on! Where have our men been? Why were they armed? And, most important of all, as Commanding Officer, why was I not informed? Sergeant Curtis, who appears to have been in charge – I use the word 'charge' in its loosest definition – of what can only be described as a rabble. Now speak up!"

"Sir, it was the District Officer's decision not to involve you, given you weren't too well. In short, Sir, a cruise ship dropped anchor yesterday a few miles off the headland and carried civilian Japanese who intended to pay their respects to their countrymen who had fallen on our island. As you know, the locals are still pretty fired up about the brutal treatment they received here during the War and everyone was worried what might happen if any Japanese landed. As it happened, Sir, they didn't land. Apparently the captain on the boat talked them out of it."

"How do you know they haven't already landed somewhere else on the island?" counters the C.O, rising to his feet. "A classic decoy and outflanking manoeuvre, which those despicable people no doubt learnt from reading our military manuals. They could well have landed on the other side of the island by now – and at this very minute be heading this way!"

"But the cruise ship has just set sail, Sir," explains Andy.

"Good heavens, man, this was a military decision. Not something to be ruled upon by some overweight, colonial idiot. Didn't you speak to one of the Sergeants?"

"Yes, Sir."

"And?"

"They thought they could handle the matter without bothering you, given your condition."

"So that was the purpose of your last visit to my bungalow, was it? To check on my *condition?* How dare you! How dare all of you."

His experience of working with Flight Lieutenant Munro has taught Andy that there are moments when it is advisable to remain silent. No question about it, this is one of them.

"My first hand knowledge of the Japanese is greater than that of the District Officer, the Police and all our personnel here put together," continues the C.O. "This was precisely the emergency which demanded my presence. I am now returning to my bungalow.

Tomorrow, first thing, you will send for the D.O and that Charlie Chan Police side-kick of his. We'll thrash out this whole mess. Also, make sure that Sergeant Curtis is available for questioning. Something about him I don't trust."

18

"How long's it been since you last heard from Sandra?" enquires Martin.

Andy pretends not to hear the Music Man's question and continues re-making his bed, moving smartly from one side to the other to unleash an angry punch on the defenceless pillow.

"You're probably off her Christmas Card list by now. Out of sight and all that. Mind you, not as if you're married and…"

"We *were* engaged," snaps Andy. "Last minute decision, but nevertheless engaged."

"Oops! sorry," replies Martin.

"There's a film on here tonight. I'm going, interested?" asks Andy, in an attempt to change the subject.

"Depends what it is."

"It's a musical *Young at Heart,* Doris Day and Sinatra. In colour, too, Curtis told me."

"Can't wait. Give me a shout when you're going – but if I'm asleep, don't disturb."

Martin's ongoing interest in Andy's faltering relationship with his fiancée has thrown the eighteen year old off guard. He decides to take a stroll outside, where the temperature has dropped into the more comfortable seventies. To his surprise, he catches sight of Ken, the cook, alongside the neighbouring billet, leaning over a tripod.

"Hey, Cookie, didn't know you were interested in photography."

Ken spins around.

"Oh, pictures and all that? Na, I just think some of the sunsets here are great."

"What camera have you got?"

"Nothing special, box camera type. Bought it from 'Lost Property' on Changi. Told me they weren't sure whether someone had lost it or thrown it away. Anyway, got it really cheap."

"And the tripod?"

"Found it, straight up. Always seem to start shaking with a camera in my hand and the tripod stops all that. Did you know that?"

"You'll have to show me your photo albums sometime," replies Andy enthusiastically.

"Haven't got none. Most of the buggers don't come out, so I just keep what does in an old shoe box – but if you really wanted to see them…"

"'Course, bring them down to the office with the C.O's morning coffee."

"You bet, but I'll only show you the best ones."

Ken, the butt of many camp jokes, not only for his cooking but for his memorable display of nudity in front of the washerwomen, now appears uncharacteristically relaxed. He even manages a warm smile. Andy heads back to his billet having seen a different side to the Yorkshire lad.

"Hey! Andy before you go," comes a shout from Ken. "It's the flicks tonight, and Curtis is our best projectionist. Never breaks down when he's doing it. Have you noticed?"

"Yes, Cookie, he's got the knack but don't forget he's our only trained projectionist," replies Andy.

"Might see you there then? I could bring along my box of pictures, just for a bit of a laugh."

"You do that, I'd really like to see them."

A dozen or so Airmen are seated in the modestly constructed camp cinema, open-sided and topped by a corrugated iron roof. They sit chatting and joking, waiting expectantly for Sergeant Curtis to arrive. One of the resident stray dogs makes a late decision to join the gathering, threading its bony frame under the seats before flopping down in front of the screen. Threatening dark clouds hang overhead.

Curtis's recent masterly command of the party that rebuffed the threat of a landing of Japanese civilians has given him an added touch of authority, so much so that his late arrival fails to draw the customary comments of derision.

From his operational position at the rear of the audience, standing on a raised platform constructed from broken paving slabs, he introduces the forthcoming entertainment in his inimitable style: "Good evening, cinemagoers. Tonight, through the miracle of celluloid, I can bring to you a truly musical gem from Hollywood, starring Doris Day and Frank Sinatra. And – wait for it, gentlemen – it's all in colour! And the title is *Young at Heart,* no doubt an apt description for all you soft-hearted buggers who turn up for films like this."

A trickle of laughter is mixed with a few groans.

"Just get it rolling, Sarge, before the bad weather hits us," comes a curt suggestion from the front of the audience. Andy feels a nudge on his arm. Ken has joined him for the picture show.

"I've brought the box with all my best photos," he whispers. "Thought you could have a look after the film has ended," adds the cook enthusiastically.

"Sure," replies Andy, without turning his eyes away from the empty screen.

Ken gives Andy another unwelcome prod before pointing to a couple of the camp's washerwomen squatted together at the front.

"Don't know why they bother to come here. Always laugh in the wrong places, can't speak the language, so can't understand what the film's about – so what's the attraction?"

Before he has finished asking the question, Ken is already regretting his words. He knows full well the direction Andy's mind is taking.

"Could be you, Cookie. Might just be a ploy, hoping to catch you taking another shower."

Andy's comment is met with silence.

The soundtrack bursts into life with the title song and a sweeping overhead camera shot, closing in on a homely row of cottages, neatly separated by white painted picket fences.

But the audience are soon distracted from the folksy American lifestyle being reeled out before them. Reality strikes. Without warning, there is a crack of thunder.

Almost immediately the heavens open and the rain is soon hammering down on the corrugated iron roof. The absence of any guttering compounds the problem. The film continues but its sound has already lost its battle to be heard above the noise from the downpour. Mother Nature is winning, hands down!

On screen, Sinatra is seated at a piano, singing, but as far as the cinemagoers are aware, he is miming. With the cinema being open-sided, the rain is sweeping through, reaching the feet of almost everyone, except the elevated projectionist who has already donned a rain cape and a tattered, white waterproof hat.

Within minutes, the soaked audience have left the makeshift

cinema and are seeking refuge in the nearby Mess. Sinatra and Doris Day are now engaged in a silent duet, while Sgt Curtis is left alone to curse as he struggles to put the equipment away.

Meanwhile, in the Mess, Andy watches as Ken, slowly and meticulously, spreads his collection of pictures across one of the dining tables. The other Airmen, waiting for the rain to subside before making a dash to their billet, gather around to view an unscheduled photographic exhibition that is unfolding in front of them.

"Where d'ya get those pictures from, Cookie?" comes the first question.

"Right professional stuff you've got there, mate," comments another with more than a hint of incredulity in his voice.

"You really think so?" replies Ken innocently.

"Don't try and tell us *you* took 'em," laughs Jock, leaning forward to take a closer look.

Andy jumps immediately to Cookie's defence.

"All his own work, I can vouch for that," counters Andy to the others now giving closer attention to the countless snaps. The compliments begin to flow.

"Cookie, you should re-muster as a photographer. You're in the wrong trade, mate, we'll all vouch for that." "Hey, that's a good one of the airstrip – and this one of the palm trees, too." "And I'd like a copy of this." "Keep it up, that's my advice." "Who knows, after you leave the Air Force you could be a wedding photographer or do baby portraits." "Good money in that, so I hear."

The camp cook is welcoming the unexpected praise from his mates. The Mess clears, leaving Ken and Andy alone to file away the pictures in the shoe box.

"Yeh, Cookie, I reckon you've got a hidden talent for this," adds Andy. "And if you take a bad picture you can always throw it away, not like a badly cooked meal."

"You're absolutely right. I won't forget that piece of advice," smiles the Yorkshireman.

The heavy rain continues throughout the night. The Airmen awake to a camp which is under water. The monsoon ditches surrounding each of the three billets are coping admirably but elsewhere the large pools of brown coloured water are getting larger.

Martin emerges from the Signals hut, takes a quick look up at the grey clouds then, head down, makes a dash for SHQ clutching a piece of paper.

Andy is standing in the shelter of the doorway, looking in the other direction, watching as the broken guttering on the cookhouse roof prepares to surrender to the forces of nature.

"Bad news," announces the almost breathless Music Man, his jacket totally soaked.

He hands over a soggy, crumpled piece of paper. The pair go inside.

"Can hardly read it, it's so damn faint," complains Andy, trying to flatten it out on his desk top.

"I'll read it for you:

PRIORITY: DUE TO ADVERSE WEATHER CONDITIONS, FLIGHTS TO YOUR DETACHMENT ARE SUSPENDED UNTIL FURTHER NOTICE. IF NECESSARY, DRAW ON EMERGENCY RATIONS.

"And you'll have to let the Old Man know about this ASAP," adds Martin, removing his shoes and socks.

"You bet, as soon as this lot stops, I'll be over to his place on my bike."

"It won't stop: it's the bloody monsoon season. Go over now. By the way, how long is it since we last saw him on the camp.

"O.K, Martin, I'll go now. But first I'll have to let the servicing crew and firemen know the news. Bet they'll be glad of the break."

"Andy, before you go, check with the cookhouse on the level of emergency rations."

"Because… ?"

"Because – I'd be surprised if we have any. When was the last inventory taken?"

"Probably a month or two ago," comes the defensive answer. Andy recalls the C.O's earlier request that he should check the stores.

"Anyway, I'd check now with Broadside in the cookhouse before you speak with the C.O."

Moments later Andy arrives at the cookhouse, breathless and dripping wet.

"Where's Broadside?"

"He's not well today," comes a voice from behind a tall wooden cupboard. "Who's asking?"

"It's Andy, I need to speak to him urgently."

"You'll find him in his billet."

"What's wrong with him?"

"Not sure, could be food poisoning."

Ken steps into view.

"Sorry about not bringing your coffee over, I was waiting for the rain to stop."

"It won't stop: it's the monsoon season," answers Andy abruptly. "I need to know how we're placed for emergency rations. Do you know, or must I speak to the Sarge?"

"Yes, you'll have to speak to him. Just between you and me, there's not much."

"Oh dear," sighs Andy.

"Problem was Christmas, the parties and then we ran into a heavy run of birthdays. Never seemed to stop. And then a couple of lads twisted our arm with a few dollars here, a couple of dollars there and…"

"That's enough, I get the picture."

"Who's been asking?"

"Well, there'll be no flights in here until the weather improves and, if that doesn't happen, we'll be using our emergency rations."

"Bloody hell," groans Ken.

Andy returns to the office to gather his thoughts. He decides he must first speak to Flight Lieutenant Munro before actually establishing the true position of the cookhouse reserves. The C.O cannot be left in the dark, as he was over the aborted Japanese landing. The rain continues as Andy braces himself for an uncomfortable cycle ride in the driving rain to the bungalow.

Meanwhile, Ken is having to employ some nimble footwork to avoid the large puddles as he makes a dash from the cookhouse to his Sergeant's billet. Andy's questions about the emergency rations have left him rattled, and the cook is having second thoughts on having revealed any knowledge of the true position of the reserve rations.

A sodden Andy arrives at the C.O's residence, dismounting and throwing his bike to the ground in a single movement. One of the towering palm trees overhanging the bungalow has snapped and is lying menacingly over the roof. The usually manicured lawns are deep under water. The ropes holding the tarpaulin sheeting covering the Land Rover have all but broken loose and are about to expose the vehicle to the elements. Andy raps a knuckle on the door. The C.O's servant is quick to respond, opening the door with a courteous bow. "But Masta still not well," he adds in a solemn voice.

"Let me in. Out of this filthy weather." The servant steps to one side as Andy brushes past him and makes a direct move for the lounge. "Is he awake?"

"Masta not well," is repeated, accompanied by a grimace and shrug of the shoulders.

"Where is he then?"

"In bedroom."

"Right, I've got to see him now."

The servant leads the way to the bedroom. The door is slightly open, enough for Andy to catch a glimpse of his C.O sitting up in bed, sipping from what could be either a glass of water – or gin.

"Tell him I'm here, will you?"

The servant edges in front of Andy and disappears into the bedroom, closing the door behind him. He emerges a few minutes later. "Masta see you now."

"To what do I owe this unscheduled visit, Airman?" says the C.O, with a wicked grin. "Papers to see? Papers to sign? Speak up, man."

Andy's concentration wanders until he notices a framed wedding photograph hanging directly above the bed. It is a picture of the C.O and his now departed wife. The married couple stand slightly apart in an unromantic, totally militaristic pose. The groom has the look of a condemned man, his capped head stretching upwards in a forlorn attempt to minimise the disparity in their heights. Neither can muster a smile. His bride, Dorothy, wearing a knee-length cotton dress, presents a serious pose as befits the role of the dutiful Officer's wife. Andy finds it difficult to accept that the photo was taken only a few months ago.

"I'm waiting!" snaps the C.O.

"Er, sorry, Sir. Signal received from Changi that flights to our station are grounded due to bad weather."

"And quite right, too. Now let's have a drink – it'll help to dry you out, 'cause it's dry gin." Andy manages to raise a polite smile at his Commanding Officer's rare stab at humour, unsure whether he has grasped the implications of the signal.

"Bit early for me, Sir. Perhaps later."

"Boy!" screams the C.O. "Another glass for Leading Aircraftman Marshall."

"Saw you gawking at the photo up there. What were you thinking? Come on, tell me?"

"It's very…er a very nice picture, Sir."

"Nice? Nice! It's bloody awful – and it'll be coming down, mark my words."

The servant returns, carrying a silver tray bearing an unopened bottle of gin and a single glass.

"Ah, now here's you're drink, Airman. Thank you, Boy. Now open the bottle then leave us alone and make sure all the shutters are firmly closed. You left one open last night and I heard the damn thing banging. This place could soon be under water if it starts coming through the windows as well. Go on, Boy, off you go. Chop, chop!"

Andy prepares to raise the question of emergency rations but is cut-off in mid-thought.

"So, what did you think of her?"

"Sorry, who Sir?"

"My wife, sorry ex-wife, Dorothy," comes the impatient response.

"To be honest Sir, didn't know her."

"That makes two of us. It's finished, you know, she's not coming back," says the C.O, pouring himself another generous measure.

"One never knows, you might just meet up again back home," adds Andy.

The comment is ignored.

The C.O hiccups before refilling Andy's glass.

"I was married before, you know – and that didn't work out either."

"Sorry to hear about that, Sir…"

Flight Lieutenant Munro steamrollers over Andy's words.

"And what's been going on in the camp?"

"Not a great deal, particularly because of the weather but …"

The C.O is clearly not to be interrupted.

"When I get back on my feet again, I'm going to really turn the screw. That scoundrel Curtis will be for it. One of the washerwomen tells me he does an impersonation of me, which apparently the men find amusing. That will stop, mark my words. Butlins this is not. Get those Charge Sheets ready. Boy! where are the slices of lime?" comes the cry.

The C.O drops helplessly back onto the bed, almost closing his eyes. His glass slips from his grasp and hits the floor.

Andy is beginning to feel the effects of a couple of glasses of gin.

Increasingly light-headed, he moves back to rest his unsteady body on a stool in front of the dressing table.

From a horizontal position, the C.O suddenly forces himself up to look at his visitor.

"Drink up, man, I'm having another. You know Dorothy used to sit where you are, in front of the mirror, making herself up. More often than not, made a pretty decent job of it, too. I'll give her that."

Momentarily, Andy has some sympathy for the C.O. Having himself been given the postal 'brush off' by Sandra, he has already sampled a taste of the difficulties one can experience with the opposite sex.

The Flight Lieutenant rises from his bed, shuffling unsteadily across the room, before clumsily poking the nose of the now almost half empty gin bottle into Andy's glass.

"Boy! where's that damn lime?" shouts the C.O. "That's it, young man, drink up. Another one in there won't do any harm. Boy! Where the hell are you?"

"Does he have a proper name, Sir?"

"Boy was his name when I took over here, is what he understands and therefore what he answers to. No damn point in confusing the chap, is there?"

Andy is struggling to contain his amusement at the appearance of his Commanding Officer, who is staring bleary-eyed at him through glasses perched on a severely reddened nose. Apart from a hand towel draped around his neck, his only clothing is a pair of non-matching, crumpled cotton socks.

"What's so funny?" is the predictable response.

"It must be the gin, Sir, I'm not used to it and it's making me giggle," is the first excuse that Andy can call upon.

"Silly ass," laughs the C.O. "Plenty more where that came from," he adds, shaking the bottle.

Andy slides his hand quickly over the top of the glass to prevent another re-fill.

He has witnessed his Commanding Officer becoming drunk once before, at the fateful invitation evening here for the Sergeants when he spoke at length about his active Service; but now Andy is seeing him in a more relaxed and humorous light. He decides a complete change of subject is called for.

"Where did you go to school, Sir?"

"Er...well, Private one to start with, then a first class Public one. Give me a few minutes to remember the damn name of it." He pauses. "Hold on, it's coming! My gawd, can't think! It's damn well gone again. I think the gin's getting through to me, too!"

The C.O stutters for a few moments, before playfully reeling off the names of numerous schools with bizarre and vulgar sounding names. Soon, his failure to recall the right one succeeds in both men breaking out into simultaneous laughter.

In Andy's eyes, a bottle of gin has reduced the normally serious and articulate Officer to the non-commissioned ranks.

"You'll find out about women soon enough, young Marshall," says the C.O pointing a finger at his drinking companion. "Then you'll remember my words."

A puzzled look appears on the Airman's face. "Which were, Sir?"

There is a silence as the C.O is again lost in a struggle with both his short and long-term memory. "What was I saying?" Finally accepting defeat, he returns to his bed.

His dishevelled sheets have already slipped to the floor, so he stretches out untidily on the exposed mattress.

Andy senses it is the moment to leave, turns his back and prepares to slip quietly away.

But as he attempts to exit, the C.O suddenly reactivates the conversation by mumbling:

"Ah, those elusive words, I mentioned earlier?" There is a pause before he resumes. "Yes, and very, very important they are, too – whatever they were!"

Andy smiles down on the exhausted and drunken figure, who is now struggling to keep one eye open. He turns away in the knowledge that very shortly the fight will be over and the C.O will be soundly asleep.

As Andy reaches the door, he is aware of the sound of the C.O struggling to rise from his bed.

"Hey! before you go, Airman."

"Sir?"

"Be a good idea to check on the state of our emergency rations, given the bad weather."

The words crash around Andy's ears.

To his total surprise, and despite a heavy intake of gin, the C.O has made the connection between the monsoon and the camp's level of food supplies. Climbing back on his bike, Andy is saying a little prayer for both an immediate end to the monsoon season and the continued absence from duty of Flight Lieutenant Munro.

As Andy begins to negotiate the slippery track back to the camp, he can hear distant and repeated cries of "Boy!"

19

"You're a lucky bastard, Marshall." The words are accompanied by a painful nudge in the ribs. Andy's attempt at a Sunday morning lie-in has been brought to an abrupt end by the Music Man.

"Can't you see – I'm trying to get some kip," comes the dismissive response.

"Apologies, I'll rephrase that: you lucky and miserable bastard."

"O.K, so what you on about?"

"You're off to the mainland at the weekend with the Island football team," says Martin.

"Who says?" asks Andy, not wishing to sound too enthusiastic in case it's not true.

"The lads have heard the team selection and were talking about it over breakfast. Apparently four blokes from the camp have made it – and you're one of them, you lucky bastard."

Andy is now on his feet, looking out from the billet doorway at the rain cascading down from the roof of the outside shower.

"Tell you what, Music Man, if this weather doesn't improve there'll be no match to play. Anyway, where exactly is the game being played?"

"Sounded like Sipidang or Sipitang. You'll soon find out. Apparently the District Officer has organised a launch to get the team – and a few of his drinking mates – over there."

"I wonder if the C.O will be going? Couple of days away from here might do him a power of good," ponders Andy.

"If there's a drink for him at the other end, he won't refuse," laughs Martin.

"Your guts been playing you up?" asks Andy.

"Yeh, a bit – come to think of it."

"I reckon it was that meat we had last night. Tasted most peculiar."

"I do too, thought it was just me. Hey! let's have a word with Ken. He should know, he prepared it."

Andy moves into the aisle, looking down the row of beds for the cook. He catches Ken making a hasty exit from the billet.

"Ken! Ken! Hold on a minute…" The calls are in vain.

"He's up to something you can bet. I'll catch him later," says Andy.

The Doc appears in the doorway, wearing the look of a worried man.

"A private word, LAC Marshall."

The pair step outside, taking cover beneath the Doc's umbrella as the rain continues to fall.

"Something's going on," whispers the Doc. "I've had three blokes up at Sick Quarters already. Their asses are on fire – and I reckon it's something they've eaten. I want the C.O's permission to close the cookhouse until I've had a good look round it. Is he still out at his bungalow?"

"Uh, well, yes but…"

"Good enough. I'm on my way," replies the Doc.

Andy holds up a restraining hand. "In this weather?"

"In any bloody weather!"

"Not sure whether it's a good idea to see him today, 'cause he's not too well."

"No problem, I'll take a look at him myself."

Andy's heart sinks. He has done his best to conceal the C.O's state of health and mind, hoping that somehow, there will be an improvement.

"I'll come with you, I'll race you there!" adds Andy, trying to lighten the mood.

"You're on. But you'll have to give me a start because I'll have to balance my box of tricks on the handlebars."

The competitors don their rain capes, mount their bikes and head out from the camp.

Slithering, sliding over the treacherous surface, now and then being forced to dismount, both men manage to avoid falling off as they negotiate the paths which lead them to the C.O's bungalow. The Doc trails behind, giving himself a running commentary on the success of navigating around each of the large pools of water.

Andy is first to arrive. He drops his bike to the ground and sprints to the door.

The servant stands solemnly inside, one foot pressed hard against the wooden door frame. "Not good time to see Masta," is the unwelcoming remark.

"Sorry, *got* to see him," replies Andy.

From inside, comes the sound of female laughter. Andy recognises the voice immediately: Fatimah is back in favour.

He waits for the Doc to arrive. "Typical, bloody typical," curses Andy to himself.

The Doc is now at his side. "What's going on? Aren't we going in? Sounds like a woman in there with him, doesn't it?"

"Just one of the cleaners, I think," replies Andy.

The servant is doing his best to protect his master, his foot remaining wedged firmly against the other side of the door.

"Listen, Doc, I'll go in alone and have a word with him. Wait here for the moment."

Brushing past the servant, Andy moves inside. The vocals have ceased. Slowly and quietly opening the bedroom door, he sees Flight Lieutenant Munro lying naked, face down on the bed. Fatimah is astride him, also in her birthday suit, her large dark brown hands massaging his lily-white back.

The Indian washerwoman spins her head round to look directly at Andy.

"Coomandah have bad back, Fatimah make better," she smiles.

"Just wanted a quick word, Sir?" says Andy turning his eyes away from the action.

"Airman! clear off," comes the muffled cry from the C.O, his face almost buried in a pillow.

Andy hesitates before exiting the room. It's a hopeless situation.

The Doc is waiting at the front of the bungalow. Andy joins him.

"How is the Old Man?"

Andy pauses to collect his thoughts.

"Yeh, he's looking quite relaxed. He's in good hands. No need for you to see him."

"What you mean, what did he say?" presses the Doc.

"Um, he said it was OK."

"You mean OK to close down the cookhouse?"

"Yep, that's right," says Andy.

"What about a quick check on him, while I'm here?"

"No, not at the moment. He's best left alone, take my word for it," replies Andy.

"Something odd going on, I just get that feeling. Nothing to do with that cleaning lady, is it?" adds the Doc.

The pair move outside as the rain subsides into a steady drizzle.

As they slowly cycle back to camp, weaving their way from side to side on the muddy track to skirt the flooded paths, Andy reflects on the nigh impossible ongoing task of trying to protect what remains of the C.O's dwindling reputation. Although his absence has had little or no effect on the functioning of the detachment, he clearly has a serious drink problem and the resumption of his relationship with Fatimah can only be for the worse. He recalls the ordeal of meeting with the Flight Lieutenant on his first full day at the camp, standing in front of a seemingly confident but self-opinionated, dictatorial figure whose thoughts and words were constantly slipping back into the days of World War Two. How different from the helpless character he has just seen, half-drunk, cavorting with a camp washerwomen.

The departure of his wife, together with the possibility of receiving an unfavourable report following the Wing Commander's recent inspection, has clearly taken him to the edge.

Yet, still Andy feels he should be doing something to help his C.O. Could it just be that he is responding to a virtuous inner call of duty, or is it simply a case of feeling sorry for someone sinking fast before his eyes? There is little respect or sympathy for him amongst the men, who see him almost as a caricature. Why should he think otherwise? The young Airman remains uncertain and confused about the immediate future.

It is lunchtime as the returning cyclists pass close to the Mess. Half a dozen of the men are on their knees, heads bowed, as if in prayer. The Doc and Andy dismount to witness the bizarre scene being acted out in the rain.

"Silly sods, they must be checking the water levels in the monsoon drains," laughs Andy.

"No they're not. Look! Listen to 'em, they're damn well throwing up!" cries the Doc as he charges into the Mess.

Andy dashes first towards Billy, whose fingers are attempting to remove something from his throat, simultaneously pushing the other hand hard against the pit of his stomach.

"What the hell have you been eating?"

Billy shakes his head, before depositing an unwanted mouthful on the ground.

"What's that?" asks Andy, recoiling from the unsightly deposit. "Fish?"

"Yeh, fucking fish!"

"What sort of fish?"

"Not a clue. Tasted like a piece of rubber! The haul from the cooks fishing expedition last night, that's what," adds Billy, using his wrist to wipe off grey slime hanging from his mouth.

The Doc reappears.

"Right you lot, follow me," comes his authoritative shouted order.

The sickened line of diners slowly struggle to their feet, amidst groans and bouts of coughing. The faces of the silent ones carry painful grimaces.

"Come on, you're not dying! This way – and quick."

He turns to face Andy.

"The cookhouse is closed indefinitely. And those two bloody cooks are for it."

"O.K, Doc, I'll try to inform C.O," says Andy.

"This lot I'm taking away for treatment 'cause they're ones who've eaten the fish. The greedy bastards probably got here early, jumping the queue. Serves 'em right, in a way, but the cooks are still for it," explains the Doc.

Andy decides to join a huddle of men, deep in conversation inside the Mess. He looks towards the counter but there is no sign of the two cooks.

"Anyone seen Broadside or Ken?"

"They cleared off as soon as they finished serving up," explains Martin, emerging from the Mess.

Andy is met by Curtis, as usual in a jovial mood.

"Hear what happened? The daft buggers went out fishing last night, after dark, as the emergency rations are down to zero. Apparently Broadside and his sidekick borrowed a boat, with a light rigged up at the back, turned the beam on the water and – guess what? Up jumped the fish. Result: jackpot!"

"Pull the other one" smiles Jock, joining the discussion.

"What exactly d'they catch?" says Andy.

"Well, the cooks had no idea, that's for sure!" continues Curtis.

"Must have had some idea..."

"Nope" says Curtis before suddenly breaking into song: "Pink ones, orange ones, some as big as yer 'ead – like monkfish."

"Oh, no," says Andy with an expression of disgust.

"It gets worse," adds Curtis. "Some they caught were carnivorous, with bits of other fish inside them."

"That would certainly make them carnivorous," suggests Jock.

Curtis breaks away and heads in the direction of the notice board. He snatches from it a grease stained manuscript. Arm outstretched, he returns, dangling the paper between two fingers.

"What you got there?" asks Jock.

"The lunch menu, gentlemen. It reads: 'Special fish and chips' – and there's no doubt it certainly did turn out to be special!"

"What you going to do with it, Sarge?"

"I'll keep it for the cooks court martial. Exhibit one, m'lud, shall we say?"

Andy is wondering how the Doc is coping at the Sick Quarters but decides to return to the billet. The weather has put paid to the usual Sunday morning game of soccer and there is a full complement of Airmen, except for a couple of empty beds vacated by those being treated by the Doc.

"You lot need cheering up," suggests the Music Man, moving from his bedside to the aisle to make a general address to his fellow men.

"Not now – and not with that damn music of yours –thank you," comes an immediate response.

"And not when I'm trying to get some kip!" adds another voice.

"Must have a requiem record somewhere here," teases Martin, ignoring the comment and dipping his head into his locker to check his collection.

But the attention of everyone is suddenly focused on two sickly looking characters who have just entered the billet. They stand together, ashen-faced, recovering their breath after their short walk from Sick Quarters.

They are greeted immediately with a barrage of questions.

"You all right, lads?" "The Doc sort you out?" "Manage to bring it all up?"

Heads down, the stricken pair make straight for the comfort of their beds without offering a word.

Andy slips out and heads back to the Mess, hoping to meet up with the two cooks.

The rain has finally come to a halt, the sun has broken through and in places faint clouds of steam are rising from the sodden ground.

As he leaves, he passes a couple discussing the likely menu for the evening meal.

"Likely to be something we've never had, that's for sure," laughs one.

"As long as it's not my last supper," responds the other.

Andy reaches the cookhouse. One of the stray dogs attempts, unsuccessfully, to follow him in. Sergeant Broadside and Ken are nowhere to be seen. The tables and floor are spotless, no different from the day of the Wing Commander's recent inspection. The only food on view is a sizeable bunch of over-ripe bananas, resting in the shade of a corner shelf. To his surprise, Andy discovers the freezer is empty and there is no sign, or smell, of the recent catch of fish. The Doc is now at his side.

"Doesn't look as if there's anything to close down," says Andy.

"Question is: where have the buggers gone?" snaps the Doc. "He'll know, I've seen him helping out here," says the Doc, pointing to a local Chinese boy, sitting alone outside. They scamper out to question the young lad.

"Where've the cooks gone?"

The aggressive tone of the Doc's question gains an immediate but unhelpful response.

"I come for money. Sergeant promise."

"Listen, you'll get your money but first tell us where is he?"

The boy merely shrugs his shoulders.

"Let's go to Broadside's billet and ask some of the lads, they might know," suggests Andy.

"And if you see either of them, let us know – and you'll get paid," shouts the Doc to the boy as the pair turn away in the direction of 'Tensing' billet.

The Doc stands in the doorway and, without a moment's hesitation, bellows out to the occupants: "Anyone here know where Sergeant Broadside is? It's important!"

"Probably gone fishing," comes a flippant comment.

"Not a joking matter lads," continues the Doc. "He and his mate have almost poisoned half a dozen of us and we need to speak to him. Once again, can anyone tell us where the man is?" The Doc's mood is an angry one, far removed from that of a romantic collector of sea shells.

There is a total silence.

169

"Do you think they might be hiding him?" whispers Andy to the Doc. They walk outside to consider a strategy. The Doc is deep in thought, running his fingers backwards and forwards under his chin.

"I know sometimes he goes on a 'bender' down in the village. He's come to me a couple of times, while still hung over, and asked for something. That's when he let slip he's been down there drinking the local rocket fuel. It might be worth a look there," replies the Doc.

Those of the rank of Sergeant are given a separate room at the end of the billet and the pair decide to pay it quick visit to see if there is anything which might give a clue to Broadside's disappearance. Hanging on the door knob they find a piece of cardboard on which is scrawled the words 'Do Not Disturb.' The Doc gives the door a sharp prod with an outstretched foot and it flies open, revealing an unmade bed and a dresser with its emptied drawers gaping open.

"Looks like he's made a run for it," says the Doc.

"To the village, you mean?"

"My money's on it. We'll take the ambulance."

"Being Sunday afternoon, won't it be quiet with no one around?" suggests Andy.

"Possibly, but all we have to do is find out where the locals are drinking. Simple."

The Doc wastes no time in negotiating the ambulance around the twisting, narrow road which leads down to the village. The monsoon has left the road flooded in places but this proves no obstacle to the driver as he sprays the windscreen when hitting the pools of knee-high water.

As expected, the village is asleep. There is little activity to be seen as they arrive at the single row of shops which represent the heart of local trading activity. A few bicycles lie in front of the fallen blinds which shield the shop fronts from the now blinding sun.

The pair park up and look for any Bar that might be open. Walking in the shaded area in front of the shops, they first pass a group of local Chinese, seated on wooden boxes, engaged in a game of mah-jong.

As they pause, one of the players, without looking up or turning around, points an arm further down the row. The Doc gratefully accepts the silent lead and Andy follows him as they hurry along towards one of the few shops that are not boarded up. As they approach the end of the row they catch the sounds of laughter mixed with high pitched shouting. Suddenly they can hear the unmistakeable voice of the missing Sergeant.

"Got 'im!" mutters the Doc.

Walking into an open shop, they are first met with a dizzy aroma of spices. It appears to be a general store. Immediately they spot Broadside at the rear of the shop, sprawled out behind a display of fruit and vegetables, his back propped up against an untidy collection of opened sacks. His head is rolling from side to side as he alternates between shouting then mumbling to himself. Standing over him is a slim, middle-aged Chinese woman dressed smartly in an black jacket and trousers. Her confident stance suggests she could be the owner.

Andy bends down to speak to the Sergeant, laying a consoling hand on his shoulder.

"Sarge, it's me, Andy. Time to come back to camp."

There is no response.

"Give me a hand, Andy, let's lift him up," suggests the Doc.

"Sergeant not well," intervenes the woman, stepping between the men and their cook.

"Christ! we can see that for ourselves, dear. How much has he had?" asks the Doc aggressively.

"Sergeant no longer work for Air Force. Now he work for me – here. Understand?"

The Chinese woman steps further forward, distancing Andy and the Doc from Broadside.

The two men look at each other in disbelief as the Sergeant's prospective employer places her feet wider apart and folds her arms.

With just a few movements, her body language has darkened the mood within the shop.

The Doc and Andy stand speechless. Before they can utter a word, two swarthy young Chinese men appear through a door at the back of the shop. One is holding a kitchen knife; the other a machete. Their expressions suggest the Sergeant will not be returning to the camp.

The owner steps forward. "These my two sons. You leave now – then no trouble."

The warning serves its purpose. As the two Airman turn to depart, they can hear the muffled tones of their prostrate cook breaking into song. Within minutes, the ambulance is heading back to camp, as it left, with just two men on board.

20

The Chinese skipper of the motor launch taking the island's soccer team to the mainland is beginning to show his impatience. The word is that the departure has been delayed by the non-arrival of Amelia Prenderghast, the District Officer's wife.

Meanwhile, the four RAF members of the team stand together at the back of the boat, discussing football tactics and the physical problems of playing on rock-hard pitches.

"It's the damn blisters that are the killer," complains Andy.

"Could always pop in to see the Doc about that," smiles Curtis.

"And end up with him stroking my leg again! No thank you!"

"Hold on, here she is," says Ken, as they turn their eyes to catch Amelia dashing along the jetty. In her wake lumbers the ever-loyal Malcolm, clutching a bulging brown leather suitcase.

"They must be planning to stay the weekend. Thought we were coming back this evening, not spending a blooming holiday over there!"

The Police Inspector rises quickly from his seat inside the boat, anxious to be first in position to offer a guiding hand for Amelia as she boards.

"How gallant, Inspector," is her prompt expression of thanks as she drops a tanned leg into the launch, a touch of spontaneous glamour that brings a smile to the faces of the male passengers.

"One can but try," comes the grovelling reply.

The launch's engine promptly bursts into life and heads for the open sea.

The other members of the island team, consisting of Chinese and Indian players, sit together in silence at the front of the boat. It is a sight that concerns Curtis.

"Should be talking to them, at least know their names before we get on the field.

Could prove useful when we want the ball. Come on, lads, let's go and have a word. We haven't even trained with them."

"Can't really blame 'em for staying clear of us. We usually kick the daylights out of them when they're the opposition," adds Ken.

Andy, Billy and Ken follow their Sergeant, struggling to maintain their balance as the craft picks up speed, treating the passengers to an occasional bounce in the water and an unsolicited cooling spray from the sea.

"Looking forward to the game then, boys?" asks Curtis, standing over the unknown locals of the island team.

The question is greeted with an immediate nodding of heads.

"Great, well, that's a start…"

One of the Chinese rises to his feet. "You call me 'Sir,'" he demands.

"Get him!" whispers Ken.

"You not understand. I important teacher of English in village school. All pupils call me 'Sir', so you call me 'Sir'. Understand?"

"Er, Yeh, O.K – 'Sir'."

The Chinaman offers a beaming smile of appreciation and sits down. There is no further exchange, either of names or possible tactics. The RAF members of the team return to their seats.

The sun beats down as the boat drops speed before accelerating again. The D.O and his wife shelter under the shade of a huge umbrella which is being held firmly and obediently in place by the Police Inspector, now standing directly behind them. The sporadic gusts of wind are making his task increasingly difficult but he is managing to hold on bravely to the handle.

"What a creep," observes Billy.

"Look, directly over there, I can see a few people moving around on the coastline," says Andy enthusiastically.

"The Captain says we'll arrive in about five minutes," comes the word from Curtis, returning from a second visit to the front of the boat.

"Doesn't seem much going on over there. Hope they know the match is today."

The launch slips into an isolated part of the beach, before coming to rest alongside a small pier. A group of local children are there to greet them. Led by the D.O and his wife, the passengers disembark.

"The place looks dead," says Ken.

"But just look at the smiles and laughter of those kids. Probably haven't got much but they look so happy. Don't see that much back home, do you?" observes Andy.

The D.O stops and turns to address the players. He is joined by an elderly, barefoot figure with a weather-beaten face. "This gentlemen here will show you to your hotel. It's not the Ritz but then you wouldn't expect it to be, would you?"

"What time is kick off, Sir?" asks Curtis.

"Five o'clock, when it's cooled down a bit. And a final word: while you're here you are ambassadors, so no monkey business – especially with the womenfolk. I don't want to report back to your C.O anything other than that your behaviour has been admirable."

"Get him," mutters Billy under his breath.

The four Servicemen find themselves being led along the shoreline, littered with broken and discarded fishing boats, before turning sharply away from the seafront to face what appears to be an extended bungalow.

It is a hotel in the loosest terms of the word. There is little paint left on the woodwork and the guttering gives the impression of being on the point of collapse. The men file in cautiously as a scrawny mongrel welcomes them with a subdued but continuous growl.

A line of threadbare mats cover the creaking floorboards. The accommodation appears to consist of only three bedrooms, all unoccupied. The owner, a tall Indian gentleman, emerges from one of the bedrooms to explain in perfect English that "food is not provided in this establishment."

Somewhere, somehow, the non-Service members of the team have disappeared.

"Christ, it's hot," gasps Curtis. "Where's the shower?"

"You're too late, Sarge, Billy's in there already."

Andy and Ken flop out on their beds.

"Hoping to take a look at the pitch – but not in this heat," says Curtis.

"Come on, Billy, you've been in there long enough! You'll use up all the cold water."

Billy emerges wearing a broad smile. "That was really good."

Andy and Ken leave their team mates behind to go in search of the pitch.

One of the younger locals standing in the shade outside, dressed only in a pair of swimming trunks, anticipates their question. Without speaking, he nods, then points in the direction of the beach, close to where they landed. Just to make the point, he swings a leg to kick an imaginary ball.

Within minutes, Andy and Ken are standing in the centre circle of the pitch.

As the temperature drops, dark clouds are beginning to form above them.

"Just what we need to cool us off," says Ken looking upwards.

The pair manage to return to the hotel before the heavens open. Within minutes the rain is hammering down.

Curtis and Billy join them in the doorway to witness the effects of the downpour.

"Looks like a postponement," groans Curtis.

"And an overnight stay perhaps?" adds Billy.

The Police Inspector, seeking refuge in the hotel from the elements, has overheard their conversation and steps forward.

"The match goes ahead, whatever the weather. Some of the opposition team have travelled a long way from the Interior, so we can't wait for better weather."

But slowly the weather improves and with it the humidity rises. The four Air Force players try, without success, to relax during the remainder of the afternoon. In adjacent rooms, the couples alternate between stretching out on a bed and taking a shower.

The Sipitang team are first to take to the waterlogged pitch. Their appearance is greeted with screams of delight from the few local spectators that have braved the elements. Heavy rain returns and large pools gather on the uneven parts of the playing surface and, during the preparatory 'kick in,' the visiting players are alarmed at the manner in which the ball fails to bounce, simply splashing down and then floating on the ever growing puddles. Ken, as goalkeeper, catches first sight of the opposition. He stands, open-mouthed, as the red-shirted team form up in a circle at the other end of the field, arms locked together, and begin chanting to each other. His attention is such that he totally ignores a salvo of practice shots from his own players that fly past him.

"What the hell are we up against here, lads? Take a look at this lot," he shouts.

The visitors turn to take up their positions and face the local Sipitang side.

The opposition move closer to the middle in anticipation of the kick off. Barefoot, with each player wearing a matching red bandana around the forehead, their menacing appearance suggests they are

175

preparing for battle rather than a game of soccer.

"Not a pair of boots between them! Who the hell are they?" asks Billy.

Curtis trots forward from his central defensive position to give Andy a few words of encouragement

"Got no idea where this lot have come from – but they look an evil bunch of bastards. If they start roughing you up, Andy my boy, just step on their toes."

The referee blows the whistle. The ball travels a few feet before it is caught up in an enormous puddle. A handful of players are temporarily lost from sight as they scuffle for possession in a rising cloud of spray. Billy, a fleet-footed winger, is the first to sample the intimidating physical presence of the opposition.

After neatly slipping the ball past a defender, his path is blocked by a blatant body check leaving him doubled-up, breathless and shaken. The portly Indian referee, more concerned with keeping his feet dry and moving with the dexterity of an accomplished ballet dancer over and between the countless pools of water, allows play to flow. Shortly afterwards, Andy manages to release the ball before he is tackled; but is unable to avoid the intimidating figure racing towards him. The opposing defender has no interest in winning possession, only in registering a direct hit. Despite a last-second attempt to raise his hands to protect his body, the young National Serviceman is left feeling as if he has been hit by a tank. As the Air Force members of the island team quickly adjust to the conditions by lifting the ball from the water and keeping it above ground, their team mates display a marked reluctance to challenge for the ball. Clearly intimidated, it is as if they already have prior knowledge of the opposition and know what to expect.

Meanwhile, the Sipitang side maintain a strategy similar to that practised by the underdog in the Spanish bull rings. Andy and Billy each manage to score and together with Ken, having survived a series of calculated head butts, are relieved to hear the final whistle. The scant changing accommodation, which could double as a garden shed, has yielded to the heavy rains and flooded. The visitors decide to walk back to the hotel in their playing gear, sodden with sweat and rain.

"Quite an experience, don't you think young Andy," says Curtis.

"Couldn't work out their nationality. All of them short, but immensely strong with what seemed disproportionately large heads."

"Definitely nothing like the Chinese or Indians – or the Malays," adds Andy.

"Bet the D.O knows who they are – or bloody well should do," replies Curtis.

"By the way, didn't see him at the game. Wonder where he got to? Wonder where he's staying?"

As the quartet enter the hotel, they are met by the D.O.

"How did it go, chaps? Filthy weather out there, you did damn well just to see it through. Rugger man myself, so I wouldn't have appreciated the finer points of the round ball game," come his slurred words.

"Don't think the opposition did either, Sir, but we won," replies Curtis proudly.

"Well done, anyway."

"How soon before we go back," asks Ken, raising a hand to soothe his swollen forehead.

"Ah, now there's the problem. There's a bad fuel leak on the launch which will be looked at first thing in the morning. Once that is attended to, off we jolly well go."

"So we're staying overnight, Sir?"

"That's about it. The local school children are putting on a play this evening, followed by a meal. You're all expected to attend, so no sneaking out and making a nuisance of yourselves."

Andy feels exhausted and prepares to rest. His team mates decide to leave him asleep as they leave for dinner. "Poor kid took some brutal knocks today," observes Curtis, quietly closing the bedroom door behind him.

"I did, too," pleads Ken, pointing to an eye that has almost disappeared behind an angry swelling.

Andy awakes early to a sunlit sky. He slips outside, leaving Curtis asleep.

As he passes down the corridor, he catches sight of Ken and Billy who have each taken a bed in the next room.

"Hey! where you going?" asks Billy.

"Just for a quick look around," says Andy.

Billy slides out of bed and pulls on a pair of slacks. "Hold on, be right with you."

The trio move outside.

"Why d'you let me sleep in last night?" queries Andy.

"Thought you needed it. Anyway, you didn't miss anything. The food was so bad that even Ken complained; the kids were singing in a foreign language and the beer – if it was beer – tasted awful. The only entertainment was watching Curtis trying to get off with the D.O's wife."

"Silly bugger, should have learnt his lesson after that social evening at the C.O's place. How's your leg, by the way?"

"Which one?" laughs Billy. "Never been hit so hard in my life. Wonder what those blokes feed on?"

"Probably each other. Won't forget that match in a hurry," smiles Andy. "Hear any more from that girl who dropped you?" asks Andy rather tentatively.

"Nah, not a word. Why d'you ask?"

"Got a 'Dear John' myself."

"Didn't see it on the notice board."

"Well, it wasn't really a proper one," explains Andy.

"Different words perhaps but the same message, I bet," suggests Billy.

A breathless Curtis joins them to impart the latest news on the timing of their return.

"Apparently the launch won't be ready till early afternoon, so we've got a few hours to kill and the D.O let slip that today is market day here so there might be some bargains."

The men amble along, recalling the highlights of their game the previous day. A pair of youngsters sharing a cycle suddenly race past. They decide to follow and soon reach the first of a line of stalls. They are greeted with welcoming smiles from the local people, punctuated by the occasional stare from some of the children. The Indian silk traders are present in strength but the food, fruit and drink sellers predominate. Immediately in front of them, an array of watches is being displayed invitingly on a stretch of velvet cloth.

Curtis steps forward to take a closer look. Attempts to agree a price are proving difficult, given the inability to communicate by language. Finally, a piece of scrap paper is produced and is soon passing backwards and forwards between the Sergeant and the seller. Communication between the parties is now reduced to scribbling numbers upon it. Finally, a deal is struck. But Andy's attention is now drawn to a crowd that have encircled a large tree nearby. There is frantic shouting from the spectators, spiced with the odd burst of applause. Some of the people are waving notes in the air, others are pushing forward to take a closer view of the action. He moves forward and catches the pitiful sight of a pair of cockerels locked together in a struggle for survival. Spurs have been attached to their feet to give them added powers of destruction. Feathers fly. Their wings entwined, the squawking and high-pitched screams slowly subside. Finally, a motionless, horribly torn bird is disentangled from its exhausted victor. The cheering breaks out as bets are won and lost. It is Andy's first experience of cock-fighting, and he vows it will be his last.

The visiting entourage gather at the pier. Below them, the engine of the motor launch bursts into action, throwing out a cloud of smoke. The D.O and his wife move quickly for the prime seats, followed obediently by the Police Inspector, struggling to open the umbrella. Andy and Ken are close behind, snatching seats close to the V.I.P couple. Curtis and Billy are among the last to file on, busily chatting to 'Sir', the Chinese English teacher. Their animated language and gestures suggest the highlights of yesterday's game are once again being re-enacted.

As the boat spins around, Amelia Prenderghast catches sight of Ken's damaged face.

"My God!" she shouts. "I noticed how dreadful it looked last night but it looks even worse today."

"Thank you," replies Ken. "Wish I knew where those animals came from."

"They were Iban, all but one of them," interrupts the D.O.

"Never heard of 'em," comes the simultaneous response from Ken and Andy.

"Well, for your information they are a branch of the Dayak peoples of Borneo, known to us as Sea Dayaks. Ibans were renowned for practising headhunting but, fortunately for us all, that's now a thing of their past."

"I don't think so," adds Ken. "The blighters were not just after my head, it was my whole body – and I've got the bruises to prove it!"

"But did you provoke them? That's the question," asks the D.O.

"No, all I was doing, as goalkeeper, was trying to stop them from scoring."

"I rest my case," counters the D.O with a wicked smile.

"How did they take to the invading Japanese in the last War?" asks Ken.

"Not too kindly, is the answer to that one. Our Army employed the Temengong Iban, who hunted Japanese heads in a 'bob-a-nob' scheme. Hunting in bare feet, with blow darts, the Iban killed silently and invisibly. Fearing jungle spirits were taking their men, the Japanese fled. I'll tell you something even more gruesome," continues Amelia. "I learnt, on good authority, about a party of Japanese soldiers who paid an off-duty visit to one of the coastal villages not far from here. It happened to be on a day when the men had gone to the Interior for some sort of pow-wow, leaving their families behind unprotected. True to form, the Japs raped and pillaged. The next weekend the Japs returned unarmed, obviously looking for some more sport. But this time the local men were waiting. As the Japs came off the beach they were hit by a torrent of poison-tipped darts which paralysed them. As they lay, defenceless, the Iban broke their wrists and ankles and left them crawling around in agony at the mercy of the wild pigs. Subsequently, a Jap search party found a row of their skulls on the beach, mounted on sticks, complete with military caps and glasses. The villagers suffered no further visits for the duration of the War."

"Count your blessings, Ken, I reckon you got off lightly!" laughs Andy.

21

It is now eight months since Andy landed on the island. A solitary month on detachment remains before his return to Changi.

This morning finds him in the office struggling to reassure a pair of new arrivals that their tour of duty will soon fly by. It is a daunting task but made easier by the absence of the C.O who has been summoned, at short notice, to Singapore. The purpose of the visit had not been disclosed, although the C.O had no doubts it was related to the recent Station Inspection carried out by Wing Commander Harding. "Routine procedure, no cause for concern," had been his parting comment.

One of the new arrivals is a chubby, ginger-haired lad from Wales who is relieving Jock, in the stores.

"With your colouring, make sure you cover up and don't go sunbathing," warns Andy in a fatherly tone. The advice is accepted with a thankful nod. Alongside the Welshman stands Sergeant Broadside's relief; a tall, well-built Scotsman whose dour appearance suggests that any critical comment about his culinary skills could prove unwise.

The disparity in their ranks prevents Andy from offering him too much advice, and certainly nothing of a personal nature.

"So that's about it, chaps," concludes Andy. "Any questions?"

"Heard at Changi the C.O is a bit of an odd bugger. That right?" asks the new cook.

"Well, speak as you find, Sergeant," comes Andy's diplomatic response. "He'll be back from Singapore tomorrow. Judge for yourself."

Shortly after the pair disappear, Ken arrives with Andy's morning coffee.

"Just seen your new cookhouse boss, looks a hard nut," smiles Andy.

"Well, as long as he pulls his weight there'll be no complaints from me. Old Broadside wasn't a bad bloke at heart but such a lazy, drunken bastard. Silly sod getting caught up with that woman down in the village, but it was serving up all that dodgy fish up here that really did for him. I warned him, you know."

"Let you into a secret, Ken, to this day the C.O knows nothing about your disastrous fishing expedition – and that's the way it's going to stay."

"How come?"

"Broadside did a deal with Curtis and the Doc," explains Andy.

"What sort of deal?"

"Curtis and the Doc told him they were going to spill the beans to the Old Man about the fishing trip and poisoning the men. But Broadside let them know if they breathed a word he'd explain everything to the C.O about Curtis groping his wife at the Sergeants only social evening."

"Bloody hell," gasps Ken. "I never knew that. So what was the *real* reason Broadside went?"

"Well, after he eventually sobered up and returned from that weekend in the village, he stormed straight into the C.O's office, asking for permission to marry."

"You're joking! What did the Old Man say?"

"Told him to wait till he got home. Broadside exploded, explaining that his 'wife to be' was already here, down in the village. As soon as the C.O realised she was local Chinese, he just blew a gasket. Tore him off a strip, gave him a lecture on security and had him flown back to Changi the same day."

"Wondered why everything happened so quickly. Broadside said he was needed, urgently, in Singapore for special duties. But how come the Doc got involved with the deal? Surely Broadside had nothing on him?"

"But he did. Broadside found out the Doc had been treating patients in the village, for a small consideration," explains Andy. "And it's got worse! Apparently your old cookhouse boss went on a bender when he arrived in Singapore, got caught in an 'Out of Bounds' area, picked a fight with the Police and ended by getting locked up."

Ken shakes his head in disbelief.

Back in Everest billet, Martin is confined to bed with a mysterious fever. The other occupants of the billet have already expressed their concern about his condition by suggesting, mischievously, to the Doc that he could share his accommodation in the Sick Quarters with the Music Man. A suggestion thought to be motivated more by a consensus vote to avoid being a captive audience to his classical music than a genuine concern for his health.

At lunchtime, Andy returns to the billet to check on his friend.

"How you feeling, Martin?"

"Bloody awful. Headache, sweating like a pig. Aching all over."

"Know what it is?"

"Doc came in this morning said it could be dengue fever, a virus transmitted by mosquitoes."

"Should you be in here with the rest of us? Did he say?"

"He reckoned I'm through the worst of it and I'll be all right in a couple of days. Got to drink a lot of water, though."

"Anything I can do for you?" asks Andy sympathetically.

"Not really. Heard we're finally getting a replacement storeman for Jock."

"Yep, he arrived this morning. Ginger Welshman called…"

"Don't tell me, let me guess, … Jones? Evans? Griffiths? Davies?"

"Wrong! It's Morgan," laughs Andy.

"I was getting close: there's only Lewis left and then you've covered half the population of Wales! Tell you what you can do, though. Get the new boy to replace these mangy sheets and get me a decent mattress. They're both wringing wet from all this sweating."

"O.K, I'm on to it," replies Andy.

"Oh, and while you're about it, get me a decent mossie net. The holes in this one are so big the birds will soon be flying through without touching the sides!"

As he leaves the billet, Andy spots Morgan passing the flagpole, heading for the Mess. He decides to follow him. The Welshman is now sitting in the corner of the room, sipping a glass of water.

"Sorry to bother you with work – so soon after you've just arrived – but one of our lads is pretty sick at the moment and needs a complete issue of bedding, plus mattress of course," pleads Andy.

"Haven't even been inside the stores yet to see what's there. By the way, I meant to ask you where the key is?"

"Haven't a clue. But where have you been for the past couple of hours since I saw you and the new cook?"

"Thought I'd have a good look round the camp, after all it's a nine month tour. Needed to be on my own," says Morgan plaintively. "To be honest, I'm a bit browned off at the moment. Got married just before I left England. Don't laugh, will you, but when I got here I felt like crying my eyes out. Singapore was far enough away but this place is another four hours further into the wilderness."

"'Fraid there's not much to see right here on camp," replies Andy. "But we've a good bunch of lads, great beaches – if you don't get stung by the jellyfish – a football team, and we get the odd film or two flown in. The village is pretty quiet and the Memorial Park is the place if you want to be on your own. Mind you that's quite a walk from the camp. Come on, it's not that bad. You just watch, the time will fly by," says Andy, aware as he speaks that his words lack conviction.

"Want to see a picture of my wife?" asks the Welshman.

"Of course," says Andy.

A well-thumbed, black and white snap is produced in double-quick time.

"She's a good looker," responds Andy, giving the picture just a cursory glance.

"Know what they told me when I complained about being sent to the Far East?"

"Haven't a clue."

"Well, an Officer said our separation would be a good test of our marriage. What a bloody cheek!"

"Anyway, let's find the key to the store and get that bedding for Martin," suggests Andy, in an attempt to break the melancholy mood.

Their conversation has been overheard by Ken, who comes out from behind the counter.

"I can tell you where the keys are," he says in a subdued tone.

"Where?!" shouts the Welshman in disbelief.

"Well, I went up to the strip with Jock to take a picture of him leaving and, at the last moment – just before he got on the 'plane – he suddenly remembered he still had his bunch of keys in his pocket. He threw them to me – then I forgot! Don't worry I put them back a couple of days ago."

"Put them back – but where?"

"In the lock, of course," replies Ken. "Look! they're still there."

"And on view to everyone," adds Andy, shaking his head in disbelief.

"Oh no, the store could be stripped bare by now!" groans Morgan.

"I very much doubt it, there's not much of value left in there. Not since the ammunition was moved out," explains Andy.

"So where is the ammo kept now?" asks the Welshman.

"Let's not worry about that today, let's just get hold of some clean bedding for my mate who's sick," suggests Andy.

A pleasant surprise awaits the pair. A quick survey within suggests there have been no visitors.

Morgan registers his shock at the condition of the mosquito nets, after running his fingers over the green netting. "They all seem to have a hole somewhere. Are they all like that? What's yours like, Andy?"

"Just the same," comes the reply.

"And what are all these cans for?"

"Aerosol spray. Magic for all sorts of insects and bugs, mossies in particular. A couple of big squirts are usually enough to clear a Valetta; but I've used most of one can up on a mattress to clear the bugs. Take the bed outside in the sun, and spray the seams on the side of the mattress, leave it for an hour – then watch the blighters jump ship!"

Andy returns to the office. The arrival of Morgan has served to remind him again that his time on the island is drawing to a close; and the Welshman's talk of his leaving a newly-married wife at home has also triggered thoughts of Sandra.

Like Morgan, he, too, could so easily have married, rather than got engaged before being posted abroad. Was it a blessing in disguise that it never happened? His thoughts drift back to their emotional farewell at Plymouth's North Road Station. But their prospects of an enduring relationship are now increasingly bleak. The interval between Sandra's letters is ever longer, news of how she is spending her time is reduced to a minimum. The once romantic dreams of young love are being replaced by what seems to be a dutiful, soulless report from a distant land. Perhaps it is all for the best.

Meanwhile, Flight Lieutenant Munro is on the first floor at SHQ, RAF Changi, seated in front of Wing Commander Harding.

"Let's deal with my inspection first, shall we?"

"Of course, Sir," comes the immediate response.

The inference that there could possibly be anything of real substance for discussion catches the Flight Lieutenant off guard, putting him on the defensive. What was of more interest was whether the Wing Commander had swung into action on his request for a move? Is there possibly a promotion in the offing? With Dorothy now out of his life, an extended stay in the Far East would certainly be acceptable if it meant rising to the rank of Squadron Leader. Those recent, depressing months serving at a remote detachment are being pushed to the back of his mind. Hopefully, a new start beckons. Is the tide finally turning? Some good news at last? His eyes close as he savours the thought of being addressed in the elevated rank of 'Squadron Leader.'

The Wing Commander bangs a fist on the desk.

"I said, Flight Lieutenant, do you agree with my recommendation for improved lighting in all the billets?"

"Uh, um sorry, Sir."

"Well do you? Speak up, man. Are you all right?"

"Of course, Sir."

"Take some water. Sadly, I can't reciprocate the range of spirits that were on offer on my visit to your Station." The words are spoken in a manner which suggests it is a statement, rather than an apology. The comment hits Charles Munro like a unexpected blow to the solar plexus. This can only be a pointed jibe directed at his liking for a drink. The atmosphere has suddenly stiffened.

"So, all in all, a reasonably satisfactory report," continues the Wing Commander.

"Catering and discipline are critical on a small detachment; and your Sergeant cook has, I'm told, been found more suitable – albeit cooler – accommodation here. Morale could be higher and that will be a priority for your replacement. Give the document to him: that'll be his baby. Just a few other wrinkles need smoothing out."

"But I've still got another month to do up there, Sir."

"Not necessary. Your replacement, Flying Officer Scarborough, has already been briefed. He'll return with you tomorrow, take a couple of days to show him round the place – you shouldn't need more than that – pick up your belongings and then head back here."

"And, what's for me then, Sir?"

"Nothing in prospect. You're almost tour expired, no other slots here, so you might as well prepare to make your way back home. Nothing's been decided yet."

Flight Lieutenant Munro sits numbed from the discussion, unable to offer any comment.

First his marriage, and now his career, appear in ruins. He rises to his feet, struggling to force out the words: "Thank you, Sir."

"And one more thing, Munro. The District Officer on your island sent us a confidential and rather critical report about your handling of an incident involving some Japanese tourists who had attempted to pay a visit. The fellow who wrote it certainly seems to have a misplaced conception of the role of a District Officer. Anyway, thought you

186

should know – we've decided to ignore it."

Another verbal blow hits home.

The Flight Lieutenant receives a robust, parting handshake and, head slightly bowed, slowly walks along the balcony overlooking the airstrip. The Wing Commander's final remarks have shaken him to the core. "What the hell was the D.O trying to do?" he mutters to himself, totally unaware of the deafening roar from a Bristol Freighter that is struggling to lift its belly from the nearby strip. Momentarily, he feels like going back to ask for a sight of the D.O's report; but decides that such action might serve to give the mistaken impression that it has some credibility.

Below, at ground level, laughter fills the air as a group of Airmen empty the offices and spill out onto the tarmac road, their working day at an end. A despatch rider carefully snakes his way between them before opening his throttle and speeding away. An attractive brunette 'Waf' lingers in the car park, chatting to a Squadron Leader sporting a handlebar moustache.

The Flight Lieutenant ignores the offer of a lift to the Officers' Mess, deciding to make for the quiet of the Station's 9-hole Golf course. He sits alone behind one of the greens beneath a palm tree and reflects on his talk with the Wing Commander. A couple of local children have chased each other out onto the fairway, oblivious to the danger of the oncoming balls that will soon be sending them scurrying back into the undergrowth. There is precious little to salvage from his visit to Changi. Proof that his reputation and performance have almost certainly been damaged by his time on the island is suggested by the fact that his successor will be of lower rank. He decides that his brief return there will demand a positive approach. The presentation of his successor, holding a lesser rank, might well prove tricky. But, most important of all, it is imperative to have a farewell word with Malcolm Prenderghast; and the nature of that meeting has now taken on a completely different complexion, given the Wing Commander's revelation of having received a critical report from the District Officer.

22

Not having fully recovered from his bout of fever, Martin takes his time walking the short distance from the wireless cabin to Andy's office. In his hand he carries a signal just received from Changi, bearing the classification 'Priority.'

Andy stands in the doorway, unaware of the approaching messenger, gazing in hypnotic admiration at one of the grass cutters who, with a graceful and seemingly effortless movement of one arm, is rapidly clearing an untidy stretch of wild grass with the aid of a small curved blade.

"Attention!" comes the cry in his ear. "Take a look at the passengers coming in on this kite, young man! The Old Man should be back with us before lunch!" laughs Martin.

"Crumbs, doesn't give me much time to warn the others and sort out his papers," replies Andy. "Hope the Wing Commander's Inspection Report for this place went off all right, otherwise the C.O will be returning in a foul mood."

"I saw the Doc earlier heading off for the beach, carrying his bag of shells, so could be planning to be there for the day. Worth getting him back just in case the report has said anything critical about the Sick Quarters. Let's face it, his hut is a joke," adds Martin.

"And I'll give Curtis and Ashton a call, they'll need to know ASAP," says Andy.

"Don't forget to warn the fire crew! If the C.O finds they're not up at the strip when his plane lands, he'll go crackers," teases Martin.

"I'll call on them first, give 'em time to get ready," says Andy.

Martin reiterates his advice about the need for the fire crew to be waiting in place before touch down by adding: "I can just imagine the Old Man now, at a great height, peering anxiously out from the aircraft window, waiting for the cloud cover to clear, hoping against hope that his 'plane will land *before* the fire crew have managed to get up to the runway. Then leaping down from the aircraft to tear a strip off each of them in turn as they arrive, bawling out: "You lot are a disgrace, a complete shower! This is not Butlins!" Hastily, Andy jots down a 'must-do' list. There can be no slip-ups on the C.O's return.

Meanwhile, Flying Officer Scarborough receives a firm nudge on the shoulder from his fellow passenger. "Wake up, man, we'll be landing shortly."

The lanky Officer, sporting a shock of blonde hair, gives a vigorous shake of the head then leans forward to take in the view below. The Valetta is hugging the coastline at a low enough altitude for him to pick out the occasional longhouse dwellings that lie close to the water's edge.

"Not much to see down there, I can tell you. Probably hasn't changed much in the past hundred years," comments the C.O.

"Well, as long as they're enjoying life, with enough to eat, and not bothering anyone else – does it really matter?" exclaims the young Flying Officer.

"Actually, you'll soon find out that some of them do bother the local people and it does really matter. This is precisely the area from where the pirates operate. I'll de-brief on that later. Nasty bunch altogether. Probably collaborated with the Japanese during the War, if the truth were known."

The Flying Officer decides to drop the subject.

It is a smooth landing, sufficiently smooth in the C.O's judgement to move forward and plant a soft but uncharacteristic congratulatory pat on the Pilot's shoulder before leaving the aircraft.

The two passengers disembark. Scarborough stops to take a first look at what will be 'his' detachment. The C.O pauses only to glare at the fire crew who, having been alerted, are already in position.

"Who the hell is that with the Old Man?" asks the Doc, seated at the wheel of his ambulance, having been forced to make a premature return from a shell expedition to the beach. "Surely can't be his replacement, too young and not even a Flight Lieutenant."

"Not another flaming inspection is it?" comes the immediate response from one of the firemen.

Sergeant Curtis, watching closely from the shade of the servicing shed, is waiting to collect a couple of feature films from the aircraft; but has already come to the conclusion that it is the C.O's replacement and moves off smartly in the direction of SHQ.

He arrives breathing heavily.

"Your boss has just landed but won't be here for a while. He was walking over to the control tower with another Officer who was on the flight. Could be wrong, but I reckon he's brought his successor with him."

"What makes you think that?" asks Andy.

"Well first, the Old Man's tour here is almost up and, second, the other bloke was carrying a large bag and heard him telling one of the aircrew to be careful off-loading his suitcases. He's not just staying the night."

"What did he look like?" asks Andy anxiously.

"Young, gawky but a great tan. We'll handle him, putty in our hands, no bother. Anyway, why are you worried? The Music Man told me you've only a few weeks to go."

"That's only if my replacement comes in time."

"Now then, Andy – and the reason I'm here at this moment. What happened at that social evening at the C.O's place must remain dead and buried. Got it? I've overheard the odd funny about it in the Mess but I'm trusting you, as the C.O's sidekick, not to say a word – particularly to this new bloke. Must keep the lid on it. Understand?"

"I think you're worrying unnecessarily, Sarge," replies Andy.

"I'm covering every angle. Even wondered the other night whether the C.O might have, accidentally, met up with Broadside during his visit to Changi."

"Not a chance, heard Broadside is locked up for the moment. The only person he'll be talking to is himself."

"Fantastic, great news! Andy my boy, you've made my day."

There is an undeniable spring in Curtis's step as he leaves and makes his way back towards the airstrip. The Sergeant is likely to be in fine voice at the cinema tonight, introducing the latest film, hot from Singapore.

With more than a little apprehension, Andy waits for the C.O to arrive at the office.

If Curtis is right, a change of Commanding Officer is something Andy could do without, given that he has almost reached the end of his tour. He had finally come to terms with the idiosyncrasies of the Flight Lieutenant and, in recent months, his irregular appearances at the camp

190

have allowed him more freedom of action. The C.O's bouts of drinking have continued, but Andy has established a reliable manner of communicating with his faithful Indian servant, which allows him to organise camp business.

Bicycle rides to the bungalow have become a regular feature of Andy's working week. Effectively, the camp is being run by the three Sergeants. A new C.O would almost certainly wish to stamp his authority on the men, and perhaps even order him to go through the motions of yet another pointless search for those elusive Charge Sheets.

Andy braces himself over the typewriter as he catches the familiar sound of the C.O's voice. The Flight Lieutenant is in full vocal flow and heading closer. The footsteps come to an end just outside the office.

"And this, Scarborough, is SHQ. Your working accommodation for the foreseeable future. Perhaps not the greatest example of Asian architecture but constructed of a mix of stone, wood and bamboo and thoroughly monsoon proof."

Andy is taken aback by the apparently light-hearted tone of his Commanding Officer. Could his mood be a legacy from a drunken night out in Singapore – or has he been drinking on the 'plane?

The C.O moves inside, followed by the Flying Officer.

Andy rises quickly to his feet.

"This is LAC Marshall, he'll be looking after you. Pretty reliable chap, civil servant in a previous life but we overlook that. He's a National Serviceman – and we, of course, are obliged to overlook that, too! Hails from Portsmouth, or somewhere down that way."

"Plymouth actually, Sir," interjects Andy.

"That's what I said, Airman!" snaps the C.O.

The Flying Officer offers a handshake and an understanding wink.

Andy is impressed by the deep tan and concludes he must have clocked up a few hours as a sun-worshipper on Changi beach.

"Relying on you to show me the ropes," he adds softly.

Somewhat rudely, the C.O steps in between them.

"We're about to have a private meeting, Airman, so rustle up a pot of coffee from the cookhouse. Oh yes! And you can remind me – just me – of the combination for the safe."

Andy steps forward and whispers the numbers to the C.O. With raised eyebrows, while turning his head from side to side, the Flying

Officer registers the absurdity of withholding the secret numbers from him.

Given there is only a beaded curtain separating the rooms, the meeting is anything but private, despite both officers speaking quietly. The incoming C.O is being forced to endure the same lecture delivered to Andy shortly after his arrival on the camp. Details of the Japanese occupation of the island, their reliance on the Borneo oilfields and the impending threat from Communist China flow freely. Talk of the special activities of the small Australian contingent on the island draws Andy out of his chair and closer to the curtain, but his attempt to eavesdrop is stalled as both men drop their voices to a whisper.

From catching snatches of their conversation, Andy is left to surmise that the Aussies are engaged on 'Top Secret' operations, eavesdropping on neighbouring countries. Over an hour elapses before the pair reappear.

"Airman, an urgent task for you. I need to speak with the District Officer. I'll be leaving for Changi midday tomorrow, so it's imperative I speak with him this evening. Arrange it!"

"Social or business, Sir?"

"Official business, very official business," snaps the C.O. "I've no wish whatsoever to socialise with his chi-chi wife. It's just him I need to see."

One of the MT Section returns with the C.O's hastily serviced Land Rover. The driver is dismissed and the two Officers climb in. Andy moves to the doorway.

"Airman, we're off to the bungalow. I'll be back shortly by which time you'll have arranged that meeting, without having mentioned a word to anyone about my departure," shouts the C.O.

Before the vehicle has passed out of earshot, Amelia Prenderghast is taking the call.

As usual, Andy hesitates before addressing the District Officer's wife.

"Hello? Hello?…Good afternoon, Ma'am, I have a message from Flight Lieutenant Munro."

"You mean Charles?"

"Yes Ma'am. He needs to see the District Officer urgently, this afternoon – or evening."

"Oh! Out of the question, I'm afraid. It's our Bridge evening here," replies Amelia.

"Any chance of them getting together before Bridge starts?" presses Andy.

"Well, I suppose that's a possibility as long as Malcolm is clear by seven – at the very latest – but I won't be able to join them. I have to prepare for the evening."

"I'll certainly make your apologies and I'm sure the C.O will understand," adds Andy, relieved that the D.O's wife has now excluded herself from the discussion.

"You'll find the place a bit run down and every now and then one has to give the servant a kick or two. Otherwise, it's adequate," explains the C.O, standing with his replacement outside the bungalow.

"Bit remote, all right for a married couple but, for just one, think I'll find it a bit lonely. Probably be better off staying on the camp. Closer to the men, closer to the action," explains Scarborough.

"That's a decision for you. Mind you, being at a distance does have its advantages. Unnecessary fraternisation with the men is not, of course, recommended military practice."

"So, when are you are you leaving, Charles?"

The C.O pauses before answering. "I'll introduce you to the Sergeants early tomorrow, then I'll take the midday flight out."

"No farewell party, drink… ?" begins Scarborough.

"Not necessary, no need for that sort of thing," comes the abrupt response. "Now come and meet 'Boy.'"

The pair walk through the lounge to look out across the rear garden. The servant is on his knees, tending the flower beds, unaware he is being watched.

"He looks fully grown to me, hardly a boy," jokes Scarborough.

The flippant remark brings a withering glance from the C.O. "He'll show you around. Might be a good idea for you to get your head down after you've unpacked. I'll be back here after my meeting with the District Officer."

"Wouldn't it be an idea, perhaps, for me to join you both and be introduced," suggests Scarborough.

"Not today I'm afraid. This one will be strictly 'a deux', comes the swift reply.

The distinctive sound of screeching brakes tells Andy that the C.O has returned.

"Airman, what time have you arranged my meeting?" comes the demanding voice.

Andy comes to the office doorway. "He's ready for you now, Sir."

"Excellent!"

"Can I ask what it's about?" asks Andy.

"No, not for the moment but I want you along as a witness. Hurry up, man."

The C.O remains silent throughout the ride to the District Officer's residence, carrying the facial expression of a gun-slinging, Western cowboy preparing for the final shoot-out with a long time adversary. His hands grip the steering wheel as the Land Rover is driven with little care over the rugged tracks.

Andy's thoughts are preoccupied as to what could possibly be of such local concern to the C.O to merit such an urgent meeting, given he is about to leave the island altogether. The reference to 'official business' offers no clue. In recent months, since the departure of Dorothy Munro, there had been little socialising between the two men. Andy is also intrigued at his new role as witness, patting his jacket pocket to double-check that he is suitably equipped with his pen and note pad to record the encounter. And wouldn't this have provided the perfect opportunity to introduce the Flying Officer as his replacement? Whatever is the Flight Lieutenant planning?

Amelia is waiting to meet them, dressed casually in her tennis clothes. She immediately embarrasses the C.O with a warm embrace and lingering smile. Without a word being exchanged, she leads her visitors through the house. Andy is impressed by both the size and furnishings of the District Officer's home. His eye is caught by the long hallway carrying a line of numerous framed photographs of what could be other colonial dignitaries. In pole position, above the doorway to the main office, is a much larger but faded colour picture of Her Majesty. A couple of servants shuffle away out of sight.

Amelia stops suddenly to remind the C.O just how welcome he is. "Charles, it's simply wonderful to see you again. Malcolm told me you hadn't been too well, so I'm so relieved to see you back on your feet again. So sorry to hear that Dorothy had to dash home. You must miss her dreadfully, having only just married."

"Family funeral, that's all – and Dorothy's just fine," replies the C.O.

"Yes, of course. By the way, Malcolm's got someone in there with him at the moment but he shouldn't be too long. He's been rather busy today. I'm sure people here and in London have absolutely no idea of his immense workload."

Andy sits obediently alongside the C.O, still without the slightest clue of the purpose of the meeting.

A bout of laughing erupts as a door opens further along the corridor and the D.O comes into view, politely ushering out an Indian visitor.

"And tell your chum, will you, that if the mileage is genuine I'll be very interested indeed," calls the D.O as the visitor heads for the front door. "Always useful to have a second car as a back up." He turns to face the Flight Lieutenant.

"Charles, my boy, what an unexpected surprise! And to what do I owe this rare visit?"

The C.O draws a deep breath and rises.

"This won't take too long, Malcolm."

"But first a drink, and one of course for your chap here. Andrew, isn't it? Your usual, Charles?"

"Not for me, thank you, I'm driving. And not for the Airman either – we're both on duty."

"Let's go to my study," suggests the D.O, sensing there is something serious to consider.

The trio walk further along the hall before turning into a room over-populated with book shelves and documents. One wall is covered with an assortment of maps. In a corner is a large cage, housing a small but silent parrot.

The D.O makes straight for the drinks cabinet, close to the cage.

"Lovely looking fellow, don't you think? One of the blue-crowned hanging parrot family. Fun to watch and pleasant to listen to. The chap I bought it from swears he heard it say a few words in Japanese. Haven't heard any yet! Mind you, if I did ..."

"Then you'd have to shoot the damn thing, wouldn't you, Malcolm?" interjects the C.O.

There is a pause before the D.O continues. "Not many in captivity, I can tell you. He'll be sizing you up now, Charles, so he won't be doing much talking."

"Do they make much of a mess?" enquires Andy rather tentatively.

"Good point, young man. The answer to that is in the affirmative.

Their faeces is almost liquid and can be squirted on walls and out of the cage."

Andy and the C.O take an immediate step backwards.

"So what's troubling you, Charles? Take a seat, both of you. If it's of a confidential nature, I can always take the bird outside, although the silly blighter isn't bright enough to repeat anything, take my word for it!"

Together, the C.O and Andy sink into an expensive burgundy coloured leather settee, as the D.O turns his back and heads again for the drinks cabinet.

"Well, I'd like to know what you understand to be the duties of a District Officer," demands the C.O in an assertive tone.

"Many and various, ever-changing and always challenging," comes the immediate reply.

"Which sadly tells me exactly nothing," smiles the C.O.

"Really. Put it this way, Charles, I am a servant of both the Crown and the local people. We are a colonial power here and responsible for the economy of this island and, ultimately, the safeguarding of its citizens. Shall I go on?"

"Just one question, Malcolm: do your responsibilities extend to the military?"

"Well, if the security of the island was endangered that would be of concern to me."

"Concern but not a responsibility?"

"Correct," replies the D.O.

"And if, say, the Japanese Forces did a repeat of their '42 landing, would you be responsible?" asks the C.O in an impatient tone.

"In such a scenario that would primarily be a matter for you, representing our military presence; but obviously I would need to be involved."

"Thank you, Malcolm, this leads me to my final question: so what the hell were you doing sending a report about those Japs on the cruise ship to the Group Captain at Changi.?"

"Oh! *that*?"

"Yes, *that*. You had no authority to communicate with my superior Officer about a matter that is not your responsibility."

The District Officer is clearly flustered by the barrage of questions and attempts to buy himself time by changing the subject.

"Sure you won't take a drink, Charles?"

"I'd rather have an answer!" replies the C.O, rising angrily to his feet.

"Sorry, old chap, but the possibility of those Japanese passengers from the cruise ship setting foot on this island was assessed as a real threat. You were incapacitated and it was left to me, with the able support of my Police Inspector, to deal with what was shaping up to be a major diplomatic incident. Your men, though armed, appeared to be without an Officer in command. The locals were positively incandescent with rage, and considering the treatment meted out to them by the Japs during the War, I understood exactly how they felt. Fortunately, sanity prevailed: the Japanese failed to land and a political disaster was averted. I informed Jesselton immediately and, of course, London. And just to tidy things up I kept the Station Commander at Changi in the picture. They signalled back at once to say 'comments on the situation had been noted'."

"And that, Malcolm, is the precise wordage the Royal Air Force use when replying to lunatic letters from the public reporting sightings of flying saucers carrying men with funny shaped heads."

"I'm sorry if you think I overstepped the mark, Charles, but I am responsible for this District and although your men turned up at the jetty they had no clear leader, other than a jocular Sergeant, and what's more though they had rifles, it was rumoured that they had no ammunition. Clearly not up to speed. So, in my report, I felt duty bound to detail all this."

"Well, Malcolm, rest assured that as far as the Royal Air Force are concerned, your letter has been totally ignored. In fact, it was regarded as a complete joke."

"Hold on a bit, old man, that's a bit strong. Just put yourself in my position…"

"We'll see ourselves out," says the C.O, heading for the door.

"Charles, why not stay for Bridge?" comes the despairing invitation from the D.O.

The invitation is ignored. With a nod of the head, the C.O beckons to Andy to leave.

"Charles! Before you go. You're very welcome to stay on for Bridge – I'm happy to drop out," suggests the D.O in a final attempt to defuse the situation.

Amelia bursts into the room, carrying a worried frown.

She is greeted by a high-pitched squawk from the parrot, lurching forward from its perch at the back of its cage. "Excuse me, gentlemen. Just received some bad news."

She turns to her husband, breathing heavily. "Malcolm, dear, we've just lost one of our men for Bridge tonight."

The dramatic manner of the announcement suggests to Andy there has been a sudden fatality.

"Damned bad timing," responds the D.O. "Not that damn Bannister man again, is it?"

"Charles, we're now in desperate need of an extra pair of trousers, so to speak. Can you possibly come to our rescue?" pleads Amelia, with an almost theatrical flourish.

"Too busy to play card games. Tomorrow will be a busy day for me and I must away," replies the C.O coldly.

"Don't forget to send our love to Dorothy, will you," comes the closing remark from the Prenderghasts.

Outside, the C.O is wearing a beaming smile as he takes his position behind the wheel.

"I enjoyed that, Airman, and I'm grateful to you for being there."

Andy is taken aback by the generosity of the remark.

"Thank you, Sir, but I'm not sure I did much. Didn't take any notes."

"Doesn't matter, Airman, you were there as a witness – just in case."

"In case of what, Sir?"

"In case I was forced to take matters into my hands, literally speaking!"

"You mean a fight, Sir? You looked pretty angry. I thought you might hit him!"

"You said it, Airman, not me. Quite a nifty boxer during my time as a Scout. 'A featherweight with a hammer inside each glove', was one description someone gave me."

There is a welcome breeze as the pair drive back to camp. Thoughts of the heated exchange with the District Officer have, for the moment, taken second billing to the early promise of another glorious sunset developing above them. Andy looks skywards and once again regrets his continuing failure to buy a camera.

The C.O leads the way into the office to collect the papers he needs to take away with him. He allows himself a few minutes to reflect on his time on the Island.

"Damn it Airman, I'm going out in style! Open that safe and let's have a crack at the gin."

"Not really my drink, Sir."

"It is now – and that's an order."

Unlike the C.O, Andy is soon struggling to cope with the large measure in his glass.

"Answer me this, Airman: why am I so unpopular with the men? Go on, answer me!"

Andy is completely lost for words, caught like the proverbial rabbit in the headlights.

"I don't know about that, Sir."

"Course you bloody well do. You're my eyes and ears on this detachment. Go on, tell me. I'm leaving tomorrow, so your comments will be safe with me. Off the record. No one will ever know."

Andy hesitates, before taking a quick gulp from his glass.

"That's more like it, man," says the C.O, almost immediately stretching an arm to top up Andy's glass. Andy decides his only way out is to change the subject, with a thinly-veiled serving of flattery.

"Sir, when you've returned to the UK do you think you'll still look back at the fall of Singapore in '42 as the highlight of your many Asian experiences?"

Andy waits nervously for the response to what could be taken as a highly patronising and personal question. The bait is duly taken.

"Very profound question, young man. That requires some considerable thought. You see I faced countless challenges, and in the process I was put to the test on so many occasions – but here I am. Cheers!"

Andy gives his drinking partner a further steer away from any discussion about his lack of popularity with the men. "Another drink, Sir?"

"And why the hell not!" comes the swift reply.

The gin is going quickly to Andy's head and his thoughts are turning to the evening meal.

A glance at his watch tells him the Mess will soon be closing.

Meanwhile, the C.O is moving into verbal overdrive.

"Just as well I wasn't there when the Japs arrived."

"But you said you were, Sir, when they crossed the causeway from Malaya."

"No dammit, Airman. I'm talking about that damn cruise ship. I'd have seen them off, mark my words!"

"But they didn't even land Sir," replies Andy.

"That, Airman, is an assumption not a fact. You must learn to differentiate between the two. Listen, had I been available I would have been out to the ship and ordered the captain to set sail. Instead we had the District Officer and his wife trying to take the glory for organising what I understand was little more than a fancy dress party at the jetty. Damned cheek. It was a military matter. Time for a cool, experienced head. Prenderghast should have been out of sight, practising for his Bridge evenings."

"Sir, just a little left in the bottle, can I top you up before I go?" asks Andy.

The C.O ignores the remark and again turns his wrath in the direction of the Japanese.

"That country is dead and buried. After the way in which they conducted themselves, their atrocities, flouting the Geneva Convention, that country is finished. Their behaviour will never be forgotten. Even in fifty years' time who will want to buy *anything* made in Japan? Mark my words, no one will ever want to even go there. They are destined to be the lepers of the international community."

"I really think I should try and make it to the Mess before they stop serving, Sir."

"Yes, of course," replies the C.O in an unusually understanding tone.

Andy rises unsteadily to his feet and turns towards the door. The gin has taken its toll.

"Airman, before you go. There'll only be time in the morning for me to have a quick word with the Sergeants, and I'll be seeing them at their post – not here. Anyway, thank you for your help here, you've done a first rate job. As I mentioned to you before, I do have connections with Personnel in Changi and I could put in a word for you; but I think my reputation now is such that it might hinder rather than help."

"Thank you, Sir. I appreciate that."

"And just before you go, did you ever find those Charge Sheets?"

The C.O's now reddened face breaks into a rare smile.

"Don't answer that! Let you into a secret. I've not the slightest idea what Butlins looks like. Have you or any of your family been there? Always imagined those places in the pouring rain with crowds of people from those dreadful northern cities, huddled together like cattle in small huts, all laughing their heads off and getting hopelessly drunk. A complete madhouse."

Andy returns the smile, closes the door and heads for the Mess. The C.O is left alone to re-charge his glass.

23

Half a dozen locally-engaged staff gather outside the office, waiting to be summoned in to receive their wages. For Andy, who will shortly be handing out a single, brown envelope to each of them, it is his last Pay Parade.

He glances outside to catch Fatimah, always the exhibitionist, performing. Arms outstretched sideways, as if in flight, she is humming in a deep voice. Andy decides it can only be an impersonation of an aircraft in flight. Pay Parades have always been taken very seriously, no doubt a legacy from the days of the Japanese occupation, but today the mood is different. As the washerwomen and gardeners stand in line, Andy senses a more relaxed atmosphere. The envelopes are gratefully received with the usual deep bow but there are smiles on all the faces, particularly that of Fatimah who steps forward as their spokeswoman.

"I tell friends that Friday you leave island. You honest man, never take money from envelope. So we have goodbye present for Andee."

One of the gardeners steps forward, bows then produces a huge bunch of unripe bananas from behind his back.

"I don't know what to say," comes the stuttering reply, "but thank you, I love bananas."

The staff file out of the office, except for Fatimah.

"Were you pretending to be a 'plane out there?" asks Andy.

"I show them you soon leave Island. Now, Andee, my friend, little favour for Fatimah." The Indian woman's face holds a mischievous grin.

"If I can," replies Andy cautiously.

"New Coomandah 'andsome man. You tell Coomandah: Fatimah think him velly 'andsome?"

Andy winces at the thought of another Commanding Officer becoming embroiled in a torrid romance with the Indian washerwoman and quickly reminds himself that his successor will be left to pick up the pieces. But Scarborough seems the type to be able to handle the situation.

"I'll do what I can, Fatimah," comes his measured response.

As the staff disperse, Andy notices the village hairdresser, cycling into view on a bike that is clearly struggling to cope with his ample frame. The lads have nick-named the elderly Chinese man, Fifi. Mindful that he will shortly be returning to Singapore and the need to smarten up, Andy moves to the open doorway to attract Fifi's attention.

His wave is reciprocated immediately. The bike wobbles as its rider attempts to maintain his balance. Some of the men regard his haircutting skills as being on a par with anyone back in the UK, and are prepared to overlook his effeminate manner; others dismiss him as being positively 'creepy', due to a dubious tendency to punctuate his work with the occasional soft word in the customer's ear. The hairdresser dismounts, wheels his bike across the square before leaning it to one side of the office door. With meticulous care, he removes the contents of his pannier. It is a further five minutes before the clippers are in action. Today the Chinese man is not in a talkative mood.

"You're quiet today Fifi, you all right?" asks Andy.

The question fails to draw any comment.

Fifi continues, characteristically revisiting certain areas of Andy's head, before finally downing the tools of his trade. He stands directly in front of his customer to admire his handiwork.

"You like hair? Now, you want poof-poof?"

"No thanks."

"But poof-poof make you smell nice," insists Fifi, dipping his head to whisper in his customer's ear.

"O.K, just a bit then," replies Andy, anxious to terminate the operation and return to his work.

Without a moment's hesitation, Fifi is gently patting the back of Andy's neck with a strongly perfumed powder puff. The effect is immediate. Andy bursts into a fit of uncontrolled sneezing.

"Soree, soree, too much poof-poof," concedes Fifi.

"OK, never mind. Here's your money, now, I must get on with my work."

The flannel covering Andy's shoulders is removed delicately, as if it were a surgical dressing.

Andy returns to his desk with his hairdresser in hot pursuit, still attempting to remove the excess powder which remains on the back of his jacket.

"So what's your problem, Fifi? Not much to say for yourself today, have you?"

"Fifi need new bike – but no money. You have spare Air Force bike for Fifi?"

Andy feeds a sheet of paper into his typewriter and begins to type an imaginary letter.

The hairdresser pauses, in anticipation of a reply, realises nothing will be forthcoming and slowly heads for the door.

"Thank you, Fifi," calls out Andy without turning his eyes away from the clattering keys.

The post is due today and Andy knows he can expect a letter from his parents – but will there be one from Sandra? Since his arrival on the island, he has adjusted to the fact that the woman with whom he had intended to share his life has had a change of mind.

Her letters have become increasingly short and there is little mention of their future together. Talk of the wedding has become conspicuous by its absence. With his return to England now only nine months away, Andy sometimes feels the Air Force must carry the blame for the breakdown. But at other times he wonders whether their enforced separation has perhaps done them both a favour by forcing them to face the reality of the consequences of a hastily arranged engagement. If the relationship was meant to endure it would survive. These are the thoughts which are running and re-running through his head as he returns to the billet at the end of the day.

The Music Man and Ken are waiting for Andy on his return to the billet after work.

"It's about your farewell do, Andy boy."

"Any preferences or happy to leave it to us?"

"Uh, haven't really thought about it."

"Well, start thinking. It's Monday evening now and you go on Friday, don't you?"

"Yep."

"When's your replacement arriving?" asks Ken.

"Should have been here last week. The C.O 's not too bothered, as long as he shows up before I go."

"Doesn't seem too bothered about anything as far as I can see," laughs Martin.

"By the way, Andy, there's a letter for you on your locker," says Ken as he moves off further down the billet with the Music Man.

Andy immediately recognises the handwriting on the envelope as that of his mother.

He decides to read it without delay.

Dear Andrew,

So pleased to get your last two letters. They arrived together, which was an unexpected bonus.

Hope this letter reaches you before you finish your duty in Borneo. Secretly, we'll be relieved to know you're going back to the bigger camp at Changi. Should be much safer in Singapore. Every time your father and I look at the map we always say how remote your island is.

Had one of your old Civil Service chums drop by last week. Seemed to think your National Service time was coming to an end. He asked whether you were staying on in the RAF. His face was familiar but we've both forgotten his name. Asked to be remembered to you. Your father gave him the dates and he went away happily enough.

Hope Sandra is keeping you up to date and writing regularly. Oddly enough, we haven't seen her for a little while. As you know, she came to us with her father for Christmas drinks. Didn't seem too talkative and her father was a bit abrupt, although you know we've never really hit it off with him. They didn't seem interested in talking to anyone else and left soon without saying goodbye, which was a big disappointment to me because I was hoping to talk to her about her wedding dress, the arrangements for the Church Service and, of course, the Reception. Not to mention the honeymoon and where you're planning to live. Has she said anything to you? I've got lots of ideas and suggestions for you both. I'm still assuming you'll be getting married as soon as you get back. There's also the question of where'll you live but perhaps I'm getting ahead of myself – and I know Sandra will have strong opinions on all this…"

Andy has read enough and slips the letter back into the envelope. Seven thousand miles from home, he feels totally powerless to discover what is really happening in England. Has Sandra met someone else? Are these words a prelude to her breaking their engagement? Or has she already done that? Perhaps he should now write to her to clear the air once and for all. But it will need a carefully worded letter. A few words of advice would help but who can he talk to? Certainly not the Music Man, who has declared his lack of interest in the opposite sex. Finnegan would certainly have something to say but, sadly, he is now already on his way home. Yes, Finnegan would definitely not have been short of advice – and it would have been worth hearing.

Andy's reflective mood is broken by Ken who suddenly appears in the doorway.

"Quick, lads!" he shouts, "Over to the Mess as quick as you can. The drinks are on our new C.O!"

The reaction of the men, particularly those in a horizontal mode, is on a par with a bunch of well-trained commandos responding to a fire drill. Apart from one snoring body, the billet is emptied in double quick time.

Andy and the Music Man find a place close to the bar. Flying Officer Scarborough, glass in hand, appears to be in a carefree mood. He is surrounded by a group of attentive Airmen, including Curtis, who is no doubt silently taking a mental note of any characteristics which might serve as a basis for future impersonations.

"Speech! Speech!" comes the repeated cry, as the men crowd around their new C.O.

The Flying Officer gives a dismissive wave of his hand. "All in good time," he replies.

"Another drink for our new Commanding Officer," suggests another.

Andy moves quickly to the side of his new boss.

"Don't worry about having an extra drink or two, Sir. I can get someone to run you home – I mean to the bungalow."

"Who knows? I might well decide to be accommodated here in future, with the men."

"Really, Sir? Then there'll be some bits and pieces out there which are Service property and I'll arrange to bring them in to your place on camp."

"Don't bloody well fuss. Relax and have a drink on me. Go on, cheer up you look too bloody serious."

Meanwhile, Curtis is holding court with a small group gathered in a corner of the Mess, drawing laugh upon laugh from his seemingly endless repertoire of jokes.

Andy suddenly finds himself pushed to one side as a pair of his mates succeed in lifting the Flying Officer aloft onto one of the tables positioned in the centre of the room.

Left to balance himself, Scarborough's legs begin to wobble as he looks downwards in an attempt to locate his missing glass.

"Speech, speech," is repeated in an increasingly higher decibel count.

"Well, what can I say?" come the opening words.

Before he can continue, the group in the corner break into familiar song: "Why was he born so beautiful, why was he born at all, he's no bloody use..."

"Order, order," shouts the C.O, bringing his audience to an abrupt silence.

Close to his head, a fan slowly begins to whirr into action. Taking prompt evasive action, the Commanding Officer avoids what would have been a series of nasty blows to the head.

All eyes are focused overhead as the fan is brought under control.

"You'll have to do better than that. Now who's the joker?" calls out the new C.O in an authoritative manner. Within seconds, he appears sober and in command.

There is total silence, as he turns to face the likely offenders standing close to the light switch.

"I said: who is the joker?" There is immediate silence. "No one? Right, then I'll have you two men standing next to the switch to come up and answer for your actions."

Sheepishly, two of the firemen step forward, heads bowed.

His eyes are now trained on the pair of likely suspects.

"Hold on, aren't you the two chaps I saw clowning around the fire tender when I first arrived?"

The question is met with a silence.

"Dangerous game you're playing. Striking an Officer is not a smart move. Anything to say?" adds the C.O.

"No, Sir," comes a muffled reply.

"And you?" says the C.O pointing a finger down at the other fireman.

"Speak up, man!"

"No Sir," is the second response.

The C.O pauses to observe the accused, their eyes now focused on the stone floor.

"Well, after that articulate and considered defence of your actions I suggest you pair just crawl away and reflect on the morality of, literally, acting behind someone's back. I'd have more respect had you faced me.

You'd better be bloody good at putting out fires. I'll see you both in the morning."

The words hit home. There is uneasy silence as the two men slip out of the Mess, while the C.O steps down from his chair.

"Now, the rest of you, there's still a lot of beer left, so let's get stuck into it – and that's an order!"

Andy is in no doubt that his new boss is a totally different package from his predecessor. This is clearly a Commanding Officer who actually commands. Slowly, the drinking party begins to break up. Quite noticeably, every Airman who leaves exits with a respectful comment of "Good night, Sir," or "Thank you, Sir."

Andy remains seated next to his new boss. Across the table from them, sit the two ever reddening faces of Ken and the newly arrived Sergeant cook, surrounded by an array of empty bottles.

"You two men have an important job here. Do you enjoy it?" asks the C.O.

The two cookhouse staff are caught off guard.

"Uh… well, yes. It's not a bad job really…" begins Ken.

"Not the question I asked," replies the C.O. "Don't bother for now, I'll have a word with you both later. Now, a more serious question and one for which I need an answer this evening. Someone, told me this camp runs a pretty useful soccer team. Or is that duff gen?"

Ken reacts immediately.

"Sir, we have a great team. I'm the goalie. Play in the local league – even went over to the mainland to play a match against the Iban."

"Good, I'll have to get into shape then, and I'd like to hear more about that match later," replies the C.O with a beaming smile. "And don't worry, I'm not a goalie!"

"We usually get together for practice in the evenings when it's cooler. Sometimes finishing off with a bit of volleyball," adds Ken enthusiastically.

"And you have your own cinema?"

"Yes, Sir, we sometimes get real technicolour films as well," replies Andy.

"I think that's clinched it, gentlemen, I'll definitely be staying on camp. Otherwise I'll be missing out," says the C.O.

"How soon, Sir?" asks Andy.

"Couple of days, perhaps."

"I'll sort it out in the morning, Sir, with Morgan the storeman," replies Andy, conscious the C.O's decision to live on camp is unlikely to be a popular move with all of the men.

Curtis is close at hand and has been following the conversation. He moves closer.

Tongue firmly in a cheek, loosened by a few beers, he chances a casual remark. "Does that mean, Sir, there will now be a desirable bungalow, complete with servant, available for rent?"

"No, Sergeant, what it means is that the cost of running this detachment will be significantly reduced."

Curtis puckers his lips and leaves.

"I take it he's the camp comedian," says the C.O.

"Just one of many," replies Andy, with a touch of sarcasm. "The difference is, Sir, the others are not trying to be funny. Curtis is naturally funny – and he knows it."

Ken departs to begin cleaning up the Mess. Soon the clatter of empty bottles being collected and thrown into boxes fills the air.

"Now then, young man," begins the C.O "What have *you* learnt from your time here?"

"Difficult question, Sir," muses Andy.

"Put it another way, what advice will you be giving to your replacement?"

"Well, Sir, if Flight Lieutenant Munro had still been here – quite a lot but...."

The C.O takes a deep breath, leans back, then breaks into a hearty laugh. "I like that and you've still managed to retain your sense of humour. Good for you. Odd sort of posting for a young lad like you. An experience you're unlikely to forget. I'm off to the bungalow but I suggest you give the cooks a hand in clearing up before you go."

24

Andy is in an impatient mood. Ken has obviously forgotten to deliver his morning coffee but, more to the point, yet another flight from Changi has arrived without any sign of his promised replacement. Andy reaches for the signal pad to draft a message for the Flying Officer to send to Singapore, chasing up a successor. As he ponders whether it needs more than a 'routine' priority classification, he is aware of footsteps on the concrete strip at the back of the office. He decides to investigate, stepping out on tiptoe into the blazing sunshine and rounding the corner. There is almost a collision as Andy nearly bumps into the stranger, standing alone.

"Sorry about that, didn't mean to frighten you," comes an immediate apology. "Just taking a look round."

Andy is looking at a gangling, emaciated looking figure who is sweating profusely. An appearance that could be mistaken for any of the disorientated 'Moonmen' he had seen arriving at the transit block at Changi.

"What are you doing here? Who the hell are you? Hold on a minute, you can't be my replacement…"

"That's me, SAC Denham, replacing LAC Andrew Marshall," comes the proud declaration, while wiping the lens of his horn-rimmed glasses with a grubby cloth.

"Oh, great! Come inside, we've got the fan working again, you're looking pretty whacked."

Andy puts a welcoming arm across the shoulders of the new arrival. "Just a minute, where's your kit?"

"No problem, the Corporal in the ambulance said he'd bring it down from the strip and I could pick it up from Sick Quarters. Seemed a friendly sort."

"You could say that," smiles Andy.

The men walk inside and Andy promptly offers up his chair. The prospect of leaving has suddenly become a reality. It immediately triggers his memory of his first day at the camp and hearing the ominous words: 'you'll never get off the island.' But nothing can stop him now. Just a few more months in Changi – then home!

"So why didn't they inform us you were coming up?" asks Andy.

"All a bit of a rush job. Apparently they were having trouble getting someone up here."

"How long you in for?" asks Andy.

"National Service. Just under a year to go. Take out the six month tour here and..."

"Sorry, you'll have to do your calculations again. The tour of duty here is – has always been – nine months *not* six," says Andy firmly.

"Don't think so. Before I left they said there'd been a Wing Commander's Inspection here and his recommendation was to reduce the length of tour to six months. They said he felt strongly that nine months here, in one go, was too much. And that's been agreed. Surprised no one has told you."

Andy shakes his head in disbelief. "To be honest, I'm not surprised."

"So what's the job like? And the C.O of course?" enquires Denham in a sudden burst of enthusiasm.

"The job? Well, depends what experience you've had. What were you doing before call-up?" asks Andy.

"Nothing special. Worked in a builders yard, bit of fork-lifting and tidying up."

"Was that it?"

"Just about, except in the Winter when it got quiet, I helped out in the office doing a bit of filing and double-checking invoices to see people had paid up."

"And that's the sum total of your clerical experience? Lucky to get taken in as Clerk Personnel, I can tell you," says Andy raising his eyebrows.

"Well, to be honest, I was a bit artful."

"You must have been! Lucky you're not doing two years with the Pongos."

"I applied for the Air Force and put down my civvy job as administrative work in a construction company, 'cause in a way that covered the bits and pieces of filing I did."

"And you got away with that?"

"Put down I had a couple of 'O' levels – which I don't have – and must have been lucky in the educational tests. That's about it."

"Crikey. You're artful enough to do well here. And you got your SAC through quick, too."

"Yes, only last week," comes the proud response. "I owe the Sergeant at Changi a beer for that. He was really desperate to get me up here – 'cause no one else was available – so he made sure I got through the test."

"You're joking! He can't do that."

"He did. On the morning of the test he told me the sort of questions I might be asked."

"Nothing wrong with that."

"Only they all turned out to be *the* questions! Then just to make sure, before he went to lunch leaving me on my own in the office, he said I'd find the test paper in the top drawer of his desk."

"And?" asks Andy incredulously.

"Well, I had a good look, didn't I? And when he returned from lunch I was taken to another room and he handed me the very same test paper. I was the only one in the room. Must have been there for over an hour. He came in every now and then to ask if I needed more time!"

"How d'you get on?"

"Well I'm here, aren't I?" laughs Denham. "Got over ninety per cent. The Sarge was happy, said it was the best paper he'd marked in ages."

"Not a total surprise in the circumstances though," replies Andy.

"Got to admit though, still good to get over ninety per cent," insists Denham.

"Sorry, what's your first name?"

"Brian."

"Well, Brian, you still look whacked. I'll take you to your billet."

"Thanks. I only arrived on the 'Devonshire' a couple of weeks ago. This heat kills me."

Poor bastard thinks Andy, looking down in sympathy at his replacement who is trying to cope with the heat by waving his beret in front of his face. No doubt about it, this bespectacled, pale-faced lad must have been a prime target for the welcoming old sweats when he arrived at Changi with his fellow 'Moonmen.'

"So what part of England you from?" enquires Andy.

"Southampton – d'ya know it?" Andy's replacement suddenly comes alive.

"Yeh, been there to watch Plymouth play, that's my team back home. Seems a good place, seen some of the big boats at the docks, too.

You'll have a bit of spare time on your hands here. Interested in sport, are you?"

"Not really. Love boats and like swimming, too. Used to spend a lot of time at home hanging around the docks. Used to watch the big liners come in from America."

There is a noticeable twinkle in the eyes of the new arrival as he unwinds with talk of the sea.

"Not many enjoyed travelling on the 'Devonshire', I bet?" jokes Andy.

"Blimey, no. A lot of 'Pongos' with us! Uniform, parades, up at daybreak on the trip out."

"I don't know though, a month at sea all paid. Must be worth something," teases Andy.

"Wasn't all a waste of time," continues Denham, "Learnt a lot of interesting things about the 'Devonshire' from speaking to a couple of the crew."

Despite himself coming from a nearby naval city, Andy's interest is fading fast. He turns his attention to a clutch of papers laying in his intray.

"Did you know, Andy – all right if I call you Andy? – did you know, the troopship was built in Glasgow in 1939? Took part in the Sicily and Salerno landings in the last War, carried troops to Juno Beach as part of the 'D' Day landings in Normandy and later took our men to Korea in 1951…"

"No, I didn't, to be honest," says Andy, attempting to stifle a yawn.

"Made the voyage exciting, once I found out I was sailing on a ship with so much history."

"Tell you what, Brian, I'll show you to your billet. Get your head down this afternoon and then, when it's cooled down a bit, I'll show you the beach. Who knows, you might even fancy a dip."

"Great!"

"A warning though, there's a load of jellyfish around down there."

"Any big ships pass this way?" asks Brian.

"Not really. Mind you we did have a big cruise ship come in close a little while back, caused a bit of excitement at the time. But that's a story in itself. I'm sure the other lads will tell you all about it. Why don't you take a breather now. Plenty of time later for me to show you the ropes."

"Thanks, Andy, I'll do just that."

Andy returns to the billet after work to find SAC Denham, mouth open, lying flat out on his bed. Stripped to the waist but still wearing his black, Service issue shoes. The four hour flight from Singapore and the introductory talk with Andy have taken their toll. His kit bag stands unpacked alongside his upright locker.

The Music Man is near the foot of the bed, taking his first look at the new arrival.

"I've seen pale blokes before but this one is positively ghostly. He's powdered his face, hasn't he?"

Ken feels more sympathetic, adding, "Bet he's just arrived from home, hardly had time to have a shave and they've shot him straight up here. Poor bugger."

"Andy's the lucky one, he's got his replacement in decent time. Remember Finnegan? Nearly lost his mind here waiting for a bloke to take his place," says the Music Man.

The group's attention suddenly turns to the prostrate body of the new arrival.

"Look! It stirs," says Morgan, the storeman, pointing to Denham whose eyes are opening.

The Music Man ambles around to the head of the bed to offer a welcoming handshake.

Denham responds with a weak smile.

"I'm Martin, known to one and all as the 'Music Man.' If you have an educated musical ear – I'm your man."

"What he means is he tries to inflict his choice of classical and jazz records on everyone," interrupts Ken.

"Take no notice of them, I've had more converts than Billy Graham," beams Martin.

Andy and Brian head for the beach. They follow a path through a stretch of undergrowth of swampy grassland bordering the camp, the breeding ground for the mosquitoes that plague the surrounding area, and then along a dusty track behind which lie a couple of derelict looking huts belonging to local people.

"As you're interested in history, the beach ahead is worth a good look," says Andy.

"I'm all eyes," replies Brian.

"Well, this is where the Aussies landed when they re-took the island some ten years ago."

"Bet they've all gone home by now," grins Brian

"No, not all of them. Some remain in the Memorial Park," explains Andy.

"Oh, sorry, I didn't mean anything…"

"I know. But talking of Aussies, I've never been able to discover exactly what a bunch of them are doing here on our camp. The last C.O always kept quiet about what they're actually doing. Seems all very hush-hush. You know a bit cloak and dagger!"

"Aussies, still here?"

"Yes, half a dozen of them billeted with our lads. They're all Signals men. They keep to themselves, don't even have the odd drink with us."

The two men stroll the length of the deserted beach, now and then casting a watchful eye on the incoming tide.

"Some beach this," remarks Brian. "Not a person in sight and clean sand. Nothing like this back home."

"You're right. Suppose we just take it for granted. The lads come down here a lot, 'specially the Doc who collects shells."

"But what the hell does he do with them?"

"Keeps them on display in his Sick Quarters."

"Bit of a nutcase then? Told me when I landed to see him in the morning about some paludrine tablets."

"Yes, you need those but watch his wandering hands – 'fraid he's one of them."

"So what's the C.O like? Only a Flying Officer, I'm told," says Brian.

"I reckon he's all right. Took over recently from a bloke who was a real handful," explains Andy. "Shouldn't be any trouble for you, although he's decided to stay on camp which won't be popular with some of the men."

"So what will I actually *do* each day?" asks Brian.

"Varies day to day. Telephonist, working out rotas, filing, typing letters…"

"I can't type, you know," admits the new arrival sheepishly.

"Nor can I – so that makes two of us! I'm strictly a two-finger man."

This sudden admission comes as an enormous relief to Andy's replacement who relaxes with a spontaneous, deep breath.

"But a piece of useful advice on typing. Whenever you get a letter from the C.O to type, make sure you start on it immediately – whatever else you might be doing at the time."

"Why's that?" asks Brian.

"Because Officers always seem to think of something to write at the last moment, usually when the aircraft is being loaded up. With only two fingers, the sooner you start typing the sooner you finish. It's no fun running up to the strip at the last moment, in this heat, with the mail bag in your hand and seeing the kite just about to take off, 'specially when there's an urgent letter to go with it!"

"That it, then? I suppose that the most important people here are the servicing crew who turn the 'planes round and the fire crew that cover for emergency and crash landings."

"I can tell you something special about one of our servicing crew here," begins Andy.

"I'm all ears."

"Well, from time to time we get civilian flights coming through. Just before Christmas, we had a Qantas flight which was forced to land here with engine trouble, en route from Australia to Singapore. Load of wealthy Chinese on board. Within the hour, the airline had flown in their service engineers from the mainland to fix it. Meanwhile, much to the annoyance of all the passengers, they were told to disembark and walk across the strip to our so-called Airport Hotel. Some, in first class, had already taken a quick look out through the window and decided to remain on board while the problem was sorted out. Made us realise what they must have thought of this place, preferring to stay in an oven-like temperature rather than get out in the fresh air and stretch their legs."

"So what happened next?" asks Brian, listening intently.

The conversation is broken as Andy and his replacement decide to rest in a clearing, sitting on the stump of a fallen palm tree. "Go on, Andy, I'm interested in hearing the rest of this story," says Brian.

"Well, our lads came straight out and offered to help but were told by the Qantas engineers, dressed in their flash, fancy overalls, that they weren't needed. After best part of an hour, it was clear the Aussies had no idea how to fix it. At which point, Corporal Green suggested one of his servicing crew would probably be able to identify the problem. He knew one of his team in particular could fix anything. With nothing to lose, and the passengers getting more restless, the Qantas men gave in and allowed our man to have a look. Pretty soon he had identified the fault. I tell you, it was a sight to savour. Our bloke sitting on the starboard wing, with these so called experts passing him up the tools. No doubt in our minds, if Qantas had been left to deal with it that

216

'plane would still be here! Just to round it all off, the passengers had somehow heard who was responsible for getting them airborne again. So just before they went on their way, some of the appreciative passengers came to the aircraft to thank our man personally by stuffing loads of dollar notes into his hands. A few of the women gave him a kiss and a hug! Funny what the thought of spending Christmas here can do to people."

"What a story! That pukka gen?" asks Brian.

The two men reach the beach.

"Oh yes, and there's the weekly Pay Parades for the local staff. You know, for the washerwomen and grass cutters. The old C.O used to like doing it himself, thought that receiving money from an Officer, rather than just an Erk like me, was an important reminder to them of their loyalty to our Queen and Country. Then he got fed up with it and passed it on to me. Anyway, now it's our – sorry, your job."

"Crumbs, he sounds a bit batty," says Brian.

"Another thing about those parades, don't be put off by their bowing and all that stuff. Don't forget that now, will you? And when you've got some spare time, check that all our men here don't have any grievances about their pay. If so, knock out a list of their queries, with their name and number of course, and send a letter to Accounts at Changi for them to sort out. Money's a bit tight for those sending money back home."

Andy senses from the tired expression on his successor's face that enough advice has been given for one day.

"Haven't seen any jellyfish yet,"says Brian moving closer to the water's edge. "Are they big ones?"

"Big? Some are the size of a dustbin lid."

"Bloody hell that's done for my swimming here," says Brian.

"Only joking! – they are a size but not that big. Come on now, time to head back to camp."

As they return, swapping stories of each other's square-bashing experience, Andy senses that his successor has something more serious on his mind.

"Anything else you need to know?" comes the calculated question.

"Just one thing that's seems bloody odd to me. Before I had my afternoon kip I walked around the billet and looked at the notice board. I read the letters from women dumping the blokes. Looked like real letters to me – are they real?"

217

"You mean the 'Dear Johns'? Yes, sad to, say they're all genuine," explains Andy.

"But who the hell wants everyone to know they've been dumped? Doesn't say much for the bloke, 'cause he's letting everyone know he's a failure? The whole thing strikes me as daft."

"Not necessarily, perhaps he's showing everyone it doesn't matter. Although could be the woman is doing the bloke a favour, I don't really know."

"Well, I've a 'steady' back home but what we have is private."

"Let's change the subject, shall we?" suggests Andy.

But Brian persists. "Now, just imagine you had one of those letters, would you put it on the notice board?"

Andy decides the question is best ignored.

"I've no idea how I'd react. Now, let's see what Ken and our new Sarge have got lined up for grub. You'll find the cookhouse can be full of surprises."

25

Andy has never considered the need for a Demob Chart. His view is that ticking off days, one by one, will in no way accelerate the time remaining, but serve only as a depressing daily reminder of a passage of time too distant to comprehend. However, had he kept such a chart it would show him that tomorrow will be his last day on the island, leaving a further nine months in Singapore before returning home.

So far, the day has been spent showing his successor the ropes and listening to him talk to the C.O. Only a few days for the handover but he is confident that Brian will settle in quickly. Whatever his academic shortcomings, the newcomer seems to be welcoming the challenge – and his two fingers are already moving at speed across the keyboard.

Early afternoon and the C.O's head appears through the beaded curtain: "Why don't you take the rest of the day off, Marshall? Get your packing started."

"Thank you, Sir," answers Andy gratefully, unable to dismiss the thought that such a gesture would not have been made by his predecessor, Flight Lieutenant Munro.

"I've heard you'll be having a farewell drink this evening, so you might be a bit fragile in the morning," adds the C.O.

In his hand, Andy carries away the framed black and white aerial photograph of the camp. If it was taken by the Japs, as had been suggested, it could prove to be an impressive memento to take back to the UK. The question is: would this picture, which had been hanging on the office wall for all to see, be missed? Surely not. After all, it was hardly an official document? No question about it: Andy reaches the conclusion he will be taking it home.

As he strolls back to the billet, Andy catches sight of Fatimah talking with the two other washerwomen. He decides to avoid her and turns away in the direction of the cookhouse, from where Ken has emerged to take a smoke break.

"Everything's lined up for tonight. Got your speech ready? Gonna be a night to remember, though. Just you wait and see."

"Can't stop now, Ken," says Andy, aware that Fatimah is now closing in on them fast.

"You give my message to Coomandah?" she shouts.

"Sorry, just haven't had time – and I'm off in the morning," answers Andy curtly before walking away.

"If you no tell him, Fatimah will," screams the Indian washerwoman.

"What's the message then, is it about the dhobi, the washing?" asks Ken innocently, left alone to face an angry woman.

"Not dhobi. If Andee no tell Coomandah, he give Fatimah back bananas."

A few minutes later, Ken and Andy meet up in the billet.

"What's all that about? She said something about bananas, what's she on about?"

"Not a clue, what time do we get together tonight," says Andy, anxious to change the subject and reminding himself that, before he goes, his replacement will need to be fully briefed on the female fireball that is Fatimah.

"Sevenish? After it gets dark," answers Ken.

"Yeh, that'll do fine. Mind you, just a reminder, I can't take spirits – and beer just bloats me out. Don't want to be a spoil sport but I can't have a repeat of my birthday party. Must get to Singapore in one piece, and without leaving anything behind."

"Of course, completely understand," replies Ken with a mischievous grin.

Andy is in a reflective mood as he begins to empty his locker. He recalls his first few days on the camp when he wondered how he would be able to get through nine months at this remote spot, serving with a bunch of strangers. But his father's often repeated words about the strong and enduring sense of camaraderie to be found in the Services had been borne out. Many of those once strangers had become friends, particularly Martin, alias the Music Man, and Ken – and that never to be forgotten, larger than life character, Finnegan.

The last few weeks have somehow just flown away, as if to catch him by surprise. Now, at last, Singapore and the ultimate goal of home beckon. Back to his parents, to resuming his career in the Civil Service, to watching Plymouth Argyle from the Devonport End at their Home Park ground on a Saturday afternoon and, hopefully, back to Sandra. Also to catch up on all that has happened during his absence. But first the challenge of surviving tonight's farewell party. Andy ponders how best to prepare for the unwanted ordeal. Perhaps an afternoon nap, followed by a cold shower?

At the far end of the billet, squats one of the Malay bearers, diligently polishing a collection of dust covered shoes. The teenager from the village, sporting a shock of jet black hair and an ever present toothy grin, is a popular figure with the men. Working for a pittance, his skills are in demand. Andy's interest in the villagers and especially the boy, had changed dramatically from the moment he learned that both the boy's parents had been publicly executed by the Japanese during their occupation of the island. He watches in admiration as the boy breaks into a whistle, broken only by an occasional spit directed at the toecap, then walks towards him. The boy acknowledges Andy's presence by rising to his feet.

"No, no carry on as you were," he motions with a downward movement of both hands. Andy smiles before placing a dollar note into one of the shoes. The bearer nods excitedly in appreciation and returns the smile with interest.

The collection of empty bottles of Tuborg is growing. What started as a party for four has more than trebled in size, and the signs are it won't be long before some of the partygoers burst into song. Curtis has arrived and is about to break into his endless repertoire of jokes. Martin calls for silence before introducing the lively Sergeant.

"Silence! gentlemen. I said *Silence!*" comes the shout.

"This man is without doubt the Semprini of joke-telling…"

"Sit down, Music Man, you're talking a load of rubbish. What the hell has an old piano player got to do with Curtis?" enquires Ken.

"I'll explain. Silence! Listen now, as most of us know, Semprini started each radio programme by telling listeners that he would be playing: 'Old ones, new ones, loved ones, neglected ones'."

"Sorry, still don't get the connection," says Andy.

"Well, Curtis is just the same. He comes out with old ones, new ones…"

"No he doesn't – 'cause they're all old ones! The bloody lot of them," laughs Ken.

Curtis seems stunned by the flippant comments about his ability as a joke teller and retreats away from the main table. Andy spots Ken preparing to slip away.

"Not going, are you?"

"Not likely, just going for a pee. Back in a minute. Look, your glass is empty!"

The party is stopped in its tracks with the sudden appearance of Flying Officer Scarborough standing in the doorway.

"Heard all this joviality from across the way, so I thought as Station Commander I must investigate." The words are delivered in the self-assured, educated tone, befitting an ex-public school prefect.

The men slowly begin to rise to their feet, suspecting they've now been joined by a party-pooper. In the process, a few empty bottles roll off the table and drop to the stone floor.

The C.O casts a quick look around, surveying the happy and inebriated group.

"So, now my investigation has been concluded, where's my damn beer?!" he bellows.

The men relax instantly and the party resumes.

The mainly teetotal Andy is beginning to feel confused: one inner voice is telling him that his heightened sense of happiness must be allowed to continue, another voice is trying to tell him that he will be paying for it in the morning. While his indecision continues, he takes the opportunity to grab another bottle of Tuborg. Around him, the conversation is becoming rather ragged and sentimental.

Some of the men separated from their girlfriends are describing in detail, and no doubt ambitiously, the amorous welcome that will await them on their return; others are talking more seriously of taking up a new career outside the Service. Talk is more of the future, not of the present.

Without warning, the Mess is reduced to total darkness. "Not the bloody generator again, is it?" comes the cry. A couple of men get to their feet and move unsteadily in the direction of the light switch, to the accompaniment of the sound of a few more bottles hitting the floor.

Partial lighting returns as Ken appears from one of the doors at the back, carrying an iced cake upon which are placed half a dozen large candles.

"Who's the birthday boy, Cookie?" asks Billy.

"Nobody's, it's a farewell surprise for Andy. I know the candles are too big, sorry."

Despite having disposed of too many bottles of Tuborg, Andy is both surprised and touched by the totally unexpected gesture. The icing is already beginning to run and some of the men are soon making unkind suggestions about the ingredients.

"Shouldn't have done that, Ken. But thanks. OK lads, come and help yourselves." The men quickly gather around.

The C.O is first in line, slicing a sliver for himself. He raises it to beneath his nose, pauses, then slowly slips it into his mouth. "Mmm...this tastes good, Airman, very good."

"Don't encourage him, Sir," comes a slurred voice. "If you're not careful, he'll start showing you his collection of pictures."

"Is that so, Airman? I'm a keen photographer myself, so I'd be interested in seeing them. What made you sign up for catering rather than a photographer? You know you can always apply to re-muster into a different trade, don't you?"

"Well, Sir, I only started seriously when I came here, so I'm just a beginner," explains Ken.

"Be interested to see them – any more of that cake left?"

Andy is beginning to wilt and feels the need for fresh air. He rises from his bench and after a number of tentative steps is standing outside, looking out over the monsoon ditch.

He is soon joined by Martin.

"Enjoyed it here then?" asks the Music Man.

"Turned out a damn sight better than I thought it would."

"Not going to volunteer to stay on, are you?" laughs Martin.

"Not likely, it's not been *that* good."

"Well, I tell you I've learned to love the place. Great climate. Lovely, clean, deserted sandy beaches. Breathtaking sunsets. Left to get on with your job. No Police, no pressure – except on a Sunday morning to post the soccer results from home. Grub's a bit iffy, that's my only grouse."

"Going to stay on permanently then? You could become a resident like 'Santa', that chap we met when we rowed over to the other island," teases Andy.

"Not exactly, but I'll be putting in for another tour. Can't face going back to Changi, too big a camp for me – and all those 'Snowdrops' strutting around like the Gestapo."

"Aren't you anxious to know what's going on back home, don't you want to get back to normality?"

"Andy, just listen to yourself. What is normality? How do you start to define it? All the lads here seem to think about is getting back home, putting another tick on the demob chart. For most, that tick is the highlight of their day but in years to come they'll see this time, now, as the highlight of their life. None of them seem to be living for now, particularly the National Servicemen – nothing personal, of course!"

"Think we're getting a bit too serious, let's get back to the others," suggests Andy.

"I know it's a bit different for you because you're engaged, got someone waiting for you, but you should still enjoy what's going on around you at the time. Anyway, that's my philosophy. Who knows, in years to come you might even look back on your time here with affection and regard it as the 'good old days,' just like the old boys do at home talking about the First World War."

"Either you've had too much to drink or your music has muddled your head," laughs Andy. "Come on, let's get back to the others."

"No. See you in the morning, Andy, I know when I've had enough," comes the sobering reply.

Ken is waiting as Andy steps back into the Mess.

"Where's the Music Man?"

"On his way back to the billet, I think."

"Moody bugger sometimes. Told me he's going to miss you. Must be because you're the only one in the billet who doesn't tell him to belt up when he plays his awful music," says Ken.

"Actually, if you listen to some of it – and I mean *listen* to it – you'd be surprised how enjoyable it can be…"

"Crumbs! He's certainly worked his black magic on you. You definitely are in need of another drink."

Andy winces as Ken flips off another bottle top. His head is spinning, his stomach is grumbling and an emergency visit to the monsoon drain is on the cards.

Only a handful of partygoers remain, and one of them is the C.O.

"A word, if I may, young man," says the Flying Officer, taking a seat next to Andy. "In case I don't see you in the morning, thought I'd mention Flight Lieutenant Munro considered you had done a good job for him. He mentioned it on the 'plane on our trip up."

"Really, Sir?"

"Yes, he thought it might be in your interests to sign on," continues the C.O.

"Very good of him to say that but I've already got a good job waiting for me in the Civil Service. And it's pensionable, too," adds Andy.

"That means you're already focused on retirement. So let's see, if you're... what, eighteen, nineteen now?"

"Just nineteen, Sir."

"And assuming you retire at, say, sixty, we're talking of you getting your pension in... 1997?"

"That would be about right, Sir" replies Andy his eyes still closed after the laboured exercise in mental arithmetic.

"Then my question is, what thought have you, as a teenager, given to the forty intervening years? What will you be doing while you're waiting? That's just as important because..."

"Excuse me, Sir, but I think I'm going to be sick." The C.O moves quickly to one side to allow Andy to dash outside.

"Something, I said?" says the Flying Officer to Ken.

"No, Sir, he can't take more than a couple of drinks – not your fault."

"Not to worry, I'll catch him in the morning. And don't forget to drop your pictures into the office. I'll be interested to see them.

As the C.O leaves, Ken begins the thankless task of clearing up.

"Let's give you a hand, Cookie," comes the offer from Curtis who has lost his audience.

"Thought you had gone," says Ken.

"Just had to see Andy back to his billet. Poor kid's been pretty sick. They've cleaned him up a bit, dropped him on his bed and he's gone out like a light. Still got his shoes on, though."

"Thanks, Sarge."

"Hey, before you go, want to hear my first impersonation of the new C.O?"

"Go on then," says Ken.

"I *hard* the joviality, so I decided to investigate. Butlins this is not!"

Ken hesitates before giving his verdict.

"Not one of your best, Sarge, needs a bit of work."

Never one to welcome criticism, Curtis glares at the cook then disappears outside into the darkness.

It's the 'morning after'. Head throbbing, parched mouth, Andy is forced to accept his body is in rebellion. He opts to remain completely still inside his mosquito net. The risks of lifting his head are too painful to contemplate. For the moment, the billet lies silent although the emerging light will soon herald the dawn chorus. Andy drifts in and out of a shallow sleep before the crack of a deafening gun shot from outside brings him immediately into an upright position. Around him, fellow-sleepers from moments ago are now on their feet, while a couple of naked bodies have already made it to the door. Andy picks his way gingerly across the floor to follow them. All eyes are trained on the smoking, metal rubbish bin outside the billet, now upturned, against which is draped the front part of a bloodied, motionless green snake. The lid lays a few feet away, also smoking.

"What a mess!" says Brian.

"The rest of the beast is in the bin," adds Ken. "Look over there, that bloke with the shotgun is one of our grass cutters. What on earth has he been up to? If the truth were known, I bet the bugger's probably got hold of some of our missing ammo!"

Leaning against the door of his wooden tool shed, the grass cutter waves a triumphant hand in the air and shouts a few unintelligible words to the lads.

"No idea what that's all about, let's wait for Fatimah to arrive and we'll get a translation," suggests Martin.

The uninformed spectators return to the billet still speculating amongst themselves what actually happened.

Andy skips breakfasts. With a couple of hours to spare before his flight leaves, he decides to pay a last visit to the beach. But first a quick visit to the office to give a last-minute briefing to his successor on the danger that Fatimah might present.

He finds Brian head down, in search of an elusive letter on the keyboard. Alongside the typewriter are a number of manuscripts from the C.O waiting to be typed.

Andy's instant judgement is that only a few of them will be going out on today's aircraft.

"Don't stop, Brian. I'll talk while you type."

"Must be important for you to make a special visit. Fire away."

"Not that important. Just a word of warning about one of our locally engaged staff," says Andy.

"Fatimah, you mean?" replies Brian without looking up. Andy tries to conceal his surprise.

"So what have you heard?"

"Apparently she tried to chat up the Flying Officer last night, after work."

"And?"

"He told her to bugger off and concentrate on her washing. He's got her taped, don't worry."

"Is that pukka gen?"

"Overheard them myself on my walk round the camp."

Andy breathes a sigh of relief. "Right, I'm off to the beach. But first, I wish you all the best here. And remember, it's not forever."

"Thanks, I'll try to remember that," comes the unenthusiastic response.

Andy walks away to the sound of a clattering typewriter, punctuated by expletives from his successor. Less than two hours later he is airborne, heading west, gazing down thoughtfully on the sparkling, blue waters of the South China Sea.

26

After a nine month tour of duty on detachment to Borneo, Andy is finding it difficult to adjust to life on Changi, the biggest of the Royal Air Force stations in the Far East.

During the working day, his time is spent in a long, narrow office in SHQ.

Sergeant Moore, a soft-spoken and gentle character from the West Country, is in charge of the Movements Section. Fixed to the back wall is a blackboard, listing the arrival and departure dates of the troopships. Corporal Long, a lanky, short-sighted character from Teesside, has the sole responsibility for chalking up any alterations. When not in use, the stick of chalk remains locked in the Corporal's desk drawer. The complement of four is made up by a skinny, young, locally-engaged Chinese clerk called George, who sports a mop of spiky, black hair.

Andy is involved in the onward movement within the Far East of Airmen arriving from the UK and the repatriation of those going home. In addition, arranging internal flights, rail or road transport for those on temporary duty from Changi. Andy has no problems with the paperwork and there are long stretches during the working day when there is little to do. Not surprisingly, his two superiors take advantage of any lull in business to disappear, leaving him in charge. The Sergeant is known to slip away quietly during office hours to be with his wife and two children, while the Corporal pays spontaneous visits, during official time, to the village bars. At first, Andy finds himself taking telephone messages for his colleagues but, through necessity, is soon taking a more influential and authoritative role than his rank demands. His superiors are only too willing to delegate with the words "I'm sure you can handle it," or "Just popping out, I'll leave it to you." At the back of his mind, is the thought that a promotion to SAC could be round the corner – and with it a few extra dollars in his pocket each fortnight.

After work, Andy returns to a three floored concrete barrack block, housing well over a hundred Airmen, so markedly different from the wooden hut he had grown accustomed to in Borneo, sharing with just a dozen others. The off-duty facilities, in particular the Malcolm Club and the Astra cinema, are on a much grander scale than in Borneo. Little chance here of the projectionist suddenly showing the film upside down or the soundtrack disappearing with a visit from a tropical storm! Yet somehow there seems less camaraderie amongst the men. And there is, of course, a Police presence. In his first week, Andy has already been called to account by one of the unpopular 'Snowdrops' for dressing improperly. Nothing too suggestive, but nevertheless the crime of dressing in such a way as to exceed the permitted regulation distance between the top of his knee length socks and the bottom of his shorts. He decides it is time to mix, perhaps make some new friends. Unknown to him, however, his presence has already been noticed and both his working day and leisure time are about to be transformed.

It's close to midday. In the corridor outside the office, a group of Officers are huddled in discussion. Andy moves closer to them, attempting to eavesdrop.

"It's getting rather naughty at the schools, and it could well escalate," comes one voice.

"Time to both remind the men of the riot drill and get them down again on the rifle range to sharpen them up. The way this is shaping up we could be faced with major rioting all over the island."

One of the Officers spots Andy and ushers his colleagues out of listening distance. Soon the wise men disappear altogether into an adjacent room devoted solely to advice for those aircrew who find themselves downed in remote spots. The notice on its door reads: 'Jungle Survival School.'

"Catch any of that, Andy?" asks the Corporal.

"Something about the riots starting up. Bit of a flap by the sound of it."

"Done any riot control drill before?"

"Uh, no…"

"Right then, if they need someone from this office you'll be offered up. Understand?"

"Did a bit of riot duty in Borneo. That count?" counters Andy, recalling the aborted raid by the Japanese civilians.

"Nah, doesn't count. This is Singapore, not the same," confirms the Corporal.

"Anything I can help with, Corp? Or I'll take my lunch break now."

"Off you go but I've got something important you can help me with later. Not a word to Sarge, mind you, but important it definitely is."

The Mess is almost empty as Andy takes a seat. He is soon aware of being watched and suspects, being a newcomer, he is also being talked about. Just as he takes a first bite at what appears to be an incinerated sausage, words are being whispered in his ear.

"You the new bloke in the Movements Office?"

"I am actually," replies Andy coldly. "But for the moment I'm the new bloke in the Mess, trying to eat."

"Steady on, mate. Only wondered if you got any gen about when I was going home. Name's Woodfield, SAC, 999 are my last three – should be able to remember that!"

Andy looks up to a slim individual carrying an uncomfortable looking rash around his neck, which is being dabbed with a dampened handkerchief.

"Not a clue, sorry."

"Well, if you could find out or, better still, give me a push up the list. I'll make it worth your while. You'll find me in the Malcolm Club most nights."

Andy is taken aback by the unexpected approach. He has already heard in the office of a growing unrest amongst the long-service Regulars whose tour has expired, some of whom remain in the transit billet awaiting news of a sailing or flight time home. Their mood has not been improved with the knowledge that National Servicemen receive priority, given the fear of the Air Ministry that a Member of Parliament back home might protest at the mere sniff of a two year conscription period being exceeded.

He returns to the office to find Corporal Long waiting for him.

"That bugger George has gone home early – again! Another bloody family funeral, would you believe? No need to worry any more about the Chinese population taking over the world with someone in George's family circle popping off each week!"

"What's the job you got for me, Corp?" says Andy.

"Ah, yes. Organisational skills at the ready? You see, the Corporals have their own club – just like the Sergeants and Officers – but a special group of five of us meet together every night, Monday to Friday, to discuss all sorts of questions. You know, things like work, sport, women, although not necessarily in that order. So we have to get some beers in to break the ice…"

"But I'm not a Corporal," says Andy.

"'Course you're not – and you never will be if you keep interrupting me! You see, I'm always the Tuesday Man in the group when it's my turn to play host. Till now, I've organised beer delivery from the village, and the bills. Just the sort of job for a smart kid like you, I thought. Time on your hands and all that. Might be worth a promotion for you. I've got friends. Who knows?"

"Where do your wife and children go on a Tuesday night, Corp?"

"Funny you should say that, often wondered – never asked. Probably down the Married Families Club. At first they stayed in but then said it got too noisy for the kids to sleep. Is that agreed then?"

"Yes Corp," relies Andy dutifully.

"Good. Now get your ass moving. Today's Monday! Here's a bit of paper with all the gen. And just one final thing: when the Sarge is not around you can call me 'Lofty,' most people do."

Andy smiles as he pauses to recall his father's many stories of the Air Force's historic role in the War. Somehow those heroic tales of our men, as acted out in the films of *The Dambusters* and *Reach for the Sky*, seem a million miles away from his own paltry contribution as a National Serviceman.

Talk and rumour continues about the possibility of civil unrest in Singapore, and it has been decided by the powers above that everyone should be prepared and familiar with what might happen. The Movements Section are soon working with a rifle alongside their desk, awaiting a siren call which will send each of them scurrying to a pre-arranged position, in preparation for a 'make believe' attack on the adjoining airfield. Although it represents training, the attitude of the officers suggests that serious trouble is imminent.

The siren sounds as Andy is in mid-conversation on the 'phone.

"Drop that!" screams the Sergeant. "We're under attack! Get to your position, man."

Andy obliges and follows him down the staircase, before sprinting across the Parade Ground and taking his appointed position in one of the ditches overlooking the airfield. But as he is about to leap down into his concealed position, he can see the concrete base of the drain holds more than a foot of overnight rain, yielding an unpleasant stench. Andy decides to just lower his body and spread himself in a straddle position. It is, after all, just a training exercise.

Suddenly he feels the impact of a rifle butt thrust between his shoulder blades, causing him to lose his precarious stance and tumble, headfirst, into the ditch. His rifle splashes down into the murky water.

Andy looks up to face, first, the stripes – and then the angry face – of a Sergeant from the RAF Regiment.

"Keep your bloody head down, man! Worried about getting your feet wet, were you? Well, the news is: the enemy have just blown your fucking head off. You are, technically speaking, dead."

Andy resists the temptation to enquire whether his next of kin will be informed.

The Sergeant spits into the ditch before turning away and then breaking into a sprint across the Parade Ground.

At that moment a group of young children, returning from the nearby RAF-run school, stop to watch Andy retrieve his muddied rifle from the ditch and clamber out.

"You got real bullets in that gun, Mister? Can we play?"

Their innocent request is ignored as Andy limps back slowly to SHQ, stopping en route to administer a spit and gentle rub to a couple of nasty grazes on his leg. For the moment, still very much alive, he regrets wearing shorts.

There is a predictable greeting as he enters the office.

"What the hell you been up to?" asks the Sergeant, before breaking into laughter.

"Take 'em on single-handed, Marshall, did you?" laughs Lofty.

Before Andy can de-brief, a Squadron Leader arrives at the front of the office to report the outcome of the exercise.

"A total disaster, men, SHQ was completely overrun," comes the solemn verdict.

Head down, the Squadron Leader turns away to inform the other offices of the military disaster. The members of the Movements Section exchange glances, fighting bravely to conceal their amusement. No one can recall seeing the 'enemy' or hearing a single shot being fired.

The following morning finds Andy on the Parade Ground, working hard to hide in the second row of a hastily formed, ten strong Riot Squad. Behind him, a Sergeant is in full voice; in front of him, two men are holding a banner aloft.

"So on the front it says, in Chinese, 'Disperse or we fire'; on the other side is the same message, except it's in Indian," comes the explanation.

"You'll be under the command of an Officer, so pay attention. You obey orders. We don't need any John Wayne antics. Now you can expect to be under intense provocation by the locals, but don't be tempted to lose control. Any questions?"

But the attention of the Riot Squad is now focusing on a motley group of men, some twenty strong, forming up at the other end of the Parade Ground. Some are dressed in Chinese costume, more befitting their New Year celebrations than a military exercise: others have painted faces and fancy headgear. A few are wielding brooms, sticks and dustbin lids. One is armed with what appears to be a collection of bean bags, while another struggles manfully to prevent his ill-fitting dress from dropping to his ankles. Contrary to their appearance, they are all members of the Royal Air Force.

A voice close to Andy says: "I reckon that lot must be from the Drama Club. Not a bad wheeze to get off riot duty, pretending to be rioters." The comment is not lost on Andy.

The Sergeant moves to the front, turning to face the squad.

"Stop the chattering, you lot, this is serious. In a moment the locals – they're not really locals but for the purposes of this drill they are – will advance and threaten your position. Assume we are in the darkness of night, which means? ... WHICH MEANS?" raising his voice to a scream. There is total silence.

"Which means that we will first demand them to do – what?"

"To advance and be recognised?" comes a tentative reply.

"Exactly! Thank you. Any other questions?"

"What happens if the rioters can't read our banner 'cause they're not Chinese or Indian?"

"We'll deal with that when it happens. No more smart-arse questions. Here they come! Look to your front!"

The Drama Club prepare to make their charge. Directed no doubt by the promptings of a stage manager within their midst, the rioting crew advance to within twenty yards before their taunts begin. "Go home, Johnny." "Long live, the Emperor." "Tojo for King." "Down with the Queen." "Bring back Mosley!"

The words of the protestors lack any real venom, particularly since they are mostly delivered in a polished, theatrical accent. They are immediately called to order, ushered back to their starting point and ordered to put in a more threatening performance.

"For Christ's sake, you lot, you're supposed to be rioting!" comes a despairing cry from an Officer watching proceedings from an overhead balcony.

A spokesman for the actors steps forward, looks upwards, before claiming that a lack of sufficient rehearsal time is the explanation for their below par showing. A Warrant Officer joins the shambolic proceedings. Standing in 'no man's land,' between the rioters and their target he instructs the thespians to return to their starting position.

Far from being threatened, the Riot Squad are becoming increasingly relaxed, particularly as they witness a distressed, would-be Chinese lady, finally lose the battle to save his dress from dropping to his ankles. The ripple of laughter from the rioters which follows serves only to undermine the seriousness of the practise.

Clearly unhappy with his men's performance, the Sergeant promptly dismisses the Squad, and orders them to return at the same time tomorrow. Meanwhile the performing rioters hesitate before breaking ranks, awaiting no doubt the customary applause and curtain call which usually concludes their every show. Today there are no encores. Within minutes the parade ground is deserted, except for a couple of discarded bean bags that lie well short of their intended target.

Overnight, Andy reflects on his bizarre experience on the Parade Ground. He decides that tomorrow he will attempt to join the ranks of the Drama Club and seek a role as a routine rioter. As a newcomer on the camp, and dressed in the clothes and make-up of the opposite sex, there should be a good chance that no one will recognise him. Later in the day, Andy is back in the Block, making enquiries about the personnel and activities of the Club. The response is not an encouraging one. "They're an odd bunch." "Wouldn't stand too close to them!" "You're not one of them, are you, ducky?"

Andy has heard enough: he settles to grin 'n bear it, hopefully in the back row of the Riot Squad.

With the aid of a scratchy pen and a bottle of black ink, George is slowly and deliberately transferring names from a clutch of loose sheets into a bound book, which serves as a permanent record of postings. At his side, sits Andy.

"Can't you go a bit quicker, George?"

"So sorry, me not clever, Andy very clever man," comes the reply, followed by the customary apologetic smile.

"It's only copying for Christ's sake, not translating."

"You funny man, too," laughs George.

The other members of the office are listening as the locally-engaged clerk attempts to once again smooth away his occupational shortcomings with an offering of flattery.

"Funeral went off O.K yesterday?" enquires Andy

"Oh yes. So very, very sad."

"A close relative, then?"

George evades the question. "You practise here yesterday with guns? Why do that?"

"'Cause we're told to," laughs Andy. "Don't worry, George, we won't shoot you!"

The Chinese face is looking uncharacteristically serious, which prompts the question:

"You don't know what's going on down in Singapore, do you?"

"George know nothing," comes the reply, coupled with a wry grin.

Andy leans closer in order to whisper. "Tell you what, if I met you and your friends, late at night, in the back streets of Singapore would you ignore me, shake my hand or put a knife in my back?"

"Such things never happen," says George.

"And I'm very glad to hear that, too," replies Andy.

"You see, Mister Andy, George lives in Geylang – not back streets of Singapore."

The evasive reply is delivered with an inscrutable smile. The Sergeant and Lofty wait until their Chinese colleague leaves the office before walking forward to speak to Andy. "What's all that whispering about? You know what we think of him. Could be a spy," says the Sergeant.

"Don't be daft. He's just a bit slow," explains Andy.

"Tell you what," adds Lofty, "If the balloon goes up in Singapore, I bet you ten dollars that artful bugger will be on the wrong side of the barricades, and he won't be smiling at us."

A couple of lads from Andy's billet have talked him into joining them for a night out in Singapore and, with his earlier experience of visits with Finnegan to Bedok Corner and Orchard Road, it has taken some talking. After loosening up with a couple of beers in the Malcolm Club, the would-be revellers call for a taxi before heading westward to the inviting lights of the city. After less than fifteen minutes in the car, the driver is ordered to make an almost emergency stop as someone from the back seat spots a familiar roadside bar. "Throw a right here, John," comes the demand. "And don't you go away till we tell you. Got it?" The order is obeyed and the car comes to a sudden stop. "Christ Almighty, the first taxi I've been in where the brakes work," jokes one of the men. Anxious to please, the Indian driver smiles and nods repeatedly, waits for the car to empty, then parks at the rear of the establishment.

Andy catches sight of a partially lit overhead sign which tells him he has arrived at the 'Cameron Guest House.' "Should be no problem getting served here," laughs Keith Lewis, a slim native of Merthyr Tydfil, leading the quartet into an empty bar.

Pete Pilcher, a devoted Arsenal supporter from Islington, shuffles in cautiously.

"Must go steady tonight, lads, the ulcer is still playing up. You get the beers in – mine's a fruit juice – I'll take a look at what's on the jukebox."

The rest of the party seat themselves and immediately call for service.

Within moments, a Chinese man, in a well-tailored grey suit, appears to take the order.

A pair of attractive Siamese women, making last-minute adjustments to their skin-tight clothing, emerge from the darkness of a room behind the bar.

"Good evening, gentleman, welcome to my guest house. My pretty ladies will take your order. Tonight they are your hostesses, and you may buy them drinks if you wish. But no touch!"

The greeting and warning are delivered in impeccable English.

"Get him," says Lewis under his breath, as the owner walks away with the order. "You'd think he was talking about the flaming Raffles!"

Pilcher has brought the jukebox to life and the now familiar voice of Elvis Presley is soon filling the air, as the girls break into a series of seemingly uncontrollable bouts of giggling. Round after round of drinks follow and Andy decides that the driver should be asked to return later in the evening. It appears as if the joys of Singapore will have to wait for another night.

Negotiations for a tip to cover the driver's 'waiting' time is quickly concluded and the taxi heads back to Changi. As Andy returns to the table, he notices that half a dozen uniformed men from the Kings Own Scottish Borderers have arrived. A couple look decidedly the worse for wear, particularly a huge figure carrying a bloated stomach supported by a pair of tree-trunk thighs. The two hostesses appear to have transferred their attentions from the Air Force to the Army.

"Make this our last one, lads," is Andy's immediate advice to his companions.

"Bloody hell! He's right, Lewis, let's get out quick," adds Pilcher, taking an anxious look over his shoulder.

"I'll go when I've finished my drink, not before. The trouble with you two is thinking all 'Pongos' are always looking for a fight," replies the Welshman.

"Sod you both, I'm not waiting to find out," says Pilcher, rising to his feet before making in the direction of the toilet.

"Now then, it's my round," slurs Lewis. "Don't worry about the Pilch, Andy, let him go."

"Screw the nut, Taff, I've met this lot before and they can get nasty..." Before Andy can finish his sentence, an invitation is fired in their direction.

"Come over and join us, that's an order!"

In the background, the owner can be seen at the bar, reaching for a phone. The hostesses are now standing behind the bar, no doubt fearful of what might follow.

"See, they're not all bad," explains Lewis confidently, seemingly oblivious of the danger.

Two of the Army men are walking over from their table.

"You two deaf, or just trying to insult us? Our big man has invited you over for a drink. Didn't you hear him?" The tone is unmistakably hostile.

"We'll be over in a minute. Nice of you to think of us," replies Lewis.

"You Welsh, mate? – ' cause you're in luck as our big man is married to a girl from Cardiff."

"And who the fuck are you?" asks one of the party of soldiers, turning sideways to point a threatening finger at Andy.

"Me? No one really. Just someone trying to finish a quiet drink before I go."

The 'Big' man himself is now out of his seat and ambling across to join the discussion.

His massive legs struggling to keep his upper body on a steady course, and giving a convincing appearance of someone looking for trouble.

"So we're not good enough to drink with, are we? Outside now, you!" the command is directed at Andy.

"No need for that, we'll be off shortly."

"Too late, I said outside! Let's see who's still standing in a wee while."

All conversation comes to a sudden halt. The only voice to be heard is coming from the jukebox: Doris Day, in full flow, singing once more of her 'Secret Love.' "At last my heart's an open door," she warbles. An 'open door' thinks Andy, if only!

All eyes are now trained on the two would-be gladiators.

Andy rises from his chair, a strategy already forming in his mind to sprint out of sight under cover of darkness, leaving the ponderous opponent trailing in his wake. "And give him one for me," comes a call from one of the big man's party as the duo turn round to the side of the building. As Andy leads the way outside, the feeling of intimidation is sobering him up quickly and his heart is pounding. Out of the corner of one eye, and now out of sight of the others, he catches the shadow of his pursuer on the wall, now just a few steps behind. Andy is waiting for his moment to escape to safety. Suddenly, without warning, an enormous weight is crashing down on him, first his back, then shoulder: no sensation of fist or foot punishment, more like being the victim beneath a toppling tree. Andy takes evasive action and somehow drags his legs from under the falling body. The big man has stumbled and fallen partly into the deep monsoon drain surrounding the building, in a clumsy attempt to keep up with his prey.

He now lies in an untidy, groaning heap. Andy looks down at his adversary's badly grazed face and the blood covering the back of one of his grazed hands, the result of a failed attempt to steady himself against the pebble-dashed wall.

In the background, come the discordant strains of 'I Belong to Glasgow.' Andy decides that Lewis, now in full voice, is capable of looking after himself. It is with an exhilarated sense of relief that Andy faces the prospect of a long trek alone back to camp. Too late for a bus but, with luck, he might just be able to hitch a lift.

27

As anticipated, rioting has broken out in Singapore. It is a subject which has sparked a continuing debate in Andy's Movements Section.

Corporal 'Lofty' Long has little doubt about the origins of the local unrest. During the morning tea break he stands, hands on hips, in the centre of the office poised to impart his latest thoughts to his colleagues.

"I'm telling you, this whole mess is being masterminded by the Chinese in Peking. Bloody Communists! First Korea, then Malaya and now Singapore. The buggers are trying to take over the world – and what's more they've got enough people to do it. Breed like flies, you know."

Sergeant Moore intervenes, attempting to clarify the matter and allow work to resume: "Lofty, I don't disagree about the ambitions of the Chinese, but what you've forgotten is our country's reputation took an almighty nose dive when the Japanese invaded and took over Singapore. Until then, the locals in both Malaya and Singapore thought we were invincible. That was the point when they began to doubt us and wonder whether they'd be better off running their own country. It's already happened in India. Our Empire's fast disappearing down the pan. So it's not just the Communists that are involved, it's also people seeking independence, an opportunity to run their own country."

"How the hell can this lot run their own country, they've no experience?" replies Lofty.

"On that basis, Corporal, the Brits would never have taken over from the Romans."

"I'm not talking about the Romans. That was in the last century – this is now. We're talking here of terrorists. They don't call 'em CTs (Communist Terrorists) for nothing."

"Call them what you like, Lofty, but remember we were grateful to these same people – these so called terrorists – acting on *our* side as resistance fighters during the Japanese occupation. In my book we're all being served a lot of duff gen about what's been going on."

"How d'you make that out, Sarge?"

"Well, we're all told it's an Emergency 'Up Country.' Right? So how can you call a military operation that's being going on for eight years an *Emergency*? Don't make sense? It's a flaming War, however one dresses it up, and the reason for our not calling it a 'War' is to give the impression to the wider world that it's only a minor skirmish, almost a localised disturbance, and that we're still in control and needed here."

Andy is surprised to hear his Sergeant's strength of feeling on the subject. It is the first time that he has shown any interest in politics but, more disturbingly, it suggests he is questioning the policies of people in authority who surely must know best. Where is his loyalty? Is he perhaps a Communist sympathiser?

Lofty pauses to reflect on what is being said, then drops his head. The Sergeant braces himself, waiting for a profound response from his Corporal. Lofty raises his head from his chest, eyes partially closed as if in deep thought.

"And where's that bugger George today, that's what I want to know. Can't be at another funeral can he?" comes the unexpected question.

"Don't worry about him being added to the Chinese dead count, Lofty. Didn't you just say they breed like flies?" smiles the Sergeant.

As if by divine intervention, the 'phone rings. Andy scampers to the front of the office to field the call. "Yes, George, it is me. You all right?" The Corporal and Sergeant gather at Andy's side, close to the ear piece.

"Sorry to hear that, George," continues Andy. "OK then, you'll let us know later in the week when you're feeling better. 'Bye."

"What the hell's wrong with him?" asks the Sergeant.

"Said he's been in a car accident," explains Andy.

"Accident, my arse. I bet an Army patrol shot him during the curfew," suggests Lofty, breaking into a derisive snigger.

Andy finds it difficult to share his Corporal's suspicions about their locally-engaged, Chinese colleague. Granted, George sometimes struggles with the paperwork and his mastery of the English language is at best patchy but, beneath it all, there appears to be a genuine desire to learn and as for his being involved in rioting? – not a chance!

Andy decides against entering the discussion and slips quietly out of the office. He walks around to the front of the building and lingers on the first floor balcony, looking down at the airstrip as a Handley Page Hastings aircraft begins taxiing out towards the runway. Before the 'plane reaches its position for take off, he feels a strong hand clamp down on his shoulder. "Ah, just the man we need."

Andy spins around to catch the smiling face of the Station Warrant Officer. "This way, Airman," he snaps, pointing further down the corridor.

Andy follows, unsure of the destination and what is in store for him.

"But, Sir?"

"Where are you from, Airman? I take it you work here in SHQ?"

"Yes, Sir, Movements."

"That'll do. Now wait over there by the wall until I return. Understand?"

Andy looks across at the nearby office. The painted sign writing on the strip of wood over the door tells him he is now outside the 'Office of the Commanding Officer'.

Questions are spinning around in his mind: *what on earth is all this about, what have I done wrong? Why me?*

As he racks his brain for an answer, he can hear the sound of marching feet approaching.

With a straw-coloured shock of hair, a red-faced Airman suddenly comes into view, marching straight towards him. Closely behind follows the returning Warrant Officer, who is barking out a rapid- fire beat of "left, right, left, right, halt!"

Simultaneously, he points a finger at Andy. "And you, Airman, are to be escort to this wretched creature."

The Warrant Officer turns to throw a venomous stare at the now flustered looking and disgraced Corporal. "In short, this unsavoury character in front of you."

The accused is standing upright, in a frozen pose. The trio are joined by an another Airman who has been dragged into the action from a nearby office to act as a second escort.

"When I give you the Order – and not before – I will quick march the three of you into the C.O's Office. As escorts, you will stand either side of the accused, caps off, standing smartly to attention, facing the C.O. The accused will be read the Charge, asked if there is anything he wishes to say, then judgement. This one shouldn't take too long. Remember, the escort remains silent throughout. Understand?"

"Yes Sir," answers Andy, relieved in the knowledge he is being cast in the innocent role of a human bookend.

A few minutes later, the line of three stand facing the Commanding Officer, seated at his desk. A couple of paces behind him stands the Station Warrant Officer. The seriousness of the occasion suggests that a major crime has been committed. Newsreel pictures of the post-war Nazi trials at Nuremberg flash through Andy's mind.

The charge is read slowly by the Group Captain: "At 2100 hours on the 5th September, 1956, in the Married Families Club, the accused, 4140506 Corporal Douglas Crouch, gave an unsolicited rendition of the song 'Eskimo Nell', and in so doing did cause considerable offence to those present, in particular those of the female gender."

The Group Captain looks up solemnly to take a cold, penetrating look at the accused before adding: "Have you anything to say, Corporal?"

"No Sir. Didn't think there were any ladies in the place."

The Group Captain turns his head slightly to one side to receive a whisper from the Warrant Officer. Andy strains to catch what is being said.

"…Nor do I, Warrant Officer, I can't recall having heard this song. Jot down just a few lines of it on this piece of paper."

"To be honest, Sir, it's not one I'm too familiar with myself."

Andy finds it difficult to believe either of them. There follows an embarrassed silence.

The C.O clears his throat before looking up at the increasingly embarrassed Crouch, who is now sweating profusely.

"Corporal, I require you to speak – not, I hasten to add, sing – the words of 'Eskimo Nell'."

The accused stands open-mouthed, temporarily lost for words. His eyes drift upwards to the ceiling, seemingly focused on the whirring fan. Could the doomed Corporal perhaps be making a final peace with the Big Man above?

"Come on, man, spit it out!" comes the order.

"'Eskimo Nell', Sir?"

"That's what I said."

A few muffled words are uttered in response.

"I can't hear you, man. Speak up!"

The accused draws a deep breath, clears his throat. In a soft Southern drawl, he begins:

"When a man grows old and his balls grow cold
And the tip of his prick turns blue…"

242

"That's enough, Corporal! Stop! Silence!" screams the C.O, bringing the solicited but very much abbreviated song to an end. His lingering look of condemnation directed at the accused suggests the latter is destined for nothing less than the gallows. Surely he is doomed.

"That's enough, man, quite enough. Diss...gusting. And all that filth uttered in the hearing of ladies?"

Crestfallen, the accused looks down at his shoes having been duly named and shamed.

"You are awarded seven days," comes the immediate and damning verdict.

The Warrant Officer brings the hearing to a close with the Order: "Escort and accused: Left turn. Quick March. Left, right, left right..."

Having performed more like pantomime players than men on active Service, the trio exit.

The Warrant Officer waits outside. As Andy passes him, he feels a sharp dig in the back, together with the words, "And you can get your bleeding hair cut, Airman, you're looking like a proper nancy boy!"

It is now two months since Andy's return to Singapore during which time he has tried, without success, to ignore the fact that he has failed to receive a letter from Sandra. The hope persists that she will write saying she has thought again about their relationship and everything is back to normal; but letters from his parents pay only passing reference to her, and it is clear there seems little or no contact between them. When the other lads talk affectionately of their girlfriends or wives, Andy feels at a loss, reluctant to make a contribution. In a sense, it serves as a painful reminder of something special that has slipped out of his grasp, out of his life, while he remains out of sight, thousands of miles from home and powerless to act. Yet when alone, recalling and then dwelling on the happy moments they have shared, he can convince himself to be more positive about the future. After all, in seven months time he will be back in England. Everything could so easily and quickly change for the better.

As he lies horizontal on his mattress, reflecting further on his future with Sandra, he suddenly catches sight of an envelope which has been placed on his bedside locker, almost hidden behind his tea mug. Could it be? He levers himself up, leaning to one side to take a closer look. The writing that is visible is sufficient to show that it has been addressed in the unmistakeable hand of his mother, not Sandra. Andy slumps back in disappointment. Without opening the letter, he is sure of the advice it will contain and the precise words that will be used: predictable, parental words of guidance and comfort, well-intentioned and from the heart. But at this point in time, it is a letter from Sandra that he needs.

It is the third day of rioting, during which a curfew has been imposed by the government. Not surprisingly, there have been no incidents in Changi; but elsewhere across the Island pockets of rioting are breaking out in protest against measures to suppress what are considered to be Communist inspired activities. The consensus of opinion at Changi is that the Army will take the initiative in quelling any trouble; but as Andy well knows from his recent experience of parade ground drills and a compulsory visit to the firing range, the RAF have also been preparing to play their part, if and when required.

His last couple of nights have been spent in an office at SHQ working with a small team who are liaising with the two other Air Force Stations and the Army in the deployment of personnel. It is close to midnight as Andy's four hour shift is coming to an end. His replacement has already arrived and stands alongside his desk, preparing to take over. Andy rises from his chair, stretching his arms high above his head, with the comforting thought that within the next five minutes he will be walking back to the billet for a welcome night's kip. As Andy turns and makes for the doorway, he feels a heavy hand drop on his right shoulder.

"And where the hell do you think you're going, Airman?" comes the challenging question.

He spins around to catch the familiar face of the Station Warrant Officer, who had recently enlisted his services as escort for the recitation of 'Eskimo Nell'.

"Just finishing my four hour stint – and another man is taking over...," begins Andy.

"Well, I've got news for you, Airman. You are just about to start another stint. Stay right where you are, while I make this call."

Andy looks desperately to his Sergeant for help. Together, they have spent most of the evening taking calls and chalking up figures on a blackboard, interrupted only by a periodic visit from a Squadron Leader who, having assessed the latest information, would on each occasion mutter the word 'interesting' before disappearing.

"Sarge, do you know what's going on? It's midnight and I've done my shift, what do they want me for?"

The Sergeant, clutching a batch of signals in one hand, continues writing without turning his back. "Just got word of trouble down near Bedok Corner, there's a real flap on," he begins. His chalk is soon scratching angrily on the wall-mounted blackboard. "Most of our men are down at the port or on the airstrips standing guard and we've been caught on the hop by these crafty bastards. We need to get a detail down to Bedok, so he's trying to round up a posse, so to speak."

The Warrant Officer bounces back into the room, pointing directly at Andy.

"Right, you, downstairs. There'll be transport outside in the next five minutes to take you, and the others, to the Armoury and then the Mess. The Officer in charge will brief you on what's required. You've done Riot Drill, so remember what you've been told. Got it? And what have you done to your head? – you look like a shaven convict."

Andy is one of a dozen men who have been rounded up at short notice. Towards the end of his shift at SHQ he had found himself yawning; but now he is fully awake, yet uncertain of what the next few hours might bring.

Sitting inside a Bedford truck he faces a line of anxious-looking men as they head out of camp into the silent darkness. Directly across from him, lying at their feet and neatly tied, is the banner to be raised when rioters fail to disperse. Each man is armed with an Enfield 303 rifle and twenty rounds held in four clips. On each head sits a steel helmet; around each waist a belt and scabbard, holding a bayonet. A couple of the faces seem familiar. One bears a striking resemblance to a member of the Drama Club, last seen in action doubling as a rioter on the parade ground; another to one of the bandsmen.

What the hell did I do to end up here? Why couldn't have I got a home posting? These are the questions that Andy is asking himself.

"Bet it's a false alarm. There's been plenty of them, you know," comes the hopeful but nervous voice of an Airman sitting directly across from Andy. The suggestion is met with silence: the atmosphere remains tense. The truck picks up speed, seemingly hitting every bump in the road as it races past Changi Prison. Andy recognises a couple more familiar faces in the hastily-formed riot squad. One of them a cook and another from the Station Post Office. Someone drops a packet of biscuits on the floor and immediately there is a scramble of helping hands to recover the broken pieces. Momentarily, it serves to break the tension as the men jokingly speculate on the age of the biscuits. Andy is cursing his decision to switch to the late 8 pm to midnight shift. Had he stuck to the early shift he would now be safely tucked up in bed. His mouth is dry, his heart racing.

The truck slows, edging its way cautiously into and then through a deserted Bedok Corner. The place is in almost total darkness, with the only light coming from the headlights. There is an uncomfortable silence, so different from Andy's previous visits when people thronged the place late into the night, ambling past brightly lit food stalls with constant chatter from the traders and customers alike, together with the variety of inviting smells, filling the evening air. The vehicle stops some fifty yards away from a couple of cars parked close to each other.

The Officer in charge, a short stocky character, who has been sitting up front with the driver, jumps out and races to the back of the truck. "Out you get, Men, at the double!" comes the command. His words are delivered with a strong European accent, possibly Polish. For the moment, Andy decides that any attempt on his part to place the country of origin can wait. The wooden flap at the rear of the vehicle is dropped and the men pile out, casting an anxious look in all directions.

"Form up in two rows, quickly. Quickly, I said. Quickly!"

Apart from the impatient voice of the Officer, the only sound is from the waves lapping onto the adjacent beach. There is no sign of any rioters.

"I reckon we've come to the wrong place," whispers one of the men.

Andy begins to relax. Hopefully, as someone had predicted on the ride down, it could be shaping up for a false alarm. A voice immediately behind him has already picked up his train of thought. "And, with luck lads, we'll all get tomorrow off for doing this late turn."

Meanwhile the Officer, holding a sten gun at hip level, struts off further down the road, passing a number of boarded up shops, to take a closer look at the two parked cars.

He returns, stopping now and then to take a cautionary backward glance, before reporting back to the men.

"Keep your eyes peeled and let's have that banner stretched out – just in case. Whatever the problem, it's looking pretty damn quiet now, but we'll stick around a bit longer." Close at hand, but out of sight, a dog starts barking which quickly triggers a response from a canine neighbour.

There is a sense of relief amongst the men at the Officer's assessment of the position, which is followed immediately by the nearby sound of yet another dog barking.

"I think they must agree with you, Sir," laughs one of the squad.

The flippant remark is crushed at birth.

"Shut up and listen," orders the Officer.

Distant sounds of chanting are reaching the ears of the makeshift riot squad.

"Switch your bloody lights off, Driver! If the bastards get closer then it's full beam."

The driver obeys the order without comment.

The chanting becomes louder.

Questions among the men are coming thick and fast. "Are they heading in our direction?" "How many of them?" "Can't see a fucking thing in this darkness, can you?" "Sounds like kids, don't it?" The answers come quicker than expected.

The further of the two parked cars is being rocked violently, and at the rear of the vehicle a noisy crowd, some twenty strong, are hammering against its boot. Almost immediately comes the unmistakeable sound of shattering glass.

"What the hell are they doing that for?" one of the squad asks Andy.

"Don't know and I'm not going down the road to ask them either."

The Officer spins round to assert command. "You two, get that banner up in the air! Get moving!"

"Which side do you want us to show first, Sir, Chinese or Indian?"

"Good grief, man, it doesn't bloody matter! Hang it upside down if you have to. Just get it in the air and we've done our job."

The squad watch anxiously as one of the cars topples on its side. The doors are open and the seating is being ripped out and set alight. The number of those involved in this exercise of destruction appears to have doubled. Together, the crowd move slowly and menacingly toward the squad. The Officer has seen enough. "Driver, full beam!" comes the order.

"That's it, men, safety catches off. Load! Front row, one round, over their heads: Aim and Fire!"

Andy takes a deep breath, points his rifle skywards and pulls the trigger. The order itself has been enough to send most of the mob into instant retreat; a few rioters seek safety by throwing themselves face down on the road, then scrambling away on all fours. The volley of fire which follows hardly seems necessary.

"That showed 'em," laughs one of squad nervously.

"Don't worry, they'll be back," responds the Officer. Within minutes, his words are proved correct. The now burning cars illuminate the scene as the mob re-group and, led by a couple of men holding boards over their heads, move towards the squad. At their rear, and at a relatively safe distance from the action, a pair of turbaned Indian spectators can be seen hurriedly mounting their bicycles and pedalling away furiously under the safety of darkness. "Not again," thinks Andy, conscious that any further order will be more than a volley over their heads. He feels his clammy hands shaking as he tries to take a firm grip on his rifle. The crowd stop momentarily before unleashing a torrent of abuse, followed by a hail of sticks and stones which largely fall short of their intended target. They move closer. The Officer calls the squad to attention with the command:

"Fix... BAYONETS!"

The ominous clicking, followed by the customary slap of hands on the rifle to ensure the bayonets are firmly in place, have an immediate effect on the rioters. The sight and sound of the bayonets sends them scurrying away in retreat, peeling off to both left and right. Simultaneously, to the rear of the squad, a few of the local residents have emerged to witness the proceedings, having been disturbed by the gunfire. Unaware of the dangerous situation, two of the young children break free from their parents and begin to throw Chinese crackers bouncing in the direction of the squad. They fail to reach their intended target but the distracting sound of children screaming adds a surreal touch to the proceedings. Are the pair of youngsters acting in concert with rioters or is it an independent and spontaneous reaction to what is unfolding? The twin assault from opposite flanks, one hostile and the other hopefully playful, catches the men in a bizarre position. A few of the squad spin round to look in disbelief at what is happening. "All eyes front!" screams the Officer. "For Christ's sake, it's not 'Childrens Hour'!" Andy turns to face the real action, only to see that the mob are now in full retreat.

Within minutes, there is a screech of brakes as a couple of trucks draw alongside.

With timing lifted straight from a Hollywood Movie, the cavalry have arrived. The Army have come to the rescue. Their more professional-looking warriors clad in green battledress certainly look the part as they jump down from the vehicles, boots clattering on the tarmac, before moving purposefully into position. Their formidable appearance is enough to send the local children scampering back to the protective arms of their parents.

The few remaining rioters are now presented with a more challenging foe and quickly disperse. Even the local dogs are silenced.

The return trip to Changi sees a transformation in the mood of the squad, as a huge sense of relief fills the truck. The Officer has decided to join the men in the back of the vehicle. The words, "Mission accomplished, well done," follow. Andy has mixed feelings about his evening's work: surely shooting at unarmed civilians who may well have a genuine grievance is questionable, but is their rioting and damage to other people's property the right way forward? He recalls his father had forewarned him that, during the course of any lifetime, there will be occasions when one questions how they have ended up in an impossible situation. This has certainly been one such occasion.

Apart from a couple of the squad having been hit by stones, there are no casualties. It could have been a lot worse. Rioting mobs represent unpredictable danger. Tonight, the squad could consider themselves lucky. Meanwhile, the men are beginning to talk excitedly about the events of the past hour.

"I think I got one," comes a claim from beside Andy.

"And I got one, too," adds another enthusiastic voice.

"I didn't see anyone staying down. All those who went down, got up," interjects one of the squad. The sobering remark fails to dampen the euphoric mood.

"Wasn't too bad was it, men?" says the Officer.

"No Sir. Thinking back, gave me a bit of a buzz," comes the first response.

"Me too, Sir," confirms another comment.

"Wouldn't mind doing it again," adds someone else, enthusiastically.

Andy's thoughts turn to Chinese George from the office. He couldn't possibly have been there tonight amongst the rioters – or could he? Certainly Lofty would have put money on it!

The riots peter out within days and the curfew lifts. No longer are the jeeps and vehicles to be seen on the roads fitted with black wire netting covering the windscreens. The scale of the riots and the resultant casualties have been conveniently written-down in the local

Press. The politicians have had the final say on what has been reported in the newspapers. Locally-engaged staff return to normal duty on the station and George is back at his desk, albeit in a somewhat subdued mood. Meanwhile, Andy is aware that Lofty is waiting to pounce with probing questions to their Chinese clerk as to how he spent his time during the curfew. The Corporal's patience soon evaporates.

"So you feeling better now, George, nothing trivial I hope," comes the cynical opener.

"George feeling much, much better, Corporal."

"Good, 'cause you're well behind with your paperwork. So get moving, pronto."

Andy attempts to defuse Lofty's hostility towards George by changing the subject.

"Everything all right with the Tuesday evening arrangements, Corp? In case you haven't noticed, I use the few dollars over buying some extra nibbles to go with the drink."

"Yes, young man, everything is running very smoothly. But now all the other lads have started laying on bloody nibbles. So we have the bloody things Monday to Friday! Seriously though, you're doing a good job."

"Thanks, Corp."

"By the way, as a sort of recognition of your efforts, you're invited to a special party I'm having tonight," smiles Lofty.

Andy's heart sinks at the thought of an evening in the company of someone who is reputed to have already moved to a level approaching alcoholism.

"Tonight? I'm not too sure…"

"It's an order, Airman. We meet outside the Corporals Mess at seven, sharp."

"How many going?" enquires Andy tentatively.

"My usual drinking buddies, you know, the Monday to Friday group. And I've dropped the word to the girls downstairs in Accounts – a couple seemed pretty interested."

Andy returns to the Block to prepare himself for the unwelcome ordeal of a heavy night of drinking. As he showers, he already has a good idea of the two girls who will be joining the party. One is a bubbly, attractive brunette Corporal called Joan, best known for attracting male attention with her tight fitting KD uniform and provocative off-duty outfits; the other, Mary, a plump, dour character with a mousey pudding basin haircut, with a passion for motor bikes and an obvious lack of interest in both her appearance and her ongoing body odour problem.

With time to spare, Andy takes the opportunity to read a letter from his parents.

Dearest Andrew,

Received your letter and so pleased to hear you have settled in at Changi. It must have been quite a re-adjustment for you from being on that dreadful Island.

Your dad has reminded me of the demob charts that Servicemen used to keep. I'm not sure if you have one – but we have one now!

We've been looking through your old clothes and thought of throwing some of them out, or giving them to charity. But we've decided to wait till you return. It's not as if we are pushed for room. As you'll be coming home in Winter you'll need to wrap up. Don't want you to go down with a cold or 'flu as soon as you get back!

Sad to say, no good news to tell you about your Plymouth Argyle team. Relegated last season and they've lost their first five games this season. Your dad has stopped going, so they must be bad.

Hadn't heard from Sandra for quite a time, so we popped round to see the family. Her parents were in but seemed distinctly uneasy, almost reluctant to invite us in. It was in the evening and we asked where Sandra was. We were shocked to hear that she was in hospital. "Nothing too serious, nothing to worry about," her dad said. When we asked whether we could visit her they got edgy and said she was due out shortly and there was no need. We asked which hospital it was so that we could send her flowers but they said there was no need to waste our money because she wasn't really a flower person. Must say we found the whole thing rather odd. No doubt she's confided in you with all her problems but we do feel rather shut out. After all, she will soon be our daughter-in-law! When you next write, don't forget to remind her you still have a mum and dad living only a couple of miles away

Andy stops reading and slowly slips the letter back in the envelope.

His mother's words leave him feeling numb. How can he tell his parents his fiancée has stopped writing? The prospect of any wedding or a future with Sandra seem a million miles away. Was she perhaps not wishing to worry him about a minor medical condition – or was it something serious? O.K so her last letter might be interpreted as a 'Dear John' but surely they were still friends and the door hadn't been completely closed – or had it? Perhaps it is for the best for his parents to remain unaware that their relationship is on hold. Perhaps tonight is the ideal opportunity to put it all to the back of his mind. Why not? Switch off, relax and forget. A few extra beers might just do the trick.

As he approaches the Corporals Mess, Andy catches Lofty at the wheel of his aged Standard Vanguard, waving a hand of welcome.

"Get in the front with me," comes the driver's command.

As Andy makes himself comfortable in the front seat, he is aware of the contrasting aromas wafting through from the back seat.

"The two ladies behind you, Joan and Mary, are from downstairs in Accounts. They're coming to my unofficial promotion party as well," explains Lofty.

"Promotion?" gasps Andy. "When did that happen?"

"It hasn't – yet. But I've got contacts and it'll soon be through so it means you can delete Corporal Long, substitute Sergeant Long. Good news, innit?" adds Lofty proudly.

Followed by a second car, containing three of Lofty's regular drinking group, the party drive for some twenty minutes, passing through Bedok Corner before coming to a stop at a Chinese restaurant further along the coast road. Andy's first impression of the choice of venue is a mixed one. As he steps out of the car, he is aware of the sound of the sea which immediately evokes childhood memories of his countless visits to the Hoe in Plymouth. But there is also a decidedly unpleasant smell, similar to sewage, filling the evening air. He quickly picks up the pace, passing an abandoned car which has been stripped of its rear wheels. Lofty leads the party inside. The waiters in the dimly lit place far outnumber the few customers.

One steps forward, offering first a token bow and then a welcoming smile.

"How many of you, Sir?"

"You should know that one, John, the table was booked this morning," snaps Lofty.

"Of course, Sir, this way." The waiter attempts to usher the party through a gap between the empty tables into a darkened corner.

"No, no John, if we've come all this way – and it's a special night – we might as well be outside, next to the sea." Lofty points outside to the a large, circular table on the patio. The rest of the party prepare to follow.

"But that table already booked, Sir," pleads the waiter.

"Dead right it is, and I've just booked it," laughs Lofty. "Don't worry, you'll get a good tip at the end of it all. Isn't that right, lads?"

There are grunts of support from the partygoers, one of whom walks to the edge of the patio and looks down at the water lapping just a few feet below.

"Hey, Lofty, when we've had a few beers we can go for a swim down here. Short slope – then straight in!" The suggestion falls on deaf ears.

The party of seven spread themselves around the wooden table. Lofty is seated with his back to the water and is soon holding court. The initial order for drinks receives an immediate response, and the first few rounds are despatched without delay. Andy is soon aware he is in for a night of serious drinking. Meanwhile the waiters hover close at hand, ensuring that no glass remains empty. From inside the restaurant comes the muted sound of music which, together with their continuing intake of alcohol, prompts each of the Corporals to invite Joan to dance. A pattern unfolds. As soon as she returns to the table with a partner, she is immediately whisked away into the welcoming arms of another. The competition for her attention intensifies. The drinks continue to flow. Meanwhile, Mary is left as the unwanted wallflower to seek solace in sinking a steady flow of 'Singapore Slings.' Suddenly, her head drops with a thud on the table top, narrowly missing a vase of paper flowers. Andy attempts to console her, gently putting an arm around her shoulders.

"Where's Lofty?" she mumbles, struggling to lift her head.

"He's here with us tonight, Mary. Don't worry. It's his unofficial promotion party. Remember?" The words of explanation are in vain. Mary has passed out.

Andy decides to finish what is left of one of Mary's 'Singapore Slings." Added to the 'Tiger' beers he has already sunk, he realises his legs are turning to jelly.

One of the 'dancing' Corporals slumps into the seat alongside.

"You enjoyed that, my friend. 'Ave another, Lofty's paying. By the way, where is he?"

"He's probably inside dancing with Joan."

"O.K, just wondered."

Somewhat exhausted from her continuous dancing sessions, Joan returns to the table.

"You all right?" she asks Andy. "You've had enough," she adds, taking a long look into his eyes.

A waiter returns to clear the array of empty glasses littering the table.

Having stood patiently in line to treat Joan to a farewell kiss, the three Corporals now turn to question Andy. "What's Lofty up to?" "Where is the bugger?"

"Yeh, where is the old sod?" adds Joan.

Andy takes a quick look around. "Don't worry. He's probably having a pee, I'll tell him you've gone."

"Don't think so, just been in there," counters one of the Corporals.

The discussion is interrupted by the sudden arrival of the manager, waving his hands excitedly in the air. He is out of breath and struggling to speak.

"Calm down, John, you'll be paid," says one of the Corporals.

"No, no. You no understand. Your big friend in water on way to big sea."

"What, Lofty!" gasps Andy.

There is a rush to the edge of the patio. The tide has come in and the water below is almost lapping against the wall of the restaurant.

"Look! there's a broken bit of his chair," cries Joan. "Oh my God."

"Daft bastard. Must have fallen backwards, slid down the bank and gone straight in," suggests one of the Corporals. "Where the hell is he? Oh, look, over there, that's him floating on his back. Wonder the silly sod hasn't drowned himself!"

"It bloody well is – it's Lofty!" screams Joan, pointing out to the prostrate figure.

A small boat, with two of the kitchen staff aboard, is already closing in on the floating body. Amidst cheers from the RAF contingent gathered on the patio, Lofty is slowly hauled from the water and dropped into the boat, with his weight causing it to lurch wildly from side to side.

"Hope he's still got his shoes on," says Andy.

"Why worry about his damn shoes? He's alive that's all that matters," replies Joan.

"You don't understand. Lofty got 'jumped' last month by some 'Pongos' when he was totally sloshed. They took everything from him. Ever since, he carries his money in his left shoe."

28

Summer, 1956

News has reached Singapore of the Anglo/French invasion of the Suez Canal.

While many of those serving on the camp struggle to comprehend exactly what is happening, the crisis is creating a more practical problem for the Movements Section: delays to the repatriation of personnel to the UK. Unable to use the Canal, troopships are forced to take the much longer route around the Cape, while aircraft movements are affected by over-flying restrictions operating in the Middle East. The result is that the Transit Block at RAF Changi, holding those waiting to return home, is bulging at its seams. It is the National Servicemen who have an edge over the Regulars, given the Air Ministry's concern to avoid the adverse publicity that would follow from any conscript serving in excess of two years.

Andy is made fully aware on a daily basis of the growing frustration felt by those awaiting information of their flight or sailing date, the most prominent of whom remains SAC 'Woody' Woodfield, a long-term Regular and consequently way, way down any list for repatriation. Having at first made weekly visits to the Movements Office, Woody is now resorting to daily 'phone calls. The Sergeant and Lofty decide the man has become a total nuisance and a plan of action is agreed. As they talk, yet another call is being received from him.

"SAC Woodfield here – again. Sorry to be a nuisance but I've got to get home as soon as poss."

"So do hundreds of others here…" replies Andy sharply.

"Listen, mate, I don't care whether it's by boat, 'plane or bloody rickshaw. My parents are knocking on a bit and if someone in your outfit doesn't pull their finger out soon, I could miss seeing one or both of them again before they snuff it."

"Do either of them have a terminal illness?"

"No, mate. They're both alive."

"Hold on, I'll put you onto the Corporal."

"Corporal Long here. Can you come up to the office first thing in the morning? I might just have some news for you."

There follows a silence.

"Woodfield, you still there?" asks Lofty.

"Yes, indeed Corporal. I'm very much here and thank you so much."

"See you in the morning then?"

"You bet. And thanks once again."

Lofty puts the 'phone down and the members of the office, apart from George who as ever holds an inscrutable expression, explode into spontaneous laughter.

Woody is waiting at SHQ the following morning, half an hour before the staff arrive. Bottle in hand, he greets Andy on arrival.

"Fancy a Coke? I'll get you one from the machine. No problem."

Andy declines the offer.

"No thanks. The Corporal will be here in a minute. You'll have to speak to him."

"Yeh! 'course. Hardly slept last night with the excitement of it all."

Lofty arrives with an uncharacteristically solemn look on his face.

"In you come, Woodfield."

The pair walk to the back of the office, out of earshot of anyone else.

"Now what I have to tell you is in the strictest confidence, not to be divulged to another living soul. Got it?" begins Lofty.

"Of course, Corporal, not a word to anyone."

"You see if the others waiting for news hear what we're doing for you, they'll be livid – and it will all fall through. Got it?"

"Absolutely. I've got it, Corporal," says an excited Woody.

"Right. Well here it is: you're going home by – boat!"

"That's great news – and when do I sail?"

"Ah, that's the tricky part. All hush-hush. The ship is currently on a secret mission and we won't be told of its arrival until it's almost here. Now that is strictly secret gen, so not a word to a soul. Understand?"

"Exactly, Corporal, and thanks so much. It's not a submarine, is it?"

"Hush-hush, didn't you hear me? So, no more visits or 'phone calls to this office. We'll let you know when we have some more info," concludes Lofty, placing a vertical finger to his lips.

Woody leaves the office with a new-found spring in his step.

"Daft sod, deserves all he gets," laughs Corporal Long to the other staff, "that should keep him away from here for a while."

Meanwhile, George is at the counter struggling to explain travel details to a couple of Airmen who are being sent 'up country' to Fraser's Hill in Malaya. Andy comes quickly to the aid of his colleague.

"Any problems, chaps?" he enquires casually. George retreats to his desk and begins a bogus rearrangement of his papers. Business concluded, Andy joins George to identify the difficulties the Chinese clerk has experienced.

"What was the problem then?"

"My English no clever, Andy clever." Andy suspects that George is not progressing as he should and feels in part responsible.

"I'm off for lunch now, George, we'll have a chat when I get back."

"O.K," comes the subdued reply.

Andy has barely reached the ground floor when he discovers he has left his wallet behind. He spins around and scampers up the stairs. Taking a short cut through a backroom, he re-enters quietly at the rear of his office aware that George, with his back to him, is deep in conversation on the 'phone. Andy picks up his wallet but hesitates before leaving in case his colleague might need some assistance. To his total surprise, George, unaware that there is anyone else in the room, is in an articulate mode, employing a comprehensive English vocabulary as he questions in some detail, whether his pay has been calculated correctly. "I remind you that calculation to arrive at figure in that column does not tally... if inaccuracies reappear on next slip, I have no alternative but to..." Andy stands stunned. No question about it, Lofty was right: George has been stringing his workmates along.

The following day, Andy is alone preparing to close the office. The 'phone rings.

A glance at his watch tells him the call has arrived outside office hours. He pauses before lifting the receiver.

"Hello! Hello!" comes the desperate cry.

"LAC Marshall speaking."

"Flight Lieutenant Marsh here. I'll speak to your Sergeant."

"Not here, I'm afraid, Sir."

"All right, so I'll speak with your Corporal – Long, isn't it?"

"Not here, either, Sir."

"Damn it, I'll have to speak to you. Now listen here, we suddenly have a spare seat on a BOAC flight leaving Paya Lebar late tonight. It's got to be filled and I need a name from your office. Now then, who's next on your priority list? If you can't give me a name now, find one PDQ and ring me back in the next ten minutes. It's crucial that the spare seat is taken." The caller drops the 'phone with an abrupt thud.

Andy spends the next five minutes looking for the master list, before finally locating it at the back of one of his Sergeant's desk drawers. His eye scans the names on the front page and settles on an Airman carrying a seven figure digit National Service number beginning with 275... As he waits to be connected for the return call, he flips through to the back pages and catches the name of Harry Ashton, a Regular and a former colleague on detachment in Borneo. *Perhaps? Why the hell not!* thinks Andy to himself.

"Flight Lieutenant Marsh, speaking."

"Got a name for you, Sir, Sergeant Harold Ashton."

"And he's in the Transit Block – at this moment? Ready to go tonight, I trust?"

"Yes, Sir."

"Excellent. Contact him immediately, then get back to me to confirm."

Andy locks up and dashes down to the ground floor. Fortuitously, one of the despatch riders is outside SHQ about to kick-start his machine.

"Couldn't give me a lift to the Transit Block?" shouts Andy.

"Out of my way actually – but hop on quick."

In a matter of minutes, Andy is dismounting. He bursts into the ground floor. A number of familiar faces walk towards him.

"Just the man I want to see," laughs one. "Hey, any news for me?" enquires another.

"Anyone know where Ashton is?" shouts Andy.

"On the next floor – or in the Malcolm Club," comes the reply.

Andy scampers up the stairs. Finally, he is directed towards Harry's bed. The Brummie is fast asleep, face down on his bed. He decides to prod his dangling arm.

"Harry, it's me, Andy. Got some great news for you. Come out to the balcony."

Reluctantly, Harry turns his body around, lets his feet drop to the stone floor, slips on his flip-flops, and follows Andy onto the balcony, out of range of their being overheard.

"Better be something good to ruin my kip."

"No mucking about, got you on a flight tonight," begins Andy.

"Bugger off!" comes the immediate response.

"You're on a flight tonight. I'm telling you," repeats Andy.

"Oh yeh, BOAC is it? Fuck off!"

"It is actually. And that's pukka gen, Harry, trust me."

"O.K then, show me the papers."

"Come back to the office and I'll prove it," pleads Andy, suddenly aware that his intended good turn could misfire.

"This better be good or… "

As Andy turns away, he feels Harry's hand on his shoulder holding him back.

"If this turns out to be some sort of joke, I'll knock the daylights out of you."

"Come on, Harry, we'll use a couple of bikes – I saw a few hanging around downstairs. Nobody'll mind if we just borrow them."

The pair quickly make their way to SHQ.

"Haven't done this since I was a kid," says Harry excitedly, as his bike veers dangerously close to a monsoon drain. His sceptical mood is changing by the minute.

As Andy turns the key in the office door, Harry is becoming aware that the prospects of a speedy return home are a possibility but he remains puzzled at his unexpected good fortune.

"Why haven't you put one of those National Servicemen on this flight. Those bastards always get the first shout?"

"Because I'm doing you a favour, Harry."

"That's what worries me, favours cost money."

"Not this one, I can assure you!" laughs Andy.

"Just as well 'cause you should remember from Borneo most of my money goes straight home, without me seeing it."

Harry stands listening and scratching the back of his bald head as Andy makes a call, confirming the passenger's details and receiving information about transport to the airport, check-in and baggage entitlement.

He is showing little emotion, while Andy begins to question his efforts in trying do someone else a good turn.

"That's done, let's get back to your Block. You'll have to move quickly," says Andy.

"I'll race you back," smiles Harry.

It's the first time Andy can recall seeing a genuine smile on his friend's face. The Brummie's cynical mood is fading away. The pair say their farewell at the foot of the stairs leading to the first floor of the Transit Block.

"Have a good trip then, Harry," says Andy.

"All this rushing about better be worth it, I tell you. And if it turns out to be some bloody sick joke, I'll catch up with you, I'll hunt you down."

There is not the slightest suggestion of thanks. Andy knew it was never on the cards – but it would have been appreciated.

An exhausted Andy walks into his billet. To his dismay, the unmistakeable figure of Woody is in conversation with a group of Airmen, explaining his good fortune in winning a berth home on a special boat.

Andy spins around on a sixpence, heads outside and in the direction of the Malcolm Club. Any further discussions about repatriation dates are definitely off today's menu, but a couple of Tiger beers are very much on.

The soccer season is in full swing on the camp. Most of the Sections are represented in a League from which the Station draws the better players for their First and Second Elevens. Keen to resume playing, Andy is making enquiries within the Admin Wing to discover if there is a chance of getting a game.

"Huntley's your man," advises Sergeant Moore, without hesitation.

"Understand he's quite a player. Quick, two-footed, reads the game well and truly inspirational to his team mates."

"Seen him play then, Sarge?"

"Never, but that's what he told me."

"Could have added 'modest', couldn't he?" smiles Andy.

"What *are* you talking about? Get back to that filing, now's the time to do it while things are quiet."

Andy catches up with Huntley later in the day as they queue in the Mess.

The short, plumpish character, with his chin jutting forward, is addressing the cook behind the counter in a superior manner. Andy has already seen him strutting around SHQ but never exchanged a word.

"Any chance of a game?" comes Andy's tentative opener.

Admin Wing's self-proclaimed soccer star, takes his time before responding. First, he takes a couple of paces away, clearly making an assessment of Andy's physique before pursing his lips, "Played much?" he enquires in a barely disguised tone of disinterest.

"Yeh, quite a bit back home and more recently on detachment in Borneo."

"Problem is we've now got a pretty settled team which I'm loath to break up. Had a difficult start to the season and at the moment it's beginning to come together. I'm doing my best with them but I can't do it all myself."

"So the answer is 'No,' is it?"

"'Fraid so. Mind you, we can always do with support on the line, so if you can get down to cheer us on that would be great."

Huntley turns away quickly to join a group at another table.

Before pressing his case further, Andy decides he will watch the Admin team in action.

He doesn't have to wait too long. The following evening, he arrives at the Pagar, a grassy area accommodating three football pitches and one hockey pitch. A quick glance at his watch confirms the game has been running for only a few minutes. Almost immediately, the Admin goalkeeper is retrieving the ball from the back of his net. Andy sidles up the touchline to join Joan from the Accounts Office, dressed in a pair of tight-fitting, pink slacks and a low cut top. For a moment, he wonders whether her presence is acting as an unnecessary distraction to both teams.

"Bit of a shame to concede such an early goal."

"Early goal! You're joking, that's the third one they've let in," laughs Joan. "The only attraction about this game is their left winger. Got a lovely bum."

Andy moves further on down the line. The opposition, Signals Section, are in total command and scoring at will. Huntley, stationary in midfield, is screaming in desperation at his team mates, all to no avail. Most of his side look not only hopelessly out of condition but much older than their opponents. Andy has seen enough. He heads away from the field, passing an Indian boy handing out newspapers. He accepts a copy of the *Free Press*. On his return to the billet he looks first to the back page for any soccer news from back home.

To his surprise, there is a somewhat disproportionate coverage of Service football, complete with match reports and named scorers for virtually every game, irrespective of its importance. As such, it is a publication guaranteed to have an immediate and popular appeal with many Airmen; but it also presents the opportunity for any Serviceman, with time on their hands, to drift onto the more serious pages and perhaps read and sympathise with the extreme left-wing views it expounds. Not surprisingly, the leading article contains a scathing criticism of the United Kingdom and France for their attack on the Suez Canal. Back at work the next morning, Andy overhears a couple of lads from Accounts joking about the Admin keeper who let in a dozen goals the previous evening. He wonders whether his offer to play might now be taken up.

Coincidentally, his presence at the match had been spotted by a spectator on an adjoining pitch, someone with whom he had played on detachment in Borneo. The player in question is now standing at the Office counter. His name is John O'Neill, a popular lad from Luton and now captain of both RAF Changi's First Team and the Combined Services side.

"I thought it was you chatting to that attractive girl. Got to admire your taste."

"John, it's not like that at all…"

"Andy, just joking, but why weren't you playing down there? Injured – or just lazy?"

"Having trouble getting a game here," says Andy.

"That's easily settled, come and play with Tech. Wing. We'll find you a place."

In the weeks that follow, Andy is playing regularly and well enough to gain a place in the Station First Team. As an unexpected bonus, he finds himself on one of two coaches bound for Johore to play for RAF Changi in the annual friendly match against the Sultan's Private Army. The first coach carries players, manager, medic and trainer; the second is full of officers and their wives, keen to take the opportunity for a privileged look at the Palace.

Andy and his colleagues catch their first sight of the imposing white building, with its decorative towers as they drive over the Causeway separating Singapore from Malaya. They enter the extensive grounds and, as they draw close to the Palace itself, the driver points out the balcony from which the Japanese Generals surveyed the Island of Singapore prior to its invasion in 1942.

"Why would the Sultan invite a bunch of us for a game of football here?" comes the question from a team mate sitting behind him.

"Why don't you ask the driver, he seems a bit of a know all," suggests another.

The team's Medical Officer, seated across the aisle, has already picked up on the conversation.

"Actually, the answer to that is very interesting. As soon as it became clear – back in 1941 – that the Japanese were likely to invade Malaya, the Sultan made it clear to both sides that he was going to take a neutral position, no doubt hoping to preserve his Palace and wealth. When the War ended, the news of the surrender was relayed to him at the Palace by a couple of RAF blokes – not the Army, as one would have expected. Apparently the Sultan claimed to be particularly delighted with the outcome and subsequently decided that, in return for delivering the good news, the RAF should be invited to come here each year and play against his private Army. So here we all are!"

Andy notices that the second coach is heading off in a different direction, towards the entrance to the Palace, while his driver is taking the team to what looks like a sports pavilion. The team are led into the changing rooms. The facilities are sumptuous, spotless with mirrored tiles. Slightly old fashioned, but impressive by any standards, with gold-plated taps to each of the many washroom sinks. A pile of neatly folded large white towels lay on top of each of the wicker baskets, hair brushes and small hand towels are placed alongside each hand basin, together with a generous ration of scented soap. There is also an inviting communal plunge bath. The lads are mightily impressed. They change into their playing gear, simultaneously receiving a brief team talk from their coach, Flight Sergeant Hayes. No mention is made of the opposition who are clearly an unknown quantity. The team file out of the pavilion, running down a steep grass bank onto the field, in pursuit of footballs being fired over their heads from the coach. As they reach the level surface of the playing field, they find to their surprise there is not a single goalpost in sight. They stop and question whether they are running in the wrong direction.

"Look at this turf! I reckon this is a huge bowling green. We must have come the wrong way," comments one of Andy's team mates.

"Where's the damn pitch? There's nothing marked out!" says another.

Unknown to the men from Changi, the answer is fast approaching them from behind.

Two goals, complete with nets are being wheeled out on rollers by four of the opposition players, pushing hard against the upright posts.

As the teams limber up on the field, a group of gardeners are engaged in a last-minute marking out of the touch lines; and as the referee is about to start the game a pair of workmen encroach onto the pitch in an attempt to double-check the markings of the penalty area and centre circle. The referee loses his patience and orders them from the field of play. Before leaving the field, they turn and bow to the players. Finally, the game is under way. Andy takes a quick look at the opposition who appear to have been selected solely on their strength and height. All are towering Indians, whose facial expressions suggest they will not be treating the game as a friendly.

The match assumes a frantic pace but gradually slackens as the heat affects both sets of players. Dehydration is more of a problem for the boys from Changi but by half time they have already scored enough goals to put the game out of reach of the Sultan's men. During the half-time break they are in a relaxed and jovial mood as copious amounts of iced water provide temporary relief for their overheated bodies. The opposition, heads hung low, appear to have already accepted defeat. Just as they prepare to restart, a special visitor is arriving.

Coming across the immaculate sward towards them is the Sultan himself, being pushed in a wheelchair, accompanied by a quartet of servants who are fanning him with pink and white plumes. A fifth member walks slightly behind, an umbrella held aloft to shield his master from the sun.

The match is put on hold as the Sultan reaches the touchline. Andy is but a few feet away and catches the blank expression on his tired, wrinkled face. There had been much talk on the coach of his immense riches, with figures too huge to comprehend, and yet his appearance suggests an unhappy person. Andy concludes that it also is the face of a very sick man. The servants are going into overdrive with the fans. Not a word is uttered. Without having said a single word, the Sultan bangs his hand on the arm of the chair and the party about-turn, allowing the match to continue. His time with the Changi players and their staff has been fleeting but it is a gesture that is appreciated.

On his way to take up his position for the re-start, the Changi goalkeeper stops for a brief word with Andy.

"Did you hear the creaking of those wheels on the Sultan's chair? With all his dosh, you'd have thought he could afford to have them oiled!"

The game over, the players return to the changing room. Changi have run out winners by eight goals to nil and everyone is in high spirits. The plunge bath proves popular and the singing begins.

Meanwhile, Andy has taken a quick shower and slipped outside to take a look around.

Close to the sports field is a vineyard stretching into the distance. He walks for a few minutes alongside the protective netting, noticing that most of the grapes have been allowed to rot on the vine.

Voices call out from near the changing room. "Grub up, Andy! You'll miss it, unless you're quick."

He returns to find the servants have laid out a huge spread of sandwiches and tropical fruits on tables outside the pavilion. The officers and their wives are nowhere in sight. Glass jugs of iced water with lemon slices have been provided. To the disappointment of some of the players, there is no sign of any beer.

As the coach rolls out through the Palace gates, past the sentries, a fellow passenger remarks: "Pity we didn't have time for a look round the Palace – bet the Officers did!"

"Don't worry," says another, "they missed out on the plunge bath."

29

After an absence of two weeks, the rangy figure of SAC Woodfield appears once again at the counter of the Movements Office, still desperately in search of any information about the date of his repatriation.

Anxious to avoid dealing with what appears to him as a troublesome character, George immediately ducks his head and reaches for his 'phone to make an imaginary call. Corporal Long is already out of his desk, striding forward to the counter.

"You've called at just the right time, young man, come straight through."

Woody ducks his head under the counter, emerging with a beaming smile. The two men sit together at the back of the office.

"You'll have a berth on a troopship leaving early next month," whispers Lofty.

"That secret boat you mentioned, you mean?"

"No. That's no longer possible."

"Can you tell me the name of the boat, please?"

"Yes, confidential information at the moment, but it's almost certain to be the 'Empire Windrush'."

"Oh! I'm sure I've heard somewhere about that one. Great! Thanks a lot."

"And keep it under your hat. Don't want the others to find out what we've done for you. Special treatment is given to a select few."

"Not a chance, Corporal, you can trust me," says Woody leaving the office.

There is a silence while the staff wait for him to clear the building.

"That's really cruel, Lofty," smiles Sergeant Moore. "Funny but cruel."

"He's been asking for it, Sarge. I'd really like to be there when he finds out the 'Windrush' sank in 1954," laughs Lofty.

"We're not here to give out false information, Corporal. If we have no information, that's what we tell them, nothing, so no more of it. Mind you, it *is* funny. Now back to work!"

But Lofty has other ideas. Any doubts his colleagues might have that his playful mood is at an end are soon dispelled.

"Today, gentlemen, I have decided to have my *official* celebratory drink at lunchtime in Tong Sing's. Everyone is invited."

"And remind me what are we celebrating? And why at lunchtime, when there's work to do in the afternoon?" questions the Sergeant.

"My promotion, Sarge."

"A bit premature, isn't it? But O.K as long as everyone is back no later then two. Understood? And, Marshall, you don't drink – not properly anyway – so you can hold the fort till someone comes back."

"No problem, Sarge, I've got soccer training this evening anyway so I shouldn't be drinking beforehand."

Andy moves alongside George. "You're invited, too, I'm sure the Corporal is looking forward to buying you a drink."

The Chinese clerk's response to the sarcasm is yet another inscrutable smile.

"By the way, George, have you ever thought of taking English lessons? Would help with your job and anything else you do in the future."

"No. Big money to learn. George poor man. But if help job, Air Force give George lesson money? Yes?"

"I don't think so," replies Andy, deciding to drop the matter in the knowledge he recently discovered George is already pretty fluent.

The Sergeant and Corporal leave for the village, leaving them alone.

"Why Corporal no like me?" asks George.

Andy sidesteps the truth. "Don't think he likes many people. Take this morning, look how he treated that bloke who only wanted to know when he was going home."

"People like your Corporal, upset my people."

"Not enough to riot though, surely," says Andy. "I mean if you had met the Corporal or Sergeant when the curfew was on, what would you have done?"

George looks around the empty office before raising his arm menacingly, then runs a finger slowly across his throat. There is a threatening glare in his eyes, followed by a wry grin.

"Bloody 'ell," gasps Andy. "Just as well we didn't meet up."

"You O.K, but not Corporal."

Andy is shaken by his colleague's admission and immediately recalls Lofty's speculation about finding George on the wrong side of the barricades. Perhaps his Corporal was spot on after all. Could George have been among the rioters at Bedok Corner?

It is mid-afternoon and Andy remains alone and apprehensive about what is happening in the village. Lofty's recent, unofficial celebratory outing, when he had inadvertently toppled into the sea, is still fresh in his mind. Fortunately, Tong Sing's lies some distance from the coastline. Growing increasingly worried, Andy leaves the office and walks around to the side of the first floor balcony, overlooking the car park and the road to the village. A couple of Officers, deep in conversation, stand together, their elbows resting on the wall.

Just as he is about to move on, Andy catches the strains of laughter and intermittent song. It sounds like a solitary voice but there is no one in sight. Surely, surely it can't be Lofty! Of course not, the Sergeant and the others must be with him?

Suddenly, Lofty comes into view, waving a bottle above his head. His singing comes to an abrupt end as he struggles onto the bonnet of one of the cars.

A clumsier and even slower manoeuvre takes him to a standing position on the roof.

"Bingo!" comes his cry.

Both the Officers are shouting from the balcony. "Get off there! Get down from that vehicle, man, immediately!" The other Officer scurries away with the words: "I'll get the Adjutant."

Meanwhile, Lofty is jumping from one car roof to another, displaying a remarkable sense of balance in disentangling his legs on the top of one of the cars equipped with a roof rack. He is now greeting each successful landing with the cry of 'Olé.' A couple of school children stop to gaze in amazement at the impromptu entertainment, before the Adjutant and an RAF Policeman move in to close the performance.

The following morning, there is a subdued atmosphere in the office. Sergeant Moore is pacing the floor, repeating the question: "What you hell were you thinking, you daft bastard?"

Lofty is seated at his desk, head in hands, a large mug of black coffee at the ready. Each time he attempts to apologise, his Sergeant talks over him.

"And you can kiss that promotion goodbye, you know that, don't you?"

"But, Sarge…"

"No buts about it. Apart from being drunk on duty, there's the damaged cars. Those bleeding Officers will go to town with their estimates for repair. You'll end up paying for all the jobs they've been waiting all their tour to have done."

Lofty takes another slurp from his mug of coffee.

George remains silent throughout the Sergeant's tirade but Andy senses his Chinese colleague, with his ear duly cocked, holds little sympathy for Lofty and is no doubt enjoying the moment.

The Adjutant appears at the counter. "A private word, Corporal Long. Outside now!"

Shoulders slouched, the usually talkative Lofty leaves the office, uncertain of what is in store for him.

"Right you pair, get back to work. We've wasted enough time talking about him today. Sorry to say it, the man's an idiot," adds the Sergeant.

Andy is surprised at such a frank statement. At the same time, he is also struggling to understand why Lofty returned from the village unaccompanied. After all, he had gone there with the Sergeant. How had Lofty been allowed to get into such a state, and why had the Sergeant not returned with him to the office?

Lofty slips silently back into the office.

"You all right, Corp?" asks Andy.

"No, I'm not. My promotion is not going to happen. Where's the coffee?"

"Coming right up," says the Sergeant in a comforting tone.

Lofty looks across at George. "Bet Charlie Chan over there is lapping all this up."

"I don't think so Corp," says Andy.

A smile is slowly emerging on Lofty's face. His colleagues have learnt it is an expression which inevitably precedes an outrageous comment.

"Tell you what, you could sum up my yesterday in a few words: *Sergeant Lofty, but not for Long!*"

His colleagues are at first taken aback at his trivialisation of what is a serious act of misbehaviour. Surely a man with three young children and a fourth on the way should have acted in a more responsible manner? But this is Lofty: a married man who, only a week or so before, was yet again drunk, on his back, floating out to sea. What else could they expect? Andy and his Sergeant shake their heads in disbelief before bursting into laughter. Even George is unable to conceal a chuckle. No doubt about it, Lofty might have lost his promotion but not his sense of humour.

Andy is a frequent visitor to the recently installed automatic machine on the ground floor that dispenses ice cold cans of Coke. It is a popular facility in regular use by the despatch riders who park up close to SHQ, awaiting their next assignment. Andy soon develops an interest in their machines and listens to their dubious tales of high speed performance. When one of the drivers mentions a second hand BSA 350 cc. is for sale, his interest is immediately aroused. The generous offer that Andy can be given professional training on the finer skills of driving a motorbike, plus the added bonus that the machine can be serviced on the camp, free of charge, clinches the deal. A price is agreed, albeit on the basis of staged payments. The machine arrives within days and a period of instruction is quickly underway.

At first, Andy rides pillion watching closely as the drivers move effortlessly through the gears, braking and accelerating smoothly, yet always observing the discipline of good positioning on the road. Then, alone, he progresses to balancing the machine at almost walking pace in the car park, while threading it through cones placed closely together. Within a week Andy is going solo, albeit with 'L' plates. The freedom of movement it offers is soon being put to full use.

At weekends, he drives down to Changi Beach. Gradually, he begins to use the machine in the evenings to travel further afield. Once on the open road, ignoring the safety of a helmet, the humidity of Singapore is lost in seconds as the cool air rushes through his hair. It is a new-found and liberating sensation. The run to Bedok Corner, in particular, becomes a popular outing, occasionally with a mate as pillion passenger, for company.

Tonight, Andy is returning to the camp having stopped briefly en route at the 'Cameron Guest House' for a single bottle of Tiger beer. As he passes Changi Prison, he suddenly decides to pull off from the main road to explore a minor, unlit road leading out to the naval base at Loyang. It is shortly after midnight and his only company are the flies smacking into his face, as usual attracted by the headlight, which reveals the road is beginning to narrow. Its uneven surface is causing the machine to bounce. Andy grips the handlebars tightly, steering the bike to one side, as he accelerates into a left-hand bend. The turn proves tighter than anticipated and catches him unprepared.

Suddenly, his headlight catches a fleeting glimpse of someone in a white suit standing in the road directly in his path, frozen like the proverbial rabbit in the lights. Instinctively, Andy stabs his foot on the brake pedal, and swings the machine wildly to the left to avoid hitting the man. In so doing, he loses control. The rear wheel slithers from beneath him. He is thrown to the ground, bounces, rolls, then drops down into the monsoon drain. His evasive action has been in vain, the pedestrian having stepped backwards directly into the path of the rider-less bike. Together they now lie side by side in the road. Andy remains out of sight, a few feet below ground level. Over an hour elapses before a passing vehicle stops at the scene to find a man and a motorbike lying together in the road.

The injured man is soon taken off in an ambulance and shortly afterwards a local rescue truck arrives to collect the BSA machine. No one spots the unconscious Andy, and he is left overnight, motionless in the smelly ditch.

A downpour greets the dawn. The drain is filling fast and the cold water gathers around Andy's supine body. The level is rising as he regains consciousness. A couple of vehicles pass each other on the road beside him, totally unaware of his plight. Still, being close to the main road, he is aware of the faint buzz of the early morning traffic heading into Singapore. He tries to lever himself up but on each occasion his bruised legs buckle, sending him splashing back into the dirty water and slime. He is aware that his left eye has closed and his right arm is badly grazed. Miraculously, no bones feel as if they have been broken. His left wrist, having brushed against the machine's exhaust pipe as he fell, is badly blistered and giving a burning sensation. Frantically, Andy runs his hand over his face, searching for any other injuries. Simultaneously, his tongue is raking its way around his parched gums, engaged on an impromptu inventory check on his teeth. The incessant rain is diluting some of the caked blood around his mouth and forehead and his nails and finger tips are soon coated in red. He is trying desperately to ignore a throbbing headache. After a few more laboured attempts to rise from the drain, Andy succeeds in levering himself onto the side of the road, his feet still dangling in a couple of feet of water. His prized pair of black leather shoes bought only last week in Changi Village are done for, ruined.

He soon realises that both the pedestrian and the machine have disappeared. Another car passes. It brakes further down the road, pauses with engine running, before continuing on its way. Andy finally rises to his feet, takes a few unsteady steps, totters into the road and collapses again in a heap.

"And this chap here?" asks a doctor, engaged on his rounds of the ward.

"Motor cycle accident, Sir. Admitted early this morning. Suspected skull fracture with multiple bruising, burnt wrist and minor lacerations," replies the male orderly.

"He'll need an x-ray ASAP, and you'll need to adjust the head bandage – its covering his eyes," adds the doctor.

Andy lies fast asleep, unaware that he is now a patient in the Air Force's Changi Hospital. The doctor leaves and the chatter between patients resumes.

But all conversation comes to a sudden halt as the curtains are being drawn swiftly around the bed adjacent to Andy. A nursing attendant, pushing a trolley with surgical instruments, follows to join the hidden patient. The ward falls silent.

From behind the curtain comes sobbing, followed by a series of screams. Out of sight, there is a shuffling of feet and words of comfort are quickly being offered.

The sounds are enough to awaken Andy. His left eye is hidden behind an angry swelling, but his right eye opens to meet the darkness caused by a triple layer of bandage.

"Oh no," utters a panic-stricken Andy, running a hand across his forehead. "Not that."

Desperately, he claws the lower bandage down and away from his face.

An orderly is soon at his side. "What the hell are you doing? It's there for a reason."

An enormous sense of relief fills Andy, as gradually he begins to smile. He can still see.

"Got a nasty crack on the head, we'll be taking you down for an x-ray later. Should have worn a helmet, shouldn't you? Too bloody late now."

"What's wrong with the bloke behind those curtains?" asks Andy.

"Little Malayan chap. Lovely fellow. Captured 'Up Country' then systematically cut up by the terrorists, he's on four-hourly dressings, poor blighter."

"How long has he been in?" says Andy.

"Don't worry about him. I'll be back shortly to re-bandage you and clean up your face."

"What's it look like?"

"I've seen worse, much worse. Nothing for you to worry about."

Andy turns his head gently on the pillow. It is still throbbing but the relief that his eyesight has not been lost is overwhelming, dwarfing any concern he has for the rest of his aching and bruised body.

30

The following days witness a quick recovery for Andy. The male nurses are both attentive and in control, offering sound advice; but somehow their matter of fact approach to patients strikes him as being in sharp contrast to the bedside manners practised by their female civilian counterparts back home. Soon he is managing short walks out onto the balcony. He is keen to return to work and, on one of the routine daily ward visits by the medical team, he surprises one of them by saying he now feels ninety per cent better.

"Ah, that may be so, but it's that missing ten per cent that's all important, particularly with head injuries," comes the disappointing reply.

"But there's nothing broken, is there Sir?"

"According to the plates, that is correct but we'll take a closer look at you later in the week."

"Yes, Sir," replies Andy in a sullen tone. It is not the answer for which he had been hoping.

There is little banter between the patients and time seems to drag. The badly injured Malayan soldier in the next bed can hardly be expected to say much but the rest of the ward talk sparingly, for the most part lying stretched out with eyes closed and headphones clamped to their ears.

Andy decides to leave the larger part of his evening meal of boiled fish and mash, but speedily disposes of the small helping of jam roll and custard. Unlike the UK, visiting hours at Changi Hospital attract few visitors. The Movements Office have been informed of his accident but he is not expecting a visit from any of his work colleagues or pals from the billet. Feeling pleasantly tired, he leans back to take a nap as the first couple of visitors arrive. But soon his slumber is interrupted by a volley of wolf whistles that immediately draw a couple of male nurses into the ward in an attempt to quell the excitement. Eyes closed, he ignores the noise, totally unaware that a surprise visitor is heading his way.

"Come off it, Andy, you're not asleep. 'Cause if you are, I'm walking straight out!"

Without even looking up, the soft north country accent and strong perfume have already given the game away: it can only be Corporal Joan from Accounts.

"Silly bugger, aren't you, falling off that bike? Didn't think you went fast enough to have an accident. That's what the MT boys tell me."

"Uh, thanks for coming," stutters Andy, struggling for words as he brings his body up into a sitting position. Why, he thinks, has Joan – Joan of all people! – decided to visit him?

As usual, she is dressed to kill. A smart, powder blue body-hugging jacket and skirt accentuate her curves and, as she gently takes up a seated position on the side of the bed, she slips off her jacket to reveal an equally tight-fitting dark blue, silk blouse.

As she begins to talk, Andy is beginning to appreciate another and previously unseen side to her character. In verbal overdrive, Joan is bringing him up-to-date about her colleagues at SHQ in both a sympathetic and humorous manner. Meanwhile, her presence has certainly registered with one of male nurses whose sights are well and truly fixed upon her, while those patients within listening distance of the pair struggle to catch their conversation.

Is this the same Joan who partied into the early hours at Lofty's infamous promotion celebration when the Corporal almost drowned, and danced her partners to a standstill between drinks?

"Anyway, can't stop too long. Off to the Astra tonight to see something called *Friendly Persuasion* about some Quaker family in the American Civil War. Not my type of film but a couple of our girls thought it would be interesting. So, how ya feeling and when ya coming out?"

"End of the week, hopefully."

"Good – and when you do *we'll* have a drink to celebrate," adds Joan with a warm smile.

"How's Lofty?"

"Silly bugger's been charged, but got off lightly."

"Some evening at his promotion party, wasn't it?" asks Andy, disappointed to see Joan reaching for her jacket. "Do you have to go now?" pleads the patient.

Her reaction is one of surprise. She pauses before replying.

275

"Why, want me to stay a bit longer?"

"Don't want you to miss the film?" says Andy without any conviction in his voice.

"No, you're right, mustn't let the girls down."

Joan leans forward as if to kiss Andy but at the last moment lifts her head, settling instead for an affectionate pat on his shoulder.

"I'll tell the lads back at the office you're on the mend. Bye!"

She spins quickly around.

"Thanks for coming…"

But his words fail to reach her ears. Joan is already striding away out of the ward, heels clicking on the stone floor with each step, her exaggerated hip wiggle being monitored by every pair of male eyes.

Her disappearance is immediately followed by a stream of remarks, all directed at Andy, "You lucky bastard!" "What does she see in a kid like you?" "Next time, tell her a kiss would make me better."

Andy fields the back-handed compliments with silence. He is flattered that one of the best looking girls on the camp has taken the trouble to visit him but at the same time dubious of her motive. Surely she wasn't on the look out for a special flight home?

No, that didn't make sense, she could have spoken to the Sergeant, or even Lofty.

Perhaps she had taken a shine to him? No, that didn't make sense to him either. Everyone knew Joan flirted with men but her romantic focus was directed primarily at the Officers.

Andy knows that within the hour Joan will be in the camp cinema, waiting at the top of the gangway for the lights to dim before sashaying the length of the aisle to a chorus of whistles and cat calls. It was a regular and popular performance from the camp's number one pin-up – and this was the same woman who had just paid him a voluntary visit. Wow!

His spirits buoyed by the unexpected female visitor, and now spending more time on his feet than his back, Andy applies further pressure on the medical staff to be released.

A few days later, after one of the meal breaks, he manages to catch one of the male doctors leaving the office at the end of the ward.

"Sorry, Airman, I'm in a hurry, can't stop."

"Feeling one hundred per cent better, Sir," says Andy enthusiastically.

"You might feel you're back to normal but you've sustained severe concussion and my recommendation is that you remain here for a further week. However, it's basically your decision. If you wish to be discharged, it can be arranged. We'll discuss this tomorrow."

"If we could, Sir," pleads Andy.

"On your own head be it," adds the Officer with a barely concealed pun. "I'll see you here, same time tomorrow."

The following day, Andy walks out of the hospital, having effectively discharged himself against the advice of the hospital staff. His brisk step is soon reduced to a laboured stroll as the heat takes its toll on his weakened body. En route to the billet, he finds it necessary to rest on a strip of grass by the side of the road. A motorbike passes by, triggering a question in his mind.

"Where the hell is my bike?" he ponders.

After a few minutes, he slowly rises to his feet. The fate of his treasured machine has moved to the forefront of his thoughts. His pace quickens. *"The MT lads will know,"* he reassures himself.

It is early afternoon and the billet is empty. Andy had intended to call in at the office, but opts to rest on his bed. His jacket is soaking wet with perspiration, clinging tenaciously to his back like a tight vest. The hospital warning is sounding more sensible by the minute, perhaps he should have both listened and acted upon it. Just before he begins to stretch out on his mattress, he glimpses a couple of letters resting on his bedside locker. Sandra's flowery hand immediately identifies the sender of one – but the other one? The handwriting is unrecognisable, almost certainly that of a child. The envelope is grease-stained, carrying a 'Birmingham' postmark. *"Who do I know in Brum?"* Andy asks himself, as he rips it open. There is no letter inside, just a Postal Order for five shillings.

The penny drops. It can only be from Harry Ashton, the Sergeant he worked with on detachment in Borneo, and for whom he arranged a last minute flight home on BOAC.

"Silly sod," chuckles Andy, *"What bloody use is a Postal Order here?"*

Andy turns to Sandra's letter. It could be one of the last ones he will receive, given his tour of duty is soon due to end. She should know about his accident but at the same time there is no need to alarm her. No need either for the dramatic detail, particularly since he has been discharged. After all, there should be no long-term damage. He stretches his legs out fully, gently lowering his head to the pillow. As usual, the typed pages are scented.

Dear Andrew,

So sorry not to have replied sooner to your two – or was it three? – letters. It's been absolutely frantic here in the Office. Business has been booming and properties have been selling like proverbial hot cakes.

Daddy will be opening another branch in the City in the next couple of weeks and it's going to be a race against the clock to get everything done in time. He's been speaking to the local papers and arranging the maximum publicity. Secretly, I think he's planning to put me in as manager, once it's up and running.

You must be getting excited about coming home after so long overseas. I'm sure your mum is planning something special for your return. We've all missed you terribly and can't wait to hear your tales of life in the Far East. Hope you're a bit more talkative than my uncle who spent a couple of years in Burma during the last War and, for some peculiar reason, never seems to want to tell us anything about the place or what he got up to! Funny thing is, he is so chatty about everything else.

Bumped into your dad last week and he thought you'll be really fit and tanned after getting so much sun and playing football in that heat. Don't forget to let me know which airport you will be flying into – and, of course, when. The way business is going, I haven't a prayer of meeting you when your plane arrives but I'd like to think I can make it to North Road Station when your train pulls in.

I'm afraid Argyle are having another bad season. Must be so disappointing for you having to wait for the newspapers to arrive from England and then finding out they've lost again!

Daddy suggests you switch your allegiance to another team or to start supporting one of our two rugby sides, preferably Plymouth Albion. I told him you were too far gone for all that – and he just laughed.

Love as always, Sandra

Andy takes a deep breath, slips the letter back into the envelope and casts his eyes upwards at the ceiling. There is now little doubt in his mind that Sandra has, psychologically, moved on. Her words, 'You must be excited' are left in mid-air.

Isn't Sandra excited? 'Sure your mum is planning something special.' Doesn't Sandra *know* what his mum is planning? More to the point, does she care? The way things are shaping up, he'll probably end up giving her a call when he reaches Plymouth. Certainly not the way he had envisaged his homecoming. But after more than eighteen months abroad could he have expected more? Anyway, at least he can count on his mum and dad.

The letter from his parents reminds Andy of the need to pay a much overdue visit to Changi Village for a serious look at possible presents to take home. He knows his mum has a weakness for scarves and his father enjoys wood carving, but Sandra will be the problem. With her wealthy parents doting on their only child, she is already totally spoilt. One earlier thought had been to buy her an impressive silk night gown but, when he had enquired on an earlier visit, Andy realised he didn't even know his fiancee's dress size. An Indian shopkeeper, anxious to clinch a sale, had already claimed he could tell Sandra's waist measurement from just seeing a photograph but the possibility she had either lost or gained weight in the interim suggested it was a risk not to be taken. So what can he get for a girl who has everything – including her own horse?

Andy decides to settle for a bottle of Tiger as he reaches the village and makes for the Changi Milk Bar. He hesitates outside on hearing the raucous laughter. A quiet drink is all he needs but still he decides to go in.

As he enters, he catches sight of Joan and Mary in the company of a couple of older New Zealand Officers. Joan looks up at Andy then quickly looks away, without offering a word. Meanwhile, Mary is looking the worse for wear, trying unsuccessfully, to gain the attention of the men by performing an elusive card trick. Andy has a change of mind and heads for George's Photographic Store. He stands in front of the shop looking at the range of cameras on view but with thoughts still firmly centred on the 'brush off' he has just received from Joan, the girl who made a special trip to visit him in the hospital. It doesn't make sense.

Suddenly, he feels a sharp dig in his back. "You're a sensitive kid, aren't you?"

Without looking around, Andy recognises Joan's voice.

"If you'd had waited till Mary had done her special card trick, you could have joined us. She reckons she needs total concentration and no interruptions when she's performing."

Andy turns to face the attractive brunette. A few drinks have

279

brought a glow to her appearance. He could be wrong but she looks in a playful mood.

"Where's Mary now?" he asks.

"She's gone off with those two Kiwis. They were angling for both of us to join them for a fun evening in Singapore, a few drinks followed by an overnight stay in some hotel. Didn't fancy it myself but Mary was game. She doesn't get too many offers, you know."

"Probably 'cause she's no good at card tricks," laughs Andy.

"I think you're right. Now then, are you going to buy me that drink you owe me."

"Yes, sure, of course."

They make for Tong Sing's where the Chinese proprietor promptly threads his way though the empty tables to the door to greet Joan by name. They sit alone in the restaurant, close to a silent jukebox.

"What made you join the Air Force?" asks Andy.

"Well, straight from school, I went to work in the Co-op in Rochdale. Think one of my friends at school talked me into it. Pretty soon, I'd taken a long look at the married women there and decided it – and Rochdale – wasn't for me. The thought of ending up like them, scratching for a living with a couple of screaming kids running round my feet didn't appeal to me. They all looked so bloody miserable."

"But why not just move away from the Co-op and Rochdale? Why join up?"

"I reckon a couple of travel films I saw as a kid at the flicks got stuck in my mind. You know the stuff, palm trees and long, empty sandy beaches. And here I am!"

The waiter brings the conversation to a grinding halt.

"Ready to order, Sir?"

Joan responds with a withering look, followed by: "Bugger off, will you? We'll tell you when we're ready!"

Andy is now being treated to the abrasive side of her nature.

"Bit hard on him, weren't you?"

"Don't worry about him. If that's the worst he gets, he'll be lucky. Trouble with you, Andy, is you're too bloody sensitive. It's a tough world out there, you've got to remember that. If you're firm, people will respect you; dither and you're lost."

The waiter is now keeping his distance, waiting to be called.

"You being such a hard nut, surprised you came to see me in hospital."

"Oh that! Moment of weakness, don't flatter yourself."

The Chinese proprietor brushes past the waiter to stand at the table. "Good evening, Corporal Joan. Anything I can get you?" he asks, turning to Andy as an after thought.

"Two bottles of Tiger, please," replies Andy. "That all right with you, Joan? That's what I saw you drinking in the other place."

"Those were Mary's bottles you saw. When the Kiwis are paying, mine's always a large gin and tonic. But now, seeing as you're paying, I'll let you off with a single. Don't forget, being in Accounts, I know exactly what everyone on camp get's paid."

The proprietor drops a menu on the table before scampering off.

"What's the attraction with the New Zealanders? Those blokes didn't look extra handsome?" says Andy.

"Quite simple. Both were single and available. What's more, there's currently a chronic shortage of women in their country so most of them are on the lookout for a bride to take back home. Officers' pay and all that – and a better climate. Handsome doesn't come into it. Even Mary's got a chance of being whisked away into the sunset."

"Sounds a bit cold-blooded to me," says Andy.

"As I said, it's a tough world. You'll find out when you start going out with girls."

Anxious to sound knowledgeable on the subject of relationships, Andy responds. "Actually Joan, I'm already engaged."

Slowly, she places her glass on the table, takes a deep breath, and begins to shake her head slowly from side to side. "Engaged to be married! How old are you? How long since you last saw her? Bloody lucky you haven't had a 'Dear John' by now."

"Oh no! We'll be getting married as soon as I get home."

As he attempts to explain, Andy is mentally re-appraising his future with Sandra.

"Same age as you, is she?" presses Joan.

"No, a couple of years older."

"Got a picture of her?"

"Not with me."

"That's the wrong answer! Most of the boys out here carry one in their wallet, next to their heart, and can pull the picture out in a flash. How often does she write?"

Andy is becoming increasingly uncomfortable at the questions being fired at him.

"Hold on, Joan, this is getting more like an interrogation."

"Just trying to help. Want another drink – I'm paying."

"Not bothered really. Actually, I came out tonight to get some presents to take home. Got any ideas for something for my girl?"

"I take it she has a name," teases Joan.

"Sandra."

"Good. Right, that's a start. Hobbies? Interests?"

"Uh, well, horses really. Bit of travelling, reading and going to pictures."

"Do you like horses?"

"Not particularly."

"And this is the girl you're planning to spend the rest of your life with. Someone who could continue all those interests without involving you – and probably will. Are you sure you know what you're letting yourself in for?"

"But she's really good looking…"

"Can I ask whose idea it was to get engaged."

"Well, mine, I think. Just before I left she got quite tearful and said she hoped our friendship would not be ruined through our enforced separation."

"And then you suggested an engagement. Does she mention the wedding in her letters? You know, the date, the dress and where you're going for a honeymoon?"

"Come to think of it, no. She hasn't mentioned it at all."

"So where are you going for your honeymoon?"

"Haven't decided yet, to be honest."

"Andy, sounds to me like your posting over here has already scuppered your relationship with this girl," concludes Joan.

"Can we change the subject, I don't want to talk about it any more." A couple of Army lads arrive and the jukebox bursts into life.

They pay the bill and leave the restaurant. Although embarrassed by her questioning, Andy appreciates having had the opportunity to talk about his future with Sandra.

"I think I'll take a stroll along the beach to clear my head." He hesitates for a moment before adding tentatively, "Fancy joining me?"

"Just the two of us on a deserted beach in the fading light? Can I trust you to behave yourself?"

"Course you can," replies Andy, suddenly aware that she is once again teasing him.

Together they make for Changi Beach, strolling first along the

282

planked boardwalks in front of the shops which serve to protect pedestrians from falling into the numerous potholes.

It is a quiet night for the local traders in the village with the fronts of many shops already boarded up: but with the fortnightly RAF Pay Parade due tomorrow, business will soon be taking a turn for the better.

As they reach the deserted beach, Andy points to the silhouetted shack of the coffee shop, usually a hub of activity for the many Servicemen who gather there on weekends.

"No queuing there tonight!" he quips.

The joke is lost on the now barefoot Joan who lags a few paces behind, shaking the sand from her shoes.

"Not such a good idea, this late night stroll," she adds caustically.

Andy reaches down and collects a few stones to send skimming back into the water. It is a clear night as they now stand together watching the incoming tide drawing ever closer to their feet.

Some two miles out to sea, and through the gathering darkness, they can pick out the outline of Pulau Ubin Island, the modest home of both Chinese and Malays who quietly fish the local waters.

"Well, if I've come this far, I might as well go the whole hog."

"What do you mean?" asks Andy.

Without a moment's hesitation, Joan is removing her clothes. Her skirt is soon lying on top of her blouse, bra and pants in an untidy pile as she hot-foots her shapely figure in the direction of the sea.

Andy remains rooted to the spot, speechless, but immediately aroused at the outline of her figure silhouetted against the water. With a high-pitched scream, her legs are first to falter as she hits a wave before stumbling uncontrollably into an involuntary 'belly-flop.' He decides to follow to the waters edge. Some ten yards separate them.

"Coming in?" she shrieks, rising to stand waist high in the water.

"Not tonight, I'm afraid."

"Right, you party pooper. So now you can dry me off with your shirt. Go on, take it off!" Totally uninhibited and totally naked, she races back.

Andy is still struggling to drag his shirt tail over his head as Joan sprints out of the water. She crashes into his chest, almost knocking him over.

"Oh, I'm so, so cold – I need a good rub down."

His arms reach out, desperate to envelop her inviting body. His heart is pounding. Instinctively, Andy knows how he wants the situation to develop. It is a fantasy scenario that has run through his mind on countless occasions but one for which he is sadly unprepared. He reacts by draping his shirt around her shoulders, drawing them close. Now locked in an uncomfortable embrace, Joan begins to shiver, while he looks over her shoulder, unsure of his next move.

"You're not doing much of a job of drying me. Come on, don't you want to touch me? Are you afraid?" Slowly she presses her soft breasts against his excited frame. He can feel the water from her legs slowly sinking into his slacks, a discomfort he can readily accept. Andy responds by giving her back a frantic and abrasive rub with his shirt.

"Don't you find me attractive?" she purrs in a seductive voice, nestling her head under his chin.

"Course I do – you're... beautiful ..."

"Well, you can start by *not* drying me as if I'm some dog coming out of the water."

Joan takes a couple of steps backward and looks him coldly in the eyes.

"Haven't you had it off with your Sandra yet? You haven't, have you?"

"Well, not exactly but..." begins Andy.

"Hold on, you're still a bloody virgin, aren't you?"

Her words crash around his ears.

"No, not at all. I've..."

"Forget it." Her words kill off any chance of Andy enjoying his first serious, sexual encounter. "It's time to go," she adds in a monotone voice.

All her bounce and enthusiasm has suddenly vanished. All his has disappeared, too – and with it the expectation of something memorable, something exciting about to happen.

He cuts a sad and almost apologetic figure as he watches Joan dress. A golden opportunity has literally slipped through his fingers. He follows as they retrace their steps across the sand.

Hardly a word is exchanged as they walk back through the village. A couple of Indian traders step out from their shops in an unsuccessful attempt to get a late night sale. It serves to remind Andy that his intended shopping expedition is a second casualty of the evening.

Andy escorts Joan to the WRAF Block. He feels he has been a disappointment to both himself and his impromptu date but is uncertain of the words to use.

A warm smile comes to Joan's face as she gives him a soft, farewell kiss on his cheek.

She senses his mood. "Don't worry about it, Andy. You're a nice kid. Just make sure you get your act together before you go on honeymoon with your Sandra. If you don't, you won't get any brownie points from her."

Most of the lights are already out as Andy enters his billet. His mind is still racing about what happened on the beach, and he knows full well it will be some time before he can get to sleep. Joan is difficult to understand. At times, soft, gentle and understanding; at others intolerant, quick tempered. Why did she agree to go to the beach? Why strip off in front of him, ask him to join her in the water and end up in a clinch? Was it just a tease, an exercise in proving she could get yet another man excited. Well, if that was the aim she had proved her point, no question about that. As he finally undresses, he suddenly speculates that everything might have turned out much differently on the beach had he shed his clothes simultaneously with Joan. Something to remember for the next time, although the chances of it being with her seem dead in the water. Joan's farewell kiss on the cheek had spoken volumes. "You're a nice kid," wasn't what he had hoped to hear. As he lies down on his bed, Andy is also trying desperately to recall every contour of the naked feminine form to which he had been treated. No doubt about it, Joan wasn't cut out for the Co-op in Rochdale.

Tonight, Sandra is more than seven thousand miles away from his thoughts – she might just as well be on another planet.

31

"Sorted out where you'll be having your Boat Party? Off at the end of next week, aren't you?" asks Lofty.

It's been some twenty months since he arrived in the Far East, and the prospect of his return has always seemed too distant for Andy to contemplate. Now it's only a matter of days away. Suddenly, repatriation is within his grasp, tantalisingly close enough almost to touch and the mention of a Boat Party has served to make it a reality.

"Sorry, Corp, miles away."

"Make it the Malcolm Club then, I've had a fall out with the NAAFI."

"What happened?" asks Andy.

"Long story in more ways than one – but I'm effectively barred."

Sergeant Moore joins the pair.

"Sorted out your presents to take home, young man? If you need some time off to take a look around the village, it can be arranged. And I've also got a surprise for you – later."

Normally, a strictly 'get on with your work' man, the Sergeant's offer of time off is totally unexpected. Andy has become aware that, for some reason, the precise details of the travel arrangements for his return to the UK are being withheld from him. He's had an assurance he will be flying back on time but nothing more. Why the secrecy? Surely he's not getting the 'Woodfield' treatment of being lined up for a boat that lies at the bottom of the ocean! He waits until Sergeant Moore has left for lunch before pressing Lofty for more information.

"Corp, what date will I be leaving? I'll need to let my parents – and my fiancée – know."

"No chance of you doing that from here. You can give 'em a ring after you've landed, it'll take time for you to clear Innsworth then travel home. That's ample warning."

"Come on, Corp, I really need to know."

"All right then, you're booked out on a flight on the 26th. But not a word to the Sarge, he's sorted it all out and it's supposed to be *his* surprise."

"Service or civvy kite?" comes Andy's enthusiastic response.

"I'm saying nothing more," replies Lofty, pointing to newly-arrived customers at the front of the office. "Now, I'll leave you and Chinese Charlie to sort out these two blokes." George is already out of his seat and moving towards them.

Andy quickly thumbs through his diary. Anticipating that he will need a couple of nights rest to recover from the effects of a Boat Party, he pencils in the evening of Saturday 23rd March, 1957 for his farewell drink.

He swings round to face Lofty: "Saturday, 23rd O.K, Corp?"

"That's a bloody weekend, isn't it?"

Andy resists the temptation to point out that most Saturdays invariably fall at the weekend.

"Not the best day for me, coming home the worse for wear, but first clear the date with all the others – and don't forget the girls downstairs in Accounts. I'm sure they're planning something special for you," explains Lofty. "Now go and help your mate, looks like he's having trouble."

Andy gulps at the way the evening is shaping up.

"Wasn't planning anything too grand, Corp. A few drinks with you and the Sarge, a couple of mates from the football team and a group from the billet. Nothing too grand."

"Get a grip man, it's a Boat Party not a bloody wake! We know you're not a drinker but this will be your finale, a chance to show us what you're really made of. You'll be sinking more Tigers than you thought possible, you'll be up on the table and singing your fucking heart out – then probably ending with Mary up against the wall of the WRAF Block. It's going to be a night to remember. A drink with a couple of mates? Nothing too grand? Don't make me laugh!"

Having first-hand knowledge of Lofty's definition of a 'good drink', Andy is viewing his farewell evening with some trepidation.

On his return to his Block, Andy feels obliged to spread the word about the date for his Boat Party. There is an immediate interest in the event, with a number of his closer mates undertaking to pass the word around. Much to his concern, it looks like being a sizeable turnout. He decides that advice is now required as to how best to prepare, physically, for his ordeal. To his surprise, advice is soon forthcoming.

Later in the day, in the Mess, he finds himself sitting across from Lawrence Gale, one of the medics he met in the hospital. A sympathetic soul, it was perhaps inevitable he would be referred to by staff and patients alike as 'Florence', given his effeminate manner and with a surname only a bird hop away from Nightingale.

After exchanging comments about his recovery from his bike accident, Andy lets slip:

"Got my Boat Party next week, was wondering…"

"In the Malcolm Club, is it? I'll be there, don't worry. Just give me the day and I'll mention it to the other lads."

"Thanks," replies Andy slowly, immediately regretting that he has unwittingly invited another person onto the guest list. "Tell you what I really need is some gen from you about the best way to handle it. You see, having a skin-full doesn't really agree with me. Can't see myself lasting the evening."

The medic immediately puts down his irons and furrows his brow. Clearly, some serious words are about to be delivered. "Pity more people don't ask for advice. You'd be amazed at the number of drunken idiots we have to stitch back together at the end of their mad nights out. If only they knew when to stop, we'd all be better off."

"But what's the secret to holding your drink?" enquires Andy.

"First, advisable to have something to eat before you start, something to soak up the drink. Same principle as blotting paper. But don't have too much to eat because you'll be blown out and uncomfortable before you start: never drink on an empty stomach.

Second, pace yourself. Gives your body a chance to absorb what you're pouring into it. Stands to reason, you'll get the wrong reaction if you treat it badly.

Third, if you're bloody daft enough to drink so much you feel sick, then throw up. Don't just sit there until your body revolts, just – throw up! Always keep one step ahead."

Andy pauses to take in the professional advice. Somehow, it all seems common sense.

"Thanks for that," says Andy.

"Just make sure you let me know when it is. With luck, I'll be able to offer first hand assistance – unless I'm already legless! Oh, and I'll mention it to the other lads back at the hospital who remember you. Sure some would certainly like to see you off!"

Andy is nodding with each layer of advice, unaware the medic is struggling to suppress a grin at Andy's apparent innocence, although both laugh at his final throwaway line.

On his way back to his Block, Andy realises he has failed to take the opportunity to enquire about the condition of the patients he has left behind in the hospital ward, in particular the Malayan soldier in the next bed recovering from wounds inflicted on him when he was tortured. Perhaps, he is getting the ritual out of all proportion. Perhaps he should concentrate on following the advice from the medic. No need to get up on the table in the Malcolm Club – and certainly no need to end up with Mary at the back of the WRAF Block!

The following morning Andy has slipped out of the office and stands downstairs waiting for the Coke machine to deliver. Behind him, Huntley, the self-proclaimed soccer star of Admin Wing, is making known his impatience with a series of sighs and foot-tapping. As Andy finally collects the ice cold bottle, he is greeted with the gruff comment:

"Clever sod, aren't you?"

"Sorry, what's that," queries Andy, surprised at the hostility of the remark.

"When you asked me for a game with our lot you didn't say you could play a bit, did you? Since then I've found out you've been playing regularly for the Station First team and RAF Singapore, too. We could have done with you. Anyway, you can always change your mind. I'll still be captain, of course, but I'll get you a regular game."

"Actually, I'm leaving for the UK on the 26th so I've played my last game out here," replies Andy.

"Well, fuck you! I could have played for both those teams, you know, but I couldn't be bothered. They were desperate for me to play in the special annual match against the Sultan's Army at the Johore Palace, but I couldn't fit that in either. You played in that match I hear, lucky sod, what a memorable experience that must've been. Anyway, when I get home I'll probably turn pro. Whole string of big professional clubs interested in signing me, you know."

As he leaves, he can hear Huntley still losing patience with the machine. His cries of "Come on you bastard machine" – "You've stolen my money," bring a smile to the face of one of the local cleaners quietly sweeping the passageway.

Having watched him in action on the field, Andy is astonished at Huntley's exaggerated opinion of his own ability. 'Shooting a line' is an accepted feature of Service life and serves as a form of amusement for those prepared to listen but on an occasion such as this it is nothing short of pathetic. Andy is immediately reminded of the tale of a boastful Airman who arrived at Changi, claiming to have been transferred from one leading Scottish professional club to Glasgow Rangers for £1,000. The claim had been taken at face value and the billets on the camp had virtually emptied to catch a glimpse of a special talent in action on the field. In the event, the player had been hauled off the pitch after a mere ten minutes, leaving his team a man short for the rest of the game, but not before revealing his skills did not extend to either the basics of controlling or heading the ball. In the process he had provided much entertainment for the spectators but leaving little credibility for those who had all too readily accepted his word.

Once more, Andy's thoughts turn to repatriation. How he will adapt to resuming his job in the Civil Service. Will he want to continue to live in Plymouth? And Sandra?

Her last letter had hurt but it had brought him face to face with the true position of their relationship. They were still engaged. Did engagements have to be officially broken, or did one just do nothing and walk away? But first, the Boat Party.

The day arrives with Andy having managed to avoid taking any alcohol for 72 hours. Lofty and the Sergeant have given him the afternoon off to prepare for what they assure him will be his 'evening to remember.' His attempts to make it an 8 pm start in the Malcolm Club have been dismissed out of hand. The lads have told him in no uncertain terms that the serious drinking will commence no later than 7pm, and a drink will be waiting for him; Lofty has let it be known he will be there an hour earlier to set things up.

Mindful of the medic's advice about having something to line his stomach, Andy pays a late afternoon visit to the Changi Milk Bar in the village. At the cost of less than two dollars, he enjoys a chicken omelette followed by a pineapple milkshake. Back in the billet, as he relaxes on his mattress, Andy wonders just how many will turn up. He knows at least a dozen from the football team should be there, probably the same number from the billet, plus a handful from SHQ. Since their 'night' together on the beach, Andy has not spoken to Joan but somehow he hopes she will make an appearance. His thoughts switch to his old pals from Borneo: Finnegan and the Music Man. What a pity they can't be there.

The drinking party have gathered outside the Malcolm Club. It is a few minutes to seven and the would-be revellers are busy checking wrist watches. Lofty emerges from within, glass already in hand, with a rallying call: "Come on, lads, let's get this show on the road!" Sergeant Moore beckons his Corporal to his side. "That bugger Marshall is going to be late. Punctual little sod for work, then turns up late for his own Boat Party. Talk about getting your priorities right!"

Meanwhile, aware that he is likely to be a few minutes late, Andy quickens his step.

The Sergeant is the first to spot him.

"Right you lot, inside now. Get the beers lined up. I want a private word with young Marshall."

"Sorry, Sarge, bit late I'm afraid," gasps Andy, having run the last fifty yards.

"Listen, you all right for readies?" comes the whisper.

"Just about, I think."

"Well, here's twenty dollars to see you through. You can let me have back anything you don't spend."

"Thanks, thanks very much, Sarge." Andy is taken aback at the unexpected generosity.

"Don't think I've gone soft. Now get in there and enjoy yourself – and that's an order!"

Andy enters to a round of applause from the rest of the party. A number of tables have been pushed together and are already littered with bottles of Tuborg, Carlsberg and Tiger. It is shaping up for a serious night's drinking.

Lofty is already in full verbal flow, drawing spontaneous laughter from a captive audience from the members of the football team with yet another re-telling of his now infamous near death experience when floating out to sea on his back. Amidst the gathering noise, Andy catches an argument developing between two rival supporters from North London who are disputing the score of a match played, sometime in the distant past, between Arsenal and Tottenham. Party-goers are still arriving and the sound of chairs being dragged across the floor fills the air. A quick count suggests that some thirty men are present. Among them is the popular figure of SAC John O'Neill, the golden boy of Singapore football, surrounded by a group of admiring fans. At his side stands his close friend, Norman Webb, a dapper, blonde-haired character from Harrow, whose immaculate dress sense has led his fellow men to dub him 'Wingco', in recognition of his appearance being more in keeping with that of a Wing Commander than an LAC. It is a label that has stuck and one he will no doubt carry into civilian life.

Remembering the advice he had been given, Andy is quietly pacing himself, unaware that he is being watched. Suddenly, he finds Lofty standing over him.

"You're not keeping up with the rest. At this rate, you've got no chance of getting pissed. What the hell you playing at?"

Before Andy can say anything, his Corporal's attention is distracted by the arrival of a couple of 'Wafs', standing in the doorway as if uncertain whether to come in.

"Bloody hell, it's Mary and that sexpot Joan," gasps one of the party-goers.

With a dismissive wave, the two girls acknowledge a robust chorus of invitations to join the party, then turn their backs and make for the bar.

"Could be your lucky night, Andy, I'll take the Corporal and you can have Mary," laughs one of the football team.

"She's spoken for," comes another voice.

"What Joan?" asks Andy.

"No, Mary. Didn't you know? She's got herself a Kiwi."

"Doesn't surprise me. Ending up with a cuddly little bird that can't fly away is probably the best she could hope for."

"No, stupid. Not the bird – a New Zealand Officer."

"Does he do card tricks?" enquires Andy.

"What the hell's that got to do with it. She does favours for anyone, take my word for it! I've been there. You need another drink. By the way, d'you know whose party this is?"

"Not a clue," smiles Andy, "but I'll take that drink."

Despite his best intentions, he can feel the beer taking its effect as the evening unfolds.

Taking a much-delayed visit to the toilet, his legs falter beneath him and he is reminded that there will be a price to pay for tonight's over-indulgence but, he thinks, what the hell?

On his return, he is aware of Joan in deep conversation with one of the Sergeants from Signals Section. Mary is nowhere to be seen. Andy pauses, wondering whether to ask them both to join the party. However, before he can approach them they turn away and leave, hand in hand.

As he gets back to the table, he is aware of a familiar figure sitting in his chair.

No mistaking the man: it's 'Windrush' Woody, the victim of Lofty's dark humour.

"Heard it was your Boat Party, so I thought you and your Corporal could buy me a drink or two for having a bloody good laugh at my expense."

"Well, to be fair, you were getting to be a damn nuisance…"

"Do you know, I wrote home telling my parents that I was booked on that frigging boat. Even they knew that it was already on the ocean floor."

Lofty intervenes. "This bloke causing trouble?" he asks menacingly, simultaneously struggling to maintain his balance.

"No, Corp, I invited him along," explains Andy.

"Right then you can both get me another Tuborg, I'm just getting into the swing of it. Christ, I've had a few tonight, I can tell you."

Lofty rises unsteadily to his feet and turns proudly to his drinking mates for confirmation: "Have I, or have I not, had enough to sink a battleship?" he bellows.

"Enough to sink the whole fucking fleet, Lofty," comes the unanimous and anticipated response.

Judging by his beaming smile, the words are sweet music to the Corporal's ears.

"Can I get you another?" asks Andy.

"Dead right you can – but you're falling behind," he shouts.

"I'm giving this round a miss, Corp," replies Andy.

"Are you hell! Take this one and give it a 'yam sing'." The Corporal reaches for the nearest full glass. "You know the drill: down in one. Go on, man, on your bloody feet."

Lofty struggles to lever himself up from his seat to assume the role of cheer leader.

Andy rises with him. The chanting begins. "Oh…! Oh…!Oh…!Oh…!Olé."

As the first wave hits the back of his mouth, he hears a voice: "slower, slower, slower." The advice is heeded and the glass gradually empties. There is a roar of approval from the spectators as the ritual is completed. In triumph, Andy tilts his head back but not before some of the beer has escaped and soaked the front of his shirt.

Lofty calls the party to order. "He did well, don't you think? Now the bugger deserves a song in his honour. All together now, "Why was he born so beautiful…"

The singing serves to clear the Club of its remaining non-party-goers. Some of the members of the Boat Party are now looking the worse for wear, with heads and shoulders slumped on the tables. One of the party-goers, unknown to Andy, gives him a soft pat on the head, before lurching off in the direction of the bar for a refill.

The stranger returns, having spilt most of his glass en route, to offer a personal but slurred complimentary comment on the evening: "Great party, er – um, Sandy. It is Sandy, isn't it? – best one I've been to yet."

A couple of lads have broken away to play a game of darts and are beginning to shriek with laughter at their repeated failure to hit the board. A cloud of cigarette smoke hangs over the assembled company as the chairs slowly begin to empty and men leave the building. A group of hardened drinkers roam the tables, checking whether any of the discarded bottles offers a free drink. Lofty seems to have got his 'second wind' and is now in a laboured conversation, recruiting volunteers to join him on a late night assault on the bars in Changi Village. Andy realises that his 'yam sing' has been one drink too many and takes off once more for the toilet. The door is ajar and he waits, then watches as a fellow party-goer, down on his knees, tries unsuccessfully to throw up. Suddenly aware that he is being observed, the man rises unsteadily to his feet, before staggering out of the door and collapsing into a heap outside. The cubicle is vacant and Andy attempts to perform similar self-treatment. Thrusting a couple of fingers down his throat, the task is soon completed. He returns to the table to survey the empty chairs. Lofty has disappeared. The bar staff are now busy clearing the debris of bottles and cigarette butts that litter the tables and floor. One of the Malay waiters disappears into the toilet with a brush over his shoulder and a bucket of water in hand. Andy steps outside into the cool evening air to find the camp in total darkness. A night to remember? Well, he has survived. Beer and the remnants of his chicken omelette lay on the front of his shirt and tomorrow his body will no doubt seek retribution upon him – but it's been a laugh. On second thoughts, it could, in time, prove to be an evening he'll never forget. But as he finally drops his tired body onto his mattress his closing thoughts are of his return to the UK. Home beckons.

32

Strings have been pulled by Sergeant Moore. The result: Andy takes one of the window seats towards the back of a sparsely loaded De Havilland Comet 2E, as it lines up at the end of the Changi runway. Its nose is pointed in a northerly direction, heading out over the beach where he has spent many happy hours. On board are a collection of some twenty Service personnel, either tour or time-expired, and a handful of De Havilland staff on what will be a further test flight, before the aircraft is commissioned to go into regular, long haul Air Force service.

Without warning, the aircraft shoots forward as if being catapulted, and in seconds its wheels have devoured a huge stretch of the runway. It is Andy's first experience of the sensation of jet powered travel and one he will never forget. So, so different from his flights in the ponderous, laboured piston engine planes. As the Comet climbs steeply and effortlessly into the clouds, he has mixed emotions. A feeling of immense relief that his two years of National Service are finally coming to an end, yet carrying a hundred treasured memories from his visit to the other side of the world, from places he can surely never again expect to see. And soon he will be back home.

Andy watches as the De Havilland technical team move around in the aisle playing with an array of gadgetry. Instruments are held aloft, weights are left dangling from the arms of empty seats, readings taken and countless notes are scribbled. It all seems rather serious and intense. The seat next to him is unoccupied, so he positions his legs across the extra space, lets his head drop back and quickly falls asleep.

Meanwhile the aircraft is heading toward RAF Negombo in Ceylon for its first re-fuelling stop. The 'plane lands, empties and affords its passengers the opportunity to stretch their legs. Some of the men pause to first walk around the silver coloured jet aircraft and gaze in admiration at the latest in design and development.

The second stop is Karachi, where the first overnight stay is at 'Minwallah's Grand Hotel' on the outskirts of the overcrowded city. As the building comes into view, the name of the establishment suggests more a statement of intent rather than a realistic description of its current appearance. With more carpets hanging on its walls than on its floors, it carries an air of austerity, with the footsteps of the newly arrived, transient Service clientele soon echoing from the stone floors. Located close to a railway line, and bordering a vast expanse of arid scrubland, it offers little in terms of comfort or scenic views. Andy shares a room with a fellow passenger, a tall, pale-skinned Corporal whose sole topic of conversation on the flight to date has been a constant stream of statistics about the development of jet engines. As the day draws to a close, they stand together on a balcony close to the hotel roof, watching as the silent hand of darkness descends. There is no talk of jet engines, no talk of going home. Both sets of eyes are now focused upwards on what promises to be a glorious sunset. Andy's thoughts return to the wondrous colours he often watched unfolding at dusk in the Borneo skies.

"Perhaps they should rename this place 'Minwallah's Grand Sunset', nothing else grand about this hotel," suggests the Corporal.

"How long was your tour?" asks Andy.

"Three years."

"Enjoy it?"

"Not really."

There is little doubt in Andy's mind that his travelling companion has been involved with aircraft. His enthusiastic talk of jets has more than confirmed that.

"So what exactly was your trade? Hold on! – don't tell me – something closely to do with... aircraft? Right? Servicing? Fitter? Getting close?"

"Miles away, mate."

"Really?"

"Let's get inside, I'm getting bitten. Sod the sunset, it can look after itself," says the Corporal.

"So what was your trade?" presses Andy.

"Policeman," comes the sharp reply.

"A 'Snowdrop'?"

"Yes, a fucking 'Snowdrop.' Now you know. Happy?"

There is an uncomfortable silence. Andy is well aware that the

RAF Police are not the most popular group of men on most camps, particularly given their task of maintaining discipline during off-duty hours.

"So what you going to do when you get out?" asks Andy slowly and cautiously.

"Well, it won't be joining the Police Force, that's for sure."

"Was it that bad?"

"For starters, we had to be careful where we went for a drink. The other blokes on the camp didn't want to know us. You could tell that just by the looks on their faces. We always used to enjoy a kick-around but when the Police got a team together to play against the other Sections everyone wanted to kick lumps out of us – every game!"

"Looking forward to going home?"

"Who isn't?"

"Must have had a few laughs along the way, though," says Andy

"Yeh, a few. Tell you what I *did* enjoy about being a Service copper: being in control. Back home in the civvy Police, so I'm told, if someone gets pulled in – and it's pretty serious – you've often got the family to deal with, then probably the solicitors. Then the bloody newspapers can come in to stir it all up. But well away from the UK, in the Services, the poor bastards are on their own – and we, the Police, are in control. Yes, Sir. No, Sir. Three bloody bags full, Sir. Let 'em know who's the boss."

The Corporal's words bring a sparkle to his eyes.

"Ever heard of the Military Corrective Establishment?"

"Oh yes," replies Andy, recalling having seen at first hand the condition of some of the offenders who have returned from the place and heard their tales of alleged routine brutality. There is little doubt the policeman's enthusiasm is not confined to just jet engines.

"Well, I tell you this," continues the Corporal, "the blokes in charge up there were totally in control. All the bad eggs that got sent to us thought they were smart, hard men, but never saw a single one come out smiling. But I've got a problem to sort out before we reach Lyneham, so now *I'll ask you* a serious question for a change."

"Is my answer going on record?" jokes Andy.

There is a long pause until the Corporal realises it is a intended as a humorous comment.

He offers a weak smile, before adding: "My serious question is: what do you think of my tan? Now be honest."

"Well..." Andy is taken aback by the bizarre change of subject.

"Go on, you can give it to me straight."

"To be honest, I've seen better. You haven't spent much time on the beach, have you?"

"No, when I stretched out it was usually on my pit, only very occasionally on Changi Beach. Never fancied joining the sun worshippers laying out on the roof of the block, starkers, panicking at the last minute to get a decent tan to take home. Anyway thanks for your honest opinion."

The pair are having a quick nightcap in the downstairs bar when they are interrupted by one of the other passengers from their 'plane, who relays the news that the flight departure will not be until late afternoon on the following day and then drifts into conversation about the wonders of the Comet 2. Andy leaves them together and returns to his room. Despite the humidity, he soon falls asleep.

The sound of a nearby early-morning train is enough to awaken him. He looks across to see that the other single bed is empty. At breakfast there is no sign of the Corporal. Assuming his room-mate has taken an early morning walk, Andy decides not to question his whereabouts nor to report him missing. Lunchtime approaches in the hotel and still there is no sign of the 'Snowdrop'. Andy decides to seek out the Warrant Officer, who holds the highest rank amongst the passengers and, by virtue of that distinction, has quietly assumed the unofficial role of leader of the planeload of returning men.

They meet in the lobby of the hotel.

"What's the problem, young man?"

"Haven't seen the Corporal, have you? You know, the tall lad with the pale complexion?"

"You mean the tall, pale bloke with severe sunstroke?"

"With what?" gasps Andy.

"Silly sod's on his way to hospital – could be there now."

"What happened?"

"One of the waiters spotted him going up on the roof early this morning, before breakfast. Some time later, when he was coming off his shift, the same waiter mentioned it to Reception. Straight away, they sent someone up to find out what he was doing there and found him lying on his stomach, fast asleep, starkers, with his back burning up, almost on fire. From his condition, they reckon the daft sod must have been there for at least two hours."

298

"Poor chap. He was a Policeman, you know," replies Andy.

"Now that's funny," laughs the Warrant Officer.

He hesitates then adds, "Makings of a great newspaper headline: 'Snowdrop' takes two hours to melt in Karachi!'"

"Must have been in real pain though," Andy says sympathetically.

The remark is ignored by the Warrant Officer who is still in a state of self-congratulation about his suggested newspaper headline.

"Snowdrop takes... I think that's a gem, one to remember."

Andy turns away and heads back to his room to check whether the Corporal has left anything behind.

Minus one 'well done' Corporal, the Comet takes to the air, heading in the direction of the Persian Gulf and its third stop, Bahrain.

Despite a choice of empty seats, Andy takes the same place next to the window. It is by far the longest leg of the trip and despite the smooth flight he has difficulty in sleeping.

Not surprisingly, his mind is again turning to home and, in particular, what sort of welcome awaits him. And, of course, how he will cope with the March weather?

A few of the passengers have heard about the unfortunate sunburnt Corporal and come to question Andy as to what happened to his room-mate. It comes as no surprise that each expression of sympathy or concern is soon replaced by mild amusement when they realise the sufferer was a Policeman.

The landing at RAF Bahrain is a surprisingly bumpy one. As the aircraft taxies away from the dust-bound airstrip, the passengers look out with some apprehension at the modest collection of huts and low-rise buildings. It seems a desolate spot. Compared with being posted to this place, Andy feels his time serving on the island in North Borneo could perhaps now be viewed as the equivalent of a long stay at a holiday camp. Although perhaps not quite up to the standard of Butlins!

After disembarking, the news that there is to be an unscheduled overnight stop serves only to put a damper on the mood of the party. There is relief as the temperature drops noticeably after dark.

Late for breakfast, Andy sits alone in the Mess while a painfully thin cat shuffles around under the table, occasionally rubbing its bony, grey frame against his legs.

"Not bothering you, is she?" comes the shout from a cook behind the servery.

"No, not at all. Just given it a bit of bread."

"Shouldn't be in here in the first place, but she's just had a litter out the back, so we don't kick her out unless she gets on the tables. By the way, you on that Comet job?"

"Yeh," replies Andy proudly.

"Be home in a few hours in that kite, won't you?"

"Should be, but this will be our second overnight stop since we left Singapore."

"My heart bleeds for you, mate. I came out on a troopship and I'll be going back the same way. You should count your blessings."

After disappearing into the kitchen, the cook reappears and stands over Andy with a letter in his hand.

"Couldn't do me a favour, could you?"

"Depends."

"Well, the postal service from here to home can sometimes be a nightmare. Wondered if you could take this home with you on the plane, bung a stamp on it and post it. It's urgent. I'll give you some fags to cover the stamp."

"Don't smoke," replies Andy.

"All right then, I'll get you something extra to eat – you know, on the house like?"

"Don't worry, I'll post it. Special occasion, is it?"

"Not really, it's a reply to what they call a 'Dear John.' You're too young to know about all that, but what it means is that your girl has dumped you."

"Really?" says Andy without much conviction in his voice.

"Yeh, that's what women do. Wait until you've been posted overseas – then dump you. Clever, if you think about it?"

"But sad for you," replies Andy.

"Don't you believe it, mate, doesn't bother me in the slightest. My wife divorced me a couple of years ago. The letter you're taking home is from one of the lads in the kitchen."

Within hours, Andy is once more aloft in the Comet, heading eastwards toward the Mediterranean and the island of Cyprus. The De Havilland technical staff have apparently completed their tasks and are now beginning to talk more freely with the other passengers; and the mood among the returning Airmen is becoming increasingly relaxed as they are being brought ever closer to home. Noticeably, the Warrant Officer is no longer sitting silently alone, but can be seen in conversation with the other ranks.

The word is passed back from the cockpit that bitterly cold weather will be greeting them in Cyprus. The unwelcome news draws an immediate round of boos. However, the landings are becoming smoother as the flight progresses and the faultless touch down on the island is met by an appreciative round of applause. Once off the aircraft and into the airport, the passengers come face to face with a team of stern-faced RAF Police who have been cast in a heightened security role. A trio stand behind a counter, glaring in turn at each of the new arrivals. Andy is the first to face the hostility when a board is held up directly in front of him.

"Got any of these?" comes the gruff voice.

On a whiteboard, are listed: 'daggers', 'knives', 'revolvers' etc.

"None of those," answers Andy.

"Right, well what you standing there for? Move along, you're holding up the rest!"

Having completed the security check, the passengers take their seats in a Bedford coach outside the airport. The De Havilland team and the Warrant Officer are nowhere to be seen as the coach moves off into the evening darkness. From the seat behind, a hand arrives to tap Andy on the shoulder.

"What was all that about with the Police?" comes the question.

"Probably to do with the terrorist trouble they have here."

The explanation is met with silence then, after a pause, the words: "What, here as well?"

The coach makes its way into the moonlit countryside and climbs, groaning its way through the lower gears.

"This is it! Out you all get!" shouts the driver. The journey has taken twenty minutes.

The passengers stand outside the coach shivering, surveying a vast area of tented accommodation.

"So where are we staying, not here surely?" asks one.

"Nothing to do with me," is the driver's response. "This area around here was filled with French troops for the build-up to Suez, some of their Paras were sleeping in the ditches, and they haven't got it sorted out yet. You'll find our Army – and the Paras – in some of the tents. That big tent over there – the one with smoke coming out through the top – is the Mess, that's where you've got to report. Sorry lads, nothing to do with me."

The men survey an unfriendly expanse of frozen and rutted ground, without a tree in sight. Somewhat under-whelmed by their surroundings, they file into the Mess and are given tea and toast.

"Sorry, lads, at this time of night, nothing else I can let you have," comes an apology from the cook on duty.

"So where do we sleep?"

"Well, feel free to stretch out on the tables but you'll have to be out, six-thirty sharp, tables have to be cleared by then. Mind you, there are a few, much smaller empty tents out there but you'll have to take your chance in the dark! Wouldn't recommend you disturb the beauty sleep of any of those Army hard nuts!"

Andy decides to lie overnight on one of the tables in the Mess. The temperature has fallen dramatically so there is no question of undressing. His greatcoat is quickly pulled out from his kitbag to provide some warmth. Meanwhile, a couple of his fellow passengers venture out into the darkness in search of more acceptable tented accommodation.

The morning chorus is provided by the clattering of pots and pans in the Mess.

The sound is enough to rouse Andy. He lifts his head from his holdall, which has doubled as a pillow. His legs feel both cold and stiff but he manages to roll them off the table. A cook is already standing by, a bucket of water in hand, to wash down the tables in preparation for the first arrivals for breakfast.

"That's your lot. Out you get!"

"Where's the toilet?" asks Andy anxiously.

"Round the back, mate. Open air job here."

Andy dashes out from the tented Mess. Screened behind a broken down truck, he finds half a dozen buckets of frozen urine standing in line. Eyes closed, head turned to the sky, he moves close to the nearest bucket, undoes his flies and allows nature to take its course.

The UK-bound passengers are relieved to return by coach to the airport from their night in the Cypriot countryside. Having enjoyed little sleep and being unprepared for the Winter temperature, the mood is subdued. Despite the bumpy ride, most of the men are soon nodding off. Andy wonders where the De Havilland men from the flight – and of course the Warrant Officer – had disappeared to overnight. No doubt they had been found more desirable accommodation, a reminder perhaps of the sometimes unbridgeable gap between Officers and Other Ranks.

In the comparative comfort of the Comet, the flight across the Mediterranean from Cyprus to Libya passes quickly. There is little talk from the other ranks, most of whom are still catching up on lost sleep. The aircraft lands softly on an inhospitable, dusty desert strip at RAF El Adem. Andy is immediately impressed by the cheerful manner of the permanent staff, reminding him of his days on detachment in Borneo and the natural bonding which can follow when men are posted to a remote spot. This time there is no overnight stop and soon the Comet is heading west towards the island of Malta, hugging the North African coastline. Bordering the Mediterranean, there can be seen the patchwork quilt patterns of irrigated areas and non-irrigated lands, with differing shades of green and brown. From the port side, the view below is of a terrain more resembling a lunar landscape.

The mood of the passengers is improving by the hour. Malta will be the last stop before the 'plane finally arrives at RAF Lyneham. At the front of the aircraft, a card school has been established and its players are becoming increasingly vocal. Although there are no female passengers on board, a cautionary word about noise and language can soon be expected from the Warrant Officer. As the Comet loses altitude, Andy leans close to the window for his first glimpse of the Island and its people who had won the George Cross for their bravery during the Second World War. Visibility is perfect. Brilliant sunshine, and the reflection upwards from its white stone buildings, serve to present Malta as a sparkling jewel set in the blue waters of the Mediterranean. It is now late afternoon as the passengers eat together in the Mess at RAF Luqa. Conversation is focused on what awaits them on their return. Some are more excited than others, a few seem to be taking it in their stride, as if they were returning from a weekend pass.

The last leg of the journey home is in darkness before the Comet finally touches down at RAF Lyneham. Home at last! Those in the window seats lean forward in a totally misplaced expectation of catching a glimpse of something of the Old Country but the only sight is the lights of a Bedford coach crawling out of the misty gloom to collect them. "Typical," comes a voice from the front of the aircraft, "as if we didn't know – it's bloody raining!"

The passengers look around at each other and smile. There'll be nothing to do this evening, no celebratory drink, just time to get their heads down. It has been a longer trip than expected and the men are a touch travel-weary. The exciting catalogue of memories from their shared times in the Far East, destined to be told and re-told for the rest of their lives, are for the moment being pushed to the back of their minds. The UK is where they belong and Andy feels a sudden tingle of excitement. Tonight, Wiltshire. Tomorrow, the short trip to Gloucester and RAF Innsworth to sign off. Then Devon – and home!

Leaving the aircraft, the passengers are struck by yet another drop in temperature. The men are led to one of the camp billets for their overnight stay. Although the billet is spotlessly clean, it comes as a disappointment to find no coal to start a fire. Soon they are unpacking their kit bags and donning their trusty greatcoats which have lain dormant during their Asian sojourn. Through circumstance, rather than choice, Andy and most of the men from the Comet will be sleeping in their UK uniforms.

After an early breakfast, the party are soon on their way by coach to RAF Innsworth. The paperwork formalities for release are soon completed and Andy finds himself, once more back in civilian clothes, walking out through the camp gates. The sun is shining, the temperature is climbing and, as far as civilian life is concerned, normality has been restored. Alongside him are a couple of fellow ex-National Servicemen. They walk together for a few minutes along the deserted road, before stopping at a bus shelter to check the times of the service into Gloucester. "Twenty minutes to wait. Not too bad," comes the verdict.

Not unexpectedly, the newly demobbed are in a relaxed mood as they compare the train times from Gloucester and how long it will be before they are home. But their conversation is brought to an abrupt halt as a shapely figure comes towards them from the camp gates, carrying a small, pink suitcase.

"Just get a look at those legs!" gasps one of the men, followed by a predictable two-tone whistle. He then leaves the party and from a distance is seen in conversation with the woman, his body language suggesting he is only too willing to carry her case. As the pair approach the bus stop, Andy is immediately aware that the woman's face is a familiar one. "It can't be," he mutters to himself in disbelief.

With the words, "I'm not waiting here in the road for twenty minutes," her identity is immediately confirmed. It's Joan from the Accounts Branch at Changi!

Before Andy can step forward, she is in quick retreat, thumbing a lift from an oncoming car. Without a moment's hesitation, the male driver stops, throws open the front passenger door. With Joan seated comfortably on board, the vehicle accelerates past the bus stop, leaving the men to ponder on the wiles of the weaker sex.

33

Andy stands expectantly in the corridor of the train, suitcase and holdall at his feet, as it pulls into Plymouth's North Road Station. His left hand poised to release the door handle, his eyes anxiously scanning the platform to catch sight of his parents and, hopefully, Sandra. It is a moment for which he has been longing; a moment that seemed so distant it could never happen. He is relieved the train from Bristol is bang on time so no-one has been kept waiting. Being in one of the forward carriages, Andy passes almost the length of the platform without spotting a welcoming face. Suddenly he catches sight of his always talkative mother at the ticket barrier, this time in conversation with one of the railway staff. There is no sign of his father. Not being of an outwardly sensitive nature, Andy anticipates he is probably sitting patiently in the car outside the station.

The passengers move quickly from the train. Suitcase in one hand, holdall in the other, Andy does his best to wriggle through, managing to slip past a number of the less mobile passengers. His mother spots him and excitedly waves an arm in the air. She rushes forward, pauses to look up at his face, then wraps her arms around his neck. Not a word is spoken. Tears are flowing as they make their way through the booking hall and outside to the station forecourt. The rain and grey clouds which have escorted the train throughout its journey to Devon suddenly relent, and the sun is threatening to break through.

"Your father's over there," says his mother with a raised voice, pointing to the familiar body of the family's pale green Morris Minor. As they approach, Andy's father leaves the driver's seat and with a beaming smile on his face takes a few leisurely paces towards them. "Good to have you back son," comes the restrained greeting, followed by a vigorous handshake. "And you look so well, so brown."

"With your black hair and that tan, you could be one of those natives you left behind," adds his mother.

They drive away from the station chatting happily and head in a northerly direction for the ten mile drive to Yelverton.

"Where's Sandra?" asks Andy, in a matter of fact manner. The question reduces his parents to immediate silence. Andy's father clears his throat and says "You better tell him, dear."

"Let's get home first and then I'll explain. It's all a bit complicated."

"Explain what? I'd rather hear it now," replies Andy. "What's going on? I rang her from Lyneham as soon as I landed – and then again from Innsworth – and each time she wasn't in. Her mother said she'd pass the message on, then almost as an afterthought, added 'welcome back'. It all sounded a bit odd, not exactly the welcome I expected."

Within minutes of being reunited with his parents, Andy's mood has taken a real downturn.

"Andy, please, your father is trying to drive. Let him concentrate on that. We don't want to have an accident, 'specially on your first day home. We'll talk about it as soon as we get back." An impatient driver behind them sounds his horn and accelerates past, turning his head in the process to mime a few words.

From the back seat, his mother moves into verbal overdrive, attempting to both change the subject and bring him up to date on village gossip. Meanwhile, Andy's attention is focused elsewhere. With a benign smile, he looks out on the shoppers dotted along Mutley Plain before the car drops a gear to climb up through Mannamead and past Hartley Reservoir.

Away from the busier traffic, his father begins to relax. Never a confident driver, he prefers not to engage in conversation when at the wheel. Today, however, he is making a special effort for his son. "'Fraid Argyle aren't doing too well. Didn't re-new my season ticket. Nowhere near as good as the '52/53 team, not by a mile. Can't be sure but I think they're home on Saturday. Fancy going along? It's ages since you've seen them – could go together if you like, our presence might just inspire them."

As the car pulls into the gravel drive leading to the cottage, Andy can see the heads of the two Labradors in the conservatory, bouncing up and down with excitement. He had read somewhere that dogs possess a sense of knowing where their owners are, long before they come into sound or view. Today, it is a theory he can heartily endorse. So different from people: no complications, just unconditional love. As the door opens, the two dogs are immediately engaged in a good-tempered tussle to gain his attention. Andy makes for his favourite deep brown, leather backed chair close to the open coal fire. After a flurry of circuiting his legs, Andy is able to sit down and the dogs finally settle at his feet, looking up every now and then to seek acknowledgment from their returned master.

Andy's father reaches for the coal bucket to add a few more lumps to an already raging fire. "Don't want you to catch a cold soon as you come back, do we?" exclaims his mother. "Still March, you know – just."

Andy puts his cup of tea to one side. "Mum, what *is* going on with Sandra? I need to know. I'm confused, but I think we're engaged to be married."

"You'd better tell him about last night – right from the beginning, dear," adds his father.

"How can I put this?" begins his mother, rising to her feet.

"Anyway you like, Mum, just let me know what's going on!" snaps Andy impatiently.

"Well, we think she's got someone else, in fact we're sure of it."

Andy turns his chair around, leans forward and stares blankly into the fireplace.

Numbed, lost for words, his thoughts are immediately triggered back to the Far East and the countless times he waited with eager anticipation for the next post from home. Sure, the tone of Sandra's letters had cooled but she had never been the emotional, sloppy type. And wasn't it to be expected that, with the pair of them so far apart, she would have a re-think about the future, as he had? Or had he simply not wanted to read between the lines and accept the inevitable from their enforced and lengthy separation?

His mother breaks the silence with a predictable suggestion. "First, let's all have another cup of tea."

Andy waits for his mother to leave the room. "And how long has this been going on? How soon after I left? I need to know."

His father is now standing alongside him. "Listen, son. End of last year we were doing some late-night Christmas shopping down Royal Parade and we spotted Sandra, arm in arm with this other bloke. Coming straight towards us but with eyes only for each other. Your mum pulled me to one side, we turned away and pretended to look in some shop window. We heard them laughing together as they passed by. They didn't see us."

"Why didn't you tell me?" asks Andy.

"Well, for starters, could have been innocent. Good friends and all that. Be honest, didn't seem that way to me, but you know your mum and me don't look for trouble."

"I should have been told," replies Andy.

"That was a job for Sandra, not us. We've hardly caught sight of her since you left. More recently, your mum went up to her house a few times, hoping to talk about the wedding arrangements, the dress and all that but we always seemed to get the cold shoulder. Either they were just about to go out or visitors were expected. I soon got the message but I don't think your mum wanted to face up to it. Then yesterday..."

"What about yesterday?" asks an impatient Andy.

"Well, your mum has been getting so excited about you coming home. When it got down to the final months she was talking of nothing else, when it dropped to weeks and then days she was on an absolute high. Son, you had to be here to see how she was reacting. For the past week she was ringing the Melchetts, trying to find out what they and Sandra were planning for your return. They kept saying they'd ring back but never did. So, by yesterday, she decided enough was enough and told me she was going to see them to sort it out. Course, I had to go with her."

"And?" presses Andy, hanging on his father's every word.

"Well, it got off to the worst possible start. As we drove up to the house, Sandra was on the doorstep saying goodbye to the same boy we saw her with in Royal Parade – and they weren't shaking hands."

"So what you trying to say, Dad?"

"They were locked together, all very cosy-like. Your mum erupted. She raced up the path ahead of me and tore a strip off Sandra, calling her a tramp and a two-timing bitch."

"Mum did what? She actually said those words? Mum did?"

"Oh, yes, and that was only the beginning. The Melchetts must have heard the commotion and came out to investigate. Sandra flew inside, crying her eyes out, doors being slammed, the full performance. Her parents invited us in for a drink – long time since they'd done that, I can tell you – and asked us to sit down for a rational discussion. Rational! Can you believe it?"

"So what happened?"

"Well, your mum started crying. Then Sandra's father made it clear that he had no time for the new bloke and said his daughter was really too young to settle down anyway. And in all that time, not one mention of you!"

"Doesn't really surprise me," adds Andy.

"So I asked Sandra's father why she hadn't come clean with you. Granted a tough letter for her to write but she should have been honest with you, not stringing you along all this time."

"I'm going to have all this out with Sandra, that's for sure," says Andy firmly.

"Up to you, son, but is it – or she - really worth bothering about now. Frankly, your mum and me reckon the Melchetts and their daughter are best forgotten."

"That's a decision for me, Dad, not you."

"Well, if you decide to see her again, make sure she hands back the engagement ring. It cost you a fortune."

"She lost it!"

"What! When?"

"She wrote to me when I was in Borneo saying it was lost. Never mentioned later having found it."

"So what does that tell you about her, son?"

"What did he look like?"

"Who?"

"The bloke with Sandra."

"Tall and slim, but a scruffy looking individual. Kept his head down as he passed me, and it was dark so I didn't get a proper look at his face." Andy's mother arrives with tea and biscuits on a tray.

"Your dad's told you about last night, has he? I rang them this morning. They said that Sandra was under the weather, so she wouldn't be working today and certainly not up to seeing anyone, which I imagine includes you."

"Mind if I skip the tea, Mum? I'm dog tired."

"Course, dear. We've had your room decorated since you went and we've treated you to a couple of pairs of new pyjamas. Bit of a gamble with the colours. You'll find an extra blanket on your bed and other ones – if you need them – are in the usual place in the wardrobe. And don't worry about using the two-bar electric fire, leave it on as long as you like."

As Andy climbs the stairs, his thoughts are of a day that has suddenly been transformed from a day to remember, into one best forgotten. In less than twenty- four hours his life has taken a downturn, although not totally unexpected. No doubt about it, Sandra is no longer the girl he knew. Or is it that he never really knew her in the first place? Had the tall, slim, scruffy individual actually done him a favour? Yes,

Sandra might have changed but, fortunately, his parents hadn't.

Once in his bedroom, Andy rummages through his suitcase, gently unwrapping the tissue paper protecting Sandra's present, the wooden carving of a horse bought in Changi Village. He runs his fingers over its smooth body, pondering whether it now deserves a different home. Suddenly, he spots his record player has been relegated to a less prominent place in the room, namely beneath the lowest shelf of a bookcase. Clearly it has remained inactive throughout his absence. Andy cannot resist the temptation to remind himself of the music collection he left behind. Flicking through his 78s and 33s, the names of the American singers, Guy Mitchell, Frankie Laine, Rosemary Clooney, dominate. He smiles at the thought of how Martin, the Music Man in Borneo, would react to viewing his choices. Probably with a dismissive shake of the head, followed by an invitation to… 'open your ears and your heart to this and tell me what you think about it.' Martin had not toiled in vain with his hours of indoctrination of classical and jazz music. The established American 'Pop' singers would shortly have to shuffle up and make room for the likes of Mozart and Beethoven and the giants of jazz, such as Lionel Hampton, Count Basie and Oscar Petersen. The powers of brain-washing? From downstairs, Andy can hear the sound of his parent's recently acquired long-term lodger: a black and white television set. Within minutes, sporting his new pale blue pyjamas, he is fast asleep.

A low-lying mist greets his first morning back in Devon. During his time overseas, he had almost forgotten the joy of pulling back his bedroom curtains to gaze out over the back garden, then beyond to the open moor land. He waits expectantly for the mist to clear, running his fingers in lines across the condensation that has formed on the glass.

A soft knock on the door and his mother enters, carrying a tray.

"Your first full day back, so I've done you a special cooked breakfast. Before you say anything, I know you don't usually have too much first thing. But you do look as if you need feeding up."

"Thanks, Mum."

"And those pyjamas, all right are they? Took a gamble with the colour, you know."

"They're just fine. Excellent choice."

"I don't know what you were planning today …"

"Actually, I was thinking of talking to Sandra."

"What, on the 'phone or in person?"

"Haven't decided yet. I'll have breakfast first."

"It's not really for me to say but…"

"No, it's not for you to say, Mum," interrupts Andy, as he attempts to put a comforting arm around her. "I'll have to sort this out myself."

"Well, whatever you decide make sure you eat a hearty breakfast – you've lost weight since we last saw you," adds his mother with a smile as she leaves the bedroom.

34

The Melchetts have one of the grandest houses in Yelverton. As befits a successful estate agent, Rupert Melchett, has bought well. The five-bedroomed property stands in an elevated position, on the edge of the village. From the road, Andy can see the double-garage doors lying open, with Sandra's orange coloured Mini parked modestly alongside her dad's silver Mercedes 190 SL. It is close to midday as Andy walks purposefully along the gravel path winding up to the front door. He spots Sandra's mother engaged in a bout of curtain twitching, so decides to shorten his stride, anticipating that it will give Mrs Melchett sufficient time to alert the household to his visit. Just to be on the safe side, Andy pauses to untie then re-tie his shoe laces before giving the brass knocker a firm rap. His timing is spot on. The door is opened slowly.

"So good to see you again," comes the almost breathless greeting.

Andy leans forward, uncertain whether his arrival will be met with a kiss or a handshake.

Sandra's mother opts for neither welcome, instead turning her back towards him with the words:

"Please come in, Andrew, we've all been looking forward to seeing you again."

Andy follows her into the lounge, where her husband lies asleep in a high backed armchair, a crumpled copy of the *Daily Telegraph* on his lap.

"A coffee, perhaps, or something stronger?" suggests Sandra's mother.

"No coffee's fine, thank you."

Mrs Melchett gives her husband a firm tug on the arm.

"Guess who's here?" she adds before leaving the two men together.

"Ah, it's you! Andrew, my boy. How are you? God, that's an impressive tan!"

"Couldn't really avoid it, I'm afraid."

"Don't apologise. Costs people like me a lot of money for you to get something like that. Never been as fortunate as you chaps today in getting the taxpayer to pay for your trips abroad."

"Well, it wasn't exactly a holiday, Mr Melchett," replies Andy sharply.

"But you didn't see any action, did you?"

"Yes, some."

"You mean fighting for your place in the NAAFI queue?"

Andy ignores the sarcasm.

Mrs Melchett has returned and stands in the doorway with a pained expression, suggesting she has something unwelcome to say.

"Andrew, I've just told Sandra you're here but she's not too well and she's resting this morning. Asked if she could she pop round to see you this evening, that's if she's feeling better. Tomorrow would probably be even better. Don't mind, do you?"

Andy rises from his seat and makes quickly for the door. He pauses before adding: "So what exactly is wrong with her? It must be serious if she is unable to come downstairs to see me after a two-year absence."

Sandra's mother hesitates and looks towards her husband, as if expecting him to respond.

Suddenly, Andy is reminded of one of Finnegan's favourite sayings: 'if you want to see what your girlfriend will be like in thirty years, take a look at her mum.' The thought brings a smile to his face.

"Something amusing you would like to share with us, Andrew?" asks Mr Melchett.

The question goes unanswered. Andy has just taken a lightning glimpse into the future and Ruby Melchett has done her daughter no favours.

An uncomfortable silence fills the air.

"Right, I'll be going," Andy walks toward the front door.

"So I can tell Sandra it's OK for tomorrow then?" says Mrs Melchett with an expression of relief on her face.

"No, just tell Sandra to forget it – altogether. I've travelled seven thousand miles to get here, and was so looking forward to seeing her again. Never mind that she didn't bother to meet me at the station or even return any of my calls. Now, apparently, she can't even bother to walk down a flight of stairs. We were engaged when I left – or have I got that wrong? No, tell her that's it, it's over, we're finished – she has apparently lost the ring – so there's nothing left but to just forget the whole unfortunate episode."

Sandra's father rises to his feet to stand supportively next to his wife. The *Telegraph* slips to the floor. "Now look here, old chap, no need to take that tone ..."

"Hold on, Andrew, I'll have another word with her and perhaps..." begins Mrs Melchett, for the first time sensing a more assertive side to Andy's character.

Before she can finish the sentence, and with a dismissive wave of his hand Andy turns to go, leaving Sandra's parents standing alone together.

Drawing on his rapidly diminishing reserves of tolerance, he avoids the temptation to slam the front door. His head is spinning, a rag-bag of confused thoughts. This was light years away from the homecoming he had planned. The carefully chosen and much rehearsed opening words to his fiancée were now on the scrapheap. So Sandra was too ill to manage a flight of stairs but would 'pop round' later? Who were they kidding?

As he heads home, Andy's thoughts turn to the tall, scruffy, long haired individual who has taken his place. Was he a local boy or someone from Plymouth? How long had he known Sandra? How old was he? Had he done National Service or perhaps been deferred? More to the point was it someone he already knew? No, that didn't make sense because his parents would have recognised the bloke.

Meanwhile, the Melchett household is in complete disarray following the visit from their daughter's now ex-fiancé.

"Damn cheek of the fellow, just turning up like that. Could have rung to warn us he was on his way," says Sandra's father.

"Actually dear, he did. He telephoned yesterday and his mother rang the day before, so no real surprise he showed up here today, was it?" counters his wife "After all, they *were* engaged."

Sandra bursts into the room. "And we still are!" she adds firmly.

"But you said you had written to him calling the whole thing off," replies her mother.

"Not exactly, I just sowed the seed. Well, I had to let him down gently – didn't want to be cruel. God, he should have got the message. How dim can boys be?"

"I think you'll find out he's a man now – a very angry one and he has got the message. I'd let him cool off a bit," adds her father.

"How did he look? I caught a glimpse of him from the bedroom window, storming off down the path. Didn't bring his dreadful parents with him, did he? Knowing them, they probably sat in their car while he came in…"

"No, Sandra, he came on his own. No sign of any car down in the road. Your problem, my girl, is that you have to make your mind up which one you're going to choose. The choice is now between a reliable civil servant, and a lazy, long-haired university student who – by all appearances – won't be in gainful employment for years to come. Frankly, I'd dump them both."

"But it's not your choice, Dad, is it?"

"No, it's not – but I know what's best for you."

Sandra leaves the room without further comment, slamming the door behind her.

Mr Melchett reaches down for the *Telegraph*; his wife slumps into an armchair. Not a word is spoken.

Andy returns home to find his parents are on the point of leaving to visit friends in Plymouth.

"Thought we'd hang on till you got back," says his mother.

"What she really means is: how did it go?" explains his dad.

"Waste of time," replies Andy.

The parents wait, open-mouthed, hoping for their son to elaborate. There is no response.

"OK we'll be back early evening, help yourself to anything you need. We can talk about it then. Oh, and I'm sure the dogs would love it if you could take 'em for a walk. They're so pleased you're back – you can see that, can't you?"

Andy reaches for their leads and immediately the labradors are at his side, nudging his legs. Their warmth of affection is both welcome and well-timed.

He watches from the front door as his parents drive away. He has already noticed they have changed in the past two years. During that time his father has taken early retirement and with it life now assumes a more leisurely pace. His mother, of course, continues to fuss – as all mothers do – over her only child; but, more worryingly, she had clearly become too involved in his relationship with Sandra. Hopefully, her concerns will soon cool as the matter slips into the past.

Flanked by two dogs, Andy retraces the familiar route leading him to the local golf club. As a child, it was a popular spot for him. Often, his pals would take a ball with them and find a temporarily deserted fairway for an impromptu game of football, before being chased off by the members. As youngsters, it had made little sense to them that Dartmoor ponies were allowed to roam the fairways but not the aspiring soccer stars of tomorrow! Today, there is a sharp wind but the sky is clear and a panoramic view of the open moor land is waiting to be enjoyed. In the distance, to the west, lies Cornwall. Andy stands behind one of the greens as a couple of elderly golfers prepare to hit their approach shots. At his feet, the two dogs are panting excitedly having returned together from a search through the thicker heather, beyond the fairway.

Encouraged by his parents, Andy spends the evening telling them of his experiences in the Far East. An assortment of black and white photographs are spread across the dining table, as he impresses them with an instant recall of names, places and dates.

"And these men, will you ever see any of them again?" asks his mother.

"Well, I have a note of the home address and 'phone numbers of some of them. Yes, I'll probably be in touch with a few of them."

"This man here looks a bit of a rough diamond. I bet that's one you won't be rushing to meet up with," laughs his father.

"That's Finnegan, he's a real character. Oh yes, I'll make a point of seeing him."

His mother picks up a slightly out-of-focus snap.

"And this one, with his arm around your shoulder with a hairstyle from the thirties. Look, there's other ones of him here. Good friend, was he?"

"That's the Music Man!"

"Both National Servicemen then?"

"No, regulars but I've got their details. Funny, you've picked on my two best mates in Borneo."

"And this odd looking character? Looks a bit tipsy when you took his photo."

"He probably was. That's Lofty, a Corporal I worked with at Changi. I didn't take it – it's one he gave me. In fact I never got round to buying a camera out there – and they were dirt cheap."

"Don't worry, son, you can have ours. We've stopped taking pictures," says his father.

"Your mother and I no longer look like film stars – if we ever did!"

A full half hour is given to detailed accounts from Andy of some of his hair-raising exploits including the Corporal's premature celebration of promotion, ending with his rescue from the sea.

The parents receive the story with a sense of shock.

"He could have drowned, the silly fellow! Wasn't married was he?"

"Yep, three kids with another on the way."

"How irresponsible. Together with all these pictures of football, you probably didn't have much time to do any work, did you?"

Andy smiles.

"Tell you what did worry us. When we heard of the riots in Singapore. Just as well you didn't get caught up in that. Sounded nasty," says his father.

Andy has already decided that it is an experience best committed to memory and one that his parents would find difficult to understand. He turns their attention to a collection of beach and aerial photos.

His parents endearing naivety is already taking the edge off the bitter disappointment of the reception he received at the Melchett's home.

Andy decides not to discuss his relationship with Sandra, other than to tell them that it is now finally ended. He senses they are neither surprised nor disappointed at the news.

It is good to be home again but, deep down, he is feeling restless. Does he really want to pick up all the same pieces he let drop before being posted abroad? Does he want to resume the daily, twenty mile return trip into Plymouth to work there in the Tax Office?

Past experience has taught him there is little chance of landing another job in Plymouth, and employment in the local Dockyard holds no attraction for him, so there seems no alternative but to seek employment elsewhere. Hopefully, his parents will understand. Andy is aware that, before he joined up, his mother had warmed to the prospect of her son working and living locally with Sandra and joining her father in his estate agency business. He had never really fancied that idea and it is, of course, now definitely time to close that chapter. Yelverton is a beautiful village, where he grew up and his parents still live, but it is no longer enough and he feels that he will be unable to settle back into his old life. London seems the obvious answer. With only a handful of 'O' Level passes, and without a trade skill, another job within the Civil Service would seem the obvious choice. By the time he returns home,

Andy has reflected on all these questions and accepts his time overseas has both sharpened his appetite for travel and adventure and opened his eyes to wider horizons. So soon after his homecoming, he knows this decision will need careful handling with his mum and dad.

Andy's parents return home to find their son seated in the kitchen, tea cup in hand, scanning the sports page of the *Western Morning News*.

"Thought I might have a beer this evening. Can you suggest a decent pub, Dad?"

"Taken up drinking, have you?"

"Not exactly. Couldn't really avoid it out there. Mind you, I did grow to like the taste of Tiger beer."

"Fair enough, let's pay a visit to my favourite haunt over at Meavy. Not too sure they serve Tiger. Anyway, first pint's on me."

"Hopefully, the second and third ones will be as well," laughs Andy. "I've run out of money!"

After a short run in the car, they are seated together in a quiet corner of the pub.

It is a place Andy has visited only once before, in the company of a fellow under-age drinker. This time he can relax. He casts his eyes around to admire the exposed beams and the original slate flooring.

"You've changed," says his father.

"What? In the last couple of years? You mean the tan?" jokes Andy.

"No, be serious for a moment. Your mum and I were soon aware of it."

"Really, I've only been home a couple of days and ..."

"We were just saying last night we wouldn't be surprised if you decide to move away. Not a lot down here to hold a young man who's seen a bit of the world."

"Go on," says Andy interested to hear more.

"And if you've any sense, you'll keep well away from Sandra – now that you've decided to end the engagement. Mind you, I wouldn't be surprised if she tries to get back with you. Girls can be funny that way. She might be more attracted to you now that you've walked away. You'd never have done that two years ago, would you?"

"Suppose not," replies Andy.

"Do you know, son, I've never really worked out how women think and I've lived with one for over twenty years! My experience and conclusion is that both sexes are completely mismatched, and there's simply a basic incompatibility between men and women. Some couples manage to keep it going, but they're in the minority."

"So why do people still continue to get married? Or are they just in search of the unattainable?" teases Andy.

The question is ignored.

"Any idea where you might go?"

"Possibly London, not sure yet."

"Don't think your mum would like that."

"No, you're right. Disappearing again so soon would upset her but London's not that far."

"Did you ever think of signing on in the RAF…"

Their conversation is interrupted by a chubby, elderly gentleman with a clump of untidy white hair hanging over each ear, who has come over from another table.

"It's young Marshall, isn'it?" comes the question delivered in clipped tones.

Andy recognises the face without hesitation. It is one of his former teachers at Devonport High School who, along with other members of his staff, had failed in their attempts to explain to him the unfathomable mysteries of Mathematics.

"Yes Sir," answers Andy, as he struggles in vain to recollect the name of the stooped figure.

"Well, young man, you're looking so well. Just back from holiday?" continues the teacher of yesteryear.

"Not exactly, Sir. Just completed my National Service."

"Played soccer for the first eleven, better footballer than student, if I recall?"

"Spot on!" adds Andy's father.

"Won't linger, young man, just wanted to remind you that your school has an active Old Boys Association and we could do with some young blood. Give me your address and I'll send you the necessary literature. You'll find it rewarding to keep in touch with your old school chums."

Andy hastily scribbles the details on the reverse side of a beer mat and hands it to the teacher who, with an appreciative wink, returns to his table.

"He's got a point, you know," says his father. "Come to think of it, in time you'll probably find yourself being invited to a reunion of the men you served with out in the Far East."

The thought strikes an immediate chord with Andy. Changi was probably too big a Station for a reunion: but a gathering of the men who had served on detachment in Borneo sounds promising. Most of his colleagues on the island had exchanged addresses and seemed keen to meet up again in the UK. For starters, the Music Man's home was relatively close at hand in Bristol. And Finnegan – wherever he now was – would surely be a 'must' for any get-together. Andy remains silent, mind in overdrive, as he attempts to gauge the level of support there might be for such an event.

"Andrew, you're not listening to a word I've said."

"Sorry, Dad, I was miles away, metaphorically speaking."

"Dead right, you were. I'll get us another drink."

Andy's father moves to the bar while his son reflects further on the possibility of a Borneo reunion, perhaps in a year or two's time when his colleagues had settled back in the UK and before memories of shared experiences had become blunted by the passage of time.

The pub is filling up quickly and both men are having to raise their voices to be heard.

As an asthmatic, Andy's father begins to cough as cigarette smoke fills the air.

"Time to go Dad," suggests his son.

Andy leads the way out, pausing only to exchange handshakes from a number of villagers who are genuinely pleased he is back amongst them. A few less familiar faces settle for a nod or a raised hand.

He finds himself repeating the words: "Nice to see you again. Hope to catch up with you all later."

He turns in the doorway to find his father is no longer with him.

Andy decides to wait, anticipating that he has been caught up in conversation, but his attention switches immediately to a couple engaged in a full-blooded argument, some distance away on the other side of the road. The man leans back nonchalantly against the small car, while the woman conducts her contribution to the heated exchange with one hand on the driver's door, suggesting her departure is imminent. The two-way stream of abuse is both crude and repetitive. A passing pedestrian hesitates, as if about to intervene, but opts not to get involved. The confrontation comes to a sudden end with the woman getting behind the wheel and accelerating away at speed, leaving her adversary behind. Andy moves closer to the scene, having recognised Sandra's Mini. There is little doubt in his mind as to the identity of the tall, slim and youthful gentleman who, head down, is walking slowly away in the opposite direction Meanwhile, the noisy altercation has drawn the pub's clientele out into the road.

"What the hell was that racket all about?" asks Andy's father.

"Probably a bad lot up from Plymouth," suggests another.

"You were out here, son. Recognise them? Did you catch what was going on?"

"Leave 'em to it as far as I'm concerned, nothing to do with me," replies Andy in a less than convincing voice.

35

London, 1958

It is just over a year since a 'head for head' transfer exchange with a London-based civil servant allowed Andy to take up a position as a Clerical Officer at the Treasury in Whitehall, with the other person moving down to take his place at the Inland Revenue in Plymouth. Accommodation has been arranged by his new Department and he finds himself living, with the aid of a subsidised rent, in a hostel in Cadogan Square, Chelsea, which occupies a row of three towering red brick houses built in the late nineteenth century.

In terms of property value and appearance, it is an exclusive and central part of the capital. As if to reinforce its claim to be a desirable area, a couple of foreign embassies have chosen to set up residence further along the Square. Andy's new home is but a short walk to Harrods and, in the other direction, an even shorter stroll to Sloane Square and the fashionable Kings Road. At the rear of the hostel runs a cobbled Mews, boasting a colourful collection of sports cars and window boxes. At weekends, it often becomes a rowdy venue for serious partying for the upper set.

Andy shares a third-floor room with three other civil servants, its windows opening onto a balcony overlooking a manicured central garden set within the Square. This area of well-tended shrubs and trees is fenced off, allowing access only to key-holding permanent residents who tend to use it for exercising their dogs. Having been brought up to enjoy the freedom of open moor land, Andy can only smile at one of the deprivations of urban living. The home to office travel is a three-stop journey on the Underground, usually completed – even during the 'rush-hour' period – in less than fifteen minutes. His clerical duties at the Treasury are not of an intellectually demanding nature and life in London is falling very much into a routine. Operating on modest incomes most of his fellow residents, drawn from all parts of the United Kingdom, develop a camaraderie not unlike the spirit Andy enjoyed during his National Service. In the evenings, the glut of pubs on and around the Kings Road lie close at hand to provide a welcome change of scenery, to discuss and argue topics ranging from politics to soccer, and of course women. Cash constraints dictate that each pint of beer must be savoured and consumed in a leisurely manner. Meanwhile, the more sober-minded hostel residents are drawn to the trendy coffee shops where they find they are allowed to dwell at length on a single cup. On colder evenings, a mobile food stall in Sloane Square serves to complement an evening's drinking by serving distinctive and piping hot meat pies. Despite the rumour that the proprietor has yet to summon up the courage to eat one of his own pies, it remains surprisingly popular. As for physical recreation, Hyde Park serves as a convenient spot to loosen up for the Inter-Hostel soccer matches held in Regents Park on Sunday afternoons, as well as an opportunity to either watch the boating on the Serpentine or the horse riders thundering along the sanded Rotten Row. While for the more cerebral and politically minded, Speakers Corner' becomes a regular venue.

In quieter moments, Andy reflects on his more eventful times in the Far East; occasionally taking a nostalgic look through his photograph albums. Increasingly, he begins to wonder what is now happening thousands of miles away at his old detachment in Borneo. He smiles to himself as he recalls the ambition of so many serving with him abroad to just get back home to resume a 'normal life.' Invariably, the overseas talk was more of tomorrow than today, symbolised by the daily ritual of ticking off another day on the demob charts. Yet yesterday now seems more meaningful than today. Perhaps his cognitive process was already at work, weaving its magical spell to push the tedium and duller moments he served in uniform to the back of his mind. A few of his new friends at the hostel have also completed their National Service and let slip in conversation, or over a drink, the occasional anecdote about their time in uniform. Not many of them have travelled so far afield and seem bemused and disbelieving of his tales of the Far East. Usually, the common ground is the exchange of bizarre stories relating to the days of square-bashing undertaken straight after call-up. Such recollections mean little to the uninitiated but to Andy and those who had done their two years, these stories are invariably met with a knowing nod, a smile and often raucous laughter. Amongst those who have experienced being called up, there appears an unspoken sense of now belonging to an exclusive group. To most, it is regarded as an enlightening and valued experience; to a few, an unwelcome and unnecessary distraction.

It is difficult for him to accept that a completely new set of personnel could now be serving on the Borneo island, with possibly only the local washerwomen and grass cutters of those he knew remaining. Surely the Music Man must have finished his tour of duty. Is he perhaps back in Bristol – or could he have signed on for a further period of Service? And what of Finnegan, the unforgettable fireman? Back on the island, are the fire crew still racing against the clock to reach the airstrip before the aircraft touch down? Is Fatimah still attempting to cast her spell over the C.O – whoever he might now be? Do the civilian staff still bow 'Japanese' style when collecting their meagre wages? Are the Aussies still returning in numbers to the island on Remembrance Day? And what of the little old lady from Melbourne who visited her son's grave? Has she made a return trip? Have the Japanese attempted another civilian landing? Is the storeman still issuing 'not fit for purpose' mosquito nets to new arrivals? Do the 'Dear John' letters still get pinned on the notice boards? Is the same District Officer and his flamboyant wife, Amelia, still in post, dutifully safeguarding our colonial interests? Has there been another formal camp inspection? Is Fifi still cycling in with his box of hairdressing tools? And what of the Robinson Crusoe character he met on the boat trip to the remote island. Is that man still living with two pretty native girls catering for his every need? Has he now acquired all the parts for a car that is going nowhere?

Closer to home, what has become of the eccentric Flight Lieutenant Munro? Has he been reunited with his wife, who returned prematurely to the UK? Or has he quietly left the Service? Andy reassures himself that, whatever the changes of personnel on the island, its deserted, soft sandy beaches will still each day be welcoming and bidding farewell to the tide, while gracefully accepting second billing whenever the breathtaking hues of violet and amber linger in the sky as the sun sets.

And what of Changi? Has Lofty Long finally managed to land his elusive third stripe? Has his wife had that all-important fourth child to amass the necessary points to elevate his family to the luxurious living standard of Officers Married Quarters? Is Chinese George still on the payroll? Are the Malcolm Club and NAAFI still rocking with riotous boat parties? How is the station football team progressing? A mountain of questions are destined to lie unanswered. Andy decides it is time to get in touch with his pals but, for one inexcusable reason after another, fails to put pen to paper. As with the camera he never got round to buying in the Far East, is it a task never to be completed?

Meanwhile, his parents are keeping in regular touch by letter, plus the occasional 'phone call. Andy's return trips to Devon usually coincide with the more attractive home matches on Plymouth Argyle's fixture list. To date, he has managed to avoid meeting Sandra on any of these visits although, according to his mum and dad, she has paid a number of visits to his home, seeking to contact him. Under Andy's instructions his parents are steadfastly refusing to disclose his London address. As far as Andy is concerned, the engagement withered and died long ago and Sandra's tall, thin, unidentified suitor is more than welcome to her.

This Sunday morning he finds himself in the company of a dozen or so fellow residents, sitting in the spacious hostel lounge listening to the popular BBC weekly radio programme 'Two-Way Family Favourites.' Andy has arrived early and occupies one of the sought-after leather chairs. The requests are from Servicemen based abroad and dedicated to their family at home, alternating with requests in the other direction. Apart from the occasional rustle of a Sunday newspaper, or a snore from a sleeper hung-over from the night before, the music is heard in silence.

For the second successive weekend, the rain has been lashing down and the Inter-hostel soccer match arranged for later in the afternoon has already been postponed. Today, Andy can relax. Having finished reading the sports page and, with closed eyes, he slowly lets his head rest back. Before he can switch off completely, the lounge door is thrown open with the cry: "Marshall, calling Andy Marshall, anyone seen him?"

Andy looks to the doorway. "I'm here. Someone on the 'phone for me?" he asks.

"Not on the 'phone, mate. You've got a visitor downstairs, waiting for you."

Andy hurries down the staircase from the first floor, at a complete loss to know who the visitor might be. He brushes past a couple coming up from the ground floor dining room, who obligingly step quickly to one side. Could his mum or dad have decided on a sudden visit? No, surely not – they certainly wouldn't have made the trip to London without warning him. Perhaps the unexpected visitor is one of his Air Force mates but how would they know his London address? Could they have been in touch with his parents, but mum would have alerted him when she last rang.

Andy turns into the reception area to find a couple of residents in a heated discussion with Mrs Pennywick, the Hostel Superintendent, who is taking them to task for their rowdy behaviour overnight.

He hesitates to intervene but is anxious to meet his mystery visitor.

"Excuse me, but I was told someone was here waiting for me. Can't see anyone about."

"Oh, there was a young woman in here a few minutes ago. She came in, spoke with someone who told her he'd put out a call for you. Didn't catch her name. He just ran up the stairs; she waited a few moments then went out."

"Out in that rain?" asks Andy.

"Perhaps she was in a hurry."

Without a moment's hesitation, Andy races out into the street. He catches sight of a woman crossing the road, heading in the direction of Sloane Square. Hopefully it is his mystery visitor. With just a pullover and slacks to protect him from the elements, he breaks into a run and comes alongside her.

"Excuse me..."

The woman lifts her umbrella to reveal her face.

"Christ! Sandra, it's you."

"Yes, it's me. Good of you to remember the face."

Andy recoils at the rapier response. What a damn stupid thing to say! And this from the girl of his many dreams, whose treasured photo had travelled with him to and from the other side of the world. Pretty as ever with her flowing, shoulder-length dark hair and sparkling blue eyes, but Sandra has changed. There is now an undeniable edge, an edge that wasn't there before – or perhaps one he had never wished to acknowledge. She'd changed – no doubt about it.

"Why the hell didn't you wait for me back at the hostel?" asks Andy.

"You mean that madhouse back there. I couldn't bear listening anymore to that bossy little Camp Commandant talking to those men as if they were schoolboys."

"She's not that bad really. Hey, how did you find me?"

"Doesn't matter, does it?"

"Just intrigued, that's all."

"Well, I side-stepped your parents, got in touch with your old school. They put me on to your Old Boys' Association – and bingo!"

"Let's get out of the rain. There's a coffee shop along here, opposite Peter Jones," suggests Andy.

The weather has ensured that the cafe is crowded and they wait just inside the door for a table. After a few minutes, a table tucked away in a corner becomes free, partly hidden behind a clothes rack over-laden with damp raincoats.

"Cigarette?" comes the offer from Sandra.

"Don't smoke, thanks."

"Suit yourself," is the curt response.

"Well, it's a real surprise to see you again, Sandra."

"Is it a nice surprise – or just a surprise?"

"Well, to be honest it's a shock."

"But why, we're still engaged, aren't we?"

Andy is caught totally unprepared for her question.

"Let's face it, Sandra, from the tone of the letters I got overseas and then what happened -or didn't happen – when I got back to England it seemed clear you'd had a change of mind. You made no attempt to get in touch with me when I returned. How else could I take it. Remember, I called at your house and you couldn't even be bothered to walk down the stairs to speak to me after I'd been away for nearly two years. I told your parents then, that was the end of the matter. Engagement finished, over. And that's now more than a year ago!"

"But at the time I wasn't well, with lots of problems and wasn't thinking straight."

Andy is puzzled by her response.

"Anyway what's happened to the other chap you were going with while I was away, Sandra. The one you were still with when I returned. I saw you fighting with him outside the Pub at Meavy."

"Come on now, Andrew, two years is a long time to be on your own. What about you, what did you get up to? My dad told me all about Servicemen. That chap meant nothing to me. Just a friend. You told me you loved me before you went overseas, proposed and haven't told me otherwise since you returned. In my book, you've taken time away to appraise the relationship – and so have I. Just because you buggered off to London without telling me, means nothing."

"What the hell are you talking about?" says Andy. "Appraise? What sort of word is that! As far as I'm concerned the matter is over and done with. I have nothing further to say to you."

Andy is suddenly aware that the couple on the next table have stopped talking in order to pick up on their conversation. There is a pause before they resume an octave lower.

"Well, after an awful four and a half hour train ride from Plymouth, I think I deserve to hear something positive. An answer would do for starters," suggests Sandra, ignoring Andy's statement, puckering a lip and reaching in her handbag for a handkerchief.

Each abrasive word from his ex-fiancée removes any doubts Andy may have had that their relationship has run its course.

"You made no effort to see me when I visited you after I got back. So why wait a year – a whole year – before you make contact again? It makes no sense. If you had my address here, why didn't you write first?"

"I needed time to be sure and, once I was, I had to speak to you face to face."

"Sorry, Sandra, it doesn't add up. I'm not interested in anything that you may have to say. I'm settled in London now, so there's no chance I'd throw up my job and go back to Plymouth."

Sandra leans across the table, sliding a warm hand over Andy's wrist.

"I could come up here and we could get a flat together." The words are delivered in a soft, seductive tone.

Andy lets his body drop back in the chair, shaking his head slowly from side to side. "Did you not hear what I just said. Absolutely out of the question! I'm not interested. I broke off the engagement the day I visited your house and you stayed in your room," replies Andy firmly. "Sorry Sandra, but that was the end of the story. After two years away, that was very hard to take. We have no future together. Goodbye."

Sandra drops her head, before once again dabbing her eyes with her handkerchief.

"I told you I wasn't well," comes her tearful reply.

Andy rises to his feet, leaving five shillings alongside his empty cup, and makes for the door. A feeling of immense relief comes over him as he walks back to the hostel. In keeping with his changed mood, the rain has almost stopped and the sky is beginning to brighten.

The change in the weather has brought out the dog walkers and the Square's exclusive garden is bustling with residents. Those countless, wasted hours and days overseas waiting for Sandra's letters now fall into perspective. How silly of him to place so much faith in her, to overlook the obvious. What did Sandra really think of him? And what did he really think of her? The emphasis she had placed on their still being engaged smacked more of a contractual obligation than a declaration of love. His dad was right after all: Sandra was not the girl for him. Time surely to get in touch again with his old mates from the Air Force, people that can be relied upon not to let him down.

In the days that follow, Andy endeavours to contact both Martin, the Music Man, and Finnegan. The initiative meets with mixed success. The disappointing response to ringing Martin's Bristol 'phone number is 'you've got the wrong number'; but calls to the fireman on a Manchester number finally catch a croaking, Irish voice of an elderly lady, who eventually and reluctantly admits to being Fergus Finnegan's mother.

"You want to speak to my son, do you? Well, so do I! Haven't seen him for months."

"Where's he stationed, Mrs Finnegan? I mean where's he based?"

"The name's not Finnegan, no more. Lost my first husband, got myself another one now. No bleeding better than the first one, as it turned out."

Andy warms to a dry humour that suggests a strong genetic link with her son.

"Give me your number and I'll tell him you rang."

"But if you've got his number, I can save you the trouble," suggests Andy.

"But I don't know who you are, do I? He might not want to speak to you."

"I was in the RAF with him, an old buddy. Tell him it was Andy Marshall from Borneo who rang. He'll know me straight away."

"Just give me your number will you, or I'll put the 'phone down. Can do without all this."

Andy obliges, giving both his hostel and office number, before Finnegan's mother abruptly hangs up.

A further six months elapse and it seems that his attempts to establish contact have failed.

A letter to the Music Man's address in Bristol remains unanswered.

Andy is at his desk at the Treasury in Whitehall, about to take his lunch break, when he receives a surprise call.

"That you, Andy?" The voice is that of Finnegan.

"You old bugger!" shouts Andy.

His spontaneous cry draws a round of smiles from his colleagues in the office.

"Listen, can't say too much," continues Finnegan. "This call cost me a bloody fortune before I spoke a word. The GPO must be making a bomb with these dodgy boxes, gobbling up coins like they're going out of fashion. Listen, I'll be down in London just before Christmas and we can meet up then. Till then, I'll be getting in touch with some of the others to set it all up. Leave it all with me, my friend. O.K to ring you again on this number? Even your operator sounds posh."

"Yeh, sure."

"And before I go, don't worry about the Music Man. I've already spoken with him. He'll be there, no problem."

"I tried his Bristol number, you know," adds Andy.

"That was a waste of time, he's working near London now. You've probably already have passed him in the street! Can't stop…"

Finnegan's voice is suddenly cut off and replaced by a continuous flat tone. Andy smiles to himself as he visualises the impatient Irishman at the other end of the 'phone, as if cast in the role of a drowning man, punching the coin buttons into the 'phone box as the GPO call time on their conversation. But the thought of Finnegan taking the lead in setting up a much-awaited reunion leaves Andy somewhat apprehensive. Past experience has shown he is not the most reliable character. And what of the Music Man.? Where exactly in London is he? Andy reminds himself to be better prepared when the Irishman next telephones. But the call itself has already served to lift his spirits. He strides out of the building for his lunch brake with an added bounce in his step and begins his usual circuit of the lake in St James's Park, unaware that in his excitement he has left behind his packet of sandwiches.

In the evening, back at the hostel, he moves studiously through his two albums of black and white photographs taken in Borneo and Singapore, compiled entirely from copies of pictures taken by other comrades. Effortlessly, he is putting names to all the faces, instant recall to all the places. Now and then he pauses to grin and reflect. In the days that follow, he becomes increasingly excited at the prospect of a reunion. A chance to turn the clock back? An opportunity to find out what was happening to everyone else? A merciful relief from his day-to-day working life in the Civil Service.

His mind turns back to Borneo and Flying Officer Scarborough's words of wisdom about living in the present and not giving undue importance to the future and its promise of a distant pension. Perhaps he had a point. But as far as the forthcoming get-together was concerned, it would be the past taking centre stage.

36

Andy has taken unpaid leave for today's much awaited event.

As he stands impatiently at the meeting point alongside Platform One at Victoria Station, another glance at his watch tells him that it is twenty five minutes before the agreed hour of noon to meet up with his pals from Borneo. Comfortably outside the 'rush hour,' the concourse is strangely quiet. How ironic that a reunion of those from a place of almost continual sunshine should begin in the gloom and shade of a shabby railway station in the unfriendly, cold month of December! Further calls from Finnegan had failed to totally reassure him that all the arrangements had been made.

Andy's offer to help had been brushed to one side. The Irishman had taken responsibility and promised a few big surprises. But how many would turn up? Hopefully, Curtis together with his limitless fund of jokes and story telling. And it would be great to meet up again with Ken, the cook, with his no doubt new-found confidence. Would he perhaps now be an accomplished and prosperous photographer? But some of his former colleagues might now be serving abroad, some could even have been posted to a station well away from London, which would of course mean too much travelling for today's special event. There will be so much to talk about, not just of yesterday but of today. Andy can hardly wait. Had the others, like him, also experienced difficulty in readjusting to life back in England? Did they all share his excitement about the reunion? Or would the reunion prove to be a damp squib and just a one off? No, that couldn't happen. That wouldn't be allowed to happen.

Andy's thoughts had been that the day should kick off with a celebratory drink in one of the many pubs around Victoria Station. With a little time on his hands, he leaves the station and looks out between the lines of empty buses that wait in their terminus outside. To his left, he catches a pub sign. Carefully picking his way across the bus lanes, he gets closer to the building: 'The Shakespeare.' He peers through one of the windows.

The place appears empty, apart from a couple of elderly gentlemen engrossed in a game of cribbage. A notice advertises sandwiches and light refreshment. Andy decides to look no further: an ideal spot for the first drink, particularly if the numbers exceed expectation. He returns close to Platform One as one of the hands of the overhead station clock slips past midday. To avoid being buffeted by the passengers entering and leaving the platform, Andy moves away to the back of the concourse while keeping a sharp lookout for the first arrivals. For a moment he wonders again just how many have made the journey. Could he even rely on Finnegan making the trip from Manchester? Of course he could, he had organised everything, hadn't he? And what of Martin? Always a bit of an enigma but he was now living in London, so surely he should make it in decent time.

"Stand by your beds!" the command comes loud and clear from directly behind.

The cultured delivery is a familiar one. He spins round to face the Music Man.

"You old bastard!" replies Andy. "You almost scared the life out of me."

Tactfully ignoring the fact that Martin appears to have put on well over a stone in weight and now carries a blotchy complexion, Andy feels an obligation to comment favourably on his appearance.

"You haven't changed a bit, Martin. Like the overcoat!"

"Rubbish – and you know it. If you don't, you need your eyes tested. I'm out of bloody condition, and at least a stone heavier."

"More to the point," continues Martin, "where's that Irishman?"

"He's had to come down from Manchester, don't forget."

"Let's face it, Andy, as someone who couldn't even manage to get his fire crew a couple of hundred yards up to the landing strip *before* the planes landed, what chance has Finnegan got of making the couple of hundred miles from Manchester to here on time?"

The pair break into laughter. Momentarily, the years roll back.

"Tell you what I noticed outside, young Andy, there's a shop across the road that sells Railway Lost Property. Thought I might take a peep while you wait here for Finnegan and the others. Don't mind, do you? Be back in ten minutes."

"No problem, you might even find some 'lost' classical records," smiles Andy, concealing his disappointment that a valued friend had so little to say after their time apart.

Perhaps the Music Man does not share the same excitement about today's get-together.

Another fifteen minutes elapse and the re-union appears to be heading for the rocks.

The clock is now showing twenty minutes past the appointed hour. Andy stands alone.

Martin has yet to re-appear and there is still no sign of Finnegan.

"Would Mr Marshall please report to the Station Master's Office."

The announcement comes loud and clear but fails to register with the person for whom it was intended. It is repeated before Andy realises it is directed at him.

"Bloody hell! That's me."

He scampers up a creaking staircase to the Station Master's Office, breathless but braced to take the message. The office is in a state of high confusion. The man who appears to be in charge is deep in a 'phone conversation with the Police about a series of 'pick pocket' robberies at the station, while his young fresh-faced assistant is attempting to placate an angry group of passengers whose train to the coast has just been cancelled.

Andy's mind is spinning as he tries to imagine what the message could possibly be.

His patience lasts for but a few moments.

"Excuse me, I'm Mr Marshall." The assistant steps forward.

"Ah! A message for you from a Mr Finnegan. Now where is it? Funny, had it only a minute ago."

Andy watches the young man's hands slither amongst an untidy collection of papers and timetables.

"Here we are!" With the flourish of an accomplished magician producing a rabbit from the hat, the piece of paper is proudly held aloft.

"Yes, urgent message for you, Mr Marshall, from a Mr Finnegan. He rang here to let you know he had missed his train by seconds and would be a couple of hours late. Asked if you could wait. Said he'd meet you in the same place. Make sense to you?"

"Yes, perfectly." Andy returns to the station concourse to rejoin Martin.

"Thought you might have buggered off."

"Not likely. Had to go up to the Station Master's Office to get a message from Finnegan."

"Don't tell me, he can't make it!"

"No, but he's running late."

"How late?"

"Missed his train by seconds," explains Andy with a grin.

Martin reacts by raising his eyebrows, followed by the words, "no comment."

The two men wait another ten minutes. There is now an unspoken acceptance that no one else – except perhaps Finnegan – will arrive.

"Come on, let's have a pint in 'The Shakespeare' while we wait for the Irishman," suggests Andy. "Doesn't look like anyone else is coming."

"Don't fancy getting stuck in a pub for a couple of hours. Any other suggestions?"

"Hopefully, it'll be a lot warmer than hanging around here until two o'clock."

"O.K, if we must," replies Martin with a shrug of the shoulders.

The pair walk slowly out of the station and head for 'The Shakespeare.'

"Looking forward to Christmas then?"

"Not with all the shopping, drinking and false bonhomie," groans Martin.

"What about the carols? Some pretty good songs – you must like some of them," says Andy, anxious to lighten the mood.

"Mostly lightweight to my way of thinking. You should remember, my interest is in serious music."

How could I forget, thinks Andy. The men take a seat near one of the windows.

"Right. My shout. First one's on me, so what's it going to be?" asks Andy.

"Half of shandy will do."

"What! Come on, Martin, let the first one be a proper drink."

"All right make it a pint – of shandy."

"Shandy?! It's our reunion, don't forget."

Without responding, Martin turns his head away toward the window and to the shoppers passing by outside.

As he stands at the bar ordering the drinks, Andy senses a distinct change in the Music Man's attitude. So different from the relaxed, understanding character he had known in Borneo. Was this the same man who had joined him on the adventurous boating trip, who had delivered a never to be forgotten version of the Eton Boating Song and with whom he and Finnegan had sat on a tropical beach toasting the Air Force for allowing them to be there? But now a subdued figure, clearly with little apparent enthusiasm for the reunion. Or is it that he, Andy, has totally misjudged the importance of the get-together? Perhaps the arrival of Finnegan would prove whether or not he has got it all out of proportion. Were memories best left in the past, unspoilt, undisturbed?

Attempts to encourage Martin to loosen up are proving a struggle. There is a marked disinterest as Andy, unsuccessfully, dangles the bait of a string of colleagues names from their time overseas. Perhaps it was a mistake not to bring his photo album, that might have helped. Even Andy's offer to treat his pal to lunch falls on deaf ears.

Finally, and somewhat mercifully, the lunchtime interlude comes to a close.

"Time to get back to the station. By my reckoning, Finnegan could well be there."

"Don't bank on it," adds Martin.

As the pair re-enter the station, Andy stops at the top of the steps running down to the Underground platforms. "This is the way the Irishman will be coming. Might be an idea for one of us to wait just here?"

"Christ, you're really pumped up for this, aren't you?" laughs Martin. "We're the only two who've bothered to turn up – and the organiser's already two hours late. Some reunion!"

Before Andy can respond, they catch the familiar figure of Finnegan bounding up towards them from the stairs below. The Irishman is wearing a navy-blue duffel jacket and his hair is tied in a pony-tail.

"Really sorry, lads. Missed it by seconds! Now then, where are the others?"

"You're looking at the full turnout, Finnegan," says Martin bitingly.

"How many did you expect?" asks Andy.

"Well, I must have spoken to a dozen of 'em.."

"But how many actually said they'd come?" presses Andy.

"Most said they'd do their best to come along – if they could."

"And they were all given the day, time and place?" asks Martin.

"Yes, Friday, 19th December, Platform One, Victoria Station," replies the Irishman.

There is an uneasy silence as the trio reflect on the sad outcome.

"Too close to Christmas, that was the mistake," snaps Martin.

"Come on, you two, let's get in a drink or two before they close," suggests Andy.

"Not back to that bloody 'Shakespeare' again!" groans Martin.

"Who cares, let's get moving. Lead me to it," grins Finnegan.

Inside the pub, Andy and the Irishman immediately establish an almost continuous dialogue, while Martin's attention seems focused on the crib players.

"So what you doing at the moment, Finnegan?" asks Andy.

"Well, bought myself out in April then just bummed around for a few months. Then, in July, teamed up with an old school mate selling second-hand cars. Good money in it, if you use your nut."

"But what you doing up in London, Andy? I thought you lived in the West Country."

"I got a transfer here."

"Did Sally mind moving here?"

"Sandra, you mean. No, that's all finished. You fixed up with anyone then?"

"Not bloody likely!" laughs the Irishman.

"During your ring round, did you find out how the other lads were making out since coming home?" asks Andy.

"Not much, mind you Curtis let slip a blinder about the C.O's missus."

"Marilyn Munro?"

"Yes, the very lady – or should I say woman? Apparently Curtis was worried stiff about the Old Man finding out about him groping her at that party. So he sneaked back to their bungalow one morning to apologise, when the C.O was on camp."

"Daft sod," says Andy.

"Well, apparently she accepted the apology – and a bit more! When Curtis got back home they were in regular touch for a while. Then she broke it off to marry a Wing Commander."

"Crumbs, never thought of her as being rank conscious."

Suddenly, Martin rises to don his raincoat.

"Well, chaps, great to see you both again. I'm heading back to Uxbridge before the 'rush hour' starts. Keep in touch, won't you?"

"Hold on, you can't go now. We've got the rest of the day. It's our reunion!"

The plea draws only a wry smile from Martin as he heads for the door, with a departing overhead wave of the hand.

"Let him go, Finnegan," says Andy, "something's not right with him."

"So, what you got lined up for the rest of the day? I thought tonight we would be taking in a West End club or two. Back home they say Soho is the place."

"If you've more money than sense!"

"That's no problem, I've brought a hundred quid with me," says the Irishman proudly, reaching inside his coat for his wallet.

"Good heavens, that second hand car business must be doing well. But don't forget the clubs don't open till very late. We've got a few hours to kill before then."

"Any ideas?" asks Finnegan.

"I could show you a bit of London. Interested?"

"Yes, I'll drink to that. This is only the second time I've been to London. First time was on a coach to watch an international football match at Wembley. Never got into London proper."

The pair leave the pub and, within five minutes, have walked to the Royal Mews at Buckingham Gate. The sky has darkened and a few spots of rain hit the pavement.

"Now Finnegan, just around the corner is…"

"Don't tell me, I can see it already, it's *the* Palace," shouts the Irishman, dashing a few steps ahead to catch his first sight of the building. The pair skip between the cars circling the roundabout and pause for a few minutes in front of the Queen Victoria Memorial directly in front of the Palace.

"This is bleeding fantastic. Seen pictures and TV shots of the place, but this!" enthuses Finnegan. "Where next?"

"Right now. We wait for a break in the traffic then we leg it across to the park over there. Just follow me. Now!"

The pair have timed their run to perfection, arriving breathless on the pavement overlooking St James's Park.

"I come out here from the office at lunchtime most days. Find it clears my head to have a stroll."

"Looks nice," adds the Irishman. They pause on the metal bridge in the middle of the lake to watch the ducks skimming over the water to claim pieces of bread that are being thrown to them.

"Remember seeing those chickens fighting outside Santa's house on Treasure Island? These are more civilised," smiles Finnegan.

"But this lot are ducks, not chickens," replies Andy. The pair share a laugh and move on.

Despite the attempts of the sun to break through, the chill in the air ensures that only a few visitors are seated on the wooden benches.

"Now if we keep on in this direction," explains Andy, "there'll be a few more interesting places to show you."

They walk briskly through the park, ignoring the threatening clouds above, to look out at the open space of Horse Guards Parade.

"Don't tell me, Andy. I've seen pictures of this, too! This is where the Queen rides her horse?"

"Correct. Trooping the Colour. Now we cross the road and take that cut-through up those steps and we're into a famous street."

Andy is surprised at the reaction from the Irishman, who seems somewhat overwhelmed by what he is being shown.

"Not boring you, am I?" asks Andy.

"Boring me? Boring me! Don't make me laugh. This is bleeding great. A free, escorted trip round this place?"

They enter at the park side to Downing Street, climbing the small flight of steps alongside the side entrance to the Foreign Office and linger for a few minutes looking directly across the road to No.10.

Finnegan stands speechless, eyes trained on the famous black door, in front of which stands a solitary uniformed policeman.

"Poor bastard doesn't even have a rifle. What good would he be in an emergency?"

"That sort of thing doesn't happen here. It's just not done," replies Andy.

"They'd be better off with a couple of our old 'Snowdrops'! They'd frighten off any trouble makers."

"And all the tourists," laughs Andy.

They walk together to the end of the street, before looking out into Whitehall.

"Now then, Finnegan, that's the Cenotaph down to your right and up there to your left, just out of sight, is Trafalgar Square and Nelson's Column," explains Andy.

The Irishman is nodding, taking it all in.

"You know what, Andy, I thought the highlight of the day was going to be with the lads in some dodgy West End club, drinks flowing, taking a really close look at those birds with next to nothing on."

"Still could be," suggests Andy.

"You know what? I'm sorry I buggered things up today," says the Irishman quietly.

"Don't blame yourself. Not your fault if people decide not to turn up, is it?"

"Well, the trouble was I tried to do it all on the 'phone, sending letters ain't my thing. So there was nothing in writing, that's what cocked it up. When I rang round they were all very interested but probably waiting for a letter or a piece of paper confirming the gen. Should have tied it all up then. Should have left it all to you."

"We'll remember it for next time, shall we?" says Andy.

"Next time. I've got an even better idea for next time."

"Let's have it," replies Andy eagerly.

"We go back, back to the island. If not next year, then 1960 or '61. Listen, we have a stop-over in Singapore, opening with a 'night to remember' in Changi Village."

"Are you serious? It's a long way from home and it'll cost a small fortune!"

"Dead serious. Let's face it, we're the only ones who really look back fondly on our time there. Stuff the Music Man, I think he only showed up today out of curiosity."

"Tell you what, Finnegan, we could get Ken along to be the official photographer and, once we fix that up, I reckon Martin would be back on board. We could even take that boat trip again to our little island and see how Santa is making out with those native girls!"

"And Curtis?"

"Yeh, he'll definitely be up for it. Mind you, it'll take me some time to save up."

"Don't worry too much about that, Andy, I'm making bundles of cash with the cars. I'll be there to help you out. Don't forget, I still owe you for that night out at Bedok Corner when we ended up in that 'knocking' shop with you paying for everything."

"To be honest, I've tried to forget about that evening."

"Well, I haven't! Now are you up for it? You know, a trip back to the Island?"

"That's a 'Roger,' Finnegan," replies Andy, wrapping a friendly arm around the Irishman's shoulder.

The pair walk down Whitehall in the direction of Parliament Square, passing the grey buildings of the Home Office and Treasury where Andy is employed. They cross the road and pause to gaze up at the huge clock face of Big Ben. Their eyes focus on the Houses of Parliament and then the Abbey before they turn left towards Westminster Bridge where they take a seat on the embankment overlooking the Thames. Directly across the water stands the sprawling but impressive building, housing those working for the London County Council. The rain has turned into a steady drizzle but both men remain seated, helping each other as they trawl their minds, ferreting for elusive names from yesterday and now excited at the prospect of a return to the Island.

"Got to say this, Finnegan, you've haven't changed a jot," says Andy.

"Well you have, you daft sod – 'cause you're wearing civilian clothes! More to the point, this has been a real eye opener, Andy, thanks," says the Irishman.

"So we'll have a crack at Soho this evening, will we?" says Andy.

"I bloody hope so. Promised my mates back home to tell them all about it. Even brought my mum's old camera down with me to take pictures of those busty, nude West End birds. Christ, just imagine if those flat-chested Chinese washerwoman we had in Borneo clapped their eyes on the size of their knockers!"

"Bet the girls tonight won't be in the same class as the garage ladies of Bedok," laughs Andy.

"Not a chance, my friend, not a chance," replies Finnegan.